Forever Fields

Josh Hill

Forever Fields
By Josh Hill

Wicked House Publishing

No part of this publication may be reproduced, stored in a retrieval system, or transmitted in any way by any means, electronic, mechanical, photocopy, recording or otherwise without the prior permission of the author except as provided by USA copyright law.

This novel is a work of fiction. Names, descriptions, entities, and incidents included in the story are products of the author's imagination. Any resemblance to actual persons, events, and entities is entirely coincidental.

Cover design by Christian Bentulan
Interior Formatting by Duncan Ralston
All rights reserved. Copyright © 2024 Josh Hill

Chapter 1

"You're the last one to leave. Stubborn as always," Elsie said in French to the wounded Senegalese soldier as she tried to help him stand.

The field hospital tent in Arras, France was being evacuated and it was Elsie's job as head nurse to get the walking wounded into the waiting trucks. As of yesterday, the field hospital held a hundred sick and wounded, but Elsie and her staff had been working diligently to evacuate them from the collapsing front line. The Germans were on the offensive and clashing within a few miles of Arras. Nobody thought the Huns had any fight left in them, especially after the Americans entered the war, but here they were, evacuating well behind the front lines.

"Thank you, Elsie," Diallo said with a smile.

He had been trying to learn English to impress her, even though she spoke fluent French. It wouldn't work of course, she was un-wooable, but she appreciated the effort because it made him comply with bandage changes and medications. He was the last one left to evacuate, and she yearned to leave before the Germans arrived. The constant warning sirens howling in the distance impressed on her a sense of urgency.

She draped his muscular arm around her shoulders and began to help him limp to the other side of the tent when she suddenly found herself lying on the floor. Splinters of wood, pieces of canvas, blood surrounded her. The first thought that came to her was that an orderly needed to mop this mess up. It was filthy! It wasn't until her ears started ringing that she realized what had happened.

A German mortar round impacted next to the tent and had shredded the canvas along with most of the support poles. Elsie's ears started working again and all she could hear was a high pitch ringing and a dull, muffled din of men screaming in pain. The tent had been shattered and torn open. The picturesque French town outside was on fire. Men were running everywhere in complete chaos.

Corporal Diallo was yelling at her, but she could barely hear him over the ringing in her ears and the loud thumping of incoming artillery. Diallo was pointing and shouting. The British transport sergeant ordered to evacuate them was at the entrance of the tent and motioned for them to come.

Elsie shook her head and got her bearings. Diallo was trying to stand on his own, so she crawled over to him. With Elsie's help, they both came to their feet. The British sergeant was looking past them with wide eyes as he drew his Mauser.

"What are you doing?" she yelled at the sergeant, but he ignored her and pointed his pistol.

"Get down!" he yelled as he fired.

The sergeant fired one shot before a rifle round hit him in the head, spraying blood, grey matter and little white pieces of bone everywhere. A German soldier with a muddy uniform and bolt-action rifle entered through the other end of the torn hospital tent and chambered another round into his rifle. Even as the British sergeant's body hit the floor, Diallo scrambled for the pistol, still clutched in the dead man's hand. He wrenched it free and swung it toward the approaching German soldier.

The German fired first. Diallo's throat exploded as he fell to his knees and dropped the pistol. He grasped at the wound on his neck while blood gushed from between his fingers, his face already pale from blood loss and his eyes wide with surprise and pain. The soldier swung his rifle at Elsie.

She froze.

She wanted to scream. She wanted to run. She saw her death in the barrel of the rifle as it pointed at her face.

click

"Sheist!" the German soldier said as he pulled back the bolt and reached for another clip of ammo from a pouch on his belt.

Then she could move again. She grabbed the pistol that had fallen at Diallo's feet and aimed it at the enemy. He looked up from reloading his rifle in time to see Elsie pull the trigger. He still looked surprised as the bullet slammed into his chest. He kept hold of his rifle as he fell to the ground, already dead.

Before Elsie could breathe a sigh of relief, another German soldier entered the tent. This one was different. He resembled a medieval knight and was enclosed head to toe in iron plates. The helmet completely covered the face except for two glass eye lenses, through which she could see fierce and murderous eyes staring at her. In his hands, he didn't hold a rifle like the man she just shot. He had a flame thrower, which he swung toward her.

Elsie held the pistol in both hands in front of her like a crucifix to ward off evil. She yanked the trigger several times without aiming. Two rounds struck the German in the chest and bounced off with a small shower of sparks. The third round struck his helmet. This also bounced off, but it staggered him. He stumbled back, swearing.

Now, Elsie took a second to aim and fired the remaining two shots as the bolt locked back, empty. The first shot missed, but the second shot pierced the eyepiece of the helmet, shattering the glass and painting it red with blood.

He began to fall, but in his death throes triggered the flame thrower. Bright flame and terrible heat filled what was left of the tent. Like a living snake, the stream of fire from the barrel of the flame thrower arced toward Elsie.

Overwhelming heat streaked toward her, but she was suddenly covered and thrown to the ground. Corporal Diallo, pale with loss of blood, used the last seconds of his life to throw her down and take the brunt of the flame. He screamed but only for a second and then was gone.

Elsie felt a sharp, searing pain on her arm and face, an intense and incredible agony that she had never imagined before.

The last memory she had before she blacked out was of the smell of her own burning flesh.

Elsie woke up screaming and swatted at her arm and face, trying to put out the memory of flames. Her world transformed from a blazing inferno to the gentle rocking movement of the train she rode.

Her vision and head cleared. She stopped screaming and recognized the luxurious crimson cushions of her private cabin. The cabin was expensive, furnished in all polished dark wood and brass and worth every penny. The speed at which trains traveled had always fascinated her, ever since she was a little girl.

"Are you okay, madam? Can I get you anything? A nice tonic perhaps?" whispered the middle-aged steward with the walrus-like mustache.

Elsie jumped and instantly felt embarrassed that someone had seen her in such a state.

"Oh, no thank you," she said, unconsciously turning away and playing with her hair to make sure it was covering the scars that stretched from her temple to her jaw.

"Very well, madam," he said with a smile as he left, though Elsie did not see it. She was already back to looking out the window.

After the man left, she got up, locked the door and pulled down the blinds. Once she was sure she had complete privacy, she took off her shoes, let her hair down and sat back down.

Her thoughts brought her back again to the Great War. The once verdant farmlands of rural France, torn apart, blackened and bruised by years of artillery bombardment paled compared to the broken and dead bodies of people and animals that littered the country like a toddler's discarded toys. On her first day in Arras, temporarily assigned to the British First Army nursing corps in 1917, she saw what she thought was a dirty rag, hanging on a barbed wire fence. Only when she approached did she see it was the face of a man, just the skin, mustache and all, flapping in the breeze.

She looked away from the window realizing that her breaths were coming in quick and shallow. An old Senegalese NCO taught her a trick for cases of the jitters, as he liked to call it. Elsie closed her eyes and tried to control her breathing, taking slow, deep breaths. With a mischievous wink, the old sergeant told her to think of a young and handsome movie star, but her mind always wandered to Mary Pickford, her favorite actress and the epitome of feminine beauty. It took several minutes, but eventually her breathing returned to almost normal.

The train swayed like a wave while the lush fields and woods of Nebraska rolled by Elsie's window. The beautiful scenery was only interrupted by occasional stops in small towns where people would sell trinkets and refreshments. These short stops gave her the chance to stretch her legs and look for anybody selling books, but to her dismay, no one did. Ever since she boarded the train in Council Bluffs, she did nothing but stare out the window.

The bright green of the pastures and trees warmed her heart. It provided such a contrast to the drab, horrible and muddy existence of Eastern France at the end of the Great War, or the off-white, monotonous walls of the British hospital in which she recovered for months after.

Elsie absently flipped through a travel guide of Utah, her ultimate destination, but she had read it enough times to know it by heart. Once in a while, a photograph would capture her attention, but the rest of the book became background noise. She watched the sun descend into the West and as her cabin grew darker and darker, she didn't even notice the travel guide fall from her hand as she slipped into a shallow and disturbed sleep.

Chapter 2

Elsie got off the train at her destination at Union Station in Ogden, Utah. She had the address to the house she inherited but didn't know how to get there. She needed to find a map and transportation before it got dark, or she'd have to wait until the morning.

Ogden was small in comparison to the cities in Europe or even out East, but it had the same ambiance. Homeless and street vendors competed for people's coins on one corner, while prostitutes and crooked cops shook people down on another. The infamous Twenty Fifth Street was living up to its reputation already.

Fords, Pilots and Tourings chugged down the street, barely avoiding the pedestrians and the odd horse drawn cart full of produce. The telephone and electrical cables spanned the road in the most haphazard fashion, some almost hanging low enough to get caught on the roof of a passing truck. However, no pedestrians were struck, and no telephone cables were wrenched free by an automobile. Everything seemed to work in a well-oiled but disorganized fashion.

Elsie traveled light and grabbed the two suitcases the

orderly had placed by her feet. She wore a wide brimmed straw hat low over her face to keep the sun out of her eyes and to keep people from staring at her scars. The pistol felt heavy in her handbag but she was glad it was there. A single woman in a rough town carrying bags of cash shouldn't take any chances. She thought about wearing the gun belt, but didn't want to bring any extra attention to herself.

The July heat was intense, but compared to the mortifying humidity of Washington, DC and its swarms of flies and mosquitoes, this was nothing. A bookstore called "WR Bookstore" stood ahead, the books within calling Elsie straight to it even as the kids tried to sell her bubblegum and day-old newspapers.

The little bell announced her entrance as an older, large man stood up from leaning on the counter. Elsie took her hat off but kept the right side of her face turned away from the book seller.

"Good afternoon, and welcome to the White Russian Book Store. Anything you are

looking for? My name is Abram, and I will be glad to help," he said with a slight Russian accent.

Elsie looked around the bookstore and noticed the anti-Bolshevik propaganda posters in Cyrillic, plastered over every wall. She couldn't read what they said, but Russian propaganda was never known for its subtlety.

"This is a ducky place you got here," Elsie said, and whistled, impressed.

The book seller laughed. It was a big and hardy laugh, the kind she wasn't used to in polite society, but it was contagious. She couldn't help but smile herself.

"Ducky. I like that. I'm going to have to remember that one."

The book seller composed himself once again.

"Thank you, lady. Most of these are from my personal

collection that I brought from Russia. A shame I couldn't bring my entire collection. What can I do for you today?" he said gesturing around.

"I just need a map of the local area. As detailed as possible."

"Let me see what I have," he said, going over to an old wine rack, now repurposed to hold rolled up maps. He grabbed a few and brought them over to the counter and laid them out.

"Here you go, lady."

There was a street map of Ogden, a topographical map of all Northern Utah and a map of Weber and Morgan County, including geography, roads, wells and property lines.

"Perfect, I'll take all three. Also, if you have a copy of 'The Count of Monte Cristo', I'll take that too."

"In English or French?" he said with a cocky smirk.

She left the store and walked around for a few blocks until she found a poster for a local car dealership. After stopping a young couple to get directions, she was on the way. She only had to walk a block, but she was sweating by the time she got there. Many people passed by, and she was thankfully ignored by most of them. The less attention, the better.

A wormy looking man in a suit that would have been fashionable out east when the Great War ended a couple of years ago, approached her with a smile. She assumed he thought he was charming.

"What can I do for a fine tomato like yourself?" he said wiggling his eyebrows.

Elsie ignored the remark and looked around the lot. It was mostly Fords with a few other new brands and models scattered around.

"I'm looking for something fast and rugged. What do you have?"

"Ah, your husband must be the adventuring type! Look

no further little lady, I know just the thing! I just got it in. Newest car on the market, the Cadillac Model 57. This is the cat's meow! You'd be the first one in the state to own one and you'd be the talk of the town. It has seven seats for you and all your kids," he said in an obviously fake posh accent and motioning to a beautiful car taking up the position of honor at the front of the lot, facing the street.

"I don't have a husband or children, so I won't be needing anything that large. I need something with a high ground clearance, a V-8 engine and preferably a convertible. Can you help me, or should I go to the dealership in Salt Lake City? Do you think they would have something?" she said.

"Ah baloney. Those jalopy peddlers don't know nothing about real cars. Looks like you know your onions so let me show you what I got," he said, his accent and grammar slipping from frustration.

The car dealer took her over to another Cadillac.

"This here is the nineteen-seventeen model 55. Yeah, it's a little older but still a V-8. Seventy-seven horsepower. It seats four, maybe five people if you know each other pretty good," he said chuckling at his own joke.

The car was black, like most cars and absolutely beautiful. Everything about it screamed luxury and performance. She was usually very thrifty, but she always wanted a fast car and had dreamed about owning one since the war ended.

"It can be all yours for the low price of one thousand even," he said.

She tried not to laugh in his face, but a small chuckle slipped out. She covered her mouth with her hand in a very ladylike fashion.

"Brand new that car is only worth eight hundred. It's three years old and has some scratches on the paint, here, here and here," she said, pointing to various spots around the car.

"I'll give you seven hundred."

"Out East where a fancy broad like yourself is from, maybe. But this is Utah. I had to get this shipped in from Detroit! So, with the cost of shipping, I can come down to nine twenty-five. This is a hot commodity. One of the Young family was looking at this yesterday," he said, using the standard negotiation tactic that she instantly recognized.

"Eight seventy and throw in a spare tire," she said folding her arms.

"Look, I can do nine hundred, but that's my final...hey, ma'am, I know you've been traveling and all, but it looks like you got a little something on your face," he said pointing to the right side of his own face.

Elsie moved to wipe away whatever it was, but quickly realized what he was seeing. She tried to fix her hair again to cover her face, but his eyes were already wide and his mouth hung open.

"Oh. Eight seventy-five it is."

She opened one of her suitcases and peeled off a wad of bills from the multiple stacks she had bundled inside. She counted out eight hundred and seventy-five dollars and handed it to him.

After signing some paperwork and stopping at a small grocery store on the outside of town to pick up some food and other necessities, she was on her way. She followed the maps that took her East up Weber Canyon. A cool breeze blew through the canyon and with the top down on the convertible, she enjoyed every second of it. She let her long, blonde hair down and enjoyed being free without someone staring at her scars.

She almost felt as happy as she did before the war.

Almost.

After months spent in a British hospital recovering from her wounds, she finally returned home to Alexandria, Virginia. The few times her father and older brother were not away on an excavation or business trip, their presence made it feel cold and uninviting. They never paid her any attention or even acknowledged her existence unless they wanted something from her. She was raised by the housekeeping staff and the authoritarian masters at her all girls boarding school. So, when she came home to find the house empty, devoid of any family and staff, it actually seemed more inviting.

Besides some cobwebs, the only other sign of life in the house was an envelope from their family attorney. The letter stated that due to the untimely death of her father and brother from the Spanish flu, all holdings and assets of the family had been left to her.

She felt nothing on reading this revelation. She would have felt more loss at learning a neighbor's cat had died. Her father, the famous adventurer Walter Everly, was never abusive. He never laid a hand on her, but his apathy toward her was palpable. Her brother, Thomas was a different matter. She wished he shared their father's apathy, but he was a monster in a different way. He was cruel and vile and would not be missed.

She couldn't stay in Alexandria anymore. The family's high society friends, what few remained, for the most part ignored her. Even the ones that paid token visits made her feel alienated. They were her father's friends, so she didn't want to be around them anyway. For the most part, they were as bigoted and conceited as he was. The followers of her father's philosophy, the Original Purity cult, would also pay visits. There were thankfully few of them and she would send them on their way with a few curses.

"I'm sure you can find an older, wealthy man that won't care what you look like, dear. Then you can settle down and have some children. What were you thinking becoming a nurse and going to war? It's time to become a proper lady," Aunt Cathy told her one day.

Aunt Cathy was her mother's sister and the only family

member to ever pay attention to her, though it was usually to judge and criticize.

The bustling suburb of Washington, DC made it seem like prison walls had surrounded her. Her panic attacks and depression would have driven her to become an invalid or turn to the bottle or opium if she didn't get out. She had seen that happen to far too many Great War veterans and she vowed she wouldn't let it happen to her.

She went to the attorney's office two years after she arrived back home, her mind set on liquidating all assets, gathering the cash and moving out West. Somewhere in the middle of nowhere, maybe Washington or Oregon. She didn't know and it didn't matter. When the attorney informed her of her father's property in Morgan, Utah, she was surprised. It had been built only five years prior, but she had never heard of it. He had the deed, the location and value assessment, but nothing else.

Elsie quickly sold off the house in Alexandria and the lake house in upstate New York, sold all stock and boarded a train heading out West. She wanted to see this property for herself before deciding to sell it. After all, it might be just the kind of place she was looking for. She needed a place to be alone and heal or, if she was honest with herself, just fade away and disappear.

She almost missed the turn off onto State Street, a well-used dirt road leading into Morgan. The small town was charming in its own way, and the people waved at her as she passed by. The house was a few miles outside of town and she soon exited through the south side, driving down an even smaller valley road. The valley eventually opened up with lush trees growing along the banks of a little stream and rolling hills. Following the map closely, she turned off onto another dirt road, that wound up and around a large hill on top of which she saw the large and imposing house.

The sun started to set and cast everything in an almost golden glow, including the house. She didn't know what to expect, but it wasn't this. It was a grandiose, three-story Victorian style house, complete with a tower and wrap around porch. It sat on the top of the plateau-like hill, with a commanding view of the entire property. The area in front of the house was flat but surrounded by gently sloping hills which spread into a wide field behind. The circular driveway was paved, with a large but empty fountain in the middle. She pulled up and parked the car. A garage or barn was situated off the left side and electrical and phone lines sprouted from a nearby pole, connecting to the house.

As she stood there and took in the sight, she saw movement off to the right and before she could panic, a small heard of Pronghorns lazily strolled down the hill toward the stream. One of them stopped to look at her but paid no mind and continued on.

"Home," she said, feeling calm and safe for the first time in years.

Elsie grabbed her luggage and groceries and excitedly brought them into the house and closed the door.

A man had observed her the entire time from behind a small grove of trees past the barn. He put out his cigarette and began the long walk back into town. The sun sets quickly in valleys, but the dark didn't bother this man one bit.

Chapter 3

Elsie woke from the best night's sleep in years. A thin beam of sunlight broke through the thick curtains like a nudge. She yawned and stretched, and despite a wincing pain from the tight scars on her arm and face, felt terrific. She went to flip on the electric light switch but remembered from the evening before that the electricity wasn't connected or activated or whatever got it to work. The water also wasn't working, and she wanted a bath badly. She'd need to hire someone from town to come.

She got up from bed and didn't bother to change out of her nightie. She grabbed the bottle of linseed oil to moisturize her scars, then went down to the kitchen and grabbed a bottle of Coca-Cola. The house even came with an electric ice box, but since there was no power, she hadn't bothered putting her beloved beverages inside, though she was excited to try it because she had never seen one in real life.

The morning was warm, but a slight breeze blew through her long, unkempt hair and made everything perfect. She enjoyed the morning while watching a mother moose and her calf casually make their way across her property as a couple of

Turkey Vultures made lazy circles in the sky. Elsie inhaled deeply and everything smelled fresh and clean and perfect. She couldn't sell this house. Elsie had found her home at last. Eventually her stomach rumbled, and her Coke ran dry, so she went inside and fixed some bacon and eggs on the wood stove.

After breakfast she dressed, stuffed her pistol and some cash into a handbag and took off in her new car toward Morgan. She pulled into the small but well-kept service station in town and was immediately approached by a young man in a very tidy uniform.

He whistled and tipped his cap further back on his head as he saw the Cadillac.

"You don't see many of these around here. What a beauty."

"Thank you, young man. I just bought it."

"Anyway, what can I do for you today, ma'am?"

"Just top her off and check fluids please. Also, if you could recommend a handyman nearby, I'd really appreciate it."

"Depends on what you're looking for, ma'am. Good or cheap?" he said with a chuckle.

"I want the best."

"Then there's only one option. Piper and Son at the intersection of twenty Sixth Street and Quincey Ave in Ogden. Big shop on the corner. You can't miss it. Tell them Nephi sent ya."

He finished with the car. She bought another Coke and tipped him a dollar.

"Whoa! Thank you! Any questions you have, you can come to me!" he said as she pulled out of the station and onto the road heading back down to Ogden. The car handled better than anything she had ever driven previously and before she knew it, she was in Ogden. The grid system of Utah cities made it effortless to find the shop. It was a large brick building with an attached garage right on the corner. A bright white sign with red letters read Piper and Son. Underneath, in smaller letters it said, 'you break it, we fix it'.

She parked the car on the side of the street. Before she walked in, she made sure her hair covered the scars on her face and the long gloves she wore were pulled up to hide her arm. Fully protected against the stares and stupid questions, she walked through the front door. A little bell announced her arrival.

Just a few seconds after the chime, a handsome and distinguished looking black man with small, round glasses on the end of his nose and had grey streaks at his temples. Elsie thought he looked more like a college professor than a handy man. She was surprised because this was the first non-white person she had seen since coming to Utah. She was also surprised that a white man had recommended the place. Back in Virginia, that never would have happened.

"Good morning, madam. The name is Enoch. What can I do for you on this fine day?" he said, offering his hand.

He had a warm and gentle demeanor, yet his eyes were like steel. Elsie couldn't help thinking about her own father and his hatred for everyone not of the 'master race'. When she left for boarding school, she vowed to fight against everything her father believed. Working with and caring for the brave Senegalese soldiers during the war, cemented the fact that her father was wrong.

The image of Corporal Diallo jumping in front of her flashed in her mind.

Elsie quickly shook his hand, with a firm and very un-lady like grip to dispel the nightmarish thought. The rough and calloused hands were definitely not those of a professor.

"I'm Elsie Everly. Pleased to meet you. I just acquired a house up near Morgan. It's connected to the power lines and has electrical appliances and lights, but nothing comes on. There is also plumbing, but none of the water is working either. From what I understand it was built about five years ago, but nobody has lived in it. I'd like someone to come up and get the power and water running and see what else needs to be fixed."

"I know the place. Caused quite the stir a few years back when whoever built it brought in outsiders from California. Then they suddenly left one night without a trace. It's the one up in the valley a few miles past Morgan," he said, motioning for her to sit on the surprisingly expensive looking leather chairs.

"Yes, that's the place. A three-story Victorian sitting on top of a flat-topped hill," she said, taking a seat and glad that she wouldn't have to worry about giving directions.

"You're from Virginia, aren't you?" he said suddenly.

Surprised, Elsie said that she was.

"I figured. You still have an accent, but you hide it well enough. You're Walter Everly's daughter, aren't you? I used to like his early adventure books, even though they were pure fantasy. I'm not a fan of his politics or that little cult he started. The Original Purity, I believe he called it?"

After writing a series of very popular travel, adventure and archeology books at the turn of the century, her father began to write essays, pamphlets and books about the dangers of capitalism, democracy and miscegenation. His last writings turned mystical and esoteric before he completely disappeared from public life, but he still had a small and devoted following before his death. She knew he held meetings with a small and fanatic group. However, when she returned from the war, people said he had started a doomsday cult and had dozens of devotees. She didn't know what happened to his followers when he died, and she didn't want to know.

"I am nothing like my father. Nothing like him," she said.

"Good to hear that," he said patting her hand.

"Now, I won't have anybody available until tomorrow, but

it'll be my best employee, I promise. Don't worry about billing yet. It'll be based on time and parts used, but we have the most fair and honest pricing around. Can't beat the quality of our service. Is ten in the morning good for you?"

They worked out the details and after getting Enoch's business card and another firm handshake, Elsie left the shop. She pulled over to get a Nathan's hot dog from a street cart, then started the drive home.

Elsie arrived back at the house and decided to walk the property. She unrolled the map that showed the property lines. The property behind the house gently sloped downhill to a small pond surrounded by trees where it eventually flattened out. There was plenty of room for planting crops if she ever felt so inclined. On her way back up the hill toward the house, a family of racoons bustled across her path. She stopped and watched them until they disappeared.

She walked the entire property, soaking in the fresh air and isolation and by the end, she was in love. The stream that provided some bright green foliage along its banks, the gently sloping hills filled with wildflowers and the incredible array of wild animals made this something unique and special to her. She had never seen anything like it before. Virginia had lots of trees and hills and animals, of course, but being from the city she rarely got to enjoy it. The few times she did venture out into the wilds, it was hard to see anything through all the trees and clouds of 'Virginia face flies', the little gnats that only flew in your face. Here in Utah, she could actually see the countryside and the sky, and she loved it.

Here is the place where she wouldn't be hurt anymore. Here, she would never again have a broken heart. Here, she could be herself without hiding from the world.

Feeling truly happy, she decided to inspect the inside of the house. The kitchen she knew well. The parlor and living room's geometric patterns lay everywhere and huge mirrors covered every wall.

She noticed something odd. In every room, funny vents opened through the flooring. Surely they had a purpose, but Elsie didn't know what it could be. Also in every room was some souvenir from her father's excursions. Some were from Africa, Asia or the Middle East, but what was odd, was the vast number of Aztec or Mayan artifacts. In almost every room, some ancient stone deity looked at her with weapons in their hands or tongues shaped like knives. Their fierceness and bloodthirsty countenances made her shudder.

The upstairs held five bedrooms, each adjoined by its own bath, each richly furnished and featuring large mirrors. Much to her surprise, the sixth room, the tower, was a small library. Every surface was covered in books. A large floor-to-ceiling window provided light on three sides and two plush, leather chairs beckoned her to sit and read. Electric lights hung unlit overhead. She browsed the collection and, unsurprisingly, most were history and reference books. One wall was completely devoted to her father's own writings. The Adventures of Walter Everly in the Amazon and The Adventures of Walter Everly in Egypt and Persia or Mexico and dozens of other locations. Then her father's books tried to become more scholarly. He funded digs and had many famous discoveries, mostly all hoaxes, and his writings were "juvenile and entirely dismissive of the very cultures Mr. Everly was attempting to study," as one noted historian opined in a scholastic review.

His archeology books became about the objects he would discover, about the cultures that created them and most importantly to him, how present day Western European culture was superior to them. While scholars dismissed them, they were very popular with the layman. This led to the next shelf of books, his philosophical and political thoughts. These he called his 'Original Purity' series. This is also what he called his group of followers. His cult. These books attempted to use his experiences and discoveries to justify his beliefs in the superiority of white men. One book claimed how capitalism was a Zionist conspiracy to control the world. Another book excoriated miscegenation with a special hatred of sub-Saharan Africans. One book depicted women were inferior beings guided only by emotion and should gladly submit to men. The later books, the furthest down the shelf, ostracized him from polite society. These later books spoke about the need to embrace your inherent superiority, to replace piety with vice, and in doing so, break down barriers and open a mystical third eye to sees into the spirit realm. The last book, which spoke of the destruction of all civilization through strife and murder, was so dark and vile it was actually banned in the US and the UK. Her father tried to fight the ban in court, but when he told a judge that God would guide mankind through nightmares, murder would reign and only the strong and faithful would be left, the ban was upheld. At this point, even the most esoteric bookstores stopped carrying his books. He maintained a small but devoted following and by the time she had left for college, he was holding meetings at their house in Alexandria to discuss his works and work on how to implement his ideas.

Elsie decided her father's books would make a nice bonfire to roast marshmallows over.

One thing that disappointed her even more, there wasn't a single novel. She would have to fix that.

The library did have a record player, much to her delight. She can't remember her father ever listening to music, so this was a nice surprise. It must have been an afterthought, because as she looked around, she couldn't find any records.

Typical.

She was going to have to fix that too. She loved having music surrounding her and it reminded her of her days in the dorm rooms of boarding school. Upbeat music constantly filled the bleak dorms, and the girls danced with each other, pretending it was a ball. Sometimes one of the girls would sneak in a ragtime record and the girls would go crazy. Those were some of her fondest memories.

The third floor was an open studio set up with the roof forming an angled ceiling and large, circular windows on each end, facing the front and back of the house. Unlike the rest of the house, there was no furniture or odd rugs, but there was a large cheval style, full length standing mirror in the middle of the floor.

She wondered if her father had planned for this to be a storage room for all the artifacts he pillaged from his archeological digs, hold meetings for his followers of his 'Original Purity' writings or if he just didn't get around to it before he died. Either way, she was going to fill it up with something she enjoyed.

Elsie vowed to erase every stain her father left and make this house hers. Nothing in this new refuge would remind her of her former life and she smiled at the thought. The smile, of course, brought a twinge of pain as it stretched her scar, like it always did.

Chapter 4

Elsie stood on the front porch, drumming her fingers on the butt of her pistol and looking down the driveway every couple seconds. She did not like the idea of a strange man in her house, but she really wanted that new electric ice box working. She wore her very feminine and airy 'Robe de Style' dress in pink and blue pastel with her straw hat. She wore her hair down to cover the right side of her face and long white gloves to cover the scar on her right arm. To accessorize the outfit, she wore her leather gun belt with a 'Red Nine' Mauser pistol in a thumb break holster.

This wasn't the same pistol she used to defend herself in France. A Welsh officer sold her the pistol once she got out of the hospital. He took it off the body of a German officer, but he had lost both of his hands afterward. She would rather have the standard 7.63mm C-96 because of its higher velocity, but finding ammunition would not be a problem because 9mm was much more common in the states.

After only a few more minutes she saw a Model TT truck chug its way up the hill, a large plume of dust rising behind it. The box truck with 'Piper and Son' painted on the side parked in front of the house and sputtered as the engine turned off. The person that got out of the truck was wearing a denim bib overall, with tools and pencils poking out of every pocket and a loose-fitting blue and white striped shirt with matching newsboy style hat. The driver was tall and skinny with very dark skin and two long, thick French Braids pouring over her shoulders.

The shock must have been evident on Elsie's face because the newcomer just smiled and said, "Yup, I'm a girl."

She then walked toward Elsie with her hand outstretched.

"Pleased to meet'cha. I'm Harriet. Harriet T. Piper. The T is for Theodocia, that's an old family name, but you can just call me Harriet. And you must be Miss...Miz...Missus Waverly? Sorry, my dad didn't specify," she said in rapid succession, taking Elsie's hand and shaking it vigorously. Her fingers were long and elegant, but strong and a little rough.

"Miss, but you can just call me Elsie," she said, still taken aback by the gregariousness of this girl.

Not only was the handyman a handywoman, she was also young and very pretty. Elsie thought she looked to be in her early twenties. Her eyes were large, bright and friendly and her skin looked smooth and dark and contrasted against her perfectly white teeth and eyes.

"My dad thought you'd be more comfortable with a female, seeing as you're all alone up here and he wanted to avoid any appearance of impropriety," Harriet said, the last word emphasized in an overdone, haughty accent. Using her thumb to point at herself, she proudly added, "He also promised he'd send his best, and I'm the bee's knees!"

"Well, that was very thoughtful of him."

"He's like that. He thinks of everything. He even put a doohicky in the truck to hold my sodas while I drive. Just between you and me, white women always get really antsy when they are alone with a colored man, especially after that damned 'Birth of a Nation' came out in the theatres a few years ago. Pardon me, Miss Everly. I get a little too familiar sometimes and I'm not supposed to swear. My dad says I was born without a camshaft for my brain and my mouth," she said with a slight guffaw.

"That's a mechanic joke. You see, the camshaft regulates the opening and closing of my mouth, apparently...," Harriet started to say when Elsie interrupted her.

"I get it. I am aware of what a camshaft is."

"Oh right," she said sheepishly.

Elsie thought that was really funny but tried not to smile. She had forgotten to moisturize her scars so she kept a stony face, otherwise it would be too painful. Nobody in DC society would ever talk so freely and she found it refreshing.

"Wow, you're very lucky to have such a beautiful house. Let's get to it and see what needs fix'n. If you break it, we fix it. That's our motto, like it says on the side of the truck here," Harriet said, grabbing a tool belt from the truck and strapping it around her waist.

"My dad says you're from Virginia. Love the accent. He also said your father is that crazy racist author. Besides being a crazy racist, he's also wrong about most of the stuff he writes about, so no surprise. Let's go take a look at the power and phone lines first."

Elsie walked over to the side of the house to inspect the connections, still trying to process everything Harriet was saying.

Harriet mumbled to herself and studied the wires with exaggerated concentration. It seemed as if everything this girl did was exaggerated, which wasn't a bad thing, just different from the stoicism of aristocracy.

Harriet pulled some tools from her belt, staring at all the wires again.

"You see anything wrong?" Elsie said.

"Nope. Everything looks good here. Both electricity and phone are connected. I wonder how much it cost to get this place wired up all the way out here. Some places in town still aren't connected. This must've cost a pretty penny. You mind if I take a look inside the house, ma'am?"

"Call me Elsie, and of course. Follow me," she said turning around and walking to the front door.

Elsie was now questioning her choice in wardrobe, though to be fair, this was the only clean thing she had. She thought maybe the 'Robe de Style' dress she had on might send the wrong message, like she was looking to seduce the repairman. This was accentuated by the fact she could feel how the cloth moved over her and knew this dress accentuated her rear, so she tried to walk a little more proper, making sure there was no sway in her hips, in case Harriet gets the wrong idea.

She realized this might be the only time in her life she's put something from finishing school to practical use.

Once inside the house, Harriet removed her hat and whistled.

"And I thought the outside was nice."

Elsie noticed Harriet's full lips as she whistled and blushed as she imagined what it would be like to kiss them. She noticed the upper lip was slightly larger than the bottom, which she always found both aesthetically and physically pleasing while kissing...and doing other things with the mouth.

Get a grip on yourself. You are lonely and horny and should take your leave now before you embarrass yourself.

Harriet looked around for the light switch and pressed it. Nothing happened.

"Every room has electric lighting but as you can see, nothing works. The phone and the plumbing don't work either. You have free reign of the house so help yourself to a Coke and some crackers in the kitchen if you like. I'll be out on the porch if you need me," Elsie said curtly and left the room quickly.

Elsie went to the kitchen to grab a Coke and her copy of the The Count of Monte Cristo and went out to the porch. She sat on one of the long reclining chairs and settled in, but she couldn't stop thinking about Harriet.

Before the war, she would have struck up a conversation and even flirted a little to gauge if there was any interest. She was thirty now but back when she was younger and not disfigured, she had no problems finding female companionship.

The all-girls boarding and finishing schools she attended, while very strict, gave her lots of experience in such matters and she was rarely alone. She was quite the prize and all the girls wanted to be on her arm and up her skirt. Being young, beautiful and rich had its advantages.

Almost nightly she'd slip away to an isolated corner of the school with a different girl and 'mess around', as she called it. On a few occasions, she stole the motor carriage of one of the school mistresses and took a girl joy riding. She loved living and taking risks and many of the girls were drawn to that. It was never a question if she could find female companionship, it was only a question of who it would be.

Then the war started. She read one of her father's pamphlets about how the war was a Jewish conspiracy that only benefited the Zionist cabal and everyone should overthrow their governments and create a world in which only the strong survived. His beliefs taught that civilization was a cancer. That solidified her position, so she left Princeton and immediately joined the war effort with the French military as a nurse. Her father was furious, but that just strengthened her resolve.

The Army nurse corps was so different from anything she'd experienced, and she loved it. Her background meant nothing, only her ability to excel in her field, and she did excel.

She fell in love with the people she worked with and especially the Senegalese soldiers she cared for.

The scars on her face and arm flared in pain at the memory, and she forced herself not to think about that last day in Arras.

When she came home to Arlington, everything changed. Her father's legacy had become a scarlet letter A around her neck, while the scars kept her from ever becoming close to another woman. Being rejected by everyone she knew cemented the fact that she would remain alone with nothing but the memory of love and intimacy.

So, as lithe, pretty and friendly as this Harriet was, she would keep her distance and remain aloof. The Welsh officer that sold her his gun also taught her a phrase; "only when you lose all hope, are you truly free."

The pain of hope was too much to bear.

Elsie wiped away a tear and distracted herself with her new book. The French and Senegalese soldiers were always recommending it to her because the author was French and colored, and they were very proud of that fact.

"Edmond Dantes, that's a great name," she said to herself as she forgot her troubles momentarily and became lost in the book.

Chapter 5

"... I'll be out on the porch if you need me," Elsie said.

"I'll get to it then," Harriet said to herself, watching Miss Everly walk away.

Harriet knew she talked a lot when she was nervous, and this was a big opportunity for the family business. Fixing up a big house brought in a good margin, especially when the owner was rich. She would never be dishonest and always offered fair rates, but she still hoped there were a lot of things that needed fixing. From the look of the wiring she'd seen so far, the installers had stopped halfway through the job and just left everything in place.

She didn't know what to make of Miss Everly. She seemed stand-offish, scowling next to her and shoot'n iron on her hip. A rich, high society Southern woman was bound to dislike colored folk, even if she said she's not like her horrible father. However, she did invite her in and offer food and drinks, which no one else had ever done, so she was obviously better than him, but that was a really low bar. Also, she was beautiful, in a severe, and intense kind of way. Tall like herself and utterly elegant.

She shook her head of those invading thoughts and decided to remain professional.

As Elsie turned to walk away, the wind coming in from the front door hit her hair just right and Harriet caught a glimpse of a burn scar on her face that covered most of her right cheek.

Harriet quickly looked down, as if she had seen something private that was not meant for her. She couldn't help but wonder if those long gloves covered more scars. She figured the hair and gloves were deliberate attempts to hide them, but her dad always taught her to be proud of scars. Scars meant you survived, reminded everyone of how tough you are. There must be a great and terrible story behind those scars, and she wanted to hear that story one day.

A quick impression of terror, pain and loneliness flashed in her mind.

She got these kind of impressions a lot, but they were usually very fleeting. Every once in a while, she'd get full images and emotions, like the one time she was helping her mom find her wedding ring. She saw exactly where it was in her mind, and that's exactly where it was.

She never told anyone. Either they'd think she was lying or crazy.

Harriet watched Elsie as she walked away, observing how she walked with such grace and confidence, like one of the photo models she saw when she visited the Great Salt Lake a few years ago, before the Spanish flu. Before everything changed.

She whistled again.

That is one classy and pretty lady.

She sang 'A Pretty Girl is Like a Melody' as she worked to redo what the obviously untrained electricians had started years before, and as she worked, she happily realized that this job was going to take a couple of weeks.

Harriet lost track of time and soon her pocket watch told

her it was her lunch hour. She went out to grab her lunch box from her truck and saw Miss Everly reclined on a chair, reading a book. She waved to her, but the woman was far too lost in her reading to notice.

Movement caught her eye from the other side of the house. She barely caught a glimpse of a man in work overalls and a vacant expression on his face who walked behind the barn, and then was gone. Somehow, she always knew if she was seeing a living person or a ghost. It was instinctual.

"This house is new. How does it have ghosts already?" she said to herself.

As she headed back in, she stopped by the kitchen and found that the rich Southern lady really did leave out a Coke and crackers for her. A Coke would go great with her ham sandwich. It was room temperature, of course, but then she spotted the electric ice box.

"I know what I'm fixing next!"

After a quick lunch, she got started on the wiring in the kitchen.

"Excuse me, ma'am," Harriet said, gently tapping Elsie on the shoulder.

Elsie was obviously lost in her book, because she jumped when Harriet touched her.

"Sorry! Didn't mean to startle you, but I'm done for the day,"

"What time is it?" Elsie said, still a little disoriented.

"It's after five, and I'll be heading home for supper. Let me show you what we got so far. If you'll follow me?"

She held out her hand to help Miss Everly up, hallway expecting her not to take it, but she did.

Harriet led her to the kitchen and posed in front of the light switch like a magician's assistant.

"I present to you...," Harriet said dramatically as she pressed the switch. "Let there be light!" as the electric overhead light came on.

"Brilliant! Thank you," Elsie said in delight.

"I noticed you had an electric ice box too, so I made sure that was working. That's real swanky! I took the liberty of putting your Cokes and other groceries inside. It's been on for a couple of hours already so it's pretty cold. I've heard about these but have never seen one before, but it wasn't too hard to figure out," she said proudly.

"Thank you. So just the kitchen so far?" Elsie asked.

"For electricity, yes. They must've hired semi-trained apes to wire this house because I'm going to have to rewire the whole thing. They didn't actually connect anything. It's like they just left everything in a hurry. The water was easy, I just had to wire the electric pump and turn it on. Voila! Fresh well water. Did you know you had your own well? The phone is also working now. It just had to be connected," she beamed.

Elsie finally smiled and it was radiant, like the sun coming out to melt the frost away.

There it is. I knew I could get her to smile.

Elsie's smile really was pretty and changed her face completely. Instead of cold and aloof, she looked gentle and warm. Harriet stood there smiling back, lost in that smile.

Get a grip of yourself Harriet! Be professional!

"So, this'll take a few days," she said, breaking free of the spell.

"I'll be back, and I'll also check out that barn of yours. If you want, I can keep that swell Caddy of yours running. I'm a great mechanic too. Me and my dad are building a race car together. Also, it looks like you have some kind of heating system, you see those vents all around the house? I'll have to take a look at that too."

"Thank you, Harriet. Excellent job. I'm looking forward to seeing you tomorrow," Elsie said.

"See ya Monday, Miss Everly."

"Monday? Not tomorrow?"

"Tomorrow is Sunday silly. We don't work on the Sabbath."

"Of course, I must have lost track of what day it is. Get home safe."

"Will do. See ya!" Harriet said over her shoulder as she walked out to her truck.

Harriet threw her tool belt on the passenger seat and took her hat off. She didn't know what to make of her new client. She hoped some of that coldness didn't come from the fact she was colored, but how could you be the daughter of someone famous for hating everyone with slightly darker skin and not at least think that way a little bit? Being a rich, Southern white woman, Harriet was surprised she even let her into the house, let alone fix her something to eat.

She patted the Browning M1900 pistol she had concealed in a pocket in her coveralls. Being colored and a woman in a world that hated both wasn't easy and she'd be damned if she was going to be a victim. Elsie seemed courteous and sounded unlike her father, but Harriet wasn't going to take any chances.

"Never judge anyone, Harriet T. Piper, unless you've walked a mile in their shoes," she said, imitating her father's voice as she cranked up the Model TT. Miss Everly was still on the porch watching her, so she waved again and started driving away.

Miss Everly was a strange lady, yet there was something about her she couldn't put a finger on. She thought about her during the entire drive home.

That night, safe in her bed, she thought about Miss Everly again and drifted off to sleep with dreams of the beautiful scarred white woman that lived in the house on top of the hill.

Chapter 6

Elsie watched Harriet drive away and enjoyed the nice breeze coming from the North as some coyotes yipped off in the distance. She sat back in the deck chair and instead of catching up with the adventures of Edmond Dantes, she just enjoyed the ambiance. A hawk was on the telephone pole, keeping a close eye on her fields. She watched a bachelor herd of mule deer run at full sprint coming from the back yard and rocketing past to the front.

She sat on the front porch until sunset and her thoughts eventually drifted back toward the odd and talkative Harriet. Her solitude was her best defense and only comfort, but now she felt a twinge of longing for company.

Especially company that she could kiss.

She pushed those thoughts out of her head as she noticed the wind start to pick up. She sat and enjoyed the breeze until the wind gained enough strength to blow the hat off her head. She figured it was time for dinner anyway, so she grabbed her book and hat and went inside.

As she crawled into bed much later that night, she heard the wind howling outside. It was much stronger now and reminded her of huddling scared with the rest of the girls at her boarding school during the 1903 hurricane in Virginia. That was the night of her first kiss. She was bundled in a blanket for protection with her best friend, awkwardly figuring out how to kiss.

She soon fell asleep to her pleasant memories while the night wind from the North raged outside.

Elsie slept until hunger pangs finally woke her around ten. She threw on the same dress she wore yesterday and fixed herself some bacon and eggs. She really wanted grits, but the man at the grocery store didn't even know what those were. She was going to miss Southern food.

After breakfast, she strapped on her gun belt and collected all the empty Coke bottles she had been saving, put them in a sack and went out the back door.

The wind last night apparently wasn't too bad because she didn't see any damage. All the windows were intact, and no trees had been knocked down.

Maybe trees in Utah had deeper roots to get to what little water there was. The hurricane in Virginia knocked down almost half the trees in the state when it hit.

What she did notice was a complete and palpable silence. No birds. No insects. Nothing. She didn't see any animals either. No vultures looking for food overhead. No deer walking though the property.

"The wind last night must have scared them off," she told herself with a shrug.

Then, she noticed something peculiar further down the hill. A dark spot in the middle of the field behind her house. She started walking toward it. However, as she got closer, she noticed it was a huge hole.

"What the fuck?" she said and dropped the sack of bottles to the ground.

A typical lady would never lower herself to such vulgarity,

but she had spent years amongst soldiers and the habit had worn off on her.

In the middle of her field, was a large hole, about twenty feet wide and perfectly circular. No dirt had been piled up around the edges from digging and it certainly wasn't an impact crater. She had seen plenty of those to know what they looked like.

A foreboding feeling came over her. She hesitated a little, but continued on.

She carefully approached the hole's edge to look inside. As she got closer, the hair on her arms stood on end and her heart started to pound. She felt the adrenaline surge through her, and she instinctively wrapped her hand around the grip of her pistol, scared to think about what she might see down the hole. The idea filled her with dread, but she took another half-step and inched closer. She could see the hole was deep, but as she finally got close enough to look down, it was so deep she couldn't see the bottom. She picked up a small stone with some bluish coloring on one side and tossed it into the void. She waited to hear the report of it hitting the bottom but only heard silence.

She stood dumbfounded for a few minutes staring into the darkness. A cloud must have moved in front of the sun because the bright daylight suddenly darkened. She looked up, but there were no clouds. Her head felt light, and she had to hold her head to keep from being dizzy.

Roiling waves of fear, anger and shame hit her, and she had to take a knee to keep from falling in.

Slowly the feelings dissipated, leaving her in a stupor and out of breath. She didn't want to look down into the darkness again, but she did. She felt compelled to.

Now it seemed almost welcoming.

Nothing would hurt her down there. She would be safe, away from the pain of love and the burning, unforgiving light that laid bare all her faults. The void called to her, and she wanted to go to it.

What did light, life and love ever do for her? Nobody wanted her up here. She was completely and utterly alone, but the darkness opened its arms to her. The darkness understood her and accepted her. It welcomed her with open arms as she took a step toward it.

"Good morning, neighbor!" came a cheerful voice from behind her.

Elsie blinked and shook her head. She was abruptly and consciously aware of the hole again and quickly backed away, clutching at her chest.

"Whoa, sorry! Didn't mean to startle you," came the friendly voice.

She looked around and saw a clean cut and neatly dressed middle aged man walking toward her. He was pale with a hint of sunburn on his nose and cheeks. A shock of blonde hair jutted out from under his straw hat.

His eyes wandered over her pistol, but he didn't seem concerned.

"My name is Samuel Richards. I'm the local bishop here and your closest neighbor. I knocked on the door, then I noticed you down here and just wanted to introduce myself. Nice to meet you," he said.

Elsie quickly stepped away from the hole as if it was venomous and walked toward Samuel. When she got closer, she offered her hand, which he shook gently.

"Elsie Virginia Everly. Nice to meet you too," she said nervously, still casting glances at the hole.

"I just came by to see how you were doing but I notice you have a sink hole to deal with." he said, his friendly demeanor now one of concern.

"I don't know. It wasn't here yesterday. Maybe those

hurricane force winds from last night have something to do with it. I don't know. I've never seen anything like it."

"What winds?"

"The wind was so bad last night I thought it was going to blow my house away. Then this morning I came out and noticed this."

"You should stay back. It could...uh collapse," he said as he took a step closer.

Elsie took a few steps back as Samuel walked toward the pit. When he got to the edge, he looked down, then looked back at Elsie. He stood there for a few moments then turned around and quickly walked back.

"What is it?" she said.

"Must be a sink hole. They aren't common around here but do happen," he said, voice a little shaky while casting nervous glances back at the foreboding void.

"I think it'd be best if you just stayed away from it. It could be dangerous. Do you mind if we talk back at the house?"

"Yeah, I think that'd be a good idea," she agreed and took quick steps back up the hill.

They arrived back at the house, and she took a seat at a table on the deck.

He removed his hat and sat down as well, seeming to be much more in control.

"So, you're a bishop? Where's your giant hat? A mitre, I think they call it," she said, wanting to talk about anything other than what just happened.

"Yes, ma'am. I'm the local bishop for the Church of Jesus Christ of Latter-Day Saints and no, I don't wear a big, funny hat."

She gave him a quizzical look.

"Mormons," he said.

"Ah. I know what Mormons are, but I've never met a Mormon before."

"Where are you from if you don't mind me asking?"

"Virginia, near DC."

"That would be why. Not a lot of us out East. I'd love to talk to you more about the church, but today I just wanted to introduce myself. Is there anyone else here? I'd love to meet your family," he said looking around.

Elsie was annoyed at the question but smiled anyway.

"It's just me."

"Just you? This is a lot of house for one person. You ought to find yourself a husband! Do you have any hired help?"

"Piper and Son. In Ogden," she said, even more annoyed.

"That's who I was going to suggest. You won't find better work at a better price. Good honest people too. I'm no handyman, but if you need anything, and I do mean anything, please give me a call or pay me a visit. I live about a mile north of here. Once it gets cold you can probably see the smoke from my chimney from here," he said as he slid her a piece of paper with his phone number on it.

"Thank you," she said, ignoring the paper.

They made small talk for a few more minutes but thankfully he didn't pry any further.

"Well, I better get going. It was a pleasure to meet you," he said standing up with a tip of his hat.

"Likewise."

"In all seriousness, stay away from that hole. It's dangerous."

"Of course," she responded as he turned and started walking away.

After Samuel left, she sat there in the shade of the porch. She held up a hand straight out in front of her, palm down. The hand was visibly shaking. The experience at the edge of the hole disturbed her. In her years of schooling, training and nursing in France, she had never seen or heard of anything like that. She had heard some disturbing stories from the shell-shocked soldiers she had cared for, some of which were terrifying and could be considered supernatural. She spoke to a soldier who lost his eyes to gas but swore he still saw ghosts. Another one told everyone who would listen about little gremlins wearing red hats that looted the bodies in No-Man's-Land at night. But nothing like that hole. Her father believed in all this spiritualism and mumbo jumbo bullshit, so naturally she refused to believe it. She wasn't an atheist but didn't believe in goblins or ghouls either. This, however, spooked her. She knew there was a logical and scientific explanation, but she had no idea what that could be.

Once her hands had stopped shaking, she thought about going to get the bag of Coke bottles she had dropped but thought better of it. The thought of going near the hole again sent her into a panic. Instead, she went upstairs to the library, grabbed several of her father's books, and lined them up on the porch railing. She positioned herself about twenty feet away, still on the porch, and stood in a wide legged stance an old Texas Marshal had taught her while visiting DC. She spread her feet and placed her hand on the butt of the Mauser, thumb on the break.

"Come on you Hun bastard," she whispered to herself and quickly drew the pistol from the leather holster and fired one round into each book in rapid succession. Not every shot struck dead center, but every book was knocked down.

As she set the books up again, she imagined every target was that German soldier with the flame thrower. If only she had been quicker or more accurate, Diallo would be alive, and she wouldn't have a mutilated face. As she aimed and fired each shot again, the masked and armored figure came closer and closer, raising the flame thrower toward her. She could hear his heavy footsteps on the porch and feel the heat from the terrible weapon.

Her careful, aimed shots turned into a panicky jerking of

the trigger as the German strode closer. It wasn't until she heard the soft, metallic clicking of the trigger that she noticed the bolt had locked back on an empty chamber. She looked up, and the soldier was gone.

She practiced her breathing exercises and got herself under control. She fed a stripper clip into the pistol, put it on safe and re-holstered.

Target practice wasn't the cathartic experience it usually was, so she grabbed her book, a Coke and spent the rest of the day reading about Edmond Dante's troubles and not thinking about her own.

The thought of that hole on her property never left the forefront of her mind and followed her to a sleep that was nowhere near as restful as the night before.

Chapter 7

Elsie woke with a start. It wasn't her usual bad dream, the same one she had on the train and ever since she returned from France, the events that changed her life and scarred her played over and over again as if she was being punished for some unknown sin. This time it was different. It had never been different before.

In this dream, Diallo didn't jump in front of her. She took the full blast from the flame thrower, and she felt the searing heat enter her eye sockets, nose and mouth and rush down into her lungs. She could feel herself being roasted from the inside and just like every other time, it was so incredibly vivid, it was as if she was living it. Normally she woke up when she felt the first sting of pain. This time, she kept burning until her own screams woke her up.

She sat up quickly, panting and sweating. As she sat up and shook the dream from her head, she thought she saw some movement by her bedroom door out of the corner of her eye.

Nothing jumped out at her or seemed out of place.

She shrugged it off as a residue left over from her dream and threw the covers to the side. After her nightmares, she was usually a little paranoid. It's not the first time she thought she saw something after waking from her nightmare. Then she noticed something on the nightstand. It was the slight rocking movement that caught her eye.

A small stone with blue coloring sat on her nightstand, still moving faintly, as if someone just placed it there. It was the same stone she threw into the hole yesterday. Here. Next to her. Still rocking back and forth.

Now confident she had seen something when she woke, she jumped out of bed, threw on a dress and snatched the pistol out of the nightstand. She let the pistol lead the way as she rounded the doorway.

Nothing was there. She ran to the stairs, looking up to the third floor, then down to the first. She didn't know which way the intruder went, but she decided to go down first. She could check the first floor, maybe see if the person ran outside, and then clear the house.

She checked the house room by room. The wood floors creaked under her bare feet as she threw each door open.

Most rooms were furnished with drab furniture and brown wallpaper only her father would have liked. The only other decorations were the endlessly boring paintings of hunting scenes and generals inspecting lines of troops.

One room after another proved empty, but with each room she checked increased her anxiety. It was like playing Russian roulette. Each room was like the cylinder of a revolver, and each empty one only increased the chances of the next one ending with a bang.

Only there was no bang. Every hallway, room and closet was empty.

She checked everywhere outside, including the barn, then went back in to check the house again, with no sign of anyone having been there. She stopped on the front porch, still in her nightgown, panting with exertion as she clutched her Mauser.

"Maybe I imagined it. Maybe I am going crazy," she said to herself.

She decided to keep the doors locked. Living out in the middle of nowhere, she didn't think she would have to, but for her own peace of mind she was going to from now on. However, when she got to the front door, she noticed something. There were no locks.

"What the hell?"

The back door lacked locks too, as did every single window.

"She went to the kitchen. Though it was still morning, she grabbed the Piper and Son business card and called them, because she didn't know what time they would be in. After a few minutes, she was patched through.

"Good morning, this is Piper and son," said Enoch's friendly voice.

"This is Elsie Everly, has Harriet left yet?" she said, with a shaky voice.

"Not yet. Is there something you need?"

"Um, yes. I was wondering if she could install some door and window locks for my house...today. It needs to be done today. Please. I'll pay extra."

"Not a problem at all, Elsie. How many will you need?"

Elsie gave him the information and hung up after a polite goodbye.

She tried to calm down and think rationally.

I have shell shock. I am alone in an unfamiliar house in the middle of nowhere. I am prone to bad dreams and paranoia.

Most likely this was all a trick of the mind. The chances of a stranger breaking into her house to put a small rock on her nightstand were astronomical. There was no logic behind it, so she decided it was all a trick of her fevered mind.

With that decided, she pulled out her pistol and checked her entire property again, making sure nobody was there.

Enoch hung up the phone, concerned. He judged that Everly woman to be a rather calm and stoic person, but he could hear anxiety in her voice, maybe even a little panic.

Harriet walked in the office with a doughnut in her mouth, carrying a spool of wire.

"That for the Everly house?" he said.

"Yeah. Whoever wired the house when they built it were complete dummies. Kinda looks like they dropped what they were doing and left, right in the middle of it. Other than that, the house is really something. All electrical appliances, including an ice box, how swanky, right? There's an electric pump and even some kind of central heating system I've never seen."

"Speaking of which, that was Miss Everly on the phone just now."

"Oh? She kicking us off the job already? Quick, but hardly a record," Harriet said only half joking.

That kind of thing happened with alarming frequency. Most people around here would rather have other white people working on their stuff, even if the quality or prices are worse.

"No, nothing like that. Actually, she's giving us more work. She must have been impressed with you. Who could blame her? She wants you to install locks on all her doors and windows. See what we have any matching ones in stock. If not, go to the hardware store and pick some up. Remember, they have to be matching," he said with a mock stern look and a smirk.

"Yes, boss," she said with an exaggerated eyeroll.

"You'll never let me forget that one time I installed mismatched locks. It was our own house, so I don't think that counts."

"Harriet. I got a serious question for you," he said, looking over the rims of his glasses at her.

"Yes dad?" She also became serious.

"How does Miss Everly strike you? What do you make of her?"

"I'm not sure. She seems cold and distant, yet...not unfriendly. It's like she wants to be left alone but not because she's mean or angry. She just seems sad. But you can tell she's lonely, you know? I bet those scars on her face have something to do with it."

"I noticed that too. Please don't bring that up with her. Don't ask her about those scars. Those are the kind of scars that go a lot deeper than the skin, if you understand me."

"Oh, I won't dad. I know better than that. It's a shame though. She shouldn't feel bashful about it, she's still really pretty."

Enoch stared at her with a look of warning.

"It's not like that dad," Harriet said, frustrated and a little ashamed.

"I just mean she could probably still get any man she wants wrapped around those elegant, lily-white fingers."

"I think you'll find most men aren't as understanding about that kind of thing as you are, and wounds like that will keep a lot of men away. Men are superficial things. Even me sometimes. Still, something seems a little off. Don't get too close with her. She's a high society, Southern lady. Cordiality is the most to expect, which still puts her head and shoulders over most people around here. She seemed...different on the phone just now, though. She seemed spooked. You still have that bean shooter on you?" he asked.

Harriet patted the pistol in the center pocket of her overalls.

"Good girl. Not that I expect you'll need it with Miss Everly but keep it on you regardless. If something scared her all the way out there, it could be anything. Maybe even a bear or cougar, or something else," Enoch said, trailing off with that last word.

Enoch seemed to ponder something before speaking again.

"Harriet, I want you to be careful while you're up there. If you see anything out of the ordinary, anything odd at all, you come straight home. We can worry about contracts and the like later."

"Odd? Like what, dad?"

"Are there a lot of mirrors in the house?"

"Now that you mention it, there sure are. Whoever furnished the place must have been completely in love with their own image."

A worried look crossed his face.

"Just...be careful and keep an eye out. If you see, hear or even feel anything out of the ordinary, drop what you are doing and come home."

"You're starting to worry me, dad."

Enoch's face and posture softened, and he turned back to the Model T ignition he was working on.

"On another note, Isaac came asking about you yesterday. He's sweet on you, you know," he said with a smile.

"Ugh! That's just because I'm the only single colored Mormon girl in town."

She wasn't the only one. However, she was the closest to Isaac's age and in her own unbiased opinion, the prettiest. Harriet had no interest in Isaac or any other boy around. As a result, she never had a boyfriend. The other girls always caught her eye. She loved the feminine virtues and form but was taught that wasn't what a young lady should do, so she pushed her feelings down and told herself she was far too busy helping her dad with the shop and building their race car to bother. Isaac wasn't really interested in her anyway.

He just wanted to marry the first girl he could get his hands on so she could cook and clean his house and raise him a billion children. She didn't want any part of that kind of life.

"That's not even true. Next time you come back in the office, there better be a doughnut for me too, and be careful," he said with a smile.

"There's a whole box on the counter. Bye!"

She did find enough matching locks in their inventory, thankfully. She breathed a sigh of relief because she hated going to the hardware store. Even though she'd been going there with her dad as far back as she could remember, they always hassled her when she went there alone. It wasn't a good-natured teasing either. Sometimes they would harass her for being colored, other times for being a woman, but no matter what, it was never friendly.

The model TT cranked up as always and she was on the way to the Everly house, cold Coke in the bottle holder. Something bothered her about what her dad said earlier, or rather what he didn't say. Something spooked him, and he didn't spook easy. He knew she carried a gun, he insisted on it, but had never asked about it before.

This bothered Harriet the entire drive up to the Everly house.

When she pulled up, Miss Everly was waiting for her in a long dress, straw hat and gun belt like before. She also looked like she'd had a rough night. Her hair was long, loose and uncombed, and she didn't bother covering the scar on her face with her hair like she did before. Harriet got a good look at it this time and her heart ached for the pain this poor woman must have suffered. It covered most her right cheek and went back to her ear, what little of it remained. Her right arm also had some burn marks, though not as severe as her face. She averted her eyes, not wanting Miss Everly to catch her staring.

Miss Everly must have been so concerned with what was going on that she forgot to hide her scars.

"Thank god you're here," Miss Everly said, voice full of an almost desperate relief.

"Good morning, Miss Everly! I brought your locks," she said holding up a bag full of window and door locks.

"Perfect. If you could get those installed right away, I'd be much obliged. There is sliced ham, crackers and drinks in the kitchen, so help yourself."

"Well, then I'm much obliged! Thanks, Miss Everly," Harriet said, trying out the Southern colloquialism herself.

"Please, just call me Elsie," she said with a smile.

Harriet noticed a slight twitch in Elsie's face when she smiled. It must have caused her some pain because she brought her hand up to touch her scar. Elsie turned away as she covered her face with her hair. When she turned back around, Harriet gave her the sweetest and most caring smiles she could. Her eyes crinkled at the corners with a hint of tears threatening to fall.

"You don't have to do that around me, Miss Everly."

"Yes, well...let's get started," she said turning around and walking toward the house, looking embarrassed.

Harriet strapped on her tool belt, grabbed the locks and followed Miss Everly.

As Harriet neared the house, something felt different. She couldn't explain it, but even though it was a bright summer day, it grew darker and colder as she approached. Harriet paused for a second and tried to figure out what she was feeling, but everything returned to normal as soon as she realized the feeling was there.

She wondered if this was the oddness her dad was talking about and thought about what he said about leaving.

"Everything okay here, Miss Everly?"

"Yes, everything is fine," Miss Everly said with an unconvincing smile.

Miss Everly went up the front steps and stood near the door.

"Can we start with the front door, please?"

"You got it, ma'am," Harriet said as she kneeled in front of the door and started measuring.

She noticed that this time Miss Everly didn't retreat to the porch with her book, instead she hovered nearby, not keeping an eye on what Harriet was doing, just looking all over like she was expecting something. Maybe her dad was right to be spooked.

"You okay there Miss Everly? You seem a little out of sorts," she said after a few minutes.

"Just not used to living in a big house in the middle of nowhere by myself I guess," she said, looking around distracted.

They both sat there in an awkward silence. Harriet brought out her sketch pad and doodled the layout of the room, taking glances at Miss Everly, hoping she'd open up. She then sharpened a pencil until Harriet felt she needed to say something.

"You know, since you're new around here, I can give you some good advice on where to go for groceries or clothes or anything you might need. They say there's some really good restaurants in Ogden, but I wouldn't know. Most of them don't allow us negroes in. For groceries, I go to the Hoskisson in Ogden. For everything else, I go to ZCMI. Did you know that is the nation's first department store? Well, we got one here in Ogden too and it's fantastic. They got everything from clothes to food storage. You should check it out. I'm sure they have some nice fancy clothes for a lady like yourself too."

Harriet cringed inside. She hated it when she babbled on and on and wondered why she was still so nervous.

Miss Everly chuckled.

"Yeah, I am a real fancy lady," she scoffed.

"Oh, don't give me that. You got the elegance and polish of a real fine lady. You must've gone to a finishing school or something, I bet. Unlike most of them, you just happen to have some practicality, which puts you head and shoulders above every other high society lady I've ever met. Heck, most rich folk wouldn't even let me in the house. You fix me snacks. High society has got nothing on you, Miss Everly," Harriet said all at once.

Miss Everly looked surprised and couldn't make eye contact. Harriet thought she saw the hint of a blush.

"Umm, thank you," she said quietly, looking away, adorably bashful.

Harriet realized she probably went too far with the compliments.

"I guess what I'm trying to say is thank you. Thank you for the work and for..."

Harriet paused to think of the right words, but couldn't, so she just finished with,

"...for being you."

"You're welcome, Harriet," she said, looking deep into Harriet's eyes for the first time.

Harriet hoped it wasn't the last.

Harriet looked back into her eyes and felt a little warm around her collar and cheeks. Miss Everly's smile, though subtle and lopsided from the burns, was friendly and gentle. The lines around her eyes hid a tenderness Harriet didn't expect.

It was Harriet's turn to look away and went back to drilling holes in the door. Her cheeks flushed and she couldn't help but smile.

"Goodness, its warm in here," Harriet said to herself,

despite a noticeable cool, Northern breeze blowing through the front of the house.

Chapter 8

It took most of the day to install all the locks on every door and window. Though Harriet thought it was unusual for her client to follow her around the entire time, she did enjoy her company. Miss Everly was a great conversationalist, and her descriptions of Virginia were fascinating, as was the train ride she took to get here and even about the architectural style of the house.

Her clients have followed her before, but only when they were scared that the strange colored person in their house would make off with Grandma's expensive silverware. She could tell that Miss Everly was doing it for a different reason. She was scared of something.

Harriet looked away from Miss Everly, closed her eyes and concentrated.

A quick but very vivid image of Miss Everly chasing something through the house with her gun flashed in her mind. The sense of fear was so intense, it startled her.

"Did you see something out here, Miss Everly? Did something scare you...here in the house? They say being isolated can cause cabin fever and make folks jump at their own shadows. I don't think that's what happened, but something's got you scared."

"I'm not sure. Maybe a mountain lion...I don't know. I'm just a cautious person I guess."

Harriet knew she was lying but didn't want to pry. She'd get it out of her sooner or later.

"Well, that kitty won't be getting in here now. That's the last of them. Every door and window is now locked. You are as secure as can be, especially with that bean shooter always on your hip," she said, pointing to the pistol that never left her side.

"Yes, it is my constant companion. The one souvenir from...my trip to France," Elsie said, not wanting to get into the usual barrage of questions that always followed when she mentioned she was in the Great War.

Harriet gave a little snort.

"Most people get post cards or those little funny spoons with the pictures on them. You get a shoot'n iron. Much more practical...even if it's not a Browning," Harriet said with a wink.

"Maybe I like the mystique of living in what is left of the Wild West. You never know when a gang of outlaw bandits might try to ransack my home and steal my cattle," Elsie said, covering her mouth, following courtesy and chuckling lightly at her own joke.

Harriet loved Elsie's soft and quite laugh. It was very pleasant and feminine, and she laughed along with Elsie.

"If you think this is the Wild West, I ought to take you out past Kessler Peak toward Reno. It's still wild out there. Nothing but desert and ornery cattle ranchers," she said, in her best imitation of a gruff cowboy voice as she pointed finger guns at Elsie.

"Sounds exciting. I do love to drive, so maybe we will one of these days. In the meantime, I will have to settle for the mean streets of Ogden. I need to do some shopping anyway. I brought very few changes of clothes and need to stock up on other things. I will visit some of those stores you suggested. Any requests for refreshments? Any tools or equipment you need for the house?" Elsie said.

"Well, if you're offering, the Cokes are just fine, and I like fruit. As for the other stuff, unless you want to get us one of those fancy, new Black and Decker air compressors and drill for the shop, I think I'll do just fine with what we got, thank you."

"No problem."

"Now, here are the keys to the front and back door. The windows only lock from the inside. These'll keep any riff raff or wild animal out of the house for sure. I bet it gets mighty quiet out here, so this'll give you some peace of mind. I'm not sure I myself could sleep when it's so quiet."

Harriet looked at her watch.

"It's quitting time a little early today. I have some errands to run in town, so I'll head out and be back tomorrow."

She looked into Miss Everly's eyes as they said their goodbyes and felt the same strong, warm reaction as before. Instead of looking away, her gaze lingered. Elsie didn't look away and kept their eyes locked until Harriet forced herself to break eye contact.

ELSIE WAVED goodbye to Harriet as the woman cranked up her truck and drove off. She leaned against one of the large pillars of the front porch and felt her good mood evaporate, melancholy taking its place.

"Damn it."

She missed Harriet's company already. Maybe enjoying her

peace and solitude wouldn't work out the way she thought. This did not fit into her plan of isolation and fading away.

That was a problem. She couldn't get too attached to Harriet or think of her as more than an acquaintance. Young, pretty, with gorgeous brown eyes, such a friendly personality and infectious laugh; she wouldn't want anything to do with a broken down woman such as herself.

"Don't mistake her friendly demeanor for interest in you, Elsie Virginia Everly. She's a decent person who didn't let my scars bother her. Besides, I'm sure she has every boy in town wrapped around her finger. You are a paycheck. If she found out you were Sapphic, she'd probably think you're a freak of nature and want nothing to do with you."

She sighed and went back inside, locking the door behind her and thinking how great it would be if they could at least be friends.

Her father would be rolling in his grave so much, he could generate electricity if he found out his flesh and blood befriended a colored woman.

Elsie laughed at the idea of visiting her father's grave in Hollywood Cemetery in Richmond, to tell him. The smile quickly faded as she realized she couldn't remember the last time she'd had a true friend. She had friends in school, but after that she was too busy with the war effort and was ostracized by society when she returned.

"Would anybody attend my funeral?" she wondered for the thousandth time, though she knew the answer.

No.

In the first few months after she got back to the states from the war, she had often asked herself that same question with her pistol pointed at her temple or under her chin. Even though she knew the answer was 'no', she never pulled the trigger. She didn't know if it was cowardice, bravery or a kernel of hope that kept her finger still, but it had been months since she had done that.

She put her hand on the butt of her pistol. She felt the longing for an end like an opium addict would feel the pull of the pipe, but she put it away in a tiny box in the corner of her mind. But the box was always there, and it tugged at her.

She pulled her thoughts away from those terrible impulses and put her mind to the task at hand; getting ready to go shopping. One step at a time. The alienist at the hospital drilled that into her mind, do not dwell on the negative.

Easier said than done.

Once she showered and started getting dressed, she noticed the little rock that was still on her nightstand. She felt much more secure now that she had locks for the house, but she still felt a little violated. Someone had been in her house. She wasn't seeing things.

Did someone climb down the hole to retrieve the rock, or was someone already down there and brought it up?

Whatever it was, she wouldn't like the answer. She would be on alert from now on. Nobody else was getting in here.

After getting ready, she put her pistol and the small rock from her nightstand in a handbag and headed to the car. She checked the house and the property for intruders one more time. She didn't see anything, so she started the car and drove to Ogden.

Elsie arrived in town around five in the afternoon, parked her car on a side street and fixed her hair before getting out. Harriet's advice sounded wise, so she visited some of the shops she had suggested. She didn't like to shop anymore. She hated being starred at, so she wasted no time and bought several new outfits, including some trousers and a pair of men's jeans, telling the clerk they were presents for her nephew.

Her next stop was the WR Bookstore, where she was greeted like an old friend by Abram and stocked up on enough novels to last a few years. Abram also had a pile of records stacked in the back. She looked through the stack, ignoring the odious marching tunes her father loved so much and found some gems like John Steel, Nora Bayes, Al Jolson and Ted Lewis.

Elsie returned to the car and locked the clothes, records and books in the trunk just as her stomach started to grumble.

"Okay, let's get you fed," she said to herself.

Despite being in the middle of summer, the weather was very pleasant, so she walked around, looking for a restaurant to catch her fancy.

She decided to treat herself and settled on an expensive steak house with outdoor seating. She used to be embarrassed about it but was now used to asking for seating for one.

She sat on the patio sipping a tea, waiting for her steak to arrive. The Philistines out here had never heard of sweet tea, so she settled for a plain iced tea. She was going to have to make her own as this would not do.

It was after the steak arrived that she felt a chill. The hairs on her arms stood on end and she had a distinct feeling that she was being watched.

Elsie put her tea down and inspected all the people walking by, but nobody paid any attention to her. Men in suits and hats and women with plain, but nice-looking dresses roamed the streets doing last minute business or enjoying the summer evening. Cars zoomed through the streets, going either too fast or too slow.

She tried to go back to her meal, but the feeling was still there. She looked around again and this time, she saw someone. He stood out because he was standing still and facing her direction. It looked like a large man in a long, black duster type coat and a wide, flat brimmed hat. People kept walking by, so she didn't get a good look at his face. The figure disappeared in the crowd, but she thought it looked like he might have been wearing a white mask. Maybe he just had really pale skin.

Elsie stood from her seat to try and get a better look, but he was gone. She went back to her meal and finished it while keeping an eye out for anyone watching her. Was this her paranoia from the trauma and shell shock of France or was this real and somebody was actually stalking her? She didn't know, and the doubt and anxiety took all the flavor from her meal. She left a generous tip and walked to the grocery store, looking over her shoulder.

The Hoskisson grocery store was impressive and had almost everything she needed, except grits. Apparently, nobody in this state knew what grits were. She stocked up on everything she needed, including more Coke, and some fruit specifically for Harriet, and paid a boy to carry them to her car.

When the back seat and trunk of her car were filled with books, clothes and food, she tipped the boy a dime and sent him away. He ran back to the store yelling "the scary lady gave me a dime!"

Her heart dropped down into her stomach and her lip quivered. She should be used to this by now, but it never got easier. She thought she looked scary too.

It still hurt though.

Elsie composed herself and went to start the car when she saw movement out of the corner of her eye. She looked up in time to see a white masked face duck quickly back into an alley a half block away. It scared and startled her but if someone was following her, she was going to find out why. Was it the same person in her house?

She drew her pistol from her purse and ran over to the alley shouting, "who's there?!"

Of course, no one answered.

When she got to the entrance of the alley, she held the Mauser in both hands, pointing ahead.

It was a dead end, and except for some wooden pallets and garbage cans, it was completely empty. It went back fifty feet and ended with a brick wall, which was the side of a four story building. There were no doors or windows and nowhere for someone to climb to. She looked all around but couldn't see anywhere they could have gone.

She let the barrel of the pistol drop.

Now she really questioned her sanity. Was her shell shock and paranoia winning the war against her mind?

Elsie wanted to retreat to the comfort and security of her house. She started the Cadillac and drove home. On the way home she remembered the little stone with the blue coloring in her handbag. She took it out and tossed it into the Cottonwood Creek as she drove past.

Chapter 9

Elsie got home, checked all the locks to make sure nobody came in, changed into her new jeans and put her groceries away. It was dark now, but she lit a lantern and sat on one of the deck chairs, enjoying the night air. She had her copy of *The Count of Monte Cristo* in her lap but didn't open it yet. She was still a little shaken from what happened in Ogden and, not for the first time, questioned her sanity.

Is there an alienist in town I could talk to?

She was sick of being broken and would do anything to be whole again.

She sipped on her Coke, wishing it was something far more potent and listened to the noises of the night. However, just like yesterday, she didn't see or hear anything, which disturbed her. The sounds of wildlife soothed her, and its sudden and abrupt absence was unsettling.

Denied the therapy that nature provided, she opened her book and started reading.

After several minutes, she shot up from her seat surprised by what she'd just read.

In the book, Edmond Dantes, as the new and mysterious

Count of Monte Cristo, was visiting the Opera with the beautiful Haydee by his side. The daughter of one of Edmond's original enemies, the pretty and musically talented Eugenie Danglars, when questioned about the Count's appearance at the opera, can only see Haydee's beauty and remarks about how the diamonds only detract from her beautiful neck and wrists. Earlier in the book it described Eugenie as having Minerva's shield and something tickled the back of Elsie's mind.

Elsie took the book with her and went inside, climbing the stairs to the library. Thankfully her father kept a large assortment of reference books and she quickly found one on Greek mythology. She remembered something from her poetry class in boarding school and after only a few flips of the page, she found what she was looking for.

Under the entry for Athena/Minerva, she found a reference to the goddess' shield. It said, 'see Sappho'.

"Dumas, you wrote a sapphic character and hid her in plain sight!"

Sappho was a name she remembered from her poetry class. She was never a big fan of poetry, but she remembered this ancient Greek poet because she wrote of a subject that she cared a great deal about, the love between women. Her poems were very memorable for a young woman exploring her feelings. She lost her virginity to a Jewish girl named Alice while she whispered Sappho's poems into her ear.

It had been almost six years since she had had any kind of intimacy, and she missed it dearly. Memories of Alice from boarding school flooded her mind. The soft whispers of Alice's poetry in her ear caused a warmth to build up inside her and she enjoyed the feeling as it spread through her body. She desperately wanted to release it, to feel that elation and feel alive again.

She went to her bathroom and started to draw a hot bath.

While still a rarity, she had hot and cold running water in Alexandria as well, so she was used to this particular luxury. The spigots of the tub were shaped like Aztec feathered serpents. She didn't remember her father being that obsessed with native art and shrugged. Once the water was the right depth and temperature, she lit a couple of candles, took off her clothes and slid in. The hot water pained her scars, but it soon subsided, and she was able to relax. She preferred showers, but once in a while she liked a good hot soak.

She glided her soapy hands over her arms and legs and tried to imagine it was someone else's hands moving over her. At first, she thought of Alice and her expert touches and beautiful, poetic voice, but as she continued, her thoughts turned to a certain lithe, dark-skinned girl with two braids falling over her shoulders, beautiful large, brown eyes and a smile that forced her to smile back through the pain.

She touched her breasts and her center until she climaxed through gritted teeth, gasping for air.

She relaxed back into the tub with a smile on her face. It had been months since she last did that. Her depression, shell shock and physical pain had kept her from feeling in the mood. Now she wanted to feel alive. Maybe she didn't want to fade away into oblivion. Then she laughed. It would be hard to look at Harriet the same after this.

"The scary lady gave me a dime!" jumped into her mind without warning, almost as if it was a disembodied voice in the room.

The smile quickly fell from her face with that sobering reminder of how other people saw her.

"Only when you lose all hope, are you truly free," she reminded herself and slunk further into the tub.

She wallowed in self-pity until the water turned cold and forced her out of the tub. She dried off but didn't get dressed right away. She stood there and looked at herself in the mirror of the vanity. Her body was covered in small shrapnel scars from the mortar round that destroyed her field hospital. Her skin looked like someone tried to draw a Sunday morning newspaper maze and did a bad job of it. She gently moved her hair so she could see the right side of her face. The bright red and pink scar covered her entire cheek and spread back to her ear. There was very little left of that ear, mostly scar tissue that resulted in an almost total loss of hearing on that side.

She fiddled with her hair until it covered all of her scars. Just looking at the one good side of her face made her remember how she used to be. Young, pretty, gregarious and full of life. Now she stood here, a shell of her former self. A living personification of the Nordic goddess Hela, the 'two-faced terror'. A myth to scare children.

That German trooper with the flame thrower died quickly, but in doing so, he took everything from her, leaving her to die slowly over the years.

The only friends and lovers I'll have from now on will be my own memories.

The weight of her depression pressed down on her with a strength that was almost physical, and she swore the room had become darker than it was before. It looked like a shadow had built up around the corners and were growing bigger and darker.

"You win, you goddamn Kraut," she said to the reflection in the mirror, tears welling up in her eyes.

She reached out to wipe the moisture off the mirror, but when her finger touched the glass, a small wisp of dark smoke floated up from where her finger made contact and dissipated just as quickly as it appeared. As it did so, the room seemed to brighten, and she felt the weight and oppression being lifted from her.

Elsie stepped back, not knowing what just happened. She

reached out a tentative and trembling finger and gently touched the mirror again.

Nothing happened.

She touched it a few more times, increasing pressure with each contact, but no smoke appeared.

"What the hell?"

A thin trail of smoke clung to the floor, coming from the other room. She put on her robe and quickly walked to her bedroom. The large mirror that stood in the corner of her room oozed faint strands of light smoke that moved slowly and silently over the carpet. She stood in front of the full-length mirror and slowly reached out to touch it. The smoke stopped seeping out and evaporated into the air.

Elsie grabbed the Mauser from her nightstand and started to check all the locks in the house. Everything was locked tight, and nothing else strange happened. She paused at the back door and looked out the rear of the house, over her fields through the dark of a mostly moonless night, the mysterious hole in the ground stood out because it was even darker, as if it swallowed any light that came near it. Looking at it made Elsie uneasy, and she quickly looked away.

She finally made her way back to the bedroom, took off the robe and got in bed, pistol still in hand. The excitement had caused her to momentarily forget her troubles, but as she sat there in bed, in the dark, it slowly came back.

She quickly put the pistol back in the nightstand as if it was a venomous snake.

The July heat was considerable, but she dared not open any of the windows, so she laid there, nude, uncovered and sweaty.

Eventually she drifted off to sleep, with dreams of flame and death snapping at her heels.

Sleep was not restful, and she woke before the sun rose.

She put on a light dress and a simple shirt with the ever-present pistol at her side and went downstairs to fix breakfast, only after checking every window and door first. This time, she noticed how many mirrors actually were in the house. Every room had at least two mirrors, some considerably more. The house in Alexandria didn't have so many. Was this a new fetish of her late father's? She was going to have to get rid of most of them. She didn't want constant reminders of what she looked like.

She didn't feel like eating. She didn't feel like reading. She didn't feel like doing much of anything and sat on the front porch, looking over her property. She tried to look at the beauty around her, the rising sun casting red and gold beams, the little purple wildflowers that sprout up everywhere and the bright green trees that lined the creek, but it didn't cheer her up. She didn't know if anything could. Right now, she wanted to be alone and didn't want to drag anybody else down into her depression.

She decided to make a quick phone call.

HARRIET WALKED INTO THE OFFICE, finding her father working on the financial ledgers of the shop.

"Miss Everly called a few minutes ago," her dad said, putting the pencil down.

"What? Is she kicking us off the job finally?" she said fully joking. She knew Miss Everly wouldn't do that now.

"Well...kind of," he said.

Harriet almost spit out the doughnut she was chewing on.

"What?!"

He laughed and held up a placating hand.

"It's not like that. She told me that you don't have to drive up there today and that you should take the day off. She said she'd still pay for the full day and even threw in ten extra dollars so you can have fun and treat yourself."

"Wow! That's very generous of her," she said beaming.

She thought of Miss Everly smiling, which made her a little lightheaded. Those lips, the crooked smile and the slight crinkles at the corners of her eyes made her cheeks grow warm.

His expression darkened a little and he looked down.

"She sounded really down in the dumps. I'm not sure what to make of it," he said shaking his head.

"Well, if I'm not heading up to Morgan now, what do you need me to do today?"

"I need you to take the day off and go have fun. That's what the client wanted and that's what I agreed to."

He opened the cash register, took out ten one-dollar bills and handed them over to her.

"You should go find Isaac and see what he's up to. I know he'd love to spend some time with you. Go have a nice lunch together," he said with a wink.

Harriet rolled her eyes so much she almost hurt herself, but not so that her dad could see.

"Sure thing dad, I'll think about that."

She dropped her tool belt on the work bench and stepped outside.

Her little brother, Leroy, was out front scrubbing off the latest round of vandalism. Someone had painted a misspelled 'NiGGEr' on the front of the store last night and, thankfully, her dad found it early. He'd set her eleven-year-old younger brother to cleaning it before most decent folk were awake. Nothing about this was shocking. It happened at least once a week. Whatever the vandal had used was coming off quickly because Leroy was just finishing up.

"Morning, sis!" he said with a toothy grin.

"Morning, Roy."

"Where are you off to? Going to that rich lady's house up in the mountains?"

"No, I'm on a secret mission," she whispered.

His eyes grew wide.

"Really? What's the mission?" he whispered back.

"Well, if I told you, it wouldn't be a secret anymore," she said.

Her brother said "hey!" behind her as she walked away.

Their house was behind the store, so she didn't have far to go and walked in to see her mother listening to the gramophone while cleaning the dishes from breakfast and humming along to the tunes. She went to her room, which was small, but all her own. Until last year, her three brothers had had to share a room. Now it was just the two.

The happiness of having a day off quickly departed as she thought of her older brother Hyrum, the 'Son' part of 'Piper and Son'.

She lay back on her bed, arms outstretched. Thinking of her brother's death always saddened her, and she tried to distract herself by thinking about what she was going to do with a day off and ten bucks burning a hole in her pocket. She thought about going back to the shop to work on the race car they were building, but she could do that any time.

Her mother walked by with a basket of dirty overalls and work shirts and stopped when she saw Harriet looking glum.

"When you are feeling down, the best thing to do is to lift someone up," she said, and continued on down the hallway, humming as she went.

Harriet was always grateful for her mother. She could spot a problem a mile away and instantly come up with a solution.

She thought about Miss Everly as she stared at the ceiling. It seemed as if every waking thought was about that beautiful but mysterious lady.

As she lay there, the bed seemed to drift away as the ceiling disappeared. She learned early that trying to concentrate and force her mind's eye to see something as it wandered, usually ended the vision, so she relaxed and opened her mind further.

There!

She found Miss Everly, walking around her house with a gun in her hand, scared and alone with eyes still moist from crying recently.

What are you so scared of?

Two images came to her mind.

Smoke and mirrors.

She didn't know why that popped into her head and didn't know what it meant, but Miss Everly was scared, sad and alone.

Her bedroom ceiling snapped back into sharp focus and she sat up on her bed.

"Thanks, mom," she whispered.

She got up and looked in her dresser for some suitable casual clothes, but everything looked too plain or too old.

"It's not like you are trying to impress anyone, Harriet," she said to herself, but still, nothing looked right.

She grabbed her hat and walked a couple blocks to the ZCMI department store. She found some nice dresses out of her price range. Unlike a lot of girls, she didn't like shopping and just wanted to find something nice and leave. She quickly checked a few stores and finally found a secondhand store with a pretty sailor top and knee-length skirt in the front window. It was perfect.

They wouldn't allow any colored folk to try on their wares, but the measurements seemed like they would fit so she bought it. She also bought knee-length black socks, a flat brimmed, flat-topped hat and a pair of small, round, purple sunglasses. Those, she absolutely loved and still had plenty of money left over.

Harriet hurried home to try everything on and after

looking at herself all dolled-up in the mirror, she decided that she was going to be irresistible.

"Who are you trying to be irresistible for?" she asked herself, but the answer made her uncomfortable.

She went to the kitchen to grab a basket, a blanket, some napkins, plates, glasses and cutlery. She then went to the local grocery store and bought some bottles of Hires root beer, Orange Crush, potato salad, cherry pie, cold cuts, tomatoes, lettuce and condiments. She had never prepared a picknick before and wanted to cover her bases.

She took her basket filled with food to her work truck and cranked it up. She put the basket on the floorboard of the passenger side, put on her new sunglasses and started the drive up to Miss Everly's house.

Chapter 10

Harriet puttered up the road toward Morgan in her truck, and not for the first time, she wondered what she was doing.

"Of all the things I could be doing on a day off, you are driving up to your work site to visit your client. What kind of day off is that? Do I even know how to have fun anymore?"

Halfway there, the thought occurred to her of what if Miss Everly really didn't want any visitors. What if she really meant it?

What if she was turned away?

She didn't even consider a plan B. Miss Everly was going to be there, she was going to cheer her up and everything was going to be great.

Even so, she said a quick, little prayer that her efforts wouldn't be in vain.

As she entered the town of Morgan, she became very nervous.

"What are you really doing here, Harriet? Is this really about cheering up a sad and lonely woman or is this about you?"

Her thoughts flashed back to when she was twelve and her father walked in on her and Angelica Chavez kissing. She hadn't done or even thought about anything like that since then. She was just a little girl and didn't know better. Besides, kids always get curious and make mistakes. That was part of growing up. What she was doing now was nothing like that. It's not like she'd kiss a girl again.

Or would I? Was it a mistake?

Banishing all thoughts of her youthful indiscretions, the reality of what she was doing shook her when she took the right turn onto the road that led to Miss Everly's house.

"It's not too late to turn back. This could be a huge mistake. What if she's so insulted, she fires you? Dad would be so pissed, and it'd be all my fault!" she told herself.

She started to look for a place to turn around, but the path up to the house was narrow and steep on both sides. The only place to turn around was the circular driveway of the house itself. For better or for worse, she was committed.

She came up the long driveway and the large, imposing house came into view.

"You just want to cheer her up. When you are feeling down, the best thing to do is to lift someone up!"

Any thoughts of turning around and escaping were dashed when Harriet saw Miss Everly sitting on the front steps, head in her hands. Miss Everly looked up and Harriet could see the startled expression on her face.

"You're committed now Harriet Theodocia Piper," she said, putting a nervous smile on her face and parking the truck.

She saw Miss Everly walking toward her, but couldn't see if she was happy or angry.

She got out as Miss Everly rounded the truck and came toward her.

"I'm sorry for intruding..."

Harriet couldn't finish the sentence because Miss Everly wrapped her arms around her and hugged her tight.

"Thank god you are here," she said to Harriet, her voice trembling.

Relief washed over her as she hugged her back. Now she knew she'd made the right decision. Maybe she was even inspired to make the visit.

"Well, by some miracle, I suddenly found myself with a day off and I couldn't think of a more perfect way to spend it than to have a picnic," she said, pointing to the large basket in the truck, while slowly and reluctantly breaking off the hug.

"A picnic? I've never been on a picnic before. How thoughtful," she said with obvious emotion.

Harriet figured it'd be rude to bring it up, but her mouth started talking before she could shut it off.

"You have a rough night, Miss Everly?"

Miss Everly smiled, then blushed fiercely. Her one perfect cheek blushed enough for both, and she shyly looked away.

"You could say that. Is it that obvious? What say you come in, put those drinks in the ice box while I get a little more presentable. You look absolutely adorable by the way. I love the outfit," she said with a smile.

It was Harriet's turn to blush and look away.

"You know, I just threw any old thing on."

She grabbed the basket and followed Miss Everly toward the house. She looked over the rims of her sunglasses and once again admired how this woman moved. The thin fabric of her dress perfectly accentuated her backside as she walked up the front steps of the house and Harriet couldn't help but be a little jealous. She always thought of herself as too lanky and flat chested but didn't think she was unattractive by any means. However, she wouldn't mind having a body like those models she saw by the lake that one time...or like Miss Everly's.

Harriet was snapped out of her thoughts when she

reached the house and put her foot on the front steps. Just like the day before, she felt a darkness, an almost tangible shadow gathering around the house, despite being in the middle of the day with a clear sky and bright sun. Just like yesterday, the oppressive feeling left as soon as she realized it was there. When she entered the house, everything seemed fine again, so she questioned if it happened at all.

She sneaked another appreciative glance at Miss Everly as the woman ascended the staircase. She leaned against the counter and looked around the kitchen. She had seen it many times, but she was still impressed by it and wondered what kind of meals her mother could make in a kitchen like this.

Maybe I should learn to cook. I mean, it's got to be similar to working in the shop, right? You follow the instructions and put pieces together.

Movement from the dining room interrupted her thoughts. She turned her head toward the room but didn't see anything. The room was situated behind the kitchen at the rear corner of the house, with a commanding view of the property.

She carefully walked toward the doorway, looking for anything that could have moved.

"Hello?"

She wasn't sure why she was calling out. Miss Everly was here alone. Then she heard a barely audible shuffling sound come from the dining room, as if someone was dragging their feet in a crippled gait.

She rushed into the dining room, but nothing was there except a large table made out of one megalithic piece of timber and enough chairs to seat a dozen. She knew she saw and heard something, but the room was open and almost empty except the tables and chairs, and it was impossible for anything to hide here.

As she searched around, she looked out the window into

the fields behind the house and saw something. It looked like a huge hole in the middle of the field. There was no excavating equipment or piles of earth gathered around the hole. It was just a perfectly circular and clean hole. As she squinted to look harder, she thought she saw a dark cloud or mist come up from the hole and quickly dissipate into the air.

"What the heck is that?" she asked herself, but before she could think about it anymore, she heard Miss Everly coming down the stairs.

"Harriet?" Miss Everly called out.

"I'm in the dining room!" she answered.

Miss Everly walked in, wearing a white, one-piece chiffon dress with a fashionable black belt around her waist. Harriet noticed she combed her hair to conceal half her face like she usually did. She wasn't sure why, but she felt a tinge of disappointment in that.

"What are you doing in here?"

"I thought I saw...do you know you have a huge hole in your field?" Harriet asked.

"Yeah, it just appeared there a couple nights ago. The neighbor thinks it's a sink hole. He says it's dangerous and could collapse further. Whatever you do, don't go near it." Miss Everly whispered the last sentence, not taking her eyes off the hole.

The hairs on Harriet's arms stood on end and she shivered.

"Well, let's not have our picnic there!" she said with a little laugh, trying to ease the tension that snuck into the room.

"Come on, I know the perfect place," Harriet said, taking Miss Everly to the kitchen.

They grabbed the picnic basket and the drinks from the icebox and headed out of the house.

"Let's take my convertible."

"Capitol idea my lady! Let us proceed!" she said in an exaggerated, posh voice.

She placed the picnic basket in the back seat and rushed around to open the door for Miss Everly.

"Why, thank you, young lady," Miss Everly said in an exaggerated Southern Belle voice and a big smile on her face.

Harriet's heart beat a little faster every time Miss Everly smiled, and she wished she smiled more often.

"You know, I was hoping one day I'd be able to take a ride in this fancy convertible of yours. I do so love cars," Harriet said, unable to hide her excitement.

"I just love going fast. I love the wind on my face. It makes me feel alive again," Miss Elsey said as the engine started.

Harriet caught the use of the word 'again' and the smile on her face slipped.

Did she not feel alive now?

"This has a seventy-seven-horsepower engine, right? V-8?" she asked, enjoying the thrum of the engine as it came to life.

"Why, yes it does," she said, looking impressed.

"My dad has this crazy notion of putting a Clerget 9B rotary engine in a race car. That's a hundred and thirty horsepower! Can you imagine?" Harriet said, giddy from excitement.

"Well, if he does, let me know because I'd love to drive it!" Miss Everly said, taking off her hat and putting it in the back seat.

"So, where is this spot you have in mind?"

"Just head toward Ogden and I'll guide you from there."

Miss Everly paused and gave her a wry smile before she started to pull out of the driveway and onto the dirt road that led toward Morgan.

Neither one could stop smiling as Miss Everly sped down the road. Harriet looked over at Miss Everly, her beautiful, long and slightly wavy blonde hair was pulled back by the wind and a smile never left her face. She also noticed that Miss Everly put on red lipstick, highlighting her full lips and making her smile brighter. This created a pleasant sensation below her belly that caused her to shift in her seat.

Is this how she was before the accident...or whatever caused those scars? Vivacious and wild?

Miss Everly got on the main road heading to Ogden and sped up, going as fast as the car could go. They both shouted with excitement as the engine roared and the wind blew in their faces.

Harriet had to shout to be heard, "In a few minutes, you'll have to slow down and take a right turn!"

Miss Everly nodded, and when the turn came, she took it a little too fast, causing the tires to squeal. Miss Everly laughed and slowed down, since they were now on a dirt road. A small sign said, 'Mountain Green'.

Harriet told Miss Everly where to go and they soon found themselves parked at the foot of a small hill with a single tree on top.

"I've never been on a picnic before, but when I imagined one, I imagined it looking just like this. This is perfect," Miss Everly said, fixing her hair and putting her hat back on.

They marched up the hill and spread the blanket at the foot of the tree. It was a hot summer day, but the shade of the tree and a slight breeze made it very pleasant.

Miss Everly popped the caps on two sodas and held hers up in the air for a toast.

"I propose a toast. To us. And if I may be sold bold, to our friendship."

Harriet beamed.

"Absolutely! To our friendship!" Harriet said, tapping her bottle against Miss Everly's and took a long sip.

"Oh god, I wish this was wine."

Harriet laughed but then stopped when she realized Miss Everly was serious.

"But that's illegal," Harriet said in a quiet voice.

"Don't worry, I won't tell anyone," Miss Everly said with a wink.

"Nah, even if there wasn't prohibition, I don't drink. I'm a Mormon," she said matter of fact.

"I don't drink either, honestly. I've seen drink destroy the lives of too many veterans. It does not mean that I don't miss it."

Harriet waited for her to elaborate, but Miss Everly became quiet and looked down at her bottle.

She didn't pry but instead took out the food and started to fix the sandwiches and put the potato salad on the plates.

"You want to know about the scars," Miss Everly said. It wasn't a question.

She didn't say anything at first. She placed the plate of food in front of Miss Everly.

"Only if you want to talk about it."

"I don't, but I want you to know."

Harriet didn't touch her food while she listened to Miss Everly's story. She explained everything that happened to her in France, the shooting and burning and of her recovery and how she came to inherit the house and live in Utah.

Harriet listened to the whole story, picking up mental images of a man in an iron suit, flame and pain. A pain so intense it made every muscle in her body tense. When Miss Everly finished speaking, Harriet took her own hat off and with one hand, slowly moved the hair that was covering the scars. She leaned over and placed a gentle and chaste kiss on Miss Everly's scarred cheek.

"Thank you for telling me. I'm proud to know someone who could spend four years up to their elbows in guts and blood, patching up wounded soldiers and not lose themselves in it."

Miss Everly put her hand to her cheek with an astonished look on her face.

"How are you the only person not scared or disgusted by my scars?"

Harriet shrugged.

"Scars are just a physical reminder that you are tougher than what hurt you. Heck, I have a burn scar too. I was eleven years old and thought my dad's acetylene torch looked fun. When I turned it on, I got so scared, I dropped it on my foot. Now I know acetylene torches aren't toys. I know that doesn't compare, but just know that they don't bother me. I like scars. Scars make you tough. So, you know, you never have to hide your scars from me. Ever."

Miss Everly's pale blue eyes clouded with tears.

"Thank you. I'll keep that in mind," she said with a sniff.

"Now I have a question for you, if you don't mind."

"By all means, Harriet. Ask me anything."

"Most white folks wouldn't be caught dead spending time and having lunch with a colored person. Yet you, a Southern lady, daughter of one of the most vehement racist authors ever, are doing exactly that. Is it because a colored soldier saved your life? Is that why?"

"No. That's not why. My father spent so little time with me, his beliefs never stuck, thankfully. By the time I left for boarding school, I promised myself I would go against everything my father believed in. As his writings became more insane and murderous, that became easier. Even if I did believe what my wretched father taught me, France would have changed my mind. The Senegalese soldiers I cared for were some of the most honorable and brave people I have ever met. They had the humanity that my father and brother both lacked. So, no. Diallo saving my life was not the reason I don't hate colored people, but it is one of the reasons I love them."

"Cheers to that!" Harriet said, tapping her bottle against Miss Everly's.

As she took a long drink of her Orange Crush, she realized

she had never heard a white person say such things before. Sure, some were friendly and bore them no ill will, but most either didn't care or were openly hostile. She thought of all the times she had been kicked out of a business or all the times she had to help clean graffiti off the front of their own store. Miss Everly was different.

Different in so many ways.

"I have a question for you if you don't mind," Miss Everly said.

"Fire away."

"Well, it's a two-part question really. How old are you and how come a man hasn't snatched you up yet? If I may clarify, you are gorgeous, funny, smart, wise, talented and an excellent dresser. If I was a gentleman, I'd be ring shopping about now. In my thirty years and all my travels, I have never met anyone quite like you, Harriet. You are truly unique."

It was Harriet's turn to look away as her eyes watered.

Miss Everly looked terrified.

"I didn't mean to offend you. If I said something unkind or too forward, I assure you I meant..."

Harriet took Miss Everly's trembling hand and looked up into her eyes.

"It's nothing like that. It's just that nobody has ever said anything like that to me before. It caught me off guard and I promise I'm not offended. Thank you, Elsie."

Elsie cupped her hands around Harriet's face and leaned in close.

Harriet's heart almost jumped out of her chest as she realized Elsie was going to kiss her.

She was quite surprised when she realized she wanted to be kissed.

She wanted to kiss this woman.

The last time she ever kissed anyone was Angelica when she was twelve. She didn't know what to do.

Are my lips wet enough? Are they supposed to be wet? Do I close my eyes? How does this work?!

Harriet didn't know what to do, so she froze and let Elsie lean in.

"You called me Elsie," she said in her ear then chuckled and backed away.

A great sense of relief and disappointment washed over her. She didn't know which it was, and she laughed.

"Well, of course silly. We are friends now. First name basis," Harriet chuckled nervously.

"And you still didn't answer my question," Elsie said taking a bite of her sandwich.

"Umm, what was the question again?"

"How old are you and why hasn't anyone snatched you up yet? Do you have a boyfriend?"

"Oh, right. I'm twenty-one and no, I don't have a boyfriend and never have."

"I find that exceedingly hard to believe."

"I want to say it's because I won't even give them the time of day. I'm too busy helping with the family business to mess with that foolishness. Really, there just aren't a lot of options. I've never found anyone I've been interested in."

"Surely someone has tried though?"

"Yeah, I've had gentlemen callers, but I give them the cold shoulder. There's a young man on my heels right now. I'm no bluenose, I've been kissed before, but I'm just not interested."

"Why aren't you?" Elsie said, cocking her head to the side.

"Oh, he's a sheik all right. Everybody says he's so handsome and that I'm crazy for ignoring him."

"Maybe you are?"

"No. He wants to put me in a cage. He wants me at home, apron around my waist, cooking and cleaning all day just to greet him with a kiss and a seven-course meal when he comes home from work. He wants to fill my belly up with five-hundred babies while he puts his feet up and I take care of them. To hell with that! I'm going to live my life."

Harriet looked over at Elsie who was looking over the tops of her sunglasses and biting her bottom lip.

"I feel the same way. I will not be put in a gilded cage either. It was my choice to go to war. I'm living with the consequences, but it was my goddamn choice. I promise no man will ever own me. You never cease to impress me Harriet Theodocia Piper, and here's to blazing our own trails," Elsie said, raising her bottle.

"Salud!" Harriet toasted.

"Now, tell me about this race car you and your father are building," Elsie said with a big smile.

It wasn't until the sun was going down, all the bottles, plates and pie tins were empty, that they realized they had talked for hours.

"Oh, forgive me, but I gotta get back home. My folks are going to be worried," Harriet said reluctantly.

"Of course. I think we've done enough damage here. Let's get you back," Elsie said with an exaggerated pouty lip that Harriet thought was adorable.

As they packed up the car to leave, she wondered what she would have done if Elsie did try to kiss her. The fact that she didn't know, frightened and excited her.

Chapter 11

Elsie hid her very real disappointment with a childlike pout. She knew they would eventually have to leave, but it would be lovely if it could have gone on forever.

She sighed and helped Harriet load the car. As she went to start the car, she wished it would sputter and die and they'd be forced to spend the night here, under the stars. That would be so romantic.

Unfortunately, the car roared to life.

Romance and hope?

Oh god, you have a full-blown schoolgirl crush on her! You want to buy her flowers and chocolates and read her poetry!

She told her inner mind to shut up.

Don't mess this up Elsie. This is the first and only friend you've had in years. Letting her know how you feel would ruin everything. It's a good thing you stopped yourself from kissing her!

That cute outfit, her long shapely legs, her silky black hair tied in braids and her beautiful large eyes almost made it impossible to resist kissing her. It was almost physically painful to do so.

Harriet got into the passenger seat and gave her a huge smile.

"Do I need to hold on for dear life again?"

"Naturally, my dear," she said as she spun the tires before taking off down the dirt road.

The huge engine of her Cadillac didn't allow for much conversation, unless they shouted at each other, so they kept glancing and smiling at each other during the drive home.

It didn't take long before they were back at the house where she parked and turned the engine off.

Neither one of them exited the car yet.

"Harriet, I need to say something,"

Harriet looked worried, but just nodded.

"I don't know what possessed you to come here and spend the day with me, but I am most grateful you did. This has been the most pleasant day I've had in years…in many years, and it is all your doing. You are a wonderful person, and I hope I'm not being too bold, but I would love to do this again. As you noticed earlier, I was…am having a difficult time. My situation is not enviable or pleasant. Sometimes I let it get to me and drag me down into despair, but you Harriet, you have been a shining beacon in my dark days. I thank you from the bottom of my heart."

Elsie took Harriet's hand and softly kissed the top of it.

"Yeah, we do need to do this again. You are my friend and if you ever need to talk, give me a call. Our house phone number is five one, four one. If my dad answers, hang up."

"Oh? And why is that?"

"It's complicated. It doesn't have anything to do with you though, so don't worry about that. My dad likes you just fine. It's me he's worried about. I wish we could keep going, but I really need to get back now," Harriet said while they both got out of the car.

"I'll see you tomorrow, right?"

"Absolutely and I'll see about getting power to that library of yours."

"That would be delightful. You get home safe." She beamed.

With final goodbyes, Harriet started her truck and left, waving out the window the entire time.

Elsie stood there on the front step and watched her leave. Her heart still beat fast as she went over the day's events in her mind. She held out her hand, watching it shake as her adrenaline subsided.

Just being around her made her feel alive.

Reality came back, and she realized she was alone in this house once again. Ever since she got the locks put on her doors and windows, there has been no sign of an intruder, only that odd little thing with the mirror. However, if she was honest with herself, that very well could have been her imagination. Her father would probably chalk it up to 'female hysteria' or the fact she read too many fanciful novels.

As always, the doors and windows were still locked. Finally able to relax, she went inside and locked the door behind her.

The night passed peacefully, very much like the first night, and she woke up rested and in a great mood. She took a shower and combed her hair, wearing it loose and down, bucking against the current styles. The attempt to look good needed to not look too obvious, so she wore her jeans, a pretty blouse she just bought and a little bit of makeup, giving her eyes a hint of smokiness and her lips, just slightly more red.

She stepped out onto her front porch and once again, it was a beautiful day. She hoped to see or hear any signs of wildlife, but still nothing. Some Turkey Vultures circled off in the distance, but she saw nothing near her property.

The thought brought no comfort. It did raise a lot of questions though.

Just then, the tell-tale dust cloud of Harriet's truck came up the dirt road.

She couldn't stop smiling as the truck pulled up.

Harriet got out in her usual uniform, except she was still wearing the small, round purple sunglasses she had on yesterday, which Elsie adored.

"I brought you a present. Well, I brought us a present since I'll be enjoying them too. Something this good has to be shared, right?" she said, strapping on her tool belt and walking over to the passenger side of the truck. She reached through the open window and came out with a box of fresh doughnuts.

"Oh heavens! Are those doughnuts? It has been so long since I have had those. How fortuitous, because I forgot to eat breakfast." She laughed.

"Well, they are pretty much my favorite thing in the world. I figured they'd be pretty hard to get all the way out here."

"How thoughtful of you. Let's bring them into the kitchen."

Elsie took the box and started walking up the steps of the front porch.

In the reflection of the glass on front door, she saw Harriet staring at her as she ascended the porch. It looked like she was staring at her jeans.

Elsie looked back, catching Harriet still staring.

"Have you never seen a woman wearing jeans before?"

Harriet looked embarrassed and looked away.

"Oh! Oh yeah, the jeans. It's the jeans I was staring... looking at. Very fetching."

"They are infinitely more practical than a dress. I'll have to buy more. I'm surprised you're so taken aback by them. You wear denim almost every day."

Harriet chuckled nervously and followed Elsie inside.

She put the box of doughnuts on the counter and took one for herself. She bit into the soft and sugary pastry as her eyes rolled back from pleasure.

"Oh, my heavens I forgot how delicious these are. Thank you so much Harriet," she said, ignoring all etiquette and talking with her mouth full.

"My pleasure."

Harriet took one for herself and took a bite.

"I do have to confess...this isn't my first one today," she giggled as she chewed.

"I don't blame you one bit."

"You saw that sink hole in the field out back. Who would I contact to get that filled in or covered up?" Elsie said after finishing her second doughnut.

Harriet gave it some thought, scrunching her face cutely as she did so.

"There are a few crews that could do it. I could call my dad and ask who he'd recommend."

"By all means please do, the phone is right there," Elsie said, pointing to the rotary candlestick style phone on the counter.

Harriet picked up the earpiece and dialed the number to the shop.

After a brief conversation, she explained to her father about the sinkhole, then she covered the mouthpiece with her hand.

"He says he knows a guy that can come up here later today and check it out."

"That would be great. Send him up."

"Did you hear that? Yeah, she said to send him up...Yeah, I saw it. It's pretty big. Okay, I gotta get back to work. Love ya," Harriet said, and she hung up.

Elsie couldn't imagine talking to her dad like that or saying 'love ya'. She wondered what it would be like to have parents you could talk to.

"Thank you, Harriet. That will be a big load off my mind."

"No problem. Now, let's go up to the library and I'll get it connected."

They went up to the library and Elsie plopped herself down in one of the comfy leather chairs while Harriet spread out her tools.

"So, you have a good relationship with your father?"

"Oh yeah. I love my dad, he's great. We have a very close family. There's a lot of family back east in Georgia, but we never see them. Maybe one day. Who knows?"

"Tell me about your family," Elsie said, popping the caps off two bottles of Coke and handing her one.

"Well, you met my dad. My mom runs the house and helps around the shop when she has time. I have two annoying little brothers, Leroy who's eleven and Orson, who's eight. When they're not at school, they also do little things to help. I had an older brother, Hyrum, but he died last year from the Spanish Flu. He was supposed to be the 'son' part of Piper and Son. I guess that'll go to Leroy now."

"I'm so sorry Harriet. My condolences. I can't even imagine what it would be like to lose a sibling you were close with. Me and my brother were...not close."

"It's hard. It's been really hard, but I know we'll see him again. So, why weren't you close to your brother?"

"You know about my father. Well, my brother Thomas worshipped my father and believed everything he did, only he was more spoiled, petulant and pathetic. The last time I saw him, I was still a little girl, and I was happy to never see him again."

"What about the rest of your family?" Harriet asked.

"Unfortunately, my mother died when I was a baby. My

father and brother died from the Spanish Flu. I assume this sounds bad, but it was a relief when I found out. He and my brother were monsters. I hope I don't sound too indelicate, but I envy you and your family. It must have been a blessing to grow up with a family that loves you. You see those empty shelves over there?" she said, pointing to the bookshelves.

"That's where my father's books were. I took them out on the porch and used them for target practice. I was planning on doing it again later today."

Harriet laughed.

"Honestly, I didn't think there ever could be a use for those horrible books, but you just proved me wrong. Maybe I can take a crack at it with you? I'm a pretty good shot."

Elsie sat up interested.

"Are you suggesting a friendly competition?" she said with a raised eyebrow.

"I wasn't, but I am now. But if there's a competition, there must be stakes involved. When I beat you, what do I get?"

Elsie thought about it for a minute, then decided.

"The loser must cook dinner for the winner."

Harriet burst out laughing.

"You wouldn't be saying that if you saw my cooking. It's more like the loser has to eat my cooking. I could bring you dinner, but I can't cook. My mom has been trying to teach me for years, but it's not taking, apparently."

"Okay, deal. I'll finish up here, then you will bring me dinner tomorrow night. Sounds splendid to me," Elsie said.

"Ha ha. That's pretty funny white woman. I look forward to wiping that smirk off your face. I hope they taught you to cook in those fancy boarding schools," Harriet said, looking for her wire cutters.

"I'd ask you to cook me some lovely shrimp and grits, but they don't have either out here, I'm afraid. Such a lack of culture."

"Why would you want to eat something with grit in it? Isn't that used for sandpaper? Rich white folk are weird. Maybe that mortar round conked your noodle a little too hard."

Elsie watched the expression on Harriet's face as it went from smiling to horrified as she realized she took her joke too far.

"I'm sorry, Elsie! I didn't mean..."

Elsie wanted her to stew but holding in her laughter gave way to a very unladylike guffaw.

She could see a wave of relief flow over Harriet.

"You're too distracting. I'm never going to finish this room at this rate. Why don't you sit there like a good little girl and read a book while I fix this mess those supposed electricians left me?"

"Why don't I read aloud to you? That way you are not working in silence."

"That's a grand idea, as long as it's not by Emily Bronte. I can't stand 'Wuthering Heights'. The other Bronte sister is fine."

"Awww, I like 'Wuthering Heights'. I'm in the middle of 'The Count of Monte Cristo'. I could read that but there would be a lot of catching up."

"As fun as it would be to hear you explain the plot of a seven-hundred-page book, I've already read it. A famous novel written by a colored man, of course I've read it. So, you can just start where you left off. It's been a couple of years, but I'll catch up," she said as she started cutting wires.

"Very well, as you wish."

Elsie stood up and strode into the hallway. She entered the bedroom and grabbed the book from the nightstand, but as she did, she felt the room grow cold and saw her breath frost in the air. She held the book to her chest as the feeling of being watched came over her. A shadow in her peripheral vision moved and she jumped and backed toward the door. Her eyes were drawn to the south facing window, to the void in her field. It was as if something wanted her to look. For a fraction of an instant, she thought she saw something dark and formless sinuate back into the hole. It was oily and left a trail of shadow as it passed.

She leaned in, her frozen breath hanging in the air and listened.

Despite her damaged hearing, a faint voice, unrecognizable as man or woman, drifted in the air. It turned her blood cold.

"Elsie."

The voice came from the hole. It had to.

She stood there motionless, trying to catch another glimpse, scared that if she moved, it would cause her to miss seeing it again.

"Elsie? You okay? You've been in here several minutes," Harriet said as she poked her head into the bedroom.

"I'm fine," she said in a soft voice.

Harriet came up and stood beside her, trying to see what she was looking at.

"The hole? That thing gives me the creeps. Can't wait until you fill that in," Harriet said with a shiver.

Harriet took Elsie by the hand and brought her back to the library. The warmth and strength of her hand instantly made Elsie feel better.

Back in the library, Elsie sat in the leather chair, opened the book and re-read the chapter where she left off.

Elsie found herself really enjoying reading out loud to Harriet and the time passed quickly. Right before lunch, Harriet stood up, taking her gloves off.

"Ladies and gentlemen, if I may have your attention. Behold the marvelous modern wonder of the world...Ta da!"

Harriet flipped the switch and a barely perceptible glow emanated from the light bulbs.

"Well, I'm sure it will be much more impressive when it's dark outside. But you now have reading lights in the library," she said with a bow.

"You are a miracle worker indeed Harriet. Thank you. Unfortunately, one miracle you won't be able to accomplish is beating me in a marksmanship contest. I'll go get my gun. You go out to the front porch and set up ten of my father's books on the railing. I'll be right there."

Elsie hurried to the bedroom to fetch her pistol and ammo. She strapped on her gun belt, slid the pistol into the holster and went down to the front porch.

Harriet had just finished putting the targets up on the railing by the time Elsie came down.

"For the first time, I'm glad he wrote so many of those horrible books. We have plenty of targets," Elsie said, putting the pistol on the table.

Harriet looked at the C-96 Mauser pistol and shook her head.

"It's a shame. You're practically next-door neighbors with John Moses Browning, and you use a German pistol. What a shame," she tsked.

"Wait, Browning as in Browning firearms? Browning lives up here?"

"Yeah, well, he lives in Belgium now I think, but his shop is in Morgan. You should give it a visit and replace that obsolete piece of Teutonic garbage with an American made Model 1911."

Elsie put a protective hand over her pistol.

"I could never replace this. Holds too much sentimental value. I will, however, go pay that shop a visit."

Harriet picked up the pistol and inspected it.

"Good. See that you do. The sights on this thing are...less than ideal and the grip is uncomfortable if I'm being honest," she said looking over the gun.

"Already thinking of an excuse for when you lose?" Elsie said with a wink.

"Why don't you go first so you can show me how this antique works?"

Elsie showed her how to load the pistol and how the safety worked.

"Now, we are judging on accuracy. The gun holds ten rounds. You get one shot at each target. My father insisted on having his name in large print on the front cover of every book, so I'll aim for the 'W' and you aim for the 'Y'.

She planted her feet perpendicular to the target and raised the pistol in one hand, carefully aiming toward the books. She took the safety off, and carefully started putting pressure on the trigger. The trigger gave a little before meeting resistance and as she exhaled, she fired, knocking the first book off the railing.

Elsie put the sights on the large, gaudy letter 'W' on the second book and fired again, knocking it down. She took her time, pausing and aiming between each shot, and hit every book, knocking them all down.

"Congratulations. You hit the targets, but don't start celebrating yet," Harriet said as she went to collect the books.

Harriet gathered them all and set them back up on the railing. She then went to the table and picked up the pistol. She loaded it as if she'd done it hundreds of times before and stood with only her right side facing the target and put her left hand in her pocket. She brought the gun up and casually fired ten quick shots, knocking every book down.

Elsie was pretty sure she felt her jaw hit the ground.

"Hmmm. Now, what should you fix me for dinner?" Harriet said.

"You were fast, but were you accurate? Let's find out."

She gathered the books and brought them to the table for inspection. Sure enough, Harriet's shots were more accurate.

Every letter 'Y' was punched through close to the center while only half her own shots were dead center.

"I want steak. Medium well. Pan seared with butter. Oh, and seasoned with just salt and pepper. Let's order some diced potatoes. A side of green beans as well. And for dessert, a pineapple upside down cake, please. Do you need me to write that down?" Harriet said with a huge, smug smile on her face.

"How? You...how?"

"My dad would take me and Hyrum shooting every weekend. When he was a kid, his dad, my grandpa, was almost lynched by a mob. This was in Georgia mind you. He saw the whole thing. My grandpa taught them all to defend themselves and never be a victim. My dad taught me. Most people here seem content to ignore us colored folk, but some want to hurt us, and we won't let that happen."

"I have never been humbled so thoroughly in all my life. Steak and potatoes it is. I'll have to do some shopping. Let's see, I need to buy some—"

A low growl interrupted her.

Elsie and Harriet quickly looked to where the growl came from. At first, they didn't see anything, then they both saw movement in the tall prairie grass near the driveway.

A large cat crawled from its hiding place in the grass and crouched low warily, as if it was stalking. Its yellow-green eyes stared directly at them and left no guesses on what it was hunting.

Its body was thin, the ribs and spine clearly visible through its mangy and spotted fur. It looked sick and starved but the throaty growl it made gave a clear impression it was still very dangerous.

"That's a mountain lion." Harriet said, slowly backing up toward Elsie.

"It's a cougar."

"Same thing."

"Slowly back up and head to the front door."

Harriet slowly gave Elsie the pistol and pulled out her own she had been concealing. The mountain lion stopped and tracked their motions, moving its head along with the movement of their hands. When Elsie took the pistol, the mountain lion growled again, this time louder and more threatening.

Ignoring the growls, she reached in a pouch on her gun belt, pulled out a stripper clip and slowly loaded her pistol as carefully as possible. She flipped the safety off and put the front site on the mountain lion's head.

The mountain lion crouched lower, slowly moving toward the porch stairs. It let out a long but barely audible growl as it started to adjust its stance to make a leap.

Harriet came up beside Elsie and pointed her pistol at the large cat. The two women looked at each other and gave a determined nod.

They fired in unison, but the cat moved so fast, their shots hit nothing but dirt. It darted back into the weeds and out of sight.

"You hear that?" Harriet asked.

A Ford Depot Wagon soon came into view, sputtering up her driveway. 'Davis Contracting' was written on the side of the wagon.

"It's the contractor coming to look at the sink hole. Harriet, get inside and close the doors. I have to warn him away."

"That's not gonna happen. I'm coming with you."

Elsie didn't have time to argue and with Harriet right behind her, rushed down the porch, waving her arms to warn the contractor.

The driver of the wagon noticed them and waved just as the mountain lion, startled by the intruder, leapt from the weeds onto the vehicle. Its front claws dug into the wood paneling on the top of the wagon, as its hind legs ferociously kicked at the front wind shield.

The driver came close to losing control as he swerved and almost drove off the side of the road. The lion's kicks shattered the glass and Elsie could hear the driver screaming.

Elsie fired her pistol into the air, hoping to scare the thing away, but the cat ignored her, trying to reach inside the wagon.

The Ford wagon came to a halt as the driver flailed uselessly at the lion as it clawed through the broken wind shield and sliced its legs in the process. Blood splattered everywhere as the cat gouged itself further on the glass in a desperate attempt to get at the driver. Flesh peeled from the cat's legs as it inched further into the truck. Mr. Davis jumped out of the cab and landed on his back, his eyes wide and mouth silently screaming as he tried to scoot away. The cat saw him leave, but was so impaled on the broken glass it struggled to break free and leap after him.

At full sprint, Elsie quickly reached the contractor and came to a halt, raising her pistol at the cougar Harriet right beside her, aiming her little Browning.

They both fired at the same time and splashed the Ford with more blood as the rounds struck home. The cat jerked as it was struck, then went limp as it slowly slid down the side of the wagon, leaving long trails of blood streaking in its wake.

Mr. Davis, chest heaving and wide eyed, was covered in glass and blood. None of it was his from what she could tell.

Elsie just stood there, breathing heavy and holstered her pistol.

"What the heck just happened?" Harriet said, not breathing heavily at all.

"I don't know but let's make sure it's dead."

They both approached the motionless form lying in the middle of the dirt road, and as she got close, she saw that one of their rounds had opened up its skull, leaving no doubt the cougar was dead.

"That was my shot," Harriet said, pointing with her pistol.

"What in all that is holy is going on here?" Mr. Davis said, shaking the glass off his clothes.

"I'm terribly sorry, Mr. Davis. We were out on the porch and that cougar came out of nowhere and tried to attack us. Poor thing must've had rabies or was starved out of its mind," Harriet said apologetically.

"You can't fool me. You two were goading it, driving it toward me."

"Now, Mr. Davis. You can't possibly believe...," Elsie tried to say but was cut off by Mr. Davis, who had replaced his fear with anger.

"No burned up hag or tomboy coon is going to tell me what I can or can't believe. I know what I saw. There ain't been a lynching here in Utah, but after I tell everyone what you two chippies did to me, there might be. Better start packing your bags."

He gave an audible 'hrumph!' and got back in his Ford and drove away as fast as he could.

Elsie leaned over to Harriet.

"What does 'chippy' mean?"

"It means slut."

Chapter 12

Harriet walked side by side with Elsie to the barn to get some shovels to bury the cougar.

"Must've been out of its mind with hunger and disease. But this seems to be more than that," Harriet said, thinking out loud.

She was still a little shaky as the adrenaline started to wear off and put her hands in her pockets to keep them from shaking. Her gift let her see spirits of those that had departed. This was the first time she saw a spirit in a living thing.

When the mountain lion had come out of the grass to stalk them, she could have sworn she saw something. She didn't want to believe it at first, dismissing it as a trick of the light or her nerves, but she saw the spirit of the poor animal and it wasn't that of a mountain lion.

It looked like the spirit of a jaguar was inside the body of the cougar. She didn't want to tell Elsie what she thought she saw because she didn't want to get thrown into the looney bin by such a charming woman, but the more she thought about it, the more sure she was, even though it didn't make sense.

When they both examined the carcass, she noticed the

pads of its paws had been worn down and were bloody, infected sores. The unfortunate animal must have been in agony.

"I've never heard of anything like this happening. Like it was possessed," Harriet said, whispering the last sentence to herself.

A dark look spread over Elsie's face, and she paused before answering.

"I don't know. It was diseased and insane. It wasn't in its right mind. We did right to put it down."

"You don't think that creepy hole behind your house has anything to do with it? I don't like the way it feels. Can you honestly tell me you haven't felt...or seen anything?"

Harriet remembered the dark mist she saw near the hole and figured Elsie must have seen something too.

She thought of the times when she set foot on the property, only to feel a dark sense of foreboding surround her. There was something wrong with this house and that hole in the ground had something to do with it.

Elsie didn't say a word but looked down at her hands.

"Have you?"

"I don't know. I'm a broken woman, Harriet. I never know if what I'm seeing is real or just my shell shock. Maybe that mortar round did conk me on the head too hard. Every day I relive my worst moment in a waking nightmare. My nightmares become a reality I live with always. The only thing I can cling to, the only thing I know is real around here is you, and when you are not here, I cling to the thought of you like a drowning woman to a life raft."

Harriet was taken aback and stopped mid-step.

Elsie must have realized what she'd said, because she turned bright red and started to stammer.

"I mean...I...I mean you are my friend. I'm a thirty-year-old, reclusive eccentric who sees dark mists near holes that mysteriously pop up in my back yard, people in my house and smoke coming out of mirrors, yet here you are, looking for shovels to bury a dead cougar after helping me shoot it. You really are something."

For the first time in her life, Harriet didn't know what to say. She had no words, so she gingerly took Elsie's hand and held it. She looked into Elsie's eyes, shining with barely contained tears.

Harriet opened her mouth to start to tell Elsie what she thought of her, but something she said struck her.

"Wait, you said you saw dark mists? Near the hole?"

"Perhaps. I'm not sure what I see now days."

"I saw a dark mist near the hole yesterday too. It was there for a split second, then it disappeared."

"You saw it too? It is so hard to tell psychosis from reality."

"Unfortunately, it's not only in your mind. I'm seeing it too and a mountain lion of all things, just attacked your contractor. Oh geez, I need to call my dad. I bet news already spread around town. I gotta use your phone."

"Of course. I'll look for the shovels, you call your father."

Harriet nodded and took off running toward the house. She ran up the steps of the front porch in two bounds and went to the kitchen and grabbed the phone.

"Piper and Son. You break it, we fix it. Enoch speaking," her dad said.

"Hey, dad."

"Hey, Harriet. How's the job going? Did Jim Davis make it up there yet? He said he'd be there after lunch."

"Yeah dad, he made it. Unfortunately, we hit a little snag."

"What do you mean?" he said.

"As he was pulling up in that old Ford wagon of his, he was kinda...attacked by a ja...mountain lion. Yup, a mountain lion. I don't think he was hurt, but it tore up his truck something fierce. He was so mad. He called us terrible names and dad, he threatened to lynch us."

"He threatened to what? To lynch you? How dare he! I'll talk to him and the other contractors around town so this doesn't boil over. Are you okay? Is the mountain lion still there?"

"No, we had to shoot it, poor thing. It looked crazed and sick. I'm going to help Miss Everly bury it."

"Thank goodness you all are okay. If it was sick, it's a good thing she put locks on her doors. I shudder at the thought. It's a good thing you keep that little Browning on you."

"Do you think Mr. Davis will tell other contractors not to come here? He said some pretty awful things to us, dad."

"I'll try to get to Jim before he starts spreading word all over town that Miss Everly sics her pet mountain lions on people. Now, since you are helping her dig a hole, there is a secondary fee for excavating. Make sure it's on the receipt for the day. Good work darling. Stay safe."

She said her goodbyes, hung up the phone and hurried back outside to find Elsie.

When she found her, Elsie had two shovels in her hands and was looking at something on the ground. Harriet came up beside her.

On the ground next to the cougar's body, were clear, bloody paw prints made by the mountain lion, leading off to the south, behind the property.

An image popped into Harriet's mind of a home, or lair the cat came from.

"I...I think we should follow the tracks. Bet it stayed bedded down somewhere close before it attacked us."

"I just want to get this over with and go back inside."

"I got a feeling about this. Just trust me. Drop the shovels and follow me," Harriet said as she made sure her pistol was reloaded and followed the tracks.

Elsie shrugged, dropped the shovels and trailed Harriet into the weeds.

Despite the vegetation being thick, it was mostly brown and dead, so it was easy to follow the cougar's path.

The path took them down the slope of the hill and out of sight of the house. They came to a gulley, where the bloody tracks seemed to originate.

"The tracks go south, down this gulley. C'mon!"

"Are we sure this is completely necessary? The thing is dead. Do we really need to know where it bedded down for the night?" Elsie said.

"Just keep your gun ready, just in case. Just a little further."

Elsie nodded and followed.

While the area around the house was professionally cleared and prepared, here everything was brown, dirty and was nothing but thorns, tumble weeds and dirt. There were some wildflowers still clinging to life after the spring showers, but most of them were dead and wasted away.

Another five minutes of walking and the tracks suddenly veered off, seeming to jump out of the gulley. Harriet could see where the big cat scrambled down.

"C'mon, help me up," Harriet said, motioning for Elsie to give her a boost.

Elsie cupped her hands and Harriet used it as a step.

"Harriet. Before you jump up, take a peek first. Make sure the area is clear."

Harriet nodded and looked over the edge. Elsie gave a helpful lift at the end that boosted Harriet up and over the lip of the gulley. She then turned around, laying on her stomach and reached down to help Elsie.

Elsie took her hand and scrambled up. Harriet grunted as she lifted Elsie up over the lip and in a very unladylike manner, fell on top of Harriet with a loud 'OOF'.

Harriet lay there in the dust, surrounded by prickly weeds with Elsie looming over her. Her long blonde hair had come lose and hung between them, framing her beautiful face. Even without the lipstick she had on the day before, her lips looked full, warm and inviting, just asking to be kissed. Elsie's eyes, usually a pale blue, looked large and dark. Her lips were parted just a little as she breathed in shaky breaths, her arms and legs trembled against Harriet's own.

Instead of looking away and retreating, Harriet looked back into Elsie's eyes, daring her to continue and finish what she didn't at the picnic.

More than anything, Harriet wanted to taste those beautiful lips. She brought her hand up and placed it against Elsie's scared cheek. Elsie closed her eyes and leaned into her hand. Elsie started to lean closer to her and Harriet closed her eyes for the expected moment of bliss.

Harriet was brave enough to admit what she wanted now.

She wanted Elsie.

Instead, she heard Elsie gasp and sit up.

Harriet quickly opened her eyes and looked around as Elsie disentangled herself and stood up.

Ten feet away, hidden in the weeds and small trees, stood a small, stone structure. The walls had partially crumbled, leaving a four foot tall wall to mark the outline of the building. It reminded Harriet of the cliff dwellings of Southern Utah that she had seen in a magazine, stacked stones, no cement. Even though most of the walls had fallen, she could still see where a door and window had been. Large, bloody paw prints led inside.

"This is where it came from," Harriet said.

"Let's take a look," Elsie whispered and took a step toward it.

"Wait!" Harriet said, placing a hand on Elsie's shoulder.

As Harriet looked closer, despite the bright sunlight, a

shadow formed over the ruins, just like it did at Elsie's house, only this time the shadow was far darker and radiated malevolence.

"Do you see it?" Harriet whispered.

"See what?" Elsie said, voice trembling.

"There is a darkness surrounding this place. Something really bad happened here and whatever it was, stained it," Harriet said, not knowing exactly how she knew it. She just did.

"I won't go in, but I'll take a look."

Elsie put her hand on the butt of her pistol and slowly and carefully approached the ruins.

She watched Elsie creep closer, and the closer Elsie got, Harriet swore she could hear whispering in the air, though she couldn't make out what it said. The whispering grew louder as Elsie approached.

"Careful!" Harriet whispered, just loud enough for Elsie to hear.

Elsie crept close enough to finally look inside the ruin.

The darkness grew and grew until it surrounded them, blocking out the harsh sunlight.

Harriet noticed movement in the shadows and saw the darkness congeal into a vague, human-like figure beyond Elsie. It moved slowly, like a person moving through water, and it reached for Elsie.

"Run!" Harriet shouted.

Elsie looked startled, but she didn't hesitate and ran back to Harriet as the shadow tried to grab her. Elsie grabbed Harriet's hand as she drew close enough, and together, they ran back to the gulley and jumped down.

As they ran away, Harriet could no longer hear the whispering, but as she looked back, the shadow person stood at the brink of the gulley. She barely made out a man's face and even though it was made of pure darkness, she could see his square jaw, perfect features and what looked like a scar over his left eye. The shadow man lifted off the ground, floated down to the bottom of the gulley and rushed in their direction.

Harriet looked away and said a quick prayer as she ran and didn't look back.

They ran back to where they first entered the gully and helped each other out. They stood there, in sight of the house and breathing heavily.

"What the hell just happened?" Elsie said between breaths.

Harriet didn't say anything but watched the gulley to see if that thing followed them. Once she was sure they weren't followed, she sighed with relief and caught her breath before answering.

"Let's get back to the house first. I want to get as much distance as possible from that place."

They cautiously walked back to the house. Harriet took a seat on the front porch and kept an eye out while they sat in silence for several minutes.

Harriet could see the sky brighten and a weight lift off her soul. It had nothing to do with the sun or the weather. Whatever evil spirit haunted the place, it had left for the time being and Harriet relaxed enough to talk to Elsie.

"What did you see in the ruins?"

"Why did you tell me to run?"

"I asked you first."

"Fair enough. You were right about that place. Something terrible happened there. In the middle was a great stone slab, like an altar, covered in dry blood. Next to it, was a small, short pillar with a stone bowl on top. Inside the bowl...I don't know, but it looked like desiccated human organs. I say human because there were bones and shredded clothes scattered all over the place. Now, what did you see? Why did you tell me to run and how did you know all of that?"

"I saw a literal darkness gather around the place as we got

closer. It surrounded it and was so dark I couldn't see through. Except I did see something. A figure. Like a man made of pure shadow. It reached out for you, and I'm so glad you listened to me when I said 'run' because it almost had you. It chased us, Elsie. I don't know what's going on here, but I do know there is something...not right about this place."

"Not right?"

"Exactly. Something is wrong...wicked. I've seen that same darkness around your house a couple of times, too. Even inside, I've heard things."

"I must admit, now that I know I'm not crazy, I have too. Wouldn't it be my luck to inherit a haunted house?"

"Why don't you go take it easy, and I'll bury the cougar later," Harriet said.

"That might be a good idea. It's been a busy day, with more excitement than I'm used to," Elsie said and stood to go into the house.

Am I reading too much into this? Was she going to kiss me and changed her mind at the last second? Why would she stop?

You don't want a friendly peck on the cheek. You don't want a chaste little kiss between friends. You want to taste those lips and feel her tongue in your mouth. You want her mouth on other places...

"Well, you know what I was wondering. How is it that you can see the darkness and shadows, and I can't?"

"I'm different. I could always see things others can't. Maybe something is wrong with me?"

Elsie laughed and returned to stand beside Harriet.

"That's not possible. I couldn't imagine anything that could be wrong with you?" Elsie said shyly.

"Oh, you'd be surprised."

Maybe she wouldn't be.

It's not normal for girls to only want to kiss other girls. Or is it? Harriet didn't know and was lost in her confusion.

She thought about the coincidence of Elsie reading that passage from the 'Count of Monte Cristo' that stuck with her even years after she read it. Eugenie Danglars and her Sapphic shield of Minerva. Maybe she wielded that same shield.

If only she could use that shield to protect Elsie from all the strange goings on around here.

Chapter 13

Elsie stood on her porch and waved at Harriet as she drove away. The jitters and shakes from all the excitement were long gone and the strange happenings seemed like a bad dream.

She almost kissed Harriet again and almost ruined the only good thing in her life. Tomorrow, she was going to have a nice dinner between friends. No music. No candlelight. No romance.

She walked back into the kitchen to take a look in her ice box, already looking forward to cooking for Harriet tomorrow. Steak and potatoes sounded delicious, but as she opened the ice box, she saw that she didn't have any. She went to her cupboard, but she didn't have any potatoes either.

"Well, shit."

Getting out of this house and into town, around people, might be exactly what she needed right now.

As she stood in her kitchen, the reality of her situation began to weigh on her. It could not be denied anymore that there was something dark and evil about this place. Dark mists, murderous animals and now shadow people chasing them in broad daylight could not be chalked up to her own feverish imagination.

To compound the dreadful reality of her situation, a crushing and profound loneliness engulfed her. Harriet's absence was like a candle being blown out in a dark room and left her blind and scared.

There was a small market in Morgan that would have everything she needed. This whole 'isolation' thing wasn't turning out how she thought it would and she didn't enjoy it one bit.

She changed out of her jeans and put on a dress, threw her pistol in her purse and grabbed a hat.

Within minutes, she was tearing down the road to Morgan, glad to be away from the house.

Thankfully, it didn't start getting dark until after eight and she could get there and back without even having to use her headlights.

Her mind wandered as it always did when she drove. She didn't let herself hope, but what would it be like to kiss Harriet? What would it be like to embrace, crushing their breasts together as they kissed passionately?

Of course, Harriet didn't have much in the way of breasts, which Elsie liked. Contrary to most people, she viewed small breasts as more feminine. Maybe it was all those years in France rubbing off on her. That's how the French soldiers talked about it, and they talked about it a lot.

"Anything more than what would fit in a wine glass, was excess," was a common saying.

It was more than her good looks, of course. All her lovers at boarding school and college were always temporary and she never had a real emotional connection with any of them. At the time, she wasn't looking for a connection, just a good time. However, she could see herself spending every day with Harriet.

The way Harriet smiled at her during the picnic and looked her in the eyes without fear, revulsion or even awkwardness, made her feel like a real person again. Most people she met avoided looking at her. Harriet's gaze was thirsty for it and searched her face and eyes like a person crawling through the desert looking for water. Most importantly, she didn't feel the need to be someone else around her. She didn't have to follow traditional societal norms or conform to high society standards. She could read her novels, wear jeans and shoot guns around her.

And Harriet was funny. She made Elsie laugh like she hadn't laughed since she joined the French Army.

She was still hiding the one thing that'll scare her away.

She hasn't told her she is a lesbian.

Elsie decided that she would have to tell Harriet. If this friendship were to continue, Harriet would have to know everything, and if it scared her away, better now than later.

Harriet would have to be told.

What if she runs away? What if I scare her off and she doesn't want anything more to do with me?

She is a smart woman and will figure it out sooner than later. Better be upfront about everything. Get your cards on the table. Besides, maybe it won't scare her away and maybe she also likes women? Maybe she feels....

"No! Don't do that to yourself. Just hope she still wants to be friends. Besides, kissing between friends is normal. Hell, even doing more than that is not unheard of."

The little market across the street from the gas station came into view. 'Ute Trading Post' carved in large wooden letters hung over the front door. At one time the building was painted white, but mere chips of white paint still clung to the peeling and sun-bleached wood. If it wasn't for the few cars she had seen parked there on other occasions, she would have sworn the place was abandoned.

She pulled in front of the store and turned the car off. She put her hat on and walked up to the small steps.

There was nothing welcoming about the small market, and she almost turned around. As she put her weight on the steps, they bowed and creaked and she thought that if anyone heavier than her used them, they would break.

A sign that said 'welcome, we are open' hung on the rusty and loose doorknob and as she reached for it, she stopped. It was hard to make out, but she heard chanting or rushed and angry whispering. She hesitated but reached for the door anyway and entered.

She had seen the store before, but had never seen anyone come in or out. Immediately, she saw why the place was never busy. It was small, and only lit by a couple of oil lamps. Everything was covered in dust or soot.

The proprietor of the store wasn't any better. Despite the name, the grocer wasn't a Ute. He was an older white man, rail thin with the red, bulbous nose of an alcoholic and long, stringy hair that hung past his shoulders. There was nobody else in the store.

He didn't say a word but stared at her. Despite the huge grin, it looked like his eyes were angry.

Elsie immediately felt uncomfortable and wanted to leave. She grabbed what she needed and took everything to the counter. The man behind the counter didn't look at the food placed in front of him and kept staring into Elsie's eyes.

"How much?" Elsie said, trying to coax anything from the grocer, but he didn't move or say anything.

Her urge to leave grew.

She took a dollar from her purse and threw it on the counter, not bothering to check the amount or get change.

"Keep the change, and your store is trash," Elsie said as she grabbed her things and left. His eyes followed her the whole time.

As she pulled away from the store, the grocer stuck his head out from the door and watched her leave with the same, never changing grin. The uncomfortableness of the place stuck with her the entire drive home, and she couldn't shake it.

Elsie pulled into the driveway of her house and turned the car off. She wondered if she should just sell the house, move away and be done with this accursed place. She couldn't deny any more that what is going on is supernatural in nature.

She looked up at the house, trying to see the tangible darkness Harriet spoke of.

She wished she could feel like she did when she first arrived, when animals would wander her fields and she slept peacefully at night. Now, she locked the doors and made sure the mirrors weren't doing anything odd. Why couldn't she just have a normal life?

Of course, she thought, not being romantically interested in men destined her to a life that would always be different. Most of the girls she fooled around with from boarding school were married with children and leading their idyllic lives. Some, she knew, found the idea of being with a man as repugnant as she did, but they did what was expected of them. For boys and girls, a little experimentation was only natural, even expected, while at boarding school, but the societal expectation was to settle down, marry and have kids.

Maybe she should just leave this place and live out of a hotel room until a realtor could find another isolated place for me to buy. Somewhere far away.

Far away from Harriet?

She only knew her a few days, but already the thought of not having her in her life terrified her more than living in a haunted house, or whatever was going on here. Whatever it was, she was damn sure going to get rid of most of the mirrors in the house and keep her doors locked.

Harriet stood in front of the sink, washing her hands repeatedly while she was lost in thought. This was probably the strangest day she's ever had. She won a shooting competition, killed a mountain lion which, apparently, had the spirit of a jaguar, found an old temple, was chased by a shadow and realized that she was legitimately disappointed Elsie didn't kiss her.

Harriet looked at her hands to see if they were still shaking. They weren't, but a feeling of dread overcame her. Not just for herself or Elsie, but for everyone and everything she knew.

After taking a moment to calm down, clear her thoughts and say a prayer, she grabbed her tool belt and got out of the car.

She walked by the partially disassembled race car she and her dad were building and thought about giving Elsie a ride in it. Elsie's long blonde hair would flutter in the wind and those glossy red lips would glisten in the sun.

This worked to pull Harriet's thoughts away from the terrifying events of the day, at least temporarily.

She found herself blushing and quickly walked into the shop, dropping her stuff on the counter.

"Oh, my word, I'm glad you're back. What happened? Jim Davis is saying that Miss Everly shot at him and he was attacked by a lion. Tore up his truck real bad, too," her dad said as he jumped up from his seat and embraced her.

"We saved that ol' coot! We're the ones who shot and killed that cat while he just screamed at us and drove away, the yellow belly. And how does he repay us? He'll probably be telling his lies to the whole town now."

"He already has, but I'm just glad you're alright. There's something off with that woman. I can't put my finger on it. She has a reputation now. I'll keep trying, but it'll be hard to find another contractor to fill in that sinkhole. What an odd thing though."

"Please keep trying, dad. She needs that thing filled in or covered."

"I know, I'll keep calling around," he said.

"In the meantime, Isaac was asking about you again today. He likes you, you know. When are you going to agree to date with him?"

Never.

She didn't answer.

"Look, I'm just worried about you. You're a grown woman and you've never...had a...boyfriend. I'll be honest with you. I realize there aren't a lot of options out there for you. Here's a man that's interested. He's a good man and he's sweet on you. Why don't you give him a chance?" he said.

"I'm too busy for that nonsense. I have big shoes to fill, you know that," she said looking down.

"If you need time off, I'll be happy to give it to you. I know you didn't spend time with Isaac on your last day off. What did you do?"

She wouldn't lie to her dad, but she didn't want to tell him the truth either.

"I went shopping for some new clothes and went on a picnic up in the hills in Mountain Green."

"A picnic? By yourself? Tell me, if you didn't go with Isaac, who did you go with?"

"Dinner's ready!" called her mom, poking her head through the back door.

"I made stew with dumplings!"

Saved by the dinner bell!

"I love her dumplings! I'm going to get washed up," she said, fleeing.

Harriet almost made it out of the shop.

"Harriet?" her dad said softly.

"Yes, dad?"

"I'm worried about you. This conversation isn't over. Go get washed up. Let's not keep your mother waiting."

Harriet went to her room and closed the door.

What are you going to tell him when he asks again? You can't tell him you went on a romantic picnic with a woman instead of stupid Isaac.

She stripped off her work clothes and got into a long dress.

"You got yourself into a bind here, Harriet Theodocia Piper. What are you going to do about it? You can't date Isaac and you can't tell dad you're sweet on the odd white woman that just moved in."

She sat on her bed, confused and a little scared. She looked around her room, which was covered in her drawings of pretty ladies in fancy clothes. She loved drawing fashion and always thought that if she had been born white, she would've been able to go to school to study fashion design. Even so, her talent brought her comfort as she looked around at her creations. She reached in her nightstand and brought out a well-worn copy of the church magazine for kids, 'Children's Friend'. She quickly found the dog-eared page that she had read dozens of times.

It showed a photo of two distinguished, well-dressed women, one sitting in a chair, the other standing beside and slightly behind, holding each other's hands.

It was the general president of the church's organization for children, Louie B. Felt and her first counselor, May Anderson. The article gushed about how loving they are to each other, how they live together and even how they share the same bed.

She often read this article and thought long and hard about what this meant for her. Ever since her father caught her kissing another girl, she tried her best to deny her nature but couldn't anymore. Her desires were always there, like a constant companion. Sometimes she could put it in the back seat and almost forget it's there. Other times, it would sit in the front seat and take the wheel. Pretending it wasn't there was impossible now.

This article was proof that she might not have to keep hiding who she really was. If two women who were obviously in love could be celebrated in a church magazine, why would she have to hide her true self?

Her thoughts were interrupted when her mother called. She ran to the bathroom sink and washed her face and hands before going to the dining table. She sat at her usual spot, the rest of the family already waiting for her. Once she sat down, her dad said the prayer and then they all dug in.

"How was your day, honey? Anything interesting?" her mom asked with a wink.

"Oh, nothing much. Pretty boring day actually. Usual routine. Me and Miss Everly were attacked by a crazed jaguar and shot it, thereby saving Mr. Davis's life. How was your day?" she said as nonchalantly as possible.

Her two younger brothers sat there, forks hovering in midair and faces frozen with wide eyes and mouths open so much they were almost hitting the table.

"What!? Tell us everything!" the boys cried.

"A jaguar? I thought it was a mountain lion," her dad said with a grave and dark look on his face.

"It was some kind of big cat," she said, looking away.

"Did it have spots?" he said, leaning closer.

"Yes," she said, unable to lie.

Her dad leaned back and looked deep in thought.

She spent the rest of dinner telling a somewhat truthful, but heavily embellished version of the story. She left out the part that its bloody footprints led to haunted ruins. If she brought that up, her father would either think she was crazy or believe her and forbid her from going back. Either outcome wasn't acceptable.

After dinner, she helped her mom do the dishes, reassuring her the whole time that she was physically fine and okay returning to work on the house.

When Harriet finally returned to her room for the night, she lay on her bed and thought about everything that was going on. She was chased by something made out of shadow and smoke, and she didn't know what it was. It wasn't a ghost. Heck, she had seen ghosts before. This shadow person came after them. Ghosts didn't do that. At least she had never seen one do that.

The first time she saw a ghost was her uncle's spirit at his own funeral when she was nine. He stood beside his coffin wringing his hat in both hands. Then he disappeared. Ghosts looked just like people. Usually, they weren't scary. Most of the time they didn't even know you were there. One time a ghost did scare her, though. She walked by an old, boarded up house, and she happened to look up in the attic window and saw an old lady staring back at her. The ghost had an aura of anger and contempt so powerful it made her run away.

This thing was something else entirely and had a much more loathsome feeling about it. It was dark and icky and she had an impression of rotting meat and maggots. Sometimes Elsie's house gave her the same feelings, but not anywhere as evident or prolonged as that.

Maybe it was an unclean spirit, like from the Bible. The ones that possess people or pigs.

That thought made her even more uncomfortable than she already was.

Elsie did not give her those bad feelings. Elsie made her feel good and brought light and life. Though, she had to admit, there was a darkness that followed Elsie. Despite growing up in wealth and status, she had a difficult life. She didn't have a family that loved her. She spent four years on a battlefield patching up wounded soldiers, was wounded while trying to defend herself, and then shunned by society when she returned.

Elsie said she saw things sometimes and had nightmares and shellshock, but considering all that she's been through, she seemed remarkably sane.

The image of Elsie on top of her, her strong legs straddling her and with her hair forming a curtain around them, flashed in her mind.

What would it be like to be with someone like her? To live with her and share all the time of the day with her?

What would society think of a white lady and her colored lover?

Harriet didn't care because society already hated her. What's one more thing?

As she thought about her, she figured Elsie wouldn't care about that either. She didn't care to conform to society. Harriet loved that about her.

She decided she wasn't going to hide who she was anymore, especially around Elsie. Life was too short to pretend to be something you're not. Besides, the scriptures say that 'men are, that they might have joy'. Pretending she was something she was not did not cause joy. Elsie caused joy. Tomorrow, she wasn't going to hold anything back.

As Harriet said her prayers that night, she prayed most of all that Elsie would be safe and protected from harm while she was alone at night in that house.

Chapter 14

Elsie woke up with the sun creeping through her curtains, casting rays that highlighted the dust motes in the air. She stretched her arms and yawned, immediately wincing as her scars tugged and pinched. Before she showered and rubbed linseed oil on her scars, she got up, grabbed her pistol, and in what was quickly becoming a daily habit, walked through the house inspecting every door, window and mirror.

Once that was completed, she showered, moisturized, put on what she thought was her most attractive outfit, a light and feminine dress, and did her hair and make-up. Even though she wasn't planning on being forward with Harriet, she still wanted to look good for her.

She still had an hour before Harriet arrived, so she started rounding up all the excess mirrors in the house and putting them outside by the front porch. By the time she was done, there were over twenty piled outside.

She left only two mirrors in the house, the one on her vanity, and the one in the attic, which was too big to fit down the stairs. This left her wondering how they got it up there in the first place. She would need to break it down and throw the pieces outside. However, that would take time, and Harriet was due any minute now.

She went out to the front porch and paced a couple quick circuits. She chewed her thumbnail, scratched the back of her neck, and told herself to calm down. This was just like any other day, except they were going to have a nice, but normal and non-romantic dinner afterward. A perfectly ordinary dinner.

Elsie's heart started beating faster when she saw the plume of dust from Harriet's truck coming up the dirt road. She couldn't remember how she normally stood there waiting for her and tried different poses before finally settling on leaning one elbow on a post and resting her other hand on her hip. She didn't realize that could be mistaken for being seductive until Harriet got out of the truck.

Harriet was dressed in her usual denim coveralls, work shirt and hat, hair in long braids pouring over her shoulders. She wore those little round purple sunglasses Elsie loved so much. Absolutely nothing was different, but Elsie's heart still skipped a beat when she saw her.

"Howdy, stranger. Looks like you had a mass mirror migration," she said, strapping on her tool belt and motioning with her head toward all the mirrors haphazardly piled in front of the house.

Elsie helped her move the mirrors into the back of the truck, and by the time they were done, she was sweating. It was only ten in the morning, but the sun was already ferocious. Afterward, they took a break, sipping some ice-cold Cokes in the kitchen.

Elsie, still out of breath, drank from her bottle. In a moment of bravery, she looked up into Harriet's eyes. What she didn't expect was to see Harriet already looking into hers. Harriet looked at her as if nothing else in the world mattered.

Elsie forgot to breathe as she looked into those beautiful

brown eyes. The corner of Harriet's perfect lips turned up in a sly smile, parted slightly. Even though her brain told her not to, Elsie reached over and took Harriet's hand, expecting she would recoil and draw her hand away. Instead, Harriet gripped her hand with an almost desperate strength. She didn't dare move and sat motionless, not wanting to break the spell.

Elsie rubbed her thumb lightly over the back of Harriet's hand, noticing how her remarkably dark skin was impossibly smooth, soft and without flaw, except for her hands, which were rough and scarred. Callouses, crisscrossing cuts and smudges of oil, which seemed to be a permanent fixture on what would be perfect and elegantly shaped fingers. She touched her own face and remembered to inhale as she soaked up the sensation of genuine physical contact with another human being and savored it. They stared into each other's eyes for what seemed like forever, Elsie trying to memorize every detail in case that never happened again.

God, this woman is perfect.

"Do...do you like music?" Elsie managed to say in a soft, almost inaudible voice after a few minutes.

"Of course, silly, I love music. Any kind of music suits my fancy if you can dance to it."

Harriet's smile and the way it touched her eyes, almost broke her resolve and she fought not to ravish her right then and there.

"I have a record player in the library. I bought some records. We could listen to that during dinner tonight...if you want," Elsie said, finally breaking eye contact and looking down at her own feet.

"I'd like that a lot. I've never had an intimate dinner with music before."

Harriet put an emphasis on the word 'intimate'.

Elsie blushed as she wondered where she saw that package of candles she found earlier.

"I guess that means I need to connect the dining room, huh?"

"If we want to listen to music, yes."

"Well, let's get started then. I can't do this all day. I have a dinner appointment with a beautiful woman after work. I gotta build up an appetite, don't I?"

Does she mean me?

Elsie cocked her good ear toward Harriet to make sure she heard that correctly.

"Come again?"

"Yeah, there's this beautiful white lady, I won't hold that against her, who lost a bet with me. She should have known better but is new to these parts. Thought she could outshoot me, can you imagine? Well, she owes me dinner after work, so I better get started. I don't want to be late," she said with a wink and walked out of the kitchen with a little sway in her hip, leaving Elsie speechless.

Once Elsie recovered from being called beautiful, she followed Harriet into the dining room, where she had already gotten her tools out and was about to take off an outlet.

"Pull up a chair. This room won't take long."

"Beautiful?" Elsie said, holding a hand up to her cheek.

"Yup. Pretty as a picture. You might not see it, but I most certainly do. Always thought so, too, just never had the guts to say it. Why don't you go get that book of yours and read to me as I work? It makes the time go by quicker."

Elsie didn't know what to say, so she left the room. Once she made it to the staircase, she felt *dizzy and was forced to grab the railing.*

What has come over her? She can't possibly mean what she said.

Can she?

Maybe I have a chance? That look she gave me out by the

ruins...did she want me to kiss her then? Is it possible she wants the same thing I do?

Elsie's heart threatened to pound out of her chest at the mere possibility. Hope had been such a stranger to her these last few years that it felt foreign to her, as if she barely recognized it.

Once she got to her bedroom, she shivered and immediately felt like someone was watching her.

"Piss off, ghost. Not today," she said, grabbing the book from her nightstand and hurrying back downstairs.

Harriet was laying on her stomach, twisting some wires together, feet up in the air kicking girlishly.

Elsie admired her prone form, her perfect shoulders and the elegant slope of her back melding smoothly into her shapely ass, as she took a seat and opened the book to where they left off.

Harriet turned out to be right; it didn't even take an hour before she stood up and declared the dining room finished.

"Marvelous! You are indeed a miracle worker."

"Why thank you, Miss Everly," Harriet said, giving a formal bow.

"What room would you like me to work on next?"

Elsie thought for a second.

"Actually, I'd like your help to move the record player and stand downstairs. I can't move it by myself. Then, I say we take a look at this supposed heating system and see what that's all about."

After several minutes and a few curse words that made Harriet blush, they brought both the record player and its stand downstairs to the dining room and plugged it in.

"If you want to impress little ol' me, how about we fire this thing up?" Harriet asked.

"Hold your horses. My father only had Prussian marching tunes, so I had to go buy some more appropriate ones," Elsie said, pointing to all the records she bought from the Russian.

"What'd you get? Confederate marching tunes?" Harriet said as she flipped through the choices.

She immediately went from a smirk to looking impressed.

"Irving Berlin, Al Jolson, Joe Jordan and Arthur Pryor, why Miss Elsie, I am impressed, and I do humbly apologize."

Elsie laughed.

"Humbly? I can't imagine you doing anything humbly."

Harriet looked like she was about to argue, but then she nodded in agreement.

"Be that as it may, I'm assuming the source of these vents is some kind of centralized heating system. Where's the door to the basement?"

Elsie found the inconspicuous door under the staircase that led down. There was a switch for the lights, but of course, it didn't work. However, hanging on a nail was an Ever-Ready flash light.

Harriet took it and turned it on.

"It works. Thank goodness for that," Elsie said.

They held hands as they went down the stairs. The stairs were completely enclosed so they didn't get a look at the basement until they were at the bottom.

It was big, almost half the size of the entire first floor, and on the opposite end stood a giant brass and iron contraption.

"Harriet, what is that?"

"That's got to be the heating system. Look at all the pipes coming out of it," she said, pointing with the flashlight.

"The pipes go to all the different rooms of the house from a centralized source. This is brilliant. I've never seen anything like it"

Harriet went over to the device and started inspecting it.

"Odd. There's no manufacturing information. No serial numbers, no patent numbers, no manufacturer period. I'm going to need my dad to take a look at this. I'm not even sure what I'm looking at," Harriet said, rubbing her chin with her face scrunched.

"Though on closer look, this looks like a natural gas pipe. Pipe connects here and then exits out the wall over there. Not sure where it goes, though. That would explain why there's no place for wood or coal. There's a lot of other weird stuff going on here, but it does look like you have an electrical/natural gas central heating system. I've never seen anything like this before."

"Maybe it's European. My father knew a lot of European men that dabbled in science and engineering."

"Maybe."

Harriet took out a pad and pencil and started to sketch the machine.

Elsie noticed that her drawing and notes were very neat and technical, with clean lines and tidy writing.

"Was your father planning on living out here or would this have been one of his vacation homes or something?" Harriet asked as she scribbled on her pad.

"I have no idea. He never told me about his life or plans, thankfully. I didn't even know this place existed until our lawyer told me. I sold all our other properties and moved out here. Sight unseen, as it were."

"You got some guts lady. I wouldn't've moved across the country to some weird house in the middle of nowhere that I'd never seen before. No thank you. But then again, you are pretty daring. More so than the average dame, I might add."

"Some would say stupid. Honestly, I was past caring at that point and just wanted to be alone."

"Alone? How is that working out for you?" Harriet said with a wink.

"Not very well, thankfully. So how about I cut up some fresh fruit for a light lunch before a heavy dinner?"

"Capital idea," Harriet said, taking her by the hand and leading her back upstairs.

Elsie squeezed her hand, and she squeezed back. Such a simple gesture of affection made her face grow warm and she could feel herself turn bright red.

Harriet jumped up and sat on the kitchen counter while Elsie chopped up some fruit. She cut up some strawberries and cantaloupe, along with some grapes and put them on plates, complete with napkins.

"There you go, sweetie," Elsie said, handing the plate over.

Harriet gave the plate a funny look before digging in.

"You know, I've been wondering," she said between bites. "You arrived at this house, it was fully furnished, down to the deck furniture and expensive plates, but the electricity wasn't connected? That seems backwards to me. I mean, I'm not complaining, it's a good job and allowed me to meet you, but doesn't that seem odd?"

"Honestly, I wouldn't know. Everything my father did was a mystery to me. Nothing he did made sense. I've often wondered why they left the house unfinished but never gave thought as to why they furnished it first. Maybe my father or brother already spent some time here while they were working on it? Neither one of them would go without the comforts their money afforded for any length of time. Even out on one of their trips to the jungle or African savannah, they would have attendants to set up their tents, prepare their food and care for their every need. I even overheard him one time admit he didn't even visit the ruins of Tikal, even though he wrote all about it, because he couldn't hire enough help to get him there in luxury. The man was a total fraud in more ways than one."

"Sounds like your brother was just as bad."

"He was worse," Elsie said, not wishing to explain any further.

"Sorry to hear that. It couldn't have been easy growing up in a household like that."

"It wasn't. I actually spent my holidays at the boarding school instead of going home, unless I knew they wouldn't be there. We all have our burdens. I consider growing up in an uncaring family rather mild compared to most."

"You are very strong, Elsie. Strong, brave and beautiful."

Elsie laughed nervously.

"I used to be."

"Don't do that. You are beautiful."

"I'm fully aware of what I look like, Harriet. Family members and former friends can't even look at me. They called me a monster. Here, young children call me the 'scary lady'. Every time I look in the mirror, I see exactly what I am. I'm sick of the stares. So sick of the stares. I'm not pretty and I'm most assuredly not brave. I've put the barrel of that pistol to my temple countless times just because nobody can stare at me if I'm in a coffin. I came here to hide, to flee from society."

Elsie was about to say more, but she noticed the expression on Harriet's face. She didn't know it was possible, but she almost looked...angry. She had never seen Harriet anything but cheerful.

Harriet jumped off the kitchen counter and stood in front of Elsie, eye to eye.

"Now you listen to me, Miss Everly. Nobody talks bad about Elsie, even you. She fought Krauts, faced down jaguars and tells ghosts to fuck off. You are an amazing woman and yes, you are beautiful. You are the most beautiful woman I've ever known, and I wish... I wish you could see yourself how I see you, a fierce woman who doesn't care about conforming to society. In the time we've had together, you've made me feel brave. Brave enough to admit certain truths about myself. So, if anybody says anything about my Elsie I don't like...POW! Right in the kisser!" Harriet said, waving a fist in front of her face and giving a scowl that would have been intimidating if it wasn't so adorable.

"You said a bad word."

"What?" Harriet said, momentarily losing her momentum and taking a step back.

"You said 'fuck'."

"I did not. If I did, it was because I was quoting you and you are a bad influence," Harriet said defensively.

Elsie was moved by everything Harriet had said but couldn't bring herself to believe it.

She knew where Harriet was going and what she was saying. It was everything she wanted to hear and more.

So why can't you accept it you idiot?

The pain of accepting Harriet only to find out she was mistaken, or Harriet meant something different, would hurt her so much more than just never having the privilege of being with her and staying friends. Hearing "I just want to be friends", would kill her.

You really are a coward.

"Thank you," was all Elsie could think to say.

She did say 'my Elsie'.

That did make her smile. Harriet noticed the slight smile and started beaming.

"There we go. There's that smile I love so much," Harriet said.

"You have that effect, Harriet."

They smiled at each other, content being in each other's company.

"What say we have fun the rest of the day until dinner? Watching you work makes me tired," Elsie said with a wink.

"I'll have to charge you for the whole day though, or my dad will be mad."

"Speaking of which, did you tell your father you'll be home late today?"

Harriet suddenly looked sheepish and looked down at her feet.

"I did."

"What did you tell him?"

"I just told him I would be working late and not to expect me for dinner."

It's the first time she has lied to her father.

Elsie didn't push the issue. For someone so pure, she figured it would be difficult to lie.

"Wait here, I'll be right back," Elsie said, rushing upstairs.

She went to her bedroom and strapped her gun belt around her waist, then went back downstairs.

Harriet saw the pistol on her hip and raised an eyebrow.

"Well, this afternoon isn't going the way I thought it would."

"I figured we could go for a nice walk. The pistol is in case of emergencies."

Harriet nodded.

"I can't argue with that."

Elsie held out her arm and Harriet took it, wrapping her arm around hers.

Nothing in the world felt as natural and comfortable as this moment. Harriet's strength and warmth made her feel like she did when she first arrived at the house.

They walked out into the afternoon sun, arm in arm and began a leisurely stroll, heading to the little creek that ran at the edge of her property.

Elsie didn't believe it could be better than this until Harriet leaned her head on her shoulder and gave her arm a little squeeze.

They walked in companionable silence, enjoying the beautiful day and each other's physical presence.

Elsie sorely missed the wildlife that greeted her during her first few days at the house. She now knew the reason they avoided her property but didn't know what to do about it.

"Tell me something about yourself that I don't know yet," Elsie said as they walked along the shaded bank of the creek.

"Let me think," Harriet said, scrunching her face. "I like to draw."

"I saw that very detailed sketch of my heating system. You are very talented."

"That was just a doodle. I like to draw dresses. I know I don't look like it, but I love women's fashion," she said, motioning to her denim coveralls and work shirt.

"Oh, I believe it. That outfit you wore on the picnic was impeccable. I could tell you have an eye. And you looked amazing."

"I suppose I can clean up good when I'm gussied up," Harriet said bashfully.

"You always look good."

"So, what about you. Tell me something I don't know," Harriet said.

Elsie thought about it for a second, then perked up.

"I was once arrested for stealing a car," she said matter of factly.

"What!?"

Harriet was so surprised she dropped Elsie's arm and stood in front of her.

Elsie laughed and waived it away.

"I was fourteen and still in boarding school. A few girlfriends and I were spending the Christmas holiday at school instead of going back home, and we snuck out at night and stole the Headmistress's Knox 16 motor carriage."

"You did?" Harriet asked.

"Of course. We were only teenagers and scared of getting arrested. That didn't stop me from stealing it several more times to take my friends on nighttime rides for the next few years."

"That would have been a gas! Wish I could have been there," Harriet said as she stumbled over a rock. Elise glided over quickly to help steady here and didn't let go.

"Don't worry, I'll steal you away some night and we can go joy riding in my V-8 Cadillac. Way better than that 1904 Knox. But tell me. How did you become interested in drawing and fashion? I mean, you are surrounded by nature's beauty," Elsie said, pointing to the creek and willowy trees that bordered it.

"Why not draw these fantastic mountains, wildflowers or animals?"

"I started drawing when I was young. Once I went to school, it became my passion, and I was the best artist in the school. One of my teachers told me that to become exceptional, I'd need to learn to draw the human form. So, that's what I did. I drew people. Women particularly were pretty, elegant and wore clothes that would bounce and float around the model. So much more interesting than a man in slacks and a shirt."

"Oh, on that I agree most whole-heartedly," Elsie said with smile.

"And that's what I've been drawing ever since. Once I ran out of fashion magazines to draw from, I started inventing my own dresses, hats and jewelry. I love it."

"Very admirable."

They held hands as they walked beside the little creek, sometimes talking and laughing loudly, and sometimes in complete and comfortable silence.

When Harriet's stomach started rumbling, Elsie figured it was time to head back and start cooking dinner.

In no hurry, they walked back to the house, still hand in

hand. Once in the kitchen, Harriet hopped up on the counter and watched Elsie.

"I'm going to use a French technique I learned while I was over there," Elsie said, taking the ingredients out of the ice box.

"French cooking. Fancy. Can you speak French?"

"Bien sûr je peux parler français."

"Oh la la! I like the way that sounds," Harriet purred, biting her lip.

"Je te veux tellement mon coeur me fait mal."

"I don't know what you said, but I like the way you said it."

"How about you put on a record while I cook, sweetie?"

"Terrific idea," Harriet said as she hopped down and went into the dining room.

A few moments later the upbeat song 'A Pretty Girl is Like a Melody' by Irving Berlin could be heard from the next room.

Harriet appeared, leaning against the door frame.

"Did they teach you how to dance at those fancy boarding schools?"

Without saying a word and without a further thought about cooking, Elsie walked over to her, wrapped her arm around her slender waist and took her hand. Not only did Elsie know how to dance, she knew how to dance very well.

Elsie drew Harriet close, relishing the way Harriet's body felt against her own, and began to dance. Harriet was also a good dancer, and Elsie found herself evenly matched.

Harriet took her hand off Elsie's shoulder and ran it through her hair.

"You are so beautiful," Harriet said, gliding her hand down Elsie's cheek, the one with the scars.

"You are the most beautiful woman I have ever met. I've never known anyone like you, Harriet, and I can't stop thinking about you."

Elsie could barely keep herself from shaking from fear and excitement. Harriet felt wonderful under her hands. Her lips were so close, and it took everything she had to stop herself from kissing them.

Elsie heard the lyrics of the song for the first time. "A pretty girl is like a melody that haunts you night and day, just like the strain of a haunting refrain."

"You're trembling," Harriet whispered.

"I'm scared," Elsie whispered back.

"Why?"

"I'm terrified you don't want this the way I do," she said and started to pull away.

Harriet grabbed Elsie's face with both hands.

"I promise you I do," she said, pulling her in to kiss her.

Their lips met, and all thought was lost as they melded together. Harriet's lips parted, letting Elsie's tongue in and Elsie gasped from the pure sensation of it. Their tongues explored each other as they kissed passionately, barely able to breathe but neither one daring to stop.

Elsie put one hand on Harriet's lower back, and the other hand on the back of her head, drawing her in even closer. She had never felt anything as perfect as Harriet's mouth and she explored every inch, losing herself in the taste of it.

Harriet's belly and breasts were crushed against her own. The sensation of pressing against Harriet sent a wave of pleasurable heat to her core, causing her to moan and grip her tighter.

Elsie managed to break away and catch her breath.

Nothing else existed in the world except Harriet.

"This can't be real. This is too perfect. You are too perfect, Harriet."

"Please, just kiss me," Harriet said desperately, closing her eyes.

They kissed, eyes closed for what seemed like forever. It

could have been seconds or hours, but Elsie never wanted to stop. She devoured Harriet's mouth, savoring each new playful movement of her tongue and lips.

Harriet's body writhed ever so slightly under her hands. Every movement of her taut and sinuous muscles made her head swim in fantasies of sex and love.

Oh god, I've fallen for this woman. I've never felt like this! I need her. All of her.

None of her previous sexual experiences compared to simply kissing Harriet, and her senses exploded in lust and desire. She could smell her sweet hair and taste her skin and feel the trembling muscles under her clothes.

Harriet slipped her tongue into her mouth and Elsie sucked on it. Harriet gasped, but didn't stop, pressing her lips harder into her.

Harriet grabbed the hand that was on her back and moved it lower. Elsie moaned as she grabbed Harriet's ass, which was so firm and yet soft, the fullness of it filling her hand perfectly. She squeezed hard and Harriet had to break away to breathe.

"Yes. I want this. I've always wanted this. I want you," Harriet said as her hands lowered and cupped Elsie's breasts, squeezing tightly, causing her own breath to hitch. She moaned in pure pleasure.

"You don't know how much I've dreamt about this," Elsie said, moving her other hand to cup Harriet's breast under her shirt. Her breasts were small, and she wasn't wearing a bra. She found her nipple easily, teased it and wanted nothing more than to put it in her mouth and taste her.

Harriet reacted instantly. She breathed in suddenly then let out a long, ragged moan as she put her hand on top of Elsie's, pressing it, crushing it into her own breast even harder.

"Just like that," Harriet whispered.

Elsie undid the buttons on the side of Harriet's coveralls

and slid her hand in, cupping her ass without the denim getting in the way.

Harriet wasn't wearing any undergarments.

She stopped for a second, surprised.

"I was hoping this is how the day would go," Harriet barely managed to say.

Elsie grabbed her bare ass, the skin impossibly smooth and perfect, caressing every inch. She squeezed, massaged, and pulled Harriet even closer, practically lifting her off the ground.

"I never imagined it would feel this good. I love the way you touch me," Harriet said as Elsie began kissing her long and graceful neck and nibbling her ears.

Harriet must have liked that because her eyes rolled up and she threw her head back.

Elsie released her grip on Harriet as she moved around to come up behind her, still kissing her neck and enveloping her in an embrace. She moved her hand from Harriet's rear to her smooth and flat belly, agonizingly slow, savoring each squirming movement she made and enjoyed the gentle swell of her hip.

Harriet let out a barely audible and trembling 'yes' as she put her hands over Elsie's, guiding them. Their hands together, one hand crushed and kneaded her breast as the other hand slowly lowered down Harriet's belly, coming to the soaking wet curls of her hair.

She was about to touch the crest of Harriet's center when she heard footsteps enter the kitchen.

"You unhand my daughter this instant!" came the loud angry voice of Enoch Piper.

Chapter 15

Harriet sat in the passenger seat of the work truck in silence, with tears rolling down her face. Her dad occasionally looked over and glared at her.

Harriet fought back sobs. The best night of her life had been ruined so thoroughly. Her face felt hot, and she could feel the heat creep down her neck to her chest where her heart painfully beat.

They rode in silence all the way back to Ogden. Her father pulled into the work garage and turned off the engine, but he made no move to get out. Harriet reached for the door handle, but her father's gentle hand touched her shoulder to stop her.

"For what it's worth, I'm sorry about the way things played. After I caught you kissing Angelica, I knew you were different. I see how you would look at pretty girls that walk by."

Harriet looked out the window. She thought she hid it and buried it deep, even from herself. Apparently, it was always near the surface.

"That's why I've been pushing you to go on dates with Isaac. He's a good boy and will steer you right. I'm hoping once you see what a good, wholesome relationship with a man is like, you'll forget this whole business. It's about time you stop putting so much energy into work and settle down and have kids. I'm no spring chicken. We've all had youthful indiscretions, but now it's time to grow up and think about your future. If you agree to go on a date with Isaac tomorrow night, we'll forget about all of this."

Harriet listened to her father without a word. Once he was finished speaking, she grabbed her tool belt and got out of the truck. Before closing the door, she turned around to face her father.

"That will never happen. I will never date Isaac and most certainly will never marry him or any other man," she said, raw emotions causing her voice to tremble, even though she was speaking calmly.

"Stop being so stubborn. If I hadn't stopped you tonight, you would have lost your virginity. Then where would you be? Imagine explaining that to your husband on your wedding night? Imagine explaining that to your bishop."

"Oh no, then I won't be able to go to the temple," she said sarcastically as she closed the door and walked away.

They both knew perfectly well neither one of them was allowed in the temple anyway because of the color of their skin. Her worthiness had nothing to do with it. Why should she prepare for a celestial and eternal marriage in the temple if she wasn't even allowed in?

She knew who and what she was now. Elsie, that beautiful and passionate woman, awakened something inside of her, something she knew now was always there and always would be. She could never go back to pretending with a forced smile. She said she would never marry a man. She didn't even want another woman.

She wanted Elsie.

As she threw her tool belt on the shop counter and went

out the back door, heading to her house, she thought about what happened.

She was the one that initiated the kiss. She wanted to kiss Elsie and she did. She didn't know exactly how two women could make love, but she did what felt natural. She wanted Elsie's hand on her butt, so she moved her hands there. She wanted to touch Elsie's breasts, so she did. All of it felt so right, and Elsie responded in pleasure like she did. It felt safe and wonderful.

And her dad ruined it.

Now here she was, back home, in her own room and miserable. Her night was ruined. She couldn't imagine how Elsie was feeling now, made out to be the villain when it was herself that started it. She was all alone in that dark, haunted house on the hill, probably confused, angry and sad.

She said a quick prayer to protect and comfort Elsie. Regardless, if she was sinning or not, God still heard prayers.

Was she sinning? The Bible never mentioned anything about woman being with womankind like it does for men. The Book of Mormon and Doctrine and Covenants were silent on the issue, too.

She heard her dad come in from the shop and then muffled voices as he must have been talking with Mom. She put her ear to the wall but couldn't understand a single word.

After several minutes of intense discussion, she heard her mom announce that dinner was ready.

Harriet wasn't hungry and ignored it. The last thing she wanted to do was sit and pretend that everything was okay at the dinner table, so she got undressed, got into her nightgown and stayed in bed, thinking about Elsie and how tonight should have gone.

"STOP TREATING my daughter as your personal house negro!" Enoch Piper yelled at her.

"I'm not! Your daughter is an adult and is fully capable of making her own decisions. Maybe it's about time you realize that," Elsie said, trying to remain calm.

The sheer audacity of this man bursting into her house unannounced incensed her.

"It's a good thing someone warned me about you. Someone called me and told me you were trying to seduce her and take her virginity like a trophy."

Elsie set her emotions aside and focused on that piece of information.

"Wait, who called you?"

Enoch seemed to be taken aback by the question.

"Um, well...I don't know. I didn't recognize the voice, but it doesn't matter because he was right. Needless to say, our contract is null and void. You'll have to find someone else to fix your house, and you are never to see Harriet again," Enoch said, storming out of the house.

Elsie slammed the door and locked it behind him. It wasn't until she heard the truck pull away that she collapsed against the door and cried.

Of course, she was on the verge of holding her most desired dream, only to see it taken away at the last second. How typical.

She didn't know how long she sat there and cried, but the rays of light cast through the small window in the door had deepened considerably.

She was alone again, and Harriet's life was destroyed. Elsie was beholden to no one. Harriet had to go home to face her family.

"Oh, that poor girl. I'm so sorry, Harriet."

The world would be a better place without her. Harriet was content and happy before she showed up here, and now she ran out in tears without even looking back, heading to whatever punishment her father had in mind.

Everything would be better if she didn't exist.

The thought came as if someone whispered it into her ear and clung there like a viscous residue that wouldn't leave her mind.

She repeated it in her head over and over again. Despite the oppressive July heat, she shivered as she sat on the ground, hugging her knees. She rocked back and forth as this alien thought, one she thought she had banished, took control of her and it began to make sense.

If she removed herself from the equation, maybe Harriet could go back to being happy. Everybody would be happy if she was gone. Nobody would miss her. Harriet wouldn't even want to see her after tonight. Why would she want to be reminded of this humiliation?

She was glad she waited this long to do it because at least she got to know Harriet.

Everything would be better if she didn't exist.

It became a mantra, and it repeated in her head over and over again.

Elsie had a flash of inspiration. She knew how to solve this problem for good.

She went up to the library and took out some of her father's stationary and a pen.

She wrote a letter to her lawyer back in Virginia, bequeathing the house and all of her money to Harriet Theodocia Piper upon her death and signed it.

Nobody will miss you.

Her life was over, but with a fine house and a grand sum of money, Harriet could still have a happy life. Nobody will be at her funeral.

She sealed the envelope and addressed it, then marched outside and put the envelope in her mailbox. She then went upstairs to her bedroom, grabbing her pistol belt from the kitchen on the way up.

"Hello, old friend. Looks like you are finally going to fulfill your purpose."

Elsie sat there holding the elegant looking, yet brutal thing in her hands. She had thought about this so many times in the last two years, but hope always won. This time, she couldn't think of any reasons to keep going.

Nobody will miss her. Nobody will care. A continued existence will only mean more pain with no hope of joy and happiness.

She didn't know how long she sat there with the pistol in her lap. It grew dark and cold around her.

"How long have I been sitting here?" she asked herself, looking around but deciding it didn't matter.

She put the barrel to her temple, but it struck her that once Harriet inherited the house, she'd need to clean up the mess.

The hole.

A gasp escaped her. She could do it there and wouldn't be a bother, even after death. She always intended to fade away and this would guarantee nobody would even notice.

No funeral costs either.

She went out the back door and walked down the patio steps. She walked down the hill toward the hole. She was at peace with her decision and knew it was the right thing to do.

Maybe Harriet would remember her fondly from time to time in her new house and happy life.

She leaned over the hole.

The cool metal of the muzzle pressed against her temple was like an old, familiar friend.

"Nobody will be at your funeral," she said, putting her finger on the trigger and taking the safety off.

"You love her," came a quiet, but strong voice that sounded like someone was standing next to her, talking softly.

"Who's there?" Elsie said, looking around and lowering the gun.

It was dark, but there was still enough light to see her surroundings. Nothing but empty fields.

She kept looking but found no sign that anyone had been near her.

You love her.

"I do. I do love her."

She put the pistol back on safe as clarity returned. Never before had she been that close to actually pulling the trigger.

The night receded, and to her shock, it was still daylight. The darkness that surrounded her was not the arrival of night.

"I finally have something good in my life and I was going to throw it away? What was I thinking?"

At that moment, a noise came from the hole. She could barely hear it, especially with only one good ear, but it was unmistakable. She couldn't tell if it was a growl or maybe a rumbling incomprehensible muttering, but it sounded angry.

"You did this didn't you?" she said to the hole. "Was that you that told Harriet's father? Nobody else could have known. Was that you putting these thoughts in my head?"

The angry grumbling from the hole turned to a chant. It was a language she had never heard before. "Ia Ia. In ie tlecujlixquac, in ie tlamamatlac. Itech naci in Tezcatlipoca." The chanting died away and slowly turned to laughter. Laughter that sounded like boulders rolling down a mountain. Another voice joined, this one much more recognizable as human.

The laughter slowly faded, and all was silent again.

"Whoever or whatever you are, I swear by all that is holy, I will fucking end your existence. God in his infinite wisdom won't be able to save you from me! The trials of Job will be on you! Nobody does that to my Harriet."

She went inside and went out the front door to her car.

"Sir, I am in love with your daughter. Please let me...no, that wouldn't work. Please, if only...," she rehearsed.

Enoch wouldn't let her see his daughter, but she had to try.

Elsie descended the porch and stopped dead in her tracks. A black, smoky mist formed in front of her car and congealed into the form of a large cat made of pure smoke and shadow, that looked like the one they were forced to kill.

A beam of light from her kitchen illuminated the ghostly cat and let her see the car behind its transparent form. The spirit had no features, just the outline of a large, but skinny feline.

She could feel the thing's growl reverberate in her chest and mind as it crouched between her and the car.

"Well, you don't look so scary. You're just smoke. You can't hurt me," she said, voice trembling slightly.

The ghost jaguar remained motionless, continuing to growl.

Elsie took the pistol out of her purse, thumbed the safety off, and took a few steps forward.

The cat's growl deepened.

Emboldened, she took another few steps toward the car. The cat did nothing, so she broke into a trot.

Faster than her eye could follow, the ghost jaguar lunged at her and swatted her with its paw. The force from its strike felt like being hit by that mortar shell in France, because the next thing she realized, she was laying on the stairs, head aching and her side feeling like someone hit her with a baseball bat.

She saw her pistol laying a couple feet away and tried to reach it. Her ribs felt like they were splitting into pieces. She gasped, hurting her ribs even more. She lay there in a fetal position until the pain subsided.

At least one rib was definitely broken.

"I guess you *can* hurt me," she grunted.

The ghost jaguar crept closer, slowly looking over its prey. "Shit."

Elsie gritted her teeth, reached out to grab the pistol, and through the agony, managed to stand up and limp to the front door. The jaguar came closer but made no move to attack her again. She reached the door and slammed it shut.

Could a door stop a creature made of smoke and darkness? Nothing crashed against it or managed to come through.

Her breathing took a minute to get under control.

She snuck a peak through the window. The spectral cat prowled back and forth like a sentry, guarding her car.

She fastened the dead bolt just in case. She crept to the kitchen, holding her side and her head, found some aspirin and downed it.

Her head throbbed torturously. Did she have a concussion? She wasn't nauseous and her thoughts were clear. The aspirin will help her head. But she was out of luck with the broken rib. Nothing to do but wait that out.

She took one last look outside at her car before going upstairs. The cat was still there.

She sat on the stairs facing the front door, too scared to do anything else, but as the hours passed without incident, her head bobbed more and more. She leaned against the wall.

Eventually, exhaustion overtook her and she fell into such a deep sleep, even her nightmares couldn't reach her.

Chapter 16

Elsie woke up before sunrise, completely alone and still in considerable pain. She tested her mobility, and confirmed that everything still hurt, though her head was a dull throb instead of a pounding, sharp sting.

The pistol was still in her lap, and she slowly holstered it.

It took her a few minutes to sit up, but she managed it with only a mild ache.

Her stomach growled, and she realized she never did have dinner last night. In fact, the steaks were still sitting on the counter.

What a shame.

Despite her bad hearing, she managed to catch the sounds of light footsteps coming up the staircase.

"Who's there?!" she said, grabbing the pistol and pointing it at the door.

She thumbed the safety off and lined the sights up on the entrance to her bedroom. Her heart pounded as fear gripped her once again.

The footsteps crested the stairs and started walking toward her bedroom. Her grip tightened on the pistol.

"Elsie?" came a hesitant and softspoken voice from the hallway.

"Harriet?"

Harriet poked her head into the doorway and waved shyly.

"Oh, Harriet! You can't imagine how good it is to see you. Forgive me for not standing, I seem to have broken a rib and it is too painful to bear. Please come in!"

Elsie was in tears as she put the gun down.

Harriet stepped into the room wearing the sailor outfit she wore on the picnic.

"I can't believe you are here. I can't believe you came back for me."

"You can't get rid of me that easy," she said.

Harriet looked at her with her head cocked and a slight smile on her face.

"I had a great time yesterday."

"I did too. I've never felt anything like that. I was in heaven. I must confess that I have something to tell you."

"I also have something to tell you," Harriet said, not moving.

"You go first. You came all this way."

"Oh, yes. I came all this way to tell you, I had fun, but I never want to be with you like that again."

Elsie's heart instantly sunk into the bottom of her stomach.

"You see, I just don't have feelings for you. The more I look at your scars, the more loathsome they become. You are too old, while I am young and unbroken. Why would I fall for you?"

"Why are you doing this? This isn't like you."

The hairs on Elsie's arms stood on end and she felt a chill in the air.

Something wasn't right.

The sun was starting to rise, letting her see Harriet a little better now. Harriet looked perfect and beautiful and always brought warmth and good cheer wherever she went.

This felt cold and repellent.

"Who are you?"

Harriet gave her a smile that chilled her to the bone.

"I'm your Harriet."

"No, you are not."

It was obvious now this was not Harriet. She looked and sounded exactly like her, but it was as if this was a puppet or someone in a mask pretending to be her.

"I'm your Harriet. The other Harriet is gone. You will never see her again. She doesn't want to see you," the false Harriet said, putting a knee on the foot of the bed.

"I will be with you forever. I can be your Harriet if you want. I won't abandon you," it said, putting the other leg on the bed and crawling toward her.

Her movements were jerky and awkward, as if she was unused to such things.

"I want you, Elsie."

"Get away!" she said, pointing the pistol at the thing pretending to be Harriet.

"I almost had you once, and I *will* have you. You will be mine," it growled.

It reached for Elsie and grabbed her ankle.

The pistol barked three times, each round striking the fake Harriet at point blank range. The bullets passed through the fake Harriet, which caused it to scream in pain. She was rewarded with blood splatter as its eyes went dull and the thing fell limp and lifeless as if it was a marionette with its strings cut. She heard heavy footsteps run out of the room and down the stairs.

Pursuit was out of the question. It would take her a few minutes just to get out of bed and a lifeless puppet that looked like Harriet was pinning her legs.

Elsie panted from the sudden adrenaline surge and kept the pistol pointed at the door.

She looked down and the false Harriet was beginning to dissolve. Little pieces would break off, then float away, turning to mist and vanishing. In a few seconds, the thing had completely disintegrated.

"I have to get out of here," she said, struggling to get out of bed. The pain made her wince and cry out, but she managed to get up.

Once she was standing, she walked around the blood splatter that had fallen. It looked normal until she looked closer. In the blood, dozens of little worms writhed.

Elsie's stomach heaved, and she had to look away before she vomited.

She was still wearing the prior day's clothes, so she gingerly undressed and showered, constantly looking out to make sure no one or no thing had come in. After, she put on her best dress. She was going to go talk to Enoch Piper and wanted to look as respectable as possible.

She packed a bag with some extra clothes, toiletries, more ammo for her pistol and a couple stacks of cash she had hidden under the floorboard under the bed, and then she went downstairs.

The steaks were still on the counter where she'd left them. She was not planning on coming back for a long time, and she didn't want the place to stink like rotten meat when she returned, so she picked them up with a cloth and tossed them outside. Animals now avoided the area around the house, but maybe something would sniff it out.

When she opened the door, she didn't see the phantom cat from the night before. She did see a man approaching from her driveway.

Samuel Richards gave her a friendly wave. She waved back.

"Good morning neighbor. Sorry to intrude. Looks like you are about to leave, so I'll make this quick."

Elsie stepped out onto the porch and tried to hide that she was injured. He'd probably be worried and try to help her or perform some kind of faith healing. She didn't have time for any of that. Samuel continued.

"I saw some shifty looking men loitering around your property yesterday. Ne're-do-wells. Hobos. They were dirty and had a mischievous look about them. I drove them away with some threats and a brandished rifle, but they might come back. I promise I and my boys will keep an eye out for them or any other suspicious person and I'll let you know if I see them again."

Despite the annoyance of being interrupted while she was in a hurry to leave, she was grateful for Samuel's care.

"I greatly appreciate that, Mr. Richards. Except for Piper and Sons, I am neither expecting nor wanting any strange visitors. You did right by me, and I owe you. Please keep a sharp eye out for more strangers, if you'd be so kind."

Samuel Richards blushed.

"It's no matter, Miss Everly. Just trying to be a good neighbor."

Elsie made sure Samuel was out of sight before she grabbed her bag and hurried to her car. She threw her bag in the trunk and got in. It started right up and she tore out of there, speeding toward Ogden.

She still didn't know what she was going to say to Enoch, but she had to convince him to let her speak to Harriet.

She figured he was a reasonable man, but in case he wasn't, maybe she could find her and the two of them could run off together. They could leave this place and that house and find somewhere they could be safe.

Sure, she would just leave the family she loves, her home, friends and work, just for you.

Elsie didn't want to think about that. She had to try.

Driving as fast as her car would allow, she sped west, unconcerned with her own safety and just thinking of Harriet. She soon pulled into town and parked near Piper and Son.

She got out of the car, unconcerned about her hair or scars and marched into the shop. Enoch Piper was not at the counter, but she heard noises coming from the workshop in the back. She walked behind the counter and entered the shop, finding Enoch underneath a half-built race car. Two young boys, who had to be Harriet's younger brothers, were also underneath, listening as Enoch patiently explained what he was doing.

"See, the hose connects here. So, let's tighten this first, then we'll connect it here," he said.

"Ahem. Good morning, Mister Piper. May I have a word with you?"

Enoch stopped speaking and wriggled himself from under the car, the two boys following him.

"Miss Everly," he said calmly, rising but not offering his hand.

"I would like to speak to you privately about a personal matter."

"Leroy, Orson, go find your mother and give her a hand."

The two boys left without a word.

"We need to speak about last night. Is Harriet here? She needs to be a part of this conversation."

"There's nothing to talk about, Miss Everly. Our contract is null and void, so there is nothing further to discuss regarding that matter. As for Harriet, I'm afraid she is not here."

"When will she be back? I'm willing to wait until she returns."

"She won't be returning, at least not anytime soon. You see, I sent her away to live with my relatives, to clear her head and to forget all this nonsense. Once she has time away from your influence and realizes her mistake, she'll come back, settle down and forget this whole mess."

A woman, who could only have been Harriet's mother, appeared in the entrance of the shop, a baseball bat in her hands, barely hidden behind her.

"Everything okay in here, honey?" she asked in a voice similar to Harriet's.

"Yes, everything is okay in here, Gertrude."

"Is that her?"

"Yes, dear."

She nodded, gave Elsie a once over and left without another word.

"Where is she?" Elsie asked.

"Far away from here. If you want a recommendation for another worker, I'd be glad to give you one. Good day, Miss Everly," he said, wiping his hand on a towel and walking away.

"Mr. Piper, there are things going on that you don't understand. Things that could put us all in danger. I need to see Harriet immediately."

"She was found in your hands, so of course she's in danger. My daughter has a weakness, but you will never defile my daughter and you will never see her again," he said softly but angrily.

"No, you don't understand. Something big is going on here. Your daughter's abilities, the way she sees things we can't, can help us all. You know what I'm talking about."

Enoch Piper lowered his gaze and his expression softened.

"She is a special girl, in more ways than I can count. That is why I must protect her. Ms. Everly, you really must leave. I never have and never will lay hands on a lady, but I will force you to if you don't leave of your own volition."

The look she gave Mr. Piper would have withered the

toughest of men, but he was unfazed. With nothing else to say, she left.

Elsie stood in the street and tried to think of what to do next.

She didn't know where to go from here. He said he sent her away, but he couldn't give up their family car or work truck. He must have sent her away by rail.

That meant Union Station.

She returned to her car, found Twenty-Fifth Street and followed it down several blocks until she came to Union Station.

She arrived at the train station and approached the man in the ticket booth. The tiny electrical fan blew on the man but failed to prevent him from sweating through his fine uniform.

"Yes, ma'am, how can I help you today?" he said in a bored voice, not even looking up.

"I was hoping you could help me out. I'm looking for a woman that might have passed through here earlier this morning. Her name is Harriet Piper. She's about my height, younger, dark skin and black hair. Slim figure and probably wearing small, round purple sunglasses."

"A negro woman?" he said incredulously.

"Yes, a colored woman."

"I've seen a few of them come and go all morning. I try not to pay attention."

Elsie gave an annoyed grunt but remembered that Harriet mentioned she had family back East.

"What trains have left from here this morning then? Anything going to Georgia?"

"Well, let's see. Nothing to Georgia. We had one leave for Reno, one going to Houston, Santa Fe, Los Angeles, Seattle and Boise, Idaho. That's just the ones that have already left. I have one leaving for Chicago in a few minutes."

"Can I go look? She might be on that train!" Elsie said excitedly.

"You'll have to buy a ticket to board the train, ma'am. That'll be thirty-two and seventy cents," he said, holding out his hand.

She gave him two twenties, grabbed the ticket and didn't wait for the change. She ran past the booth and looked for 'engine three six three', heading for Illinois.

By some small miracle, it was the closest train and the man yelling 'all aboard for Chicago' helped considerably.

She gave the man her ticket and jumped on board, hurrying for the back of the train to the 'negroes only' car, to the stares of the white passengers.

The law that segregated train cars stated that the cars meant for colored people must be of the same quality as the others, but when she arrived at the last car and opened the door, it was anything but. There were plain wood benches on each side, crammed with people sitting shoulder to shoulder. The straw on the floor was just an insult.

She looked at each of the confused faces as they looked up at her, but Harriet was not one of them.

"Has anybody seen a young, pretty woman about my height, French braids, maybe wearing little purple sunglasses, named Harriet?"

They responded in a chorus of 'no's, shrugs and head shakes.

Elsie was about to ask more questions, but the train lurched as it started to move. She thanked everyone then ran to the exit and an attendant helped her down.

Elsie wandered around the train station for the next few hours asking everybody she could find if they had seen Harriet.

Nobody had.

With each shake of the head or mumbled 'no', her heart

broke piece by piece and by the afternoon, she stumbled out of the train station dejected, tired and in pain.

She didn't know what to do next. People walked past her, paying her no mind as they happily went on about their day while she stood there, heartbroken and on the verge of panic.

With the broken rib and now twisted ankle, the walk back to her car took much longer. The usual assortment of scoundrels and miscreants tried to sell her things. She tried to fight it, but a sob escaped her lips and she looked around for anyone or anything that could help her.

After gingerly lowering herself into the seat, she drove to the closest hotel she could find that wasn't going to get her a disease or murdered. She found the 'Pleasant View Hotel' and was surprised when they had valet parking.

The valet, a young boy with a few hairs on his upper lip pretending to be a mustache, helped her out of the car, for which she gave him a two dollar tip.

"Treat my car like it was the president's and I'll triple that tip."

"ye...yes, ma'am!"

Reassured that her car would still be in one piece when she claimed it, she went to the front desk and asked for the best room they had.

The desk clerk handed her the key to the penthouse. The hotel was only five stories, but she took the elevator anyway. She didn't trust anyone else to handle her suitcase, so she lugged her own bag. She didn't relish the idea of carrying something up one flight of stairs, let alone five, her throbbing ribs reminding her why.

When she got to her room, she locked the door, threw her luggage under the bed, put her pistol on the nightstand and collapsed on the bed, exhausted, not bothering to take her clothes off.

"Harriet, where are you?"

Chapter 17

Harriet sat on the uncomfortable but almost empty wooden bench of the 'coloreds only' car of the train destined for Los Angeles, though her stop was in St. George. The unfinished wood tried its best to give her a splinter every time she moved and the whole car inexplicably smelled of motor oil.

The law required that the cars for whites and coloreds have the same accommodations and comfort, but in practice, it was anything but. Harriet had to walk through the lavishly decorated and comfortable passenger cars to get to this one. Her old and splintery bench was hardly the same as the brass and velvet seating of the other cars. There were no cushions. No decorations and of course, no attendants with dapper uniforms and pristine white cloths draped stylishly over their arms to offer anyone refreshments.

She didn't know, she'd have to check when she got off, but she could also swear this car was not equipped with shock absorbers, because she felt every little bump in the tracks.

It wasn't just her present accommodation that made her

melancholy. The memories of that morning came flooding back to her.

Her dad had woken her up before dawn and told her to get dressed and to pack a suitcase.

"What's going on? Where am I going?"

"Your uncle needs help on his ranch. Since you are done with your last assignment, I told him you're available and will be down for the rest of the summer."

Harriet almost fell out of bed.

"What? You're sending me away? You need me here. You can't do this by yourself."

Her dad stood in the doorway, arms folded and silent.

"Is this all because I...kissed a woman? You can't be serious, dad!"

"I will hear no argument, Harriet. This is for your own good and for your own safety. Pack a bag. Your mom already has some food packed for you. Your train leaves in an hour," he said as he left her room.

Harriet packed a bag, but she didn't have time to braid her hair. She tried to tame it by tying a bandana on her head, but a large poof of hair still hung out the back. It would have to do.

So, she packed, said goodbye to her mom and brothers and followed her dad to the train station, trying to frantically talk him out of it the entire time. The thought of not seeing Elsie for so long sent her into near panic.

If anything could be said about me, I'm a dutiful daughter.

Now, she wished she wasn't.

She wished she'd ran away, back to Elsie.

She should've taken that 'honor they mother and father' stuff and thrown it out the window, because all she could think of now was Elsie. Elsie, who was left in that house by herself. Elsie, who saw her run away without looking back. Elsie, who would think she abandoned her.

She must hate me by now.

She regretted not standing up for herself and claiming her right as an adult to make her own decisions. But she was weak. She had always lived with her family and had never stood up to her dad. She never had a reason to until now.

She could still feel Elsie's lips and hands running over her body and she craved more. She wanted to wake up this morning with Elsie beside her. It wasn't just the life altering pleasure of that night, it was also the emotional connection. That was something she had never experienced and having it taken away at the moment of discovery seemed cruel.

Now she had a ten-hour train ride to St. George to think about her mistake, about the hell she was putting Elsie through. She started to think of all the ways she would make amends to Elsie and it caused her to blush and squirm in her seat. Instead of shooing away these dirty thoughts, she welcomed them. It was a long train ride and it helped to pass the time.

She still wasn't exactly sure how two women make love, but she had a vivid imagination and catalogued everything she could think of and put them in order of what she'd want to try first once she met Elsie again.

"Excuse me, miss?"

Harriet must have dozed off because she woke with a start, unsure where she was.

She saw a little girl, maybe seven years old and in the same French braids she, herself usually wore. She had the biggest and most beautiful brown eyes she had ever seen. The girl played with her braids as she rocked back and forth on her heels.

"Hello there."

"I'm hungry."

Harriet looked around the car. The woman the little girl was traveling with, presumably her mother, was asleep but carried no baggage. Even if she was awake, she probably wouldn't have any food. Harriet's own mother had packed her some corn bread and jerky for the trip. She still had no appetite, so she dug in her bag and pulled out some corn bread.

"Here you go, honey," she said, patting the girl on her head.

"Thank you, miss."

"You are very welcome."

She watched the little girl go back and sit beside her sleeping mother, happily munching on the corn bread. They made eye contact and they both smiled at each other.

She remembered the first time Elsie smiled at her, the slight twinge of pain, the hint of shyness. She would give anything to see that smile again.

With her good deed for the day completed, she stood up to stretch her legs. She walked over to a window, braced herself with one arm as she watched the scenery roll by. The mountains to the east grew smaller and smaller until they faded away to rolling hills, then flat and barren lands. An occasional flock of sheep or small herd of cows would break up the scenery, but there was really nothing to look at.

She was about to go back to her seat when she spotted something up ahead, near the side of the tracks. She crammed her face against the window to try to get a better look, but couldn't make it out.

A few moments passed until she could see exactly what it was and then she regretted not going back to her seat.

Right next to the tracks was a burnt-out boxcar, still smoldering. Milling around were dozens of Chinese men in traditional clothing, all confused, scared, wearing vacant expressions. One of the men shook his head in disbelief as another man rocked himself while saying prayers, but they all looked tired and sweaty. Lost was the word Harriet would use to describe them.

They looked and moved as if they were alive, but the tingle in her eyes and the hair standing on her arms told her that they were dead and that the boxcar wasn't really there.

Harriet had heard rumors of the inhumane way the Chinese railroad workers had been treated, even that they had been rounded up in boxcars and blown up with dynamite or burned alive. She guessed those weren't rumors.

A few of the ghosts noticed her looking at them and reached out to her, pleading with their eyes, but the train rolled past. They were soon out of sight.

Harriet shivered, sat down and sang hymns quietly to herself until the shivering stopped.

THE TRAIN PULLED into the station and came to a smooth stop. She was the only one from the segregated car to get out, but she waved goodbye to the little girl before she did.

She had no money, but if she sold her pistol, she might get enough to buy a ticket back up North. Back to Elsie

Unfortunately, Uncle Mack was there waiting. She didn't know his real name. Everybody always referred to him as Mack. She remembered meeting him when she was eleven or twelve but didn't remember much other than that he was nothing like her father. While her dad was tall, thin and talkative, Uncle Mack was short, built like a bull and quiet. Harriet wasn't even sure they were blood related.

Mack grunted and walked away, expecting her to follow, which she did with a consigned sigh.

He brought her to an abused looking Model T and threw her bag in the back. When he got in, the car moaned and creaked, and Harriet wasn't sure if it could support his weight. Once he was settled, she squeezed herself in.

"It's about thirty miles to the homestead. Get comfortable."

His bulk pressed her into the side of the car, and she was anything but comfy.

The car reluctantly started with a couple of gasps, and they were soon off, navigating the streets of Saint George.

Harriet figured there must be fewer colored people here than Ogden because everybody stared at them as they drove by. Besides all the stares, she liked the small city. The white temple that dominated the skyline, contrasted with the red cliffs and was breathtaking.

She thought what it would be like to take Elsie here and spend some uninterrupted time together.

A bump shook her from her thoughts as the roads degraded leaving the city center.

The scenery stayed just as striking outside the city. No more long stretches of nothing. The area surrounding Saint George was covered in cliffs, canyons and rock formations. She found herself really liking this place, despite the circumstances.

The little over-burdened Ford chugged along until they came to a valley an hour later. The dirt road looked like nobody had used it in decades. Most of it was overgrown, and some parts looked like they had been washed away by flooding. A small wooden sign came into view and in block letters said, 'Duncan's Retreat'.

She had never heard of the place, but she didn't know a lot of small towns. Mack took a left onto a tiny dirt road and came to the smallest town she had ever seen. If he hadn't pulled in, she never would have noticed it. It was obvious the place had been abandoned. Most of the dilapidated homes were overgrown with weeds and many others had collapsed.

"Is this where you live?"

"Ayup."

"Are you the only one that lives here?"

"Ayup. Everyone got up and left, and I bought their land on the cheap."

He pulled up to the only house that wasn't falling apart and turned the engine off.

A woman came out of the house. She was very short, slim and looked like she was Mexican. Her hair was pulled into one long braid and wore a brightly colored skirt and loose shirt and a cowboy hat. She was, Harriet noticed, very pretty.

It made Harriet happy that she could freely admit that to herself. Yes, this woman was attractive.

She nodded at Mack as he went into the house without a word. She reached for a rope hanging near the door and rang a dinner bell. It was an actual dinner bell, something she thought was always just a figure of speech.

A few seconds later, a young girl came running from the trees nearby. She was barefoot and covered head to toe in dust and dirt. Her hair was wild, and she had a manic grin on her face. She looked in her mid-teens, but it was hard to tell with how diminutive she was.

She went and stood by her mother, clinging to her dress and giggling.

The mother leaned over and whispered something in her ear. The girl listened intently then nodded.

She walked over to Harriet with her arm stretched toward her.

"I'm Marta. Pleased to meet you," she said with a barely suppressed giggle.

Harriet took her hand, which was dirty but strong.

"I'm Harriet. It's nice to meet you, too."

"That's my mom, Lupe. She doesn't speak English, but she welcomes you to our home and invites you to come in for dinner."

"Claro que si," she said, using what little Spanish she knew.

Lupe perked up and spoke very fast, but Harriet had to stop her.

"No hablo Español. Solo se...sabe...," she struggled with the conjugation.

"Conozco un poquito," she said finally, but figuring it was still incorrect.

Harriet held up two fingers, an inch apart to show Lupe exactly how much Spanish she actually knew.

Lupe smiled and it completely changed her countenance. She looked pretty before, but when she smiled, she looked beautiful and young.

Marta took her by the hand and led her inside.

The outside of the house looked slightly better than the rest of the abandoned town, but inside was clean, warm and inviting.

"Lavarte," Lupe said to Marta.

Marta immediately let go of her hand and ran upstairs.

Mack came into the room carrying some wood bowls to set the table. The kitchen was blocked from view by a patterned, thick blanket of some kind but she could still smell something good cooking on the other side.

Lupe ducked inside and came out balancing several bowls filled with food which she set on the table.

Everything looked simple and plain but smelled delicious. Rice, beans, chilis, tomatoes, limes, some kind of aromatic, small green leafy plant she didn't recognize and tortillas.

Marta ran back downstairs, much cleaner than before, and sat in the seat opposite Harriet, practically bouncing with excitement, and staring at her.

Harriet tried to avoid eye contact with the strange girl and every time she did look, Marta giggled.

"Dig in. There are no pretenses here," Mack said, taking a couple of tortillas.

She waited for them to say a prayer before the meal, so she said a quick one in her mind and started to help herself.

"Este es muy bien!" she said to Lupe, letting her know how good it was.

"Aye gracias niña." She beamed.

Mack smiled for the first time.

Marta was a tiny girl but seemed to have a bottomless pit of a stomach because, after she cleared her own plate, she reached for what was left on Harriet's. She stopped herself, inches away, but Harriet nodded. Marta cleaned that plate, too.

Bottomless pit.

Her thoughts went to Elsie and the huge bottomless pit and worry flooded her once again. Elsie couldn't see the things that she could.

How will she protect herself if I'm not there? What if that shadow man comes back? Elsie's been through a lot and can handle almost everything thrown at her, but can she defend against something supernatural and unseen? This isn't something her pistol and good looks can solve.

Harriet Theodocia Piper always tried to be polite, so she waited until everyone else was done before standing up from the table.

"Excuse me, I've had a long day. Where will I be sleeping?"

"Go ahead and get your bag from the car. You'll be bunking with Marta in her room. She looks young but she's almost your age. She's eighteen, so it'll be fine."

Marta squealed with excitement.

"I'll get your bag!" she said as she ran out of the house.

A moment later she came running back in with her bag yelling 'follow me!' as she ran upstairs.

Mack motioned for her to follow Marta as he began to help Lupe clear the table.

Harriet followed Marta upstairs. The second floor was a

long hallway with two bedrooms on either side, and what must be the master bedroom at the end of the hallway.

I guess when you live in a ghost town, you can have your pick of houses, she thought.

Just like downstairs, everything was immaculately clean and well kept. An attractive rug spanned the length of the hallway and there were brass candle holders on each side.

Marta poked her head out of her room and motioned for her.

Inside the room is exactly how Harriet would have imagined it. There was a shelf filled with dolls in various forms of deconstruction, manic crayon drawings pinned to the walls and a small desk covered in sticks. Rocks and little odds and ends she probably found in the abandoned houses littered the remaining surfaces.

She pointed to the bunk bed.

"You want top or bottom?"

The top bunk looked well used and slept in, while the bottom bunk was home to some stuffed animals and hadn't been touched in a long time.

"I'll take the bottom."

Marta looked relieved, put her luggage on the bed, and pointed to an ancient-looking wooden trunk.

"Good. I like the top bunk. That trunk is for you. You can put your stuff in there," she said.

Harriet threw her bag in the trunk without taking anything out.

"Is there a telephone around here?"

"A what?"

"A telephone. You know, to make a call?"

Marta just looked more confused.

"A call?"

Harriet mimed holding a telephone, but still received no recognition from Marta.

"Nevermind," she said and sat on her bed.

Marta looked over the edge of the bed and stared at her.

"We're going to have so much fun together! I can show you around the town! There is so much to explore. All the houses are empty, so nobody minds. Then there are the trails, rocks and Indian places to look at. This is going to be the best summer ever!" she said with increasing excitement, bouncing up and down on the top bunk.

"I can show you around town right now if you want."

"I've had a long day. I think I'll just read until bedtime."

Really, she just wanted to curl up, feel sorry for herself, and think about Elsie. She did bring a few books with her. She didn't know what to expect living down here for the summer, but she figured she'd better bring something to pass the time.

"Books? Like stories? You have stories? I can't read but I really like stories."

"You want me to read you a story?"

Marta nodded so fast, Harriet thought her head would fly off.

Harriet went to the trunk and took the books out, placing them on the bed.

"Ok, we have *Jane Eyre*, *Dracula*, *Frankenstein*, *Turn of the Screw* and *the Three Musketeers*."

Marta just stared at her blankly.

"How about Frankenstein? It's about a man that creates a creature that escapes and returns to terrorize him," Harriet said in a low and spooky voice.

"Like Wendigo?"

"I'm not rightly sure what that is, but let's read and find out."

"Wendigo lives up the canyon. Don't go there. He's always hungry."

"Uh huh," Harriet said, confused.

She put the other books away and lay back on her bed, holding the book up in the air.

"You will rejoice to hear that no disaster has accompanied..." she started to read out loud to the strange girl.

Harriet knew that what she read went over Marta's head, but the girl was enraptured and hung on every word. She didn't interrupt, she sat there, hanging over the bunk and staring at Harriet the entire time.

She read for a couple of hours because, each time she tried to stop, Marta would become sad. She had to light a candle to continue as the sun went down.

Eventually, Marta yawned and faded as the night grew darker, and she was finally able to stop reading without complaint.

Harriet stood up and wanted to change out of her dress, but Marta continued staring at her.

I'll have to see about sleeping in one of the other bedrooms tomorrow. I'm a grown woman.

She had no choice and continued to undress. She put on a night gown and took the bandana off, not bothering to tie her hair up.

Before she blew out the candle, she got out some paper and a pencil she'd packed and wrote a quick letter to Elsie, letting her know exactly how she felt and that leaving was not her choice. She poured her heart into the letter, and in writing it down, she solidified her feelings. She was in love. Honest, true love and not some youthful fascination.

She sealed the letter with wax from the candle and blew it out. Thankfully, Marta retreated to her own bunk and stopped staring.

Sleep wouldn't come. Her heart and her body ached for Elsie and the thought of being away from her for so long brought her to the edge of tears. She was sure that Elsie would resent her for leaving because she resented herself. She had never disobeyed dad, but if she could do it all over again, she would have. Even if she got kicked out of the house, she'd go stay at Elsie's if she would have her.

It was doubtful if Elsie would understand that, but she would make it up to her. She would spend the rest of her life making it up to her.

Thinking of Elsie made her feel like touching herself. She had never masturbated before, but she certainly felt like it now, going over how Elsie kissed her and touched her in her head, over and over again.

Marta whispering and muttering to herself reminded her why masturbating wouldn't be a good idea. She wasn't sure if Marta was talking in her sleep or just to herself, but it was odd. Everything here was odd and finally, the tears did come. She was in a weird place with these nice but weird people and far away from Elsie.

She finally drifted off to sleep with thoughts of Elsie's kisses.

Chapter 18

Elsie slept fitfully that night despite the hotel room being very fancy and the bed actually being more comfortable than her own.

The thought of Harriet resenting her and the physical pain of her broken rib kept her awake late into the night until exhaustion finally took her.

Even that didn't keep the dreams away though, and the same repeating dream haunted her. The man with the armored suit and flame thrower, which she later learned was called a sturmtruppen, burned her alive. Diallo dying in front of her and the searing pain that followed, woke her up as usual. She sat up in bed, gasping from the imaginary pain of the flames and the very real pain of her rib.

The pain was so exquisite she had to catch her breath. As she sat there trying to control her breathing, she noticed the door to her room was open and she could see into the hallway. She knew she had locked it. The hallway was dark but as she looked, she saw a dim light appear as if someone with a candle walked down the hallway.

Elsie started to feel uneasy as the light grew closer and

closer. She could now hear heavy footsteps and the clanking of metal coming slowly down the hall.

The first screams reached her ear. It was faint at first, but it grew louder as new cries of terror joined them until it was a cacophony. It was as if the entire hotel woke up to her nightmare.

The light approaching from the hallway flickered like fire and she knew what was coming. She got out of bed as quickly as she could, thankful that she slept in her clothes. She grabbed her pistol and her luggage from under the bed and went to the window.

As she tried to open the window that led out to the fire escape, the steps from the hallway stopped in front of her door.

She didn't want to look back, but she did.

Standing in the doorway was the German sturmtruppen from her dreams, covered head to toe in armor, with a cracked, red eye lens dripping with blood, carrying a flame thrower.

Smoke followed him from the hallway and poured into her room.

She forced herself to look away and opened the window, throwing her bag out first, before crawling through and closing the window behind her. She gave her nightmare one last look before heading down the fire escape. The soldier stood in the doorway, but now with the flame thrower raised and pointed at her.

Elsie quickly ducked and fell on her back as a wave of flame burst through and shattered the window, showering her with burning hot shards of glass.

"Not again. Not again. Not again...," she repeated to herself as she crawled down the fire escape as quickly as her broken rib allowed.

Sparing a quick glance around, she saw that the hotel was

engulfed in flames. She could hear the screaming from inside over the roaring fire above her.

A tall man with a thin mustache hurried down the fire escape, clutching a briefcase to his chest. As he approached, he roughly pushed her aside to get past, knocking her on her butt and causing her rib to explode in pain.

"You rude piece of trash!" she called out to him through gritted teeth.

Progress was slow, and she was down two flights of stairs before she noticed the metal railings of the fire escape were warm. Windows all over the face of the hotel burst outward, sending flame and tumbling, glittering glass down onto the street.

The fire department arrived as crowds formed to watch the grand old hotel burn. She took all this in as she climbed down even faster.

By the time she reached the street, the metal fire escape was too hot to touch with bare skin. Nobody asked her if she was okay or offered to help her. All eyes were glued to the now raging fire tearing through the hotel.

She ran to where the valet was set up. There was supposed to be someone manning the station all night, but they had obviously abandoned their post. She opened the little door in the podium, quickly found her keys and snatched them up.

She found her car in the lot and started the engine. Once the engine was purring and she was safe, she looked at the clock in the dashboard of her car. It read a little past four in the morning.

Cinders and ash began to fall around her like a snowfall. The convertible's top was down, so she decided now was the time to leave. She pulled out of the parking lot, careful not to hit any of the onlookers and drove down the street looking for another hotel.

Ogden had many hotels downtown so finding another

took no time at all. The next hotel she came across wasn't as fancy, so it didn't have valet parking. She parked on the side of the street, grabbed her bag and went in.

The bored looking clerk behind the counter perked up when he saw her.

"Good morning, ma'am. Welcome to the....," he began to say, but then stopped when he noticed her face.

Oh great, another person who's never seen a burn scar before.

"I'm sorry, but please take your business elsewhere. You are not welcome at the Andromeda Hotel."

Elsie did not expect that. "Excuse me, sir, but what business are you referring to? I have no business. The Pleasant View Hotel just burned down and I need accommodations."

"Yes, your *business*," he said that last word as if the word itself was disgusting.

He showed her a police flyer, complete with a sketch of her face, burn scars and all, explaining that she was a known prostitute and thief and under no circumstances should she be given a room. There was another sketch that also showed what she would look like with her hair covering half her face.

"Now, please leave or I will be forced to call the police."

Elsie left without another word. There were plenty of hotels in the area.

She went to several more, but they all had the same warning about her and none of them would give her a room, even the disreputable ones.

The last hotel she checked, just outside of Ogden, had a few prostitutes sleeping in the lobby, worn out from a night's work.

She tried to check in, but she was refused and shown the same police bulletin.

Without saying a word, she motioned to the ladies lounging about the lobby.

"Look, I know it seems daft, but a police detective, a wormy fellow with a big scar on his face, came in and threatened to take away our business license if we let you stay. I get a small percentage of their rates in exchange for allowing them to sleep and work here. It's honest work and I can't risk it. You must have made someone mad, miss. I'm sorry."

"A scar on his face?"

"Yeah, I didn't see him, but the night shift guy told me about it. He said some fella with a scar over his eye came in here flashing a badge and handed him this."

Elsie trembled and lifted a shaky hand to her face.

"Was the scar over his left eye?"

"I can't rightly remember. Sorry, but you must leave now."

Numbly, she turned around and left.

She went back to her car but didn't start it.

Her brother had a scar over his eye because she gave it to him. She tried to scratch it out.

But he died years ago with their father, thankfully.

She knew the person with the scar wasn't her brother, but it still bothered her. She promised herself he would never have power over her, yet here she was, sitting in a car, trembling at the thought of him.

Not waiting for the trembling to stop, she started the car and drove north out of town. She turned off on a dirt road without any idea where she was going and found a place to pull off and park.

It was a dirt patch between fields of crops with no one around as far as she could see. She put the convertible top up and reclined in the back seat, leaving the windows down. Even early in the morning, the July heat was already causing her to sweat. Her Mauser dug into her already hurting side, so she slipped it out of the holster and placed it on the floorboard.

She never dwelled on those horrible memories of her

brother, but they were always there, in the back of her mind, a dark and constant companion.

Her body still trembled, so she forced herself to think of other, more pleasant things.

Harriet. Thinking of her caused her to calm down instantly as her body, rigid and shaking from anxiety, finally relaxed.

The thought of her in that sailor outfit, with the French braids, sunglasses, hat and those impossibly perfect legs made her smile. Her firm breasts, the way she moved under her touch and the taste of her mouth made her warm and wet.

She would do anything to get her back. She didn't know how, but she was going to find her. Right now, she was exhausted and in pain, so she decided to take a nap before figuring out what to do about her lodging situation and how to find Harriet.

While she fell asleep to the sweet thoughts of Harriet, the memories of her brother were lying in wait in the dark recesses of her dreams.

Elsie jumped out of the brand new 1903 Ford Model A. The family chauffer, Reginald, giving her an indulgent smile. He had seven daughters of his own, so he knew what rambunctious thirteen-year-old girls were like.

She really liked boarding school, the friends she made there and the chance to be away from her family. What she didn't like was the stern teachers or the military-like discipline that always seemed to get her in trouble.

Most holidays were spent at school with the few friends that stayed. The only thing her and her father agreed on was that they didn't want to spend time together. This Christmas, however, her father and brother were away in Mexico, and she would have the house all to herself. The staff always treated her like royalty, and they would have fresh baked cakes always on hand. Presents would be under the tree, and she would sit with the maids and butlers for a nice Christmas dinner while she told them stories of school. It was nice being treated like a princess when her family was away.

That is why her heart sank so low when she discovered her father's and brother's luggage piled up in the foyer.

"There was some civil unrest and we were forced to cancel the rest of our trip," came the booming voice of her father.

She looked up and he and her brother Thomas were standing at the top of the grand staircase, looking down at her.

"Oh, look father. The mewling little hussy came home to bless us with her presence. I'm surprised you could rip yourself away from all your whore friends," Thomas said with a sneer.

He was nine years her senior, so thankfully they never interacted much, but when they did, he always tried to torment her with insults, condescension and the occasional slap.

She was thirteen now and was learning to stand up for herself. If she didn't, the girls at boarding school would walk all over her.

"At least I can make friends, unlike you."

His pallid skin turned bright red, and he took a step toward her. Her father's hand shot out and grabbed him by the shoulder.

"Now, now Thomas. Remember what I taught you. Don't let those who are inferior dictate our actions."

"I remember, father. I need to put her in her place."

"That's right, dear boy. Now, come with me."

Thomas was thin, pale and sickly, but shared his father's square jaw and handsome face. This made his features look out of place, as if Doctor Frankenstein had placed the wrong head on a recently dug-up corpse. Hardly the paragon of the master race her father always talked about. If his body wasn't corrupted, his mind certainly was. Before she was sent off to school, there were many times she found Thomas with a stray cat or bird that he had recently caught, tortured, killed and dissected. He kept the heads of the poor animals in a box under his bed, until even their father, who didn't seem perturbed by his son's behavior, finally made him throw it out due to the smell.

Much of her time was spent trying to keep animals away from her brother. When Thomas found out what she was up to, he shoved her face into his box of rotting trophies until she begged his forgiveness. The smell stayed with her to this day.

Elsie went to her bedroom, sure that Thomas was already thinking of insults or some other way to get revenge. He was vindictive, which is why whenever they were home, she always stayed in her room. It's how everybody preferred it.

When it was dinner time, she opted to have dinner brought to her room. She began reading the collected works of Sappho and other Greek poets and didn't want to be disturbed. A nice Jewish girl named Alice from New York City suggested the book to her.

The soft knock on the door told her the servant was here with her food. She placed the book down on her bed.

"I'm coming."

She stood up, straightened out her dress and went over to the door.

She expected Agatha, who always brought dinner. Instead, Thomas stood there with a grin on his face.

"I gave most of the staff the night off. I wanted to bring you dinner personally. After all, I want to be a good brother," he said as he stepped in and closed the door behind him.

Elsie didn't know what his intentions were, but she knew they were foul.

"You are a stupid and silly girl, but you are pretty," he said, stepping toward her, eyes wide and licking his lips.

"Really pretty," he whispered. "You should want to give yourself to me, you know. It's the natural order of things, and after all, I am your superior and we must keep our bloodline pure. But if you won't give, it is my duty to take what is rightfully mine."

He shoved her back, causing her to fall on the bed. Thomas was on her instantly and even though he was sickly and frail, he was stronger than her. Elsie screamed for help and struggled underneath him.

"I sent the staff away and nobody will help you. You'll be mine forever. Please, keep screaming."

He held her down by her wrists as he positioned himself on top, looking her over.

"I always wanted to do this, to make you mine."

He let go of her right arm as he reached down to grope her breasts.

Elsie used the opportunity and grabbed the book of poems she was reading and smashed the spine of the heavy book against Thomas' temple. He made a high-pitched shriek of surprise and pain as she hit him again. This time, it caused him to bleed.

"Why, you little bitch!"

Thomas knocked the book from her hand and slapped her.

Elsie struck out and raked her fingernails across his face. Huge drops of blood fell on her like heavy rain. Thomas sat up, clutching his eye with bloody hands.

She managed to get a leg free and used it to push him off the bed with every ounce of strength she had.

He tumbled off and struck the hardwood floor, knocking the air out of his lungs. Gasping for air and still holding his eye, he managed to stand up and run out of her room. Once he was further down the hall, he must have managed to catch his breath because she heard him scream for their father.

Her father was already there, however, and stepped into her room as if he had always been there, out of sight the entire time. Listening.

"The boy is pathetic," he said looking around the bedroom.

"Father! He hit me and tried to...!"

"Silence, idiot girl. It's obvious he isn't ready, and you are too much of a distraction. I'll have Reginald drive you back to...whatever school it was you were attending and spend the rest of the holiday there. Pack your things, you leave right now."

He left her room, leaving her shaking, crying, chest heaving.

She packed her bags, eager to be away, and ran out the front door where Reginald and the car waited for her.

"My dear girl, your lip is bleeding. Are you alright?"

"I'll be better once I'm away from here."

SOMETHING STARTLED HER AWAKE.

She sat up and looked around for what woke her, but nothing was obvious. She got out of the car and looked around. No cars were in sight, nor were any animals or anything else that would have caused her to wake up. She wiped the tears away from her eyes with her sleeve.

The sun was already high in the sky without a cloud in view. She started to sweat and fanned herself when she noticed something in the distance. Surrounding her were fields of some crop she didn't recognize, all in neat rows and waist-high and stretching as far as the eye could see. Several hundred feet away, she noticed a person. It looked like a man from the broad shoulders and wide brimmed hat, walking toward her.

"Uh oh. Must be the farmer. Looks like I overstayed my welcome."

She looked around and noticed another man, equally distant stand up from in between the rows of crops.

She waved but stopped suddenly when her peripheral vision caught a third man stand up and walk toward her. The air, despite the blazing summer sun, turned cold.

They all looked different, but they walked and moved the same, in a lurching and stiff walk, like they were in a film and the projector operator didn't get the speed quite right. They drew closer and closer with each second.

A dozen men had now appeared in the fields, all coming toward her. In unison, they raised their hands toward her as if they were trying to grab her, despite still being a hundred feet away. They called out her name in rough, gravely voices that sounded like the last desperate gasps of dying men. A sound she was all too familiar with.

"Elsie!"

She reached for her gun with trembling hands, but it wasn't there. She remembered it was lying on the back seat where she left it. The leather holster, cold and empty, felt like it had betrayed her.

She side-stepped to the front of the car, keeping her eyes on the men as they crept slowly closer. Her eye caught more movement as dozens more of these men or creatures stood up from the fields. With a searing pain and great difficulty, she reached down and turned the handle to prime the engine. Each turn of the handle tortured her ribs and caused her to grit her teeth. As she did so, the approaching men stopped as if on signal.

Elsie froze, waiting to see what they would do. They were close enough now that the wind caught their scent and she grimaced. It was the scent of a mass grave and decomposing bodies. It was a scent she unfortunately knew all too well. She could also now make out some details. They were all adult men of different ages and wore vastly different clothing, from farmer's overalls to suits and ties.

When she was sure they remained motionless, she grabbed onto the fender for support and cranked the handle. The car came to life instantly and Elsie breathed a sigh of relief and thanked herself for insisting on buying quality cars. That feeling quickly died when the men who surrounded her rushed toward the car, calling out her name in a feverish intensity.

Her broken rib pulsed in agony and didn't allow her to move as fast as she wanted. She made it inside the car as one of the men grabbed for the hem of her dress and almost hooked it.

Elsie got a good look at them as they surrounded her and banged on the car with their filthy fists, leaving trails of dirt and grime with every strike. Each of the men had grim and angry expressions on their dirt covered faces. They continued to call her name and strike her car. The sound of the engine was drowned out by the banging and her name being called out in a feverish rhythm.

Her pistol remained in the back seat and she tried to reach for it, but with her side screaming in pain and the immediate urgency of being surrounded, she didn't have the ability or time and abandoned that idea. She wasn't going to shoot her way out of this.

Surrounded on all sides, the car rocked side to side as if the men were trying to flip the car over. One of the men managed to get the passenger side door open and reached a filthy hand toward her. The fetid smell was incredible, and she wanted to vomit but her training as a nurse allowed her to keep it down.

With a pain that left her breathless and with watery eyes,

she cocked her hip and kicked the filthy creature in the face hard enough she heard its nose break and was relieved when it fell back out of the car noiselessly and blank-faced with dark, coagulated blood splattered on its ugly visage. Another man tried to take its place and crawl inside when the car lurched forward as she stepped on the gas. The two men in front of her were knocked down and caused the passenger side door to close as it struck the press of bodies.

Elsie threw the car in reverse and without regard to running any of the men over, pulled out as fast as the V-8 would allow. She heard a loud 'thump' and felt her rear wheel run over something as she pulled away. The filthy, angry faces flew past her as she tore down the road.

She cast one last look behind her at the approaching figures, but they were nowhere to be seen. Instead, she saw a single man, dark skinned and dressed in feathers, with a large, black stone disc hanging from his neck and an elaborate headdress, dancing in the middle of the road. He stared at her as he danced, then vanished as if he was never there. The streaks of grime all over her car were testament that it was indeed all too real. When she found another pull-off, she did a U-turn and kept driving, still breathing heavy from the pain and the terror, nervous that one of those things could come at her at any time.

She breathed easier once she was away from that field and the men. The problem remained, she had nowhere to go. None of the hotels would take her and she didn't want to go back to the house.

She found a service station and pulled up, automatically ringing a bell to let the service staff know they had a customer. A friendly middle-aged man ran up, asking her questions. She told him to fill it up and check the fluids, but her mind was elsewhere.

Whatever was going on, it followed her wherever she went.

Even out here in the middle of nowhere, it came after her. It even burned down the hotel she stayed in, hurting who knows how many people. She left the house because she thought it would be safer, but it wasn't.

With resignation she realized she needed help, and she wasn't going to find it in Ogden.

"Excuse me, sir."

The station attendant stopped pumping gas and looked up at her.

"Do you have the Yellow Pages and a phone I can borrow?"

Chapter 19

The first rays of daylight woke Harriet. It took her a long time to fall asleep, especially with Marta talking in her sleep all night. When she eventually did fall asleep, disturbing dreams kept it from being restful.

Marta, already awake, sat in a chair on the other side of the room, staring at her.

"How did you sleep? I didn't keep you awake, did I?"

The strange girl couldn't keep eye contact with Harriet and kneaded the hem of her dress.

"I slept as well as could be expected. I had a rough day and a lot on my mind. Do you always talk in your sleep?" she asked as kindly as possible.

"In my sleep? I wouldn't know. Mama says I snore."

"Oh, I heard you talking in your sleep last night after I read you that story."

"I wasn't sleeping, silly," she said, standing up and running out of the room.

Confused, she was about to follow her out, but realized she was still in her nightgown. Glad to change clothes without being watched, she slipped out of her nightgown and put on her denim work overalls. The breakfast bell sounded, so she quickly tied her hair up with a bandana.

Downstairs, the table was set, and the smell made her mouth water. The plates were piled with eggs, beans, tomatoes and toasted bread spread with refried beans and some kind of white, crumbly cheese.

Mack and Lupe came out of the kitchen, carrying glasses of milk. The milk was cold. He must have seen the confused look on her face because he smiled and just said, "ice box."

"This place is full of surprises."

Marta came in and sat next to her, bouncing in her chair.

"Do you miss her?"

Harriet looked around confused. Mack looked uncomfortable.

"Who?"

Marta put her hand to her right cheek.

"The burnt lady."

Harriet stood up from the table and glared at Mack.

"How much did my dad tell you? Did he tell you why he sent me away? Why did you tell Marta?"

She didn't want to be stuck in this ghost town for who knows how long with strangers who looked down on her. It was nobody's business but her own.

Harriet surprised herself with her reaction. She wasn't ashamed or embarrassed, but it was her personal space these strangers were intruding into.

Marta looked scared and on the verge of tears. Lupe got up to put her arms around her to comfort her.

"Your father told me everything," he began to say when Harriet took another step back.

"No, no, no. It's okay," he said, trying to calm and reassure her.

"Please, have a seat, I'll explain."

"Por favor," Lupe said, motioning for her to take her seat again.

Harriet hesitated.

"My sister was like you, she was also in love with a woman, so I know what you're going through doesn't have, nor needs, a cure. It's just who you are. You are safe here."

The big gruff man that rarely used words, spoke in such a manner that she relaxed and felt at ease.

"Please, have a seat." he said.

Harriet slowly sat back down. Marta reached out and took her hand, squeezing it. She squeezed her hand back and leaned over to give her a reassuring hug.

"It's okay, Marta. You didn't do anything wrong."

Marta instantly changed back to her usual manic self.

"So, do you?"

"Do I what?"

"Do you miss her? The lady with the burned face."

Mack translated what Marta had said to Lupe, then they both looked uncomfortable again.

Harriet had only realized the truth about herself and come to terms with it a couple of days ago, so even talking about it was awkward to her. Mack, Marta and Lupe seemed so honest and sincere. She couldn't help but open up to them.

"Yes. I do miss her something fierce and I just want to get back to her as soon as possible."

Mack translated again.

"La amas?" Lupe asked.

Amas?

Harriet wracked her brain, going over what little Spanish she knew.

Amas....ama...amor. Amor! Love!

"Yes! Si! I love her!" Harriet said loudly.

Then she realized what she'd said and covered her mouth with both hands.

Mack chuckled and Lupe looked pleased.

"At least I think I am. I've never been in love before, not including the love I have for my family or the righteous love I have for all mankind. But to be in love, this is new for me. I think this is what love feels like, right?"

"How do you feel when you think about her right now?" Mack said.

"I feel...pain. Being away from her is almost like a physical pain that won't go away. Every time I think of her, it makes me happy and sad at the same time. Happy that such a wonderful person even exists and sad that I can't be with her. Sure, her face is burned, but that doesn't matter. She's the most beautiful woman I've ever met."

"Yeah, that's love," Mack said, taking a big bite of his breakfast.

"She's in pain, too," Marta said with a vacant look on her face.

"I'm sure she is. If she's in love with you, I'm sure she's feeling the same pain," Mack said quickly.

Harriet hadn't considered if Elsie was in love with her. The way that woman kissed, she obviously felt something, but the thought of Elsie not loving her back made her heart drop into her stomach.

Her sudden sadness must have shown through her face, she was never able to hide her emotions, because Mack and Lupe reached out to touch her hand.

"Let's make a deal. I promised your father that I would take you in and that you would have to help me with some projects. I never said for how long. I always keep my promises."

"As much as I would like to, I really need to get back as soon as possible. It's not just that I miss her. There are things going on, dangerous things, and I need to be there to help her."

Mack chewed another bite of food before he responded.

"As soon as you finish the work, the sooner you can go home. I'll buy you a ticket myself."

AFTER BREAKFAST, Harriet and Mack went out to the back of the house. There was a dilapidated barn that was bigger than the house, an ancient tractor that looked like it had an old steam engine, and a windmill.

"Here are your two projects. The first is to fix the windmill. It was your father that put this turbine contraption together. The windmill turns and creates electricity for the house. It mostly just powers the ice box and a lamp in the kitchen. Most of the time it works fine, but sometimes, even if the blades are spinning, there's no power."

"If my dad built this, I'm sure I'll have no problem. Looks easy enough."

"Good. Now here's the real hard part."

He walked over to the tractor and put his hand on it.

"This thing has been here since before I got here. It's never moved. Make it move."

She walked over to it. Steam engines weren't her specialty and this one looked complicated and really neglected.

The main body of the tractor was a large metal cylinder, which thankfully looked intact. The wheels, with wooden spokes and metal rims, were also in decent shape. If they were broken, Mack would have to get some custom ones made in town.

As she inspected the tractor, it became apparent that those were the only things in good order. Almost every connecting pipe, hose and valve was either broken or missing. Harriet's heart sunk. All hopes for getting back home quickly were dashed.

"This is going to take a lot of work and I don't have any tools with me. Heck, even in my shop back home this would take some time. I don't have time for this. I need to get back. How about I go back home, and I'll come back later to fix this."

"I promised your father. Follow me."

He brought her to the barn, which inside was exactly how Harriet thought an old, abandoned barn would look. All the wood was grey from age and cobwebs covered almost every inch. Empty animal stalls stood on one side and work benches on the other.

"There are your tools," he said pointing to lumps of rust sitting on the tables and benches.

The amount and variety of tools was impressive, but they looked like they were old when the Civil War started.

"I know it doesn't look good but give me a list of what you need and I'll get them next time I'm in town. C'mon. Let me show you the windmill."

Harriet could definitely see her dad's handiwork. It was simple yet clever at the same time and she immediately saw the problem.

"This one's easy. The belt is worn and loose. Looks like he used a standard Ford Model T engine belt. You can get these anywhere and they are cheap. The tractor though, that might get expensive."

"Don't worry about that. I got my pension from my time with the tenth cavalry, and I work as a grounds keeper at the University in town. Tax man don't come out here either. I live frugal and save my money."

"Your wife doesn't mind living all the way out here?"

"She's not my wife, we aren't together and never have been. Marta isn't my daughter, but I treat her like she is. They are both special to me."

"So, who is she then?"

"She was my sister Sophia's lover. Sophia died and now I take care of them."

Mack chuckled at the obvious look of shock and confusion on her face.

"Weren't expecting that, were you? I reckon if your father knew that truth, he wouldn't have sent you down here to get over the white woman."

"My condolences about your sister. As you know, I lost my brother, so I kinda know how that feels. But does my dad think you two are married? What does he know? I figured you aren't my real uncle, so how did you two know each other? If you were in the Tenth Cavalry that means you were a Buffalo soldier? If you don't have a telephone, how did my dad contact you? Who is Marta's fa...,"

"Easy, easy there. One question at a time. As far as your father knows, Lupe is my common law wife, and he doesn't know anything about her and my sister. All of that happened before I met your father."

"And how did you two meet?"

"Back in eighteen eighty-seven, my troop was patrolling down by Taos, Indian territory. Now, the Puebloans didn't give us much trouble, but this damn fool negro had gotten in there and riled up the whole town. We found him, just the clothes on his back, running as fast as he could, with dozens of their warriors chasing him. He was running so fast, one of his shoes came off, but that didn't slow him down one bit. He saw us about a mile away and started waving his hands like a crazy person. We wheeled around and rescued the fool and we've been friends ever since."

Harriet scrunched her face in confusion.

"What was my dad doing down there?"

"That's a question you'd have to ask him. So, what were your other questions?"

"You don't have a telephone here. How did my dad contact you?"

"He left a message with my office at the University I work at."

"Final question for now. Who is Marta's father?"

"I don't know, and she won't tell me. At first, I tried to get it out of her, but she's always refused to give even a hint. After the first year, I stopped asking and just accepted it. I think that's enough questions for the day. Write out a list of everything you'll need, and when I go to work on Monday, I'll pick them up for you. Once you do that, spend some time with Marta. She's a sweet and very special girl and I know she enjoys your company. It can get lonely out here, especially for her."

"Oh, hey, Mack? If you are going into town, could you do me a big, big favor and mail this letter for me? If I can't leave, I need to at least communicate with her."

She pulled the letter she had written the night before out of her pocket and handed it to Mack. He nodded and turned to leave, but then stopped. Without turning around, he spoke again.

"Whatever you do, don't go to Grafton. It's dangerous... for people like you."

"Like me?"

"People who are sensitive to the spirt world. They call them ghost towns for a reason, girl."

"How did you know?"

"Marta," Mack said and walked away.

Harriet was confused but shrugged it off. She had seen plenty of ghosts and they never did anything to her. She had way too much to do before she could relax anyway. The sooner she's done fixing this ancient tractor, the sooner she could get back to Elsie.

She would give anything to know if Elsie was okay.

She's probably sitting back, drinking an ice-cold Coke,

reading a book on her porch and resenting me for leaving, while some kind of spook or creature sneaks up on her, and if I was there, I could spot it.

That thought just made her want to work harder so she could get back to her to explain and ask forgiveness. She went inside the house where Lupe was cleaning in the kitchen. She looked up and gave Harriet a beaming and genuine smile.

"Hola," she said in a sweet, almost shy voice.

"Hola. Necesito un...una...," she reached back deep into her memories to remember how to say pencil or pen.

She was hoping they had one on hand and didn't want to go upstairs and dig through her stuff to find hers.

She couldn't remember, so she made hand motions to show writing.

"Aye, una pluma," Lupe said, deliberately drawing out the word pluma.

"Si! Si! And paper."

Again, she couldn't remember the Spanish word, so tried to mimic 'paper'.

"Claro. Espera."

She held a hand to tell Harriet to wait there while she left. She came back only a few seconds later with a notebook and a pencil.

She held up the pencil and said "lapiz".

"Lapiz," she repeated and thanked her as she ran back out.

She spent the rest of the day taking inventory of all the tools and seeing which ones could be salvaged and which ones she'd need Mack to buy.

The ones that were usable were covered in rust, so she wrote 'vinegar', 'baking soda' and 'wire brush' on the list, along with the other tools she had already jotted down.

She left the barn and went up to the junk tractor. Before she did anything else, she drew the tractor and diagramed how it worked. Steam engines were difficult, but she knew the basic concept.

She drew the boiler and the heat source, then tried to draw the pipes and tubes to figure it out. She pulled up an old bucket to use as a seat as she drew.

Marta tip-toed up to Harriet and quietly sat down next to her. She didn't say anything. She just watched as Harriet sketched. Harriet put one arm around her as Marta leaned her head on her lap.

Chapter 20

Elsie knew there was no help to be found in Ogden. The Yellow Pages she borrowed from the gas station pointed her to a few private detectives in Salt Lake City and without delay, she drove south. Only one of the agencies she called answered their phone, so that's where she headed.

The Great Salt Lake was big. Bigger than any lake in Virginia. The lake lay to her right and mountains on her left.

Virginia. She knew she had to return. She didn't want to spend another night here while answers lay back east. The 54th street train station in Ogden was the closest place to find a train heading back to Virginia, and she planned to leave today.

The landscape was mostly brown and flat in the valley but dotted with green fields and tiny towns. It wasn't beautiful like the lush greenery of Virginia, but it had its own rugged charm. She would like to drive west, like Harriet suggested, and see the great deserts and the salt flats.

Thinking of Harriet caused a pain that didn't originate from her rib or scars. Even though it caused heartache, she let herself dwell on Harriet's smooth, dark skin, her beautiful eyes and those full, perfect lips. She missed her healing and intoxicating presence.

As she rounded the spur of one of the mountains, she caught her first glimpse of Salt Lake City. It was dominated by the giant temple that looked like a castle. She had seen pictures, but none of them did justice. Even though Salt Lake was a larger city than Ogden, everything was clean, neat and orderly. No hoodlums or prostitutes clogged the streets. No crooked cops that behaved worse than the criminals. Here, she didn't feel the need to keep a hand on her pistol as she drove down the streets.

Like Ogden, the city was built on a grid system, and she found the address easily. It was clearly labeled 'Valentine Private Eye' with a large sign. Inside, a pretty and very tall red head behind a desk greeted her professionally.

"Good day and welcome. I'm Gloria, how may I be of assistance?" she said with a genuine smile.

"I would like to hire someone to find a missing person."

"Splendid. If you would please take a seat, someone will be out to speak with you momentarily. What is your name, ma'am?"

"Elsie Virginia Everly," she said, taking a seat in the high-backed, overstuffed leather chair.

She waited ten minutes before a tall, thin, balding man walked into the lobby. He wore pinstriped trousers and vest, complete with pocket watch and an exceedingly large revolver on his hip.

"You must be Elsie Everly. I am Roger Valentine. Pleasure to meet you."

She stood up to shake hands. "The pleasure is mine."

"Please, follow me into my office and we'll discuss."

His office was immaculate. Every piece of wood was polished to perfection, and everything was neat and orderly. Rows of certificates and diplomas lined one wall and a giant bookcase lined the other. Elsie quickly picked out an honorable discharge from the Marine Corps, a Pinkerton Commendation and degrees in chemistry and history.

The most remarkable object on the wall was a framed photo. It was the famous picture of Teddy Roosevelt with his Rough Riders standing on San Juan Hill. On the bottom right was the image of a tall man that looked remarkably like Mr. Valentine but much younger and filthier.

He sat down behind his desk in a comfortable looking leather swivel chair and steepled his fingers.

"Now, Ms. Everly, what can I do for you?"

"I need you to locate a missing person, Harriet Theodocia Piper. Well, she's not missing per se, but she's missing to me. Her family knows where she is. They sent her away because of me and won't tell me where she is. I have only recently moved here a little over a week ago, so I don't know anybody and have no connections. She is a dear friend, you see, and I would greatly appreciate it if you could locate her."

"Tell me about this Harriet Piper."

Elsie gave him a complete description of Harriet but left out all the 'beautiful's, 'perfect's and 'wonderful's she wanted to use to describe Harriet. She told him about the shop her family owns and about her search at the train station, trying to give him as much information as possible.

Mr. Valentine didn't interrupt but wrote down quick notes about everything she said.

As Elsie finished, he nodded and put his pencil down.

"Why did the family send her away because of you? What did you do?"

Elsie didn't hesitate.

"Because we are romantically involved," she said, holding her chin high.

"That's what I surmised. Thank you for being honest with me. It's so rare when clients are. I'll take your case. I will find your lost love. There is a daily fee plus expenditures. One hundred dollars up front, non-refundable. Please give all of your contact information to my assistant. It has been a pleasure to meet you. Next time we meet, I'll have the whereabouts of Harriet Piper. Good day."

They both stood up and shook hands again.

Elsie turned around to leave when Mr. Valentine called her name.

"Ms. Everly. I'm glad you didn't turn out like your father."

"Me too."

She gave her contact information and the hundred dollars to Gloria and left.

Driving home, she wondered if her father and brother were alive? She never saw their bodies. She only had a letter as any evidence they were dead at all.

If they were alive, what would it mean that they'd left this house and all their money to her in a will? What would be their purpose of faking their own deaths?

Was it her brother, here in Utah, pretending to be a cop?

How would they be linked to the supernatural events at the house and elsewhere?

If her father and brother were alive, what did they want with her? What was the purpose of setting her up in a huge house in the middle of nowhere, infested with ghosts and jaguars and other supernatural trickery?

Her father was evil and foolish, but he always had a plan and she needed to find out what that was. She drove to a place she knew well.

Abram greeted her like an old friend when she entered the bookstore.

"Ms. Everly! My best customer! Come in!"

She smiled warmly at the gregarious man.

"I bet you say that to all of your customers."

"Ya, it's true," he said with a wink. "Now, to business.

What books are you looking for today? More speculative fiction? Adventure? Horror? Romance, eh?"

"Actually, I'd like to hire you."

"Hire me? What for?"

"I'll be gone for a couple of weeks. I'd like to hire you to do some research for me while I'm gone."

"Research? I haven't done that in years, not since my days teaching at the university. What do you want me to research?"

"Mythology, folklore and legends. I need you to find any connection with mist, smoke, holes or caves, mirrors and jaguars. See if there are any stories or myths that connect these. Also, as payment, I'll give you two hundred dollars and you can use my Cadillac while I'm gone."

"Deal! I'll start today and see what I can find. Why do you need this information?" he said raising one eyebrow.

"You are aware of my father and his writings? It has to do with that. I think some of his followers are still around and I want to know more about them and their beliefs.

"I'll drop the car off before I leave," she said.

Before she left for home, she bought a couple of hot dogs at the same Nathan's hot dog stand she visited before and headed home.

The drive back home was uneventful. She didn't like that she had to return to the house, but she needed to pack and grab some more cash for a trip back to Virginia.

The road to her home wound around and she usually spotted a deer or a raccoon. This time she saw dozens that ran the same direction; away from her place.

She had been doing this for too long to not figure something was out of the ordinary and kept her pistol handy. She felt unease and trepidation as she approached the house.

Once she arrived home, she didn't notice anything, but still walked around the property and made sure nothing was out of the ordinary. Inside the house, Elsie checked the locks on all the windows and doors. Once she guaranteed everything was in order, she changed into her travelling clothes and packed a bag to leave immediately for Virginia.

As she exited the front door and was about to turn to lock up behind her, she noticed movement off in the distance. She put her hand against her forehead to block the light of the low sun and saw a figure standing in the field in front of her property.

She waved, in case it was her Mormon bishop neighbor paying another visit, but knew it wasn't. The figure didn't move, and her hair stood on end. The unnatural stillness of the person contrasted with the gently waving grass and she shifted from foot to foot.

She pulled her pistol and a couple of stripper clips out of her handbag and threw the bag back into the house. She squinted against the sun and looked at the figure again. She noticed more movement as figures rose from the tall grass of her fields.

Dozens of people, just like when she woke up in her car, surrounded her house. They walked toward the house in that same jerky, sped up motion picture way as before.

Every hair stood up on end and she knew something loathsome and unholy approached.

She tossed her suitcase back into the house and took a knee behind the deck railing and propped the pistol against it for stability. The range to the closest person looked to be around four hundred meters. She flipped up the sights and adjusted them for range. Despite all her practice, she knew Harriet was the better shot and wished she was here.

She aligned the sights center mass on the chest of the person walking toward her and waited. The sights on her Mauser could be adjusted up to one-thousand meters, but that was beyond optimistic. She waited until the person was two-hundred meters, adjusted the sight for range and started to control her breathing.

Crouching behind the railing was making her rib scream in pain, but she ignored it and put her finger on the trigger. Once she was sure she had a good shot at a hundred meters, she gently pulled back on the trigger until the pistol barked.

The shot went wild and she quickly evaluated that she'd jerked the trigger.

She adjusted her aim and fired on another approaching figure but missed again. She adjusted the sights for fifty meters and fired again. This one stumbled, then fell face first onto her driveway, unmoving.

She allowed herself a brief second to congratulate herself before taking aim again.

She managed to fell two more when she heard heavy footsteps rounding the corner of the wrap around porch.

A large and shabby man with clothes covered in grime walked into view from around the side of the house, heading toward her. His face was covered with a white mask that looked like it was made out of porcelain or some other white, hard materiel. There was a face carved into the mask. It looked like an ancient Greek theatrical mask with a sad or sorrowful expression, though not as intricate and detailed.

Elsie wheeled and put two holes into his chest.

At this close range it was hard to miss, and she was rewarded when meat and fragments of clothing shot out his back. The man stopped and looked down. The chest wounds weren't pumping or squirting arterial spray as was expected, but a slow trickle of dark, clotted blood oozed out.

The man touched the wounds as if he didn't know what happened.

She looked behind her in time to see another man, just as filthy and also wearing a mask, round the other corner of her porch, only this mask showed a neutral expression, its mouth a straight line and its eyes simple circles.

"Elsie," said the man she shot. She turned back to face him.

The thing spoke in a quiet, calm, reassuring voice.

"Come, Elsie. Become like us. Dreams upon dreams are waiting for you," it said as it walked toward her.

A feeling of malevolence came over her, emanating from the thing like a furnace emits heat. All warmth left her body and she shook uncontrollably. She could feel an aura of wrongness surrounding it and it terrified her.

She unloaded the rest of the clip into its chest, shoulder and face, shattering the mask. The mask splintered and fell away, revealing the face behind it.

The large veiny nose, dead eyes and lecherous grin were unmistakable. It was the man behind the counter at the Ute Trading Post.

His wounds oozed more of the same black, thick blood as before.

"Ia Ia. In ie tlecujlixquac, in ie tlamamatlac. Itech naci in Tezcatlipoca. You will meet him soon," he said in a voice gurgling with blood.

More of the things rounded the corners of the house and came in from each side. They drew closer and closer.

She tried to reload her gun, but her hands trembled too much. She dropped the stripper clip. Bullets scattered over the wood boards of the porch.

Painfully, she stood up and walked as fast as she could, entered the house and locked the door behind her.

A rhythmic and incessant pounding began as dozens of the things beat their fists against the door.

"Let us in, Elsie," came a gravelly female voice.

Elsie dared to look out the window and saw a white mask with an overly happy expression, framed by wild, filthy and matted long hair cascading all around it.

It pressed its mask against the glass and touched the window like it was trying to calm a lover. It wore a corset and long dress fashionable in the last century and looked like it hadn't been washed since.

"We won't hurt you. We love you. Open the door, Elsie and let us in."

Instead of answering, she reloaded her pistol, hands still trembling, and set the sights back to zero.

When she looked up again, the woman was still pressed against the window, only now the expression on her mask had changed to look like it was angry.

"Let us in. Forget about that bitch, Harriet. I'll be yours. I'll be anything you want me to be. I'll be your lover, your friend or the mother you never knew," she cooed, grabbing her own filthy breast.

Elsie, without hesitation, shot her in the face through the window. Her mask shattered into a thousand pieces, and she caught a glimpse of the horrid face underneath before she fell back out of sight. Thankfully, the window didn't break, but there was a small hole with spider web cracks all throughout. Two more of the masked things took her place. They didn't try to break the window, but they stared at her and asked her to come outside or let them in.

She backed away from the front of the house and sat on the stairs, facing the front door and windows.

She sat there the rest of the day and all night, fighting to stay awake in case they decided to force their way in, which they could easily do. The constant pounding against the door was almost hypnotic and she caught herself dozing a few times. She figured she could sleep on the train back to Virginia if she could get out of here.

As dawn approached, the knocking on the door suddenly stopped. She pulled herself up, exhausted, thirsty and starving and approached the door. She peeked out the little window in the door and didn't see anything.

She moved to one of the larger windows and searched for the things, but there was no sight of them. They had all vanished.

Tentatively, she opened the front door and confirmed that they were gone, even the ones she had shot. She searched around for evidence of their existence, but the only thing she could find were the spent brass from her pistol. She figured there might be blood stains on the porch, but she couldn't find evidence of that either.

She went around to the back of the house to see if that's where they vanished to, just in time to see in the distance someone standing by the edge of the hole. It was the dancer she had seen on the road, dressed in the same elaborate costume of feathers. Like last time, it stared at her as it danced, but instead of disappearing, it opened its arms wide and fell backward into the hole.

She thought about going over there and firing a few parting shots into the hole, but she knew it would do no good. She hurried back to the house, showered, got dressed and drove to the train station, wanting to get away as quickly as possible. She brought only one piece of luggage and bought a ticket on the first available train heading east.

She was going to get to the bottom of this and knew some of the answers lay back in Virginia. She was going to find out for certain whether her father and brother were alive.

Chapter 21

After a week of working on the homestead, she had already fixed the wind turbine. That was easy, it only needed a new belt.

The tractor on the other hand, was more complicated than it looked. After clearing out several rodent and bird nests, she discovered that the damage was more severe than she thought.

For the last week she had been perched over a bucket, soaking and scrubbing every part of the tractor's engine with vinegar and baking soda to get the rust off. She was sick of the smell.

She worked non-stop, from sunrise to sundown to get back to Elsie. She didn't care if her parents kicked her out of the house, she'd find someplace to live and work if she had to.

She dreamed that Elsie would welcome her back with open arms, even let her stay with her, but that was just a dream. Most of her dreams are what she called "kissing dreams", though they always went beyond kissing. It was a shame they were interrupted when they were by her father, because she really wanted to figure out how two women actually make love. She had an idea, based on what Elsie was going to do to her, but she wanted to know everything, even if it just fueled her dreams.

She sighed, daydreaming about Elsie's gentle hand sliding down her belly toward her privates. After a few moments of thinking of what Elsie was going to do, she had to sit cross-legged and fan herself off.

"There you are!" Marta's voice came, sounding surprised, as if she hadn't been sitting over this bucket for the last few days.

"Hey, Marta. What'cha up to?" she said, putting down the wire brush and valve she was working on.

"Come play with me. I'm bored."

This happened at least once a day. Marta would try to drag her away to go explore one of the abandoned buildings in the town. Harriet would find an excuse to get out of it and Marta would always return with some kind of treasure; a fork, a kid's shoe and one time, she even found a bundle of old Confederate money. Marta didn't understand the concept of money, but she thought they were pretty.

It's not that she didn't want to play with Marta or go exploring, but she had to do everything she could to return to Elsie. She didn't know if Elsie was safe or if she left to go back to Virginia and she'd never see her again. That thought tore at her heart, but at least she'd be away from that wicked house.

Harriet was in need of a break, though and the smell nauseated her, so she said, "Sure, let's go play."

Marta giggled in delight and took her hand. Instead of running into what was left of the town, she led her to a shed. Inside were three bicycles, all rusty and beaten but still in working order.

"Where are we going this time, Marta?"

"I want to take you somewhere special. It's down the road a couple of miles so we need these. Mack taught me to drive the car, but he took that to go to work," Marta said, pulling out the smallest of the three bicycles.

"Why not?" Harriet shrugged and grabbed one of the bikes.

Within moments, they were off down the dirt road heading east. She had never been down this direction before and had no idea where they were going.

The road was deserted and Marta sped along as fast as she could as Harriet struggled to keep up with her.

After several minutes, Marta stopped and jumped off her bicycle and started to climb down an almost dry riverbed that ran parallel to the road.

"Where are we going, Marta?"

"You'll see! Follow me!" she called as she started to skip over the rocks in the riverbed to cross over to the other side.

Harriet put her bike down and quickly followed her, not wanting Marta to get too far ahead. She dreaded thinking of Marta getting lost or injured, especially on her watch. Mack and Lupe would never forgive her.

She scrambled down the bank, then jumped on the rocks, just as she saw Marta do. Marta helped pull her up the steep bank on the opposite side.

Once she stood up and looked around, she could see a small town a few hundred feet away. It looked bigger than Duncan's Retreat but just as abandoned. What remained of the streets were overgrown and the houses, what few remained standing, were both waterlogged and crumbling from dry rot. The place looked like everyone left in a hurry and mostly all at once. The windows weren't boarded up and farm equipment, wagons and even children's toys, were left to decay. Except for the big, two-story house in the middle of town.

"You gotta be sneaky. There is still one person that lives here. He lives in the big house in the center. He never comes out, but he watches out the windows sometimes. He won't see us if we sneak around the backs of the houses."

Harriet looked at the big house but didn't see anyone looking out the windows. What was left of the dirt streets of the town were wide and small houses lined each side. A large schoolhouse or church loomed on the opposite side of the town.

The town was picturesque with orchards and fields behind the houses. Many of the houses had already started to collapse and cast an eerie shadow over the rest of the town.

"C'mon! Let's go!"

Marta, barefoot as always, leaped a fence into the backyard of one of the abandoned houses. Each house was on its own half acre, laid out in a grid and surrounded by rotting and gnarled juniper fences. The properties faced outward, toward the streets, with most of the land behind the houses. There appeared to be only two streets with the houses nestled between them. Harriet saw that if you stayed in the back yards and were willing to jump some low fences, you could cross the entire town.

Fields of weeds and abandoned crops spread out on the outskirts of the ghost town, while small hills encircled the entirety.

"I've already explored this house a dozen times. Let's go to the one across from the church. That's where they say to go."

"Who says?" Harriet asked, knowing she wouldn't get an answer.

They took off running, keeping low and sticking to the shadows like a soldier from the Great War would to avoid getting shot.

They crossed a couple of yards and jumped a few fences until they reached the house Marta had pointed out.

It had obviously been abandoned for some time because

everything around it was dead and thorny brown weeds grew over the patch of road in front.

An ancient and dead tree dominated one side of the house, casting the entire thing into shadow. An old and decrepit cemetery loomed across the street. Faded wood marked most of the graves and leaned in all different directions. There was one row of stone graves, some of which were surrounded by an iron fence. A sign said 'Grafton Cemetery'.

"This is it. Let's see what we can find."

"Grafton? This is Grafton? Mack said we shouldn't come here."

"There's something he doesn't know!" Marta whispered back.

Marta jumped up and ran up to the rear door of the house.

"Wait! We shouldn't be here!" she whispered as loud as she could.

Harriet was about to do the same and chase after her when she saw something move behind the tree. She shaded her eyes from the bright noon-day sun to get a better look.

At first, she didn't see anything, then she spotted a pale, gaunt hand reach around the trunk of the tree.

An old man in a denim overall and a flannel shirt looked around the tree but didn't see her. He did, however, look at the house, specifically the rear door where Marta just entered.

Harriet knew it was a ghost. They always looked exactly like living people, but she instinctively knew they were dead, even when they didn't know themselves.

The ghost then stepped out from behind the tree and walked toward the door Marta went through.

"Marta!" she yelled. Something wasn't right.

She had never known a ghost to harm anyone. It was rare they acknowledged the living, but the ones that did always seemed to have bad intentions.

This one didn't look angry, like the old woman in the abandoned house years before, but it wore an odd expression, with a wicked grin and darting eyes.

Harriet ran toward the house as the ghost passed through the door as if it wasn't there. She caught up a few seconds later and threw the door open. Inside, the house was bare, rotting wood, dried mud, dust and little else. It looked like a flood came through here many years ago and left its residue. A feeling of oppression and plain wrongness hung in the air, making it hard to breathe.

Neither Marta nor the ghost were in sight.

"Marta! Where are you?"

"I'm in here," came her voice from the last room down the hallway.

Harriet ran down the hallway toward Marta's voice and came to the entrance of the room. Marta stood in the middle of the room holding an old, dusty mirror in one hand and an ornate candle in the other.

The ghost was there too, standing beside her. It was trying to touch her. It was grasping at her in ways that a man should never touch a child. As it tried to paw at her, its hands passed through, and it roared silently into the still air.

Marta didn't react at all, though Harriet could see her breath and noticed goose bumps on Marta's arms. She was too busy staring into the little mirror.

"Look what I found! A mirror and a candle!"

Marta held up the mirror. It was silver and highly decorated and embossed with large cats. The glass was intact but did not reflect Harriet's face. Instead, all she saw was a roiling black mass of shadow and smoke.

"I don't think the man that lived here was a good man," Marta said, her voice monotone and her face suddenly slack.

Harriet knocked the mirror out of her hand, causing it to shatter into hundreds of sparkling shards. Harriet grabbed

Marta by the wrist and yanked her away from the evil ghost. The ghost silently shrieked. Its face pulled tight as incorporeal tendons and veins bulged and it gnashed its teeth.

They ran out of the house and its cold oppressive atmosphere and into the warm sunlight.

"Where did the mirror go?" Marta said, shaking her head as if coming out of a dream.

"Never mind that. We need to get out of here. We never should have come here."

Harriet took a second to catch her breath when her gaze fell on the cemetery across the street.

Beside each grave stood a person, each of them dressed in old clothes from the last century and each of them staring at her. She could see the hatred in their blank stares.

As she met their dead eyes, she could feel a pain behind her eyes that grew with each second. She tore her eyes away, but the pain continued and spread further into her head.

Harriet was stunned. Ghosts never had this effect before. She had, however, never seen so many ghosts at once and had never been as terrified.

At once, they all took a step toward her, several of them pointed or reached out for her and a sensation of being dunked in ice water flowed over her. She could feel herself grow weaker as the coldness enveloped her.

"We need to run, now," Harriet said, shivering and pulling Marta with her as she took off back the way they came.

They jumped fences and ran through the fields toward the dry river. Even though the first fence had mostly fallen, she had a tough time vaulting over it. The further she ran from the ghosts, the better she felt, and her strength returned. Harriet now knew she was wrong. Ghosts can harm people and she didn't want to know what would happen if they caught her.

She then remembered her Bible studies. The Witch of Endor brought doom to Saul, but it was the unclean spirits and swine she thought of. Those spirits yearned for bodies of flesh and in desperation, inhabited a herd of pigs just to feel life again. They then drove the herd into the water and killed them. The way these spirits reached for her made her think that's exactly what they wanted. They wanted her vessel. To feel again, even if it meant death again.

Harriet, now with tears streaming down her cheeks, ran faster.

The weeds and thorns clawed at her legs as she ran through the empty fields. Marta was just as fast as her, despite her shorter legs and had no problem scrambling over the fences. She supposed this was the kind of thing Marta did all the time. Harriet came to the next fence and braced her hand on the horizontal beam to leap over, but the wood crumbled under her weight. She crashed to the Earth in a cloud of dust. She landed hard and the wind was knocked from her lungs.

Harriet was disoriented and lay in the dirt, gasping for breath and tried to figure out what just happened.

Marta was immediately at her side to help lift her up.

"A race isn't fun if the other person falls. Vamos!" Marta said.

Out of the corner of her eye, a pale hand with thin fingers and jagged nails scratched at the ground where Harriet's foot had been less than and second ago. She let out a wordless scream. She didn't want to look back to see how close the ghosts were. Her own breath frosted and hung in front of her face when she breathed and knew they were too close.

Breathing hard and sweating, they approached the big house in the center of town that was still inhabited, and she saw an old man lean out a window. This wasn't a ghost. It was the last remaining inhabitant of the ghost town of Grafton.

"Better get running, girl! They're gonna get ya!" the old man cackled and choked on his laughter.

She didn't want to, but she did anyway. Harriet dared a

glance back. She hoped they had gained ground against the spirits, but her hopes were dashed. The mob of ghosts stood still, only ten feet away. Each one of them reached for her and she felt the icy pull of their anger and bitterness.

They were all ages and sexes and this time Harriet noticed they all showed the wounds and marks of their deaths. Some were gaunt from disease. Others bore wounds of an Indian massacre. The children. There were far too many ghosts of children, and they looked fiercer than the adults, each one bore white, dead eyes. They grasped for her and clawed at the air.

The town of Grafton was filled with tragedy. She didn't see it as a dark veil like it was at Elsie's house, but she felt it, nonetheless. She felt the loss of childhood death, some to disease, others from accidents. The anger at God for the loss of a spouse overwhelmed her. Her gaze was drawn to a young woman with a bloody head wound who stared at her with the same burning anger as the rest, but also with a jealousy so intense, it radiated off her like an arctic wind and it was directed at her.

"Run faster, Marta!" she yelled uselessly as Marta was ahead of her.

They came to the last fence and Harriet watched where she placed her hand this time as she leapt over. As she landed on the other side, she heard the fence behind her shatter into hundreds of pieces that flew past her face.

They made it to the riverbed, jumped down without a second thought and scrambled up the other side. The ghosts made no sound, but she knew they were there.

She breathed heavily, grabbed her bicycle, and looked back over the river.

The ghosts of Grafton stood assembled on the bank of the river, all staring at her with their dead, angry faces. One by one, they turned to walk back to where they came from, fading away as they did. The last one, a middle-aged woman in a big, fancy dress that could have once been pretty, except for the permanent scowl etched onto her dead face, stared at her as she mounted her bicycle and peddled away. Harriet knew she was the jealous ghost.

Harriet and Marta rode as fast as they could back to Duncan's Retreat. Harriet looked back one more time to see the distant ghost of the woman who still stood there, and she could feel her gaze even though she could barely make her out from this distance.

They arrived back at Duncan's Retreat and put the bicycles back into the shed. She turned to Marta and gently put her hands on her shoulders and looked into her eyes.

"Marta, listen to me, this is very important."

Marta nodded.

"You must never go back to that town, to Grafton. It's a dangerous place, especially for little girls all alone."

"Oh, I know. You woke up all the sleeping people. They sounded angry. There's no more treasures there anyway. But I found this! This candle is super important," she said cheerfully, holding up the old, half used candle.

"What do you mean 'they sounded angry'? You can hear them?"

Marta rolled her eyes in mock exasperation.

"All the people that were asleep are awake now and they are angry. It's kinda hard not to hear them. People that sleep a long time talk a lot. Don't worry, I won't go back there. I got the bestest treasure from there anyway."

Marta then skipped away, humming a tune and playing with her candle.

Harriet chased after her and followed her inside.

"Marta, wait!"

Marta had already made it upstairs when Harriet caught up to her.

"Marta, hold on. So, you can hear spirits?"

"Well, yeah. And people call me a dummy. C'mon, lemmie show you where I hide my treasures."

On the second floor, Marta went into one of the empty rooms and took out a pole with a hook on it. In the hallway, she used it to hook a ring to an attic door and pull it down.

She used the same pole to hook another ring, pulled down a ladder, and climbed up. Harriet didn't know what she would find up there but followed her anyway.

She climbed up the ladder and peeked inside before committing. She was expecting a dark and dirty place filled with cobwebs and the bones of dead mice, but it wasn't bad.

What she saw was a small attic, clean and well-lit by a large, circular window on one side. More of Marta's drawings lined the walls. There was even a mattress and blankets for Marta to nap on.

Under the window sat an ancient looking chest. Marta walked over to it and motioned for her to follow. She climbed up into the attic, went over to her, and knelt beside her.

"This is where you keep your stuff?"

Marta nodded and opened the chest.

Inside was the oddest assortment of tidbits she had ever seen. There was a broken dinner plate, a long rusty nail, a doll's head, a knife handle and various other things it would be expected for people to leave behind.

"This is now my favorite. My very favorite. It's super important, so I'm not going to play with it. All the sleeping people told me to get it though. Doesn't seem fair to me. But don't worry, you'll get to play with it soon."

With a huff, Marta gently put the candle inside with the other trinkets as if it was delicate and the slightest mishap would break it.

"So, can we talk about how you can listen to spirits now?"

Marta shrugged.

"I've always been able to. They tell me things. They told me you were coming. They told me about you and the lady that lives in the big house with the scar on her face. They tell me a lot of things. Sometimes they make me sad."

"Did they say if Elsie is okay? Did they say anything about the hole in the ground or what is going on at that big house?"

"Oh, sure. They said a lot of stuff. They said something about a broken rib and a fire in a big building. Then they said she's going somewhere to look for her family, even though she doesn't like them. The hole? They can't see into the hole. They said something about maggots and strum or sturm-something. I can't pronounce it, but some bad guy with a weapon made of fire. They said some other stuff about stars and planets and time, but I didn't understand any of it."

"What does any of that mean?"

"I'll take you somewhere tomorrow. The sleeping people that live in the cliffs can tell you themselves. I don't really understand it. C'mon, it's time for lunch!"

Marta closed the chest and bolted from the attic, leaving Harriet alone.

She sat there in silence for several minutes trying to think about everything that had happened.

A noise drew her attention to the big attic window. She walked over and looked through.

Outside was the shower that her dad built for Mack many years ago. It had a conveyor device that drew water from the nearby stream that filled a small reservoir which hung over a roofless enclosure. It was basically four wood walls with a bucket hanging over. She had used it a few times herself. She reminded herself to complement her dad once she saw him again.

Someone used it now. Without thinking, she looked further down to see who it was.

There was Lupe, washing herself. Her long, black hair,

always kept in a bun, was now wet and draped over her shoulders, hanging down to her waist, which was very shapely. Her eyes drifted to the dark curls between Lupe's legs and her breath hitched.

She had never in her life seen another naked woman before.

She forced herself to look away and duck down though. It wasn't right to watch somebody like that without them knowing.

She peeked again.

Lupe now washed her breasts and thighs. Harriet had to cover her mouth to prevent herself from making any kind of noise and continued to watch. She compared her own body to Lupe's. While her own was tall and slim, Lupe was short and voluptuous. Lupe's hair, usually tied up in a bun, hung luxuriously from her shoulders and excited Harriet.

Lupe turned around and washed her behind, which was also very lovely.

Harriet always appreciated a nice, womanly butt.

She had never done it before, but she felt an overwhelming urge to touch herself. As she sat on the floor, she spread her legs and reached under her overalls, ready to relax and indulge in fantasy after such a harrowing day.

"C'mon, silly! Lunch is ready!"

Marta's head popped up from the door to the attic. Harriet quickly ripped her hand out of her overalls and gave her a look of frustration.

"What'cha doing?"

"Nothing!" Harriet said, scrambling to her feet.

"Let's go get some lunch, Marta."

They went downstairs to the dining room table where all the fixins for tacos were laid out on the table. Her mouth drooled as she sat down and grabbed a plate.

Harriet and Marta happily devoured the food until they were full and patted their bellies.

Lupe walked in, drying her hair with a towel and spoke Spanish to Marta, too fast for her to follow. Marta answered back with a big grin.

"Y tu? Te gusta? You like?"

Harriet thought she was talking about the food, then Lupe gave her a big, obvious wink and a smile.

She knew she had been caught and didn't know how to respond, so she replied with the only phrase she knew.

"Si, me gusta."

"O'jala," she said, blowing Harriet a kiss before going back into the kitchen.

I hope?

Harriet knew she just said something inappropriate and figured she would have to learn more Spanish to figure out what it was.

Chapter 22

Once again, Elsie sat in a luxury train car watching the fields of Nebraska roll by, highlighted by a beautiful sunset. Despite the great accommodation, it was still an exhausting trip and she wanted it to be over. She didn't want to think about the fact she would have to do this all over again on the way back.

She didn't want to think about what she would find in Virginia. She longed for the knowledge that her father and brother were gone and never coming back. She desperately never wanted to see them again. There was also a small part of her that hoped they were alive, because then she would at least have some knowledge about who is behind all of this.

She was out in the commons area by herself in a booth. It was after dinner, but waiters were still about, offering coffee in their sharp uniforms.

Most of the other passengers had retired to their private cabins, leaving less than a handful of people. Most were preoccupied with private conversations or reading the newspaper.

Elsie took her book out of her handbag and started reading. She approached the end of her book and Edmond Dantes was enacting his sweet, unholy revenge on those that betrayed him.

As always happens when you try to read in public, someone sat down opposite her in the booth and tried to strike up a conversation.

"Good evening, miss. What a gorgeous sunset," said the cheerful male voice.

Elsie tried not to roll her eyes too much and looked over the top of her book to see who disturbed her.

It was a young man, clean shaven in a neat suit and she supposed most women would think he was handsome. She didn't respond and went back to her book.

"What's a pretty woman like you doing all by herself? You should have your pick of the men on this train to keep you company."

This has happened before. Until men saw her scars, they frequently flirted with her, especially when they viewed her as alone, vulnerable and needing protection. To make this man go away and skip to the end, she brushed her hair back to reveal the burn scars on her face.

"Sorry, I don't mean to be rude, but I'm not looking for any company," she said as politely as she could.

Sometimes when men got offended, they would stick around longer and try to regain the upper hand.

This man didn't react and kept on talking.

"I'm heading to Norfolk. Business trip. I'm in the ship building business. Where are you off to by yourself?"

"It is a personal matter. Please don't mind me, but I'd like to finish reading my book."

The man remained in silence for a few minutes, and she hoped that he got the hint.

"How did you get that scar?"

Apparently, he did not get the hint, so she ignored him.

"What are you reading? Is it any good?"

She inched the front cover over so he could see it better, but she didn't say a word.

"You know, I like it when they play hard to get, especially a hot tomato like yourself."

"Please, sir, leave me in peace and let me read."

"Why does a pretty lady need to read anyway? Women are like flowers. They are exquisitely beautiful, some of God's greatest creations, but should remain docile, silent and most importantly, in one place," he said in a menacing tone.

He leaned forward, keeping his hands under the table.

The man had her complete and undivided attention now.

She put the book down and moved it to the side.

"Excuse me, I didn't catch your name," she said sweetly, overplaying her Virginian accent.

"Mister Marsh, at your service."

"Well, Mister Marsh, I must excuse myself. I'm feeling rather tired all of a sudden. I'll be retiring to my quarters now. Good night," she said, grabbing her bag and moving to stand up.

She heard the hammer of a pistol pull back and click into place.

"Awww, how could you resist my handsome male charm, Miss Everly?"

He knew her name.

"Rather easily."

"Could it be you just prefer the company of women?"

"Could be. Now what can I do for you, Mister Marsh?"

"That's the question, isn't it? You can do a lot of things for me, I imagine. So many things. But what I want from you right now is at the next stop in Omaha, you will exit this train at the station, and get on the westbound train back to Utah. Here is your ticket."

Keeping one hand under the table, he slid a ticket across the table with the other. While he was immaculately clean, his hands were filthy and looked like he had had been digging in the dirt, barehanded.

"Aren't you a charmer," she said, disgusted.

She didn't move to take the ticket.

"Look, it's the carrot or the stick. I have a fully loaded big stick under this table pointed at you. If you want a carrot, your little colored bitch is already back at her home waiting for you. Consider it our gift to you."

Elsie figured he was lying, but she went along with it anyway. She would get more information out of him if he thought she was compliant, though she wanted to shoot him there on the spot for calling Harriet that. She inched her hand toward her purse.

"I would dearly love to see her again."

Even if he was telling the truth, she still needed to go to Virginia to get answers.

She reached over, picked up the ticket and looked it over before slowly moving to put it in her purse. She placed it in her purse while sliding her pistol out onto the seat beside her.

"Careful now. I know you keep your pea shooter in there. Let's stay amicable," he said, tapping his pistol against the bottom of the table.

Elsie pulled out lipstick and slowly applied it.

"I want to look good for Harriet, don't I?"

"A coffee or tonic for the couple?"

Elsie didn't hear the waiter approach, and she jumped at his voice.

A boy, barely a teenager, stood next to them, a large platter with cups of coffee and glasses of some kind of clear, bubbly drink.

"Nothing for me, thank you. Even without coffee I never sleep," said Mister Marsh.

Marsh looked up at the waiter when he spoke to him, and

Elsie used that second to slide the pistol closer and hide it under a fold of her dress.

"No, thank you. I'm about to retire. Would you be a dear and fetch me another pillow?"

"A pillow? Y...Yes, ma'am. I'll have that brought to you with haste," he said as he left the two of them alone again.

"Now, where were we?" she asked innocently.

"I believe you agreed to be a good little girl and to use that ticket to return to Utah at the next stop."

"Ah, yes. I did. But I must ask to sate my curiosity. Why are you and your friends so invested in me staying in Utah? Seems like you are playing your hand too early here."

He scowled at this line of questioning.

"You couldn't possibly understand our motivations, you burnt hag. Just do what you're told, or we'll kill your little girlfriend."

"But not me?"

He looked confused.

"Not me though. As punishment, you wouldn't kill me? I'm assuming since you never threatened me with death, you need me alive. Good to know."

He obviously looked for something to say when an attendant approached the table.

"You requested an additional pillow for your room, ma'am?"

"Why, yes I did, thank you," she said as he handed it to her, and she placed it on her left side.

"As I was saying, since your threats are meaningless now, I'll safely ignore you and continue reading my book."

She picked up the book, placing it between them so she didn't have to see his stupid face and pretended to read.

"There are worse things than killing you, you ugly bitch, and if you keep that attitude up, I'll show you. Of course, I have to spend every second with you until we get back to

Utah, just to make sure you live up to your part of the bargain. Might as well make the time with you worth it," he sneered.

"Just put that pistol away. We both know you are not going to use it and I don't want you getting all hot and bothered thinking about little old me and shoot your round prematurely."

"You stupid arrogant bitch," he muttered under his breath, but didn't move the pistol.

She ignored him and went back to her book, confident he wouldn't try anything now.

She read for another hour as people filtered back to their private cabins, leaving only themselves and a middle aged businessman passed out a couple booths away from drinking too much.

"Well, I am fatigued, Mr. Marsh. I will be retiring to my quarters, and I suppose you are duty bound to follow me."

"You are not leaving my sight."

"I figured as much. There is no reason we can't be polite. I suppose you know I have a broken rib? Would you be a dear and help me stand up?" she said, holding up her hand in a very ladylike manner.

"Of course, Ms. Everly. Chivalry is not dead," he said with a sneer.

He stood up and walked over to her side of the table, putting the large revolver into his pocket and holding out a hand.

"Why, thank you. Such a gentleman."

She grabbed the pillow in her left hand and the pistol she had been hiding with her right. Before Mr. Marsh could react, she shoved the pillow against his stomach and punched the barrel of her gun against the pillow to muffle the noise and fired two shots, one into his gut, the other into his chest. The gun jammed on the second shot. A red mist appeared behind as the bullets tore through him, slamming into the wood paneling on the other side.

He grunted loudly as he tried to ineffectually reach for the revolver in his pocket but because it was so large, it caught in the fabric. She brought the butt of the pistol down hard on his hand and was rewarded with the wet crack of a broken metacarpal.

Elsie stood up as quickly as she could, causing severe pain in her side, and put his arm around her shoulders as if she was escorting a patient back to bed.

"Shhhhh, shhh, it'll all be over soon," she said, looking around the car.

While the pistol shots were muffled, they were still loud, which is why she waited for the car to be empty. The drunk businessman sat up, looked around bleary eyed and immediately passed out again.

Once she was sure nobody would interrupt her, she escorted Mr. Marsh to the exit behind her. She felt the man getting weaker by the second and she had to move quickly before he passed out from blood loss and shock.

"Hail. Hail. Already at the edge of fire, already at the stairway. I join Smoking Mirror," he croaked, but it was barely above a whisper.

She didn't understand what he said but moved him to the exit and opened the door between the train cars.

A hot gust of air wafted in as she brought him outside. Every step became more painful as she had to support more of his weight. He was fading fast.

She barely made it outside when he finally collapsed. His weight was too much to bear, so she let him fall.

He fell on the coupling that connected the two cars. She hoped he would just fall off.

Mr. Marsh hadn't passed out from shock yet and managed to feebly get the revolver out of his pocket, but his trembling hands couldn't keep a hold of it. The gun fell between the cars and disappeared into the darkness.

"Bye bye, Marsh. This is what you get for insulting my girl, you maggot."

She waved as she kicked him off the coupling and he fell under the train as it rolled through the Nebraska wilderness, no civilization in sight.

She quickly went back inside and used a metal coffee pot from a nearby table and smashed the lock on the other side of the car. She grabbed her purse and book, smashed the other door lock as she left, and went back to her cabin as quickly as she could before anyone saw her. There was nothing she could do about the bullet holes and blood spray on the wall. She doubted anyone investigating the scene would connect them to her.

She was just a lady, after all, and not capable of such violence.

It was unknown if Marsh worked alone or if he had a partner that would come looking for him. From their brief conversation, she doubted it, but she locked her door and kept her pistol close anyway.

The rest of the trip was uneventful and as far as she could tell, the staff had questioned many passengers about what happened, but not her.

From the change in scenery, she knew instantly when the train entered Virginia. Having seen the Rockies, she could never call what Virginia had 'mountains' ever again. They were more rolling hills now and were enveloped in gray skies and a light, hot rain.

Even though this was her home for most of her life, she wasn't glad to be back and stepped off the train at the Richmond station with a dire purpose.

First things first, she needed to find a hotel. She wanted nothing more than to start but she was exhausted and would be useless if she didn't get some rest. She was sure it was fatigue from traveling, but she developed a slight cough and felt exhausted. Normally, she wouldn't be too concerned, but each cough brought with it such severe pain that on a couple of instances almost made her black out.

She saw a Model T with a 'TAXI' sign on top and hailed it.

The car pulled over and stopped.

"Where to, ma'am?" said the rough-looking but polite and soft-spoken driver.

"Take me to the best hotel in town."

Chapter 23

Harriet woke up and looked around the dark bedroom. Something had woken her, but she wasn't sure what yet.

She grabbed her pocket watch, but it was too dark to tell the time, so she put it back down. Then she heard Marta giggling. She groaned and realized that must be what woke her up.

"Marta, it's too early in the morning for this. Please go back to sleep," she grumbled.

It was quiet again, and she waited a few minutes before she closed her eyes and tried to go back to sleep. The moment she did, Marta began talking to herself again.

"Marta, please go to sleep."

Marta ignored her and kept whispering.

With an exasperated sigh, she leaned out from the bottom bunk to look up at her.

Marta wasn't talking to herself.

Harriet froze when she saw a little girl in a pioneer dress, floating horizontally a foot over Marta. Her skin was so pale it was almost translucent, and she had dark rings around her eyes. Her legs were straight and her arms at her side, with long brown hair falling around her face. Her lips moved as if she was speaking.

The ghost whispered something to Marta. She responded but Harriet couldn't hear what she said.

The ghost girl stopped speaking and her eyes flashed toward Harriet, her lips curled and she bared her teeth and glowered at Harriet.

Harriet quickly ducked back out of sight of the ghost and Marta mumbled again, only now she knew Marta wasn't mumbling to herself.

After several minutes, Marta stopped talking and all was silent again. She gathered her courage enough to take a peek over the side and saw that the ghost had gone and could hear Marta quietly snoring.

After what she just saw, it took her a long time to go back to sleep.

When she woke again, it was daylight and Marta had already gone.

She got dressed and went down to see what was for breakfast.

Marta, Lupe and Mack were already sitting at the table eating.

"Buenos dias," Lupe said, giving her a sweet smile and motioned for her to sit.

"Sorry, I didn't get much sleep last night."

"Yeah, Marta told us you met Alva," Mack said through a mouthful of egg.

"Is that her name? She startled me for sure."

"Yup, Alva. She's the one that talks to Marta the most, though there are others. Alva, as far as we can tell, is from Grafton, a victim of an Indian massacre years ago. You see why we live way out here, away from everyone?"

"Yes. Yes, I do."

"Even in St. George, all the kids knew she was different and were hostile toward her. So, we gathered our things and moved out here where no one could disturb Marta. It works and she is happy, but she does get lonely."

Lupe said something else in Spanish and Mack translated dutifully.

"She said that Marta told us you were coming. She also told us you could see spirits."

"You said that sometimes the spirits that speak to her tell her the future? What else has she predicted?"

Mack looked down and shifted in his seat, then translated the question to Lupe, who also looked uncomfortable.

"She has other predictions, but like I said, they are rarely good and it's best not to speak about them."

"Is there anything about Elsie or me?"

"The burned lady is on a train. She's far away. Alva said she used a pillow and kicked a maggot off a train," Marta said.

"A pillow? A maggot? What does that mean?"

Marta shrugged.

"Most of what she is told is incomprehensible or can be taken different ways. That's why we don't give them much thought. You could spend hours trying to piece together what she says, but you can never be certain. She did say in clear terms that something or someone is after you and you must be hidden and protected."

After breakfast Harriet and Marta left on foot heading north. The trees that surrounded Duncan's Retreat had disappeared and the sun already blazed overhead. The hard climb over the weed infested hill behind the town left her covered in sweat. She was glad she wore her boots and coveralls, because the thorns would have shredded her shoes and legs. She was ready to stop once she reached the top of the hill, but beyond was even more steep cliffs and a lot more rocks and weeds. She felt defeated.

"Where are we going?"

"I told you. I'm taking you to the sleeping people that live in the cliffs that know about the hole in the ground."

"Are these sleeping people like the ones in Grafton? Are they angry and want to hurt us?"

"No, silly. It's not far."

Harriet hoped for more reassurance but followed her regardless.

After another hour of climbing over boulders and getting caught on thorns, Harriet was about to give up and turn around. She was sure Alva told Marta to take her into the hills to let her die of exhaustion and exposure. Everything was dead around her. Every plant was brown and withered and she hadn't seen a single animal the entire time. The water in her canteen had almost become too hot to drink as she took a sip.

"Hey, Marta, this was fun, but we should probably turn back now."

"Almost there," Marta said as she pointed.

A path wound up between two cliff faces and Harriet wondered how she'd missed it. She followed Marta up the path and as it circled around to the opposite side, it ended as it opened into a large, cavernous, open area on the cliff. A small stone dwelling was built into the contours of the rock walls.

Harriet felt nervous and took a step back. It looked a lot like that crumbled stone structure on Elsie's property. The one with darkness surrounding it, where terrible things happened. She looked around but didn't see anything out of the ordinary. No shadows or mist or darkness. No eerie feelings assaulted her either.

Marta sat down and grabbed her canteen from her pack and took a drink.

"Sometimes you have to wait," she grinned.

Harriet shrugged and sat down too, keeping an eye on the cliff dwelling. They were thankfully out of the sun, but her patience was running thin. She needed to be back so she could fix that damned tractor and get back to Elsie.

"Marta, I need to head back…"

"Shoosh. I can hear them."

Harriet clamped her mouth shut and looked around.

Something in the air changed. The birds grew quiet, and everything seemed to stand still as every hair on her body stood on end and her eyes watered.

Two men stepped out of the cliff dwelling and stood in front, unmoving. Even though they looked to be flesh and blood, Harriet knew they were the ghosts she was seeking. These weren't like the ghosts of Grafton. She felt at ease.

They wore simple tunics made of leather and rough fabric, leggings, and one of them wore some kind of poncho or cape.

The ghosts looked stern, but not unfriendly, and looked directly at her.

Marta froze and looked up in the sky.

"Are you the one seeking knowledge?" Marta said in a low and eerie voice that was not her own. It was Marta speaking, but Harriet knew it was the ghost asking the question.

Harriet gathered her courage and looked the ghosts in the eyes.

"Yes."

The ghosts nodded.

"Step forward and we will show you."

Harriet stood in front of them, nervous but trying not to show it.

"Kneel," they both said, two voices coming out of Marta at the same time.

They reached out their arms and put their hands on her head.

Harriet was paralyzed as her vision blurred. She felt time pass but didn't know how long. The sun darkened and brightened thousands of times, maybe more. She witnessed the rocks change and the sky fly by as if she stood next to the tracks as a train zoomed by. The river down below ebbed and receded as the clock turned back hundreds of years.

Her vision cleared and she found herself standing on a plateau, surrounded by scared and curious people. An obsidian stone box lay on the desert floor with the desiccated bodies of two elaborately dressed men collapsed beside it. They had obviously brought it to this place and died upon completion of their duty.

These people lived in grand and elaborate dwellings built into the cliffs and were cautious by nature. They left the stone box where it lay, and all the elders gathered in their kiva underground to discuss this new and terrifying thing.

Harriet, still an unseen bystander in the dream, looked around. She didn't know how she knew it was called a kiva, but she did. It was a large circular hole built into the ground with benches lining the perimeter. Despite the heat of the day, it was cool and comfortable at the bottom.

A young and intelligent man tried to convince the group that the thing was obviously evil, that it should be taken away and buried in a deep hole after cleansing rituals were performed.

Another man, much older and well-respected amongst the council, came forward, leaning on his cane. He had known of its coming and had been preparing for years. When their people had fled from the south generations ago, his ancestors secretly kept the ways of the old gods and passed that knowledge down from father to son throughout the years.

He was told in a dream that this day would come.

In his bold and elegant voice, he convinced the council to keep the box. It was a treasure from the gods and would ensure the prosperity of their crops and end the brutal drought that had plagued the people for the last two years.

The council agreed with the older man and took the

obsidian box into their kiva. That day it did rain and the people rejoiced.

Things were good for a time. Babies were born, crops grew, and they were happy.

The young man never gave up trying to convince his people they were in danger.

Soon, the people were plagued with nightmares. Visions of their enemies finding and slaughtering them bore into their minds. They built watchtowers over their homes to stand ready, in case their nightmares were prophetic. The rains ceased once more, and crops failed. The peaceful people, little by little, turned on each other over scraps of food or drops of water. They prayed to their gods, but the nightmares and violence continued and only grew worse.

The young man became old, and he passed on his warnings to his children. He knew the box brought death. It killed the men who bore it to their home. He knew it was the source of the nightmares.

The people became paranoid, and murder and jealousy controlled their lives. Neighbor would accuse neighbor of stealing their meager provisions and fall upon them in the night and murder them. Parents brought their children into the wilderness and in secret, ancient rights, long forgotten but taught to them by the old man's descendants, sacrificed them to appease the rain god. Men were accused of aiding their enemies and thrown from the tops of the plateaus as their families watched, convicted only on what their dreams told them.

The children of the young man convinced others it was the obsidian box causing the problems and they left the cliff houses and went south, never to return.

Those that stayed worshipped the box and what was inside. Fear, jealousy and anger reigned. They tormented each other. They murdered and raped each other, and some even ate the flesh of others until no one was left and the great palaces, watch towers and temples of the people lay deserted and abandoned.

The box lay there for centuries until two people approached. An ancient woman, older than the cliff dwellers, older than the Aztecs, was guided there by a Ute, who had dreams of the box, who knew the destruction it would bring. The Ute presented the ancient, yet powerful woman with the obsidian box, knowing wherever she brought it, it would be a cancer, malignant and deadly, and he smiled. This was not the first people the god in the box had destroyed.

The ancient and magic woman held the obsidian box aloft and rejoiced. She then ripped the liver out of the Ute guide with a long and deadly finger and threw his body off the cliff. The Ute smiled as he fell, knowing that the death of his family would be avenged.

The woman took the obsidian box away, and the vision faded.

HARRIET STARTLED and jumped to her feet when the vision ended. The falling sensation of being pulled away made her stomach lurch and she vomited.

She wiped her mouth and looked around, still trying to get her bearings.

The two ghosts remained, and Marta was still in a trance, looking up to the sky.

"We could not help our people, but our hope is that we can help yours. Please find it and destroy it or it will only grow until it encompasses all lands and peoples in unholy enmity until all who are left are the husks of men who serve it. Please do what we could not. I wish you blessings and farewell."

"Wait, how do we destroy it? Where is the box? What is this thing?"

She had so many questions, but the two ghosts were gone. Everything went back to normal, the wind blew and the birds began to sing again.

"Did the two sleeping men show you anything?" Marta said, shaking her head and trying to stand up.

"They did, and I need to get back to Elsie. Now."

Chapter 24

Orson sat on the curb outside his dad's shop playing with his jacks, but he liked to call it knuckle bones. He always thought that was funny. He wasn't allowed to help in the shop yet, even though Leroy was. Dad said it was too dangerous.

He couldn't find any of his friends to play with today, so he stayed here and played knuckle bones.

He bounced the ball and grabbed several of the jacks when a looming shadow appeared.

He looked up and saw a tall, thin white man with an impressive mustache, bowler hat and fancy pocket watch smiling at him.

"Hello, little boy," he said in a friendly voice.

Orson stood up because he remembered his manners.

"Hello, sir."

"Are you Enoch Piper's son?"

"Yes, sir, I am. My name is Orson."

"What a fine name. I knew an Orson once, years ago. I was wondering if you could help me out. I'm in a bit of a bind."

"And you need my help?"

"Yes, I was looking for your uncle who lives out of town. Do you know where I might find him?"

Orson remembered his dad telling him not to tell any stranger where Harriet went.

"I'm not supposed to talk about that," he said, gathering up his jacks.

"Oh, it's okay. Thank you for your help. That's too bad though. Too bad," the man said as he began to walk away.

"Too bad? What do you mean, mister?"

The tall white man turned back around.

"Oh, I just mean that your poor uncle won't get his money. You see, someone died and left your uncle some money here, in this envelope. I was trying to find him to give it to him. But since I can't find him, I guess all this money will have to go back to the bank. You know, I've even tried paying people to find out where he is. I could've given you a quarter if you knew where he was. Too bad," he said, holding up a big official looking envelope with a wax seal and everything.

"Wait, mister! Mack lives down somewhere near St. George. I don't know where, but he should be easy to find. He's probably the only colored fellow that lives there," Orson said, mimicking what he heard his mom say about it.

"What a helpful and bright boy you are. He'll be very happy to know you helped him out. Here is your quarter, young man. Thank you."

The tall white man tossed a large, shiny quarter to him, and patted him on the head.

Orson inspected the coin, not knowing what to look for but figuring if it was a fake, he could tell.

It was real alright, and he already planned what candy he'd buy with it.

The man walked away smiling, twirling his cane.

Chapter 25

Elsie sat in bed in her luxurious hotel room, loopy from the laudanum the doctor prescribed and frustrated that she'd been there over a week. There she was, surrounded by fluffy pillows and lace embroidered sheets wishing she could do something. She wanted to be in and out of Richmond in a day, but when she checked into her hotel, the excitement and exertion of the last week gave her a coughing fit that caused her to pass out. The doctor that was called noticed her fever and ordered her quarantined and bedridden for the next week, at least and prescribed her the laudanum to suppress her cough.

While she recovered from her burns in England, the doctors prescribed laudanum for everything. As a result, many of the Great War veterans came out as dope fiends. They survived the artillery, machine gun fire, and poison gas, to be killed by the medicine that was supposed to cure them. If the overdoses or organ failure didn't kill them, they lived on as mere husks of their former selves, putting aside family and friends to chase the dragon.

Elsie didn't want to fade away and lose the fight. Elsie Virginia Everly didn't lose fights.

The coughing became unbearable, however, and she relented to take small dosages. The sickness she contracted was worse than her broken rib, otherwise she would have refused to stay in bed. She had things to do. While convalescing in her hotel room for the first few days, she couldn't even properly enjoy reading because she would catch herself reading the same sentence over and over again and still not understand what she read.

So, she drifted in and out until the fever and coughing fits receded and the rib was more of a dull ache than sharp pain.

Today, though, she felt better, so when someone came to check on her before lunch she asked the maid if she could use the hotel's phone.

To her surprise, the walk down to the ground floor where the telephone was didn't bother her at all. Except for trips to the bathroom, this was the first time she had been up and about. She felt a little weak and her side ached, but it was nothing she couldn't handle.

She asked the dispatcher to patch her through long distance to Valentine Private Eye in Salt Lake City.

Several minutes later the pleasant voice of the receptionist came on.

"Valentine Private Eye, this is Gloria speaking. How may I be of service?"

"Good morning, Gloria. This is Elsie Everly. I'm just calling to check on the progress of my case."

She pronounced each word carefully, trying to overcome the effects of the opium and sound normal.

"Of course, Miss Everly. Mr. Valentine is away, but I have his notes."

Elsie waited a few seconds until Gloria returned.

"Here it is. Yes, there has been progress on the case. Mr. Valentine has discovered that Harriet Piper has been sent to stay with an uncle down in the St. George area. He is heading down there today to coordinate his contacts and get the exact location."

Elsie was lost in the receptionist's voice. It was so sultry and pleasantly professional at the same time. Gloria was her name? What a pretty name to match the pretty voice.

She didn't realize she drifted away until Gloria brought her back to attention.

"Hello? Are you still there, Miss Everly?"

She shook her head to come back to the present.

That damn opium.

"Yes, sorry. I am here. That is excellent news indeed. I knew I picked the right agency, and please, call me Elsie."

"You'd be surprised how often we hear that. We are the best, after all."

Elsie could hear the smile and wink through the phone.

"Thank you, Gloria. As always, it is a pleasure speaking to you."

"Likewise, Miss Ev...Elsie."

They gave their pleasantries and hung up.

Elsie thought of the soft, yet vibrant voice of Harriet. Her smile with her perfect lips and teeth and her laugh. Harriet was everything she wasn't. Young, beautiful, energetic, kind, innocent and funny. Her hair was always in those French braids, but next time they met, she wanted to undo those braids, run her fingers through her hair and kiss her.

Back in her room, she drifted away into sleep with the thoughts of making love to Harriet. Harriet, an avenging angel, that drove away the nightmares that usually haunted her. Elsie slept peacefully for a long time. When she woke, she looked around, trying to get her bearings.

Her pocket watch on the nightstand said it was four thirty, and the light coming through the window meant it was in the afternoon.

She left her bed with less pain than before and took a

shower. The hot water felt as good as a massage, and she stayed in until the water turned cold. She dried off, dressed and tucked her pistol into her handbag.

Elsie looked at her pocket watch and hailed a taxi.

"Where to, ma'am?"

"Take me to the VFW on Carry Street, please."

"Yes, ma'am."

She got in the back seat of the Ford, and it pulled away from the curb.

Twenty minutes later, the car pulled up to the local Veterans of Foreign Wars building. She tipped the cab driver handsomely and got out.

The building looked like it used to be an old church, but all religious symbols had been removed. The front door was unlocked, and she stepped inside.

Dozens of men of all ages milled about, some chatting and others grabbing their coats to leave. Elsie had looked up the hours of their meetings and was glad she wasn't too late.

Every veteran stopped what they were doing and stared at Elsie. She confidently strode up to the middle of the room, ignoring the snide comments.

"Ahem! If I may have your attention, gentlemen."

"You got our attention, toots!" came a voice from the back, followed by some laughter and a few wolf whistles.

"Excuse me, ma'am, but this establishment is for veterans only. You are not supposed to be here," said an older man wearing the cap of a Spanish-American war veteran. He was polite but firm.

Elsie brushed back her hair and showed the entire room her face. The laughter and whistling stopped.

"I wasn't a soldier, but I was over there, in France, all four years of it. I joined the French nursing corps at the beginning of the war and stayed until I was wounded during the final

Spring Offensive in eighteen. I did my time," she said, beating her chest with her fist.

Nobody said a word and stood solemnly, listened.

She took that as her queue to continue.

"I am in great need of assistance. I need four men who are willing to do some hard work and get their hands dirty, for which I will pay handsomely."

Almost every hand shot up.

"I will need someone with access to shovels and we'll be out most of the night."

Many of the hands lowered.

"It will be illegal."

Three hands remained up.

"Excuse me, ma'am," said the Spanish-American war vet.

He was not one of the three men that had their hands in the air.

"Yes, sir?"

"I am Steve Diamond, the head of this post and a police officer of this city. I cannot in good conscience allow my brothers to do something illegal while helping a fellow veteran."

Nobody said a word, and the three volunteers lowered their hands.

"But, sir...," she started, but was interrupted.

"That is why I must go with you. I must assure that nobody gets punished for helping a brother...or sister out. Let's go talk in my office. You three, on me."

Elsie followed him, along with the volunteers, to a small office in the back.

Mr. Diamond sat down behind a small desk and leaned back in his chair.

"Now, what can we do for you, Miss...?" he said, fishing for her name.

"Everly. Elsie Everly, but please call me Elsie. Some of you may have heard of my father, Walter Everly, the adventurer and pseudo-archeologist?"

Everybody in the room nodded their heads.

"Good. Well, some of you may have heard that he died two years ago."

"My condolences, Elsie...," one of the men was about to say, when she cut him off.

"No need for condolences. He was more terrible than his books. I am here because I have been led to believe that he and my trash brother faked their deaths. I am asking you to come with me to Hollywood cemetery, dig up their graves, and confirm if they are alive or dead."

"That's it? That's easy. I can just flash my badge and make sure nobody interferes with us while we do the digging. You also mentioned something about a considerable compensation."

"Of course. How does fifty dollars per man sound, plus a considerable donation to this VFW post?"

All four men gawked at the large sum and readily agreed.

"Now, we need shovels and transportation."

"Sorry, miss, we'll need a spade, picks and shovels to do this properly. This is going to take most of the night, so as soon as it's dark we need to start, assuming the ground is soft. It's been raining, but it could be clay. There are two graves, two people per grave. Any more and it gets too crowded to swing your shovels. It's hard and thirsty work, so we'll need to bring water and something to eat to keep our strength up. Flashlights or lanterns will come in handy," said one of the men.

Everybody gawked at him.

"What? I was Army Corps of Engineers and worked as a grave digger for a summer for my cousin. He has a truck and all the tools we'd need."

"How soon could he be here? I'll offer him the same rate if he can be here in less than an hour. I leave tomorrow and I need these graves dug up tonight."

"Let me use your telephone, sir, and I'll call him right now. He's in Sandston, so not far."

Steve Diamond motioned to the candlestick style phone on his desk.

With the promise of two-hundred dollars, they had a truck and tools parked in front in less than thirty minutes.

Once it was dark, they piled in the truck and arrived at Hollywood cemetery after a short drive. The narrow and winding paths through the rolling hills of the cemetery were picturesque, but they didn't allow for them to drive the truck to the site. Tools in hand, they followed Elsie on foot.

They easily found the two graves. They were side by side, marked with gaudy obelisks and surrounded by a wrought iron fence. Even in the grave, they couldn't help but show their elitism.

"Loving father and brave adventurer," she read the tombstone out loud.

She tried not to laugh because it would hurt her rib, but she couldn't help a small chuckle.

"Dig'em up, boys."

The men dug with gusto. The longer they were here, the greater chance of getting caught, even with a police officer watching over them. They all felt the need for urgency.

Elsie felt guilty about not helping, but she was a lady after all, and an injured one at that. She assuaged her guilt by telling herself she'd throw in an extra five dollars per man. While the men dug, she looked over the nighttime panoramic view of the city of Richmond. It was a shame she never spent much time here, it was pretty, especially at night.

She became lost in thought, thinking about how drastically her life had changed over the last few weeks. She didn't believe in the supernatural before going to Utah, and now she was actively fighting it. Invisible intruders in her house, smoke coming out of the mirrors, ghost jaguars and cultists. What next? Frankenstein's monster? A vampire? Richmond was the home of Edgar Allen Poe, so maybe something from one of his stories will come to haunt her.

Time passed slowly, but around two in the morning, they finally hit the coffin lids. They cleared away the dirt and noticed they were secured with large padlocks.

"Never seen that before," said Mr. Diamond.

"I'll blow the locks off," Elsie said, taking her pistol out of her purse.

"No need, I have my own." Mr. Diamond drew a Colt automatic.

Everybody backed away as he aimed and shot each lock off.

The gunshots seemed infinitely too loud and echoed all around the cemetery. They stood silent and still for a few seconds to make sure no alarm had been raised. When they were sure it was clear, Mr. Diamond bent down and opened Walter Everly's coffin.

The lid moved reluctantly as the dirt slid off like a miniature avalanche.

"Well, I'll be damned," he said.

Steve Diamond stood in the way, and Elsie couldn't see what was in the coffin.

"Mr. Diamond, would you please step to the side?"

He did so, muttering an apology.

It was empty.

"Now for the other one."

It was also empty.

"I knew it," she whispered.

The men around her seemed more surprised than she was. She had suspected they were alive because no earthly or unearthly force would torment her so much as those two. Whatever evil force they were in league with, wouldn't spend so much time dedicated to her and probably wouldn't be half as malicious.

"Alright, cover them back up, boys. No need to make it look good. Let's get out of here."

It didn't take long to fill the holes, and they were back in the truck heading toward the hotel before dawn. They parked in front of the hotel and she got out.

"I'll go up and get the cash. Do you trust me, or would you prefer one of you come up with me?"

"After what we've been through tonight, I'm so tired and sore I don't think I could take another step. We trust you."

"Excellent, I'll be right back."

She walked into the hotel and took the stairs up to her room. She passed by a large mirror in the hallway and the feeling of being watched overcame her. She looked down the hallway but didn't see anyone. Every hair was standing on end. Then she looked in the mirror.

In the reflection, her father and brother stood next to her, glaring at her. They didn't say or do anything, but she could feel the anger bubbling off them.

She gave them the middle finger and continued to her room. She took the cash out of the safe and headed back outside.

Passing by the mirror in the hallway again, the reflections of her family were gone.

"Here you are, boys. I can't thank you enough for your help and your hard work. I threw in an extra five bucks per person as a bonus and here is two hundred for the VFW contribution."

They all shook her hand vigorously and thanked her with huge smiles on their dirty faces. They debated what they were going to do with their windfall as they left.

"If you are ever in Richmond again and need help, don't hesitate to call on us," said Mr. Diamond.

They parted ways and Elsie looked at her pocket watch, trying to calculate if she had enough time for a nap and shower before her train departed.

Chapter 26

Richard Brooks sat on a bench in a small park in St. George, Utah. The ravenous sun beat down on him and made him miserable. Thankfully, the swelling around his throat, armpits and groin were not noticeable, because he didn't want to stand out. The diseases and filth were a small price to pay for immortality and reigning over his own fiefdom in the New World the Original Purity had promised him.

"All the darkies, spics, kikes and savages in my fiefdom will be under my will to do with as I please. They think they are equal to us? I'll teach'em. They will serve me and please me how I see fit," he mumbled to himself.

The passersby that heard him muttering to himself assumed he was mentally ill and kept their distance. Those that couldn't hear him, still stayed away due to the smell. Richard couldn't remember the last time he'd bathed and didn't care.

The writings of Walter Everly were like living fire to him and opened his eyes to the reality of life. He didn't get fired from his factory job because he abused his position as foreman to have his way with the desperate women who worked there.

That was part of the job. He got fired because the Jewish cabal put those inferior races in his factory to get him fired. Removing the white man from power was their first goal and it was working. Now he knew what he was fighting against and what the rewards were when they won. He had been one of the first to join the Original Purity back in Virginia when there were only a dozen members and attended the meetings when they were still at the Everly house. He even remembered seeing that little slut Elsie there in passing.

She wasn't a believer. She wasn't worthy. But she'd learn. She'd learn with all the mongrels and race traitors. They'll all be slaves again…at least the ones that survive.

He chuckled at his own wit when he spotted who he was looking for. The obsidian mirror he was given had shown him the face of the man who had hidden and protected Harriet.

Orders had come down from on high. The mission had changed. They were to find and kill Harriet. Elsie had shown herself to be tougher and more resilient than expected. She was feeling less and less afraid with each passing day.

That won't do.

If fear wasn't working, then maybe despair and loss would.

He didn't know the name, but a tall, strong looking negro walked past him in the park. He recognized that face. It was the only negro he had seen since he had been down here for a couple of days, and he stood out.

He walked into the main building of Dixie College, lunch pail in hand.

"What is he? A negro professor?"

He laughed at the idea. Whatever he did here at the college, he now knew where he worked.

Richard found a secluded place behind some bushes and took out the small obsidian mirror he kept in his pocket. He drew the symbol of the Apostle on the mirror and waited as he chanted, "Ia Ia. In ie tlecujlixquac, in ie tlamamatlac. Itech naci in Tezcatlipoca." The symbol or 'glyph' as Walter liked to call it, turned bright red, then white with heat, changing the surface of the mirror into black liquid.

"The guy that's hiding Harriet is here in St. George. He works at the big school. I'll keep tailing him and see where he lives and where he's hiding Harriet," he said into the mirror.

The mirror vibrated at his voice, then turned solid again. His message would be heard. He put it back in his pocket and waited outside the school for him to come out again. He switched hiding spots but never took his eyes off the campus building.

The sweat poured off him and made the boils on his body itch. He scratched them until they burst and bled. Each boil and scab were a badge of honor. He was a true believer after all.

Around noon, a group of fancy dressed, know it all professor types walked out of the main building chatting amongst themselves. His mark, the big darkie, walked with them. They talked and laughed.

"More race traitors. They're probably capitalists too," he spat.

His mark didn't follow the group. He laughed and waved goodbye and took off in another direction.

Richard left his hiding spot and followed him from a distance.

A block away, he took a left into an ally and Richard lost sight of him.

"Shit!"

He hurried to catch up and approached the alley. He peeped around the corner to see if he could spot him. No one was there. Just some discarded paint cans, a broken piece of wood and a dumpster.

"Where the fuck did he go?" he whispered.

He had tailed many people since joining the Original

Purity, and no one had ever given him the slip. He wasn't about to let some low life get the best of him.

The ally split into a four-way a hundred feet ahead and he ran to catch up. He had to see which direction he went. Then he stopped.

What would I do? I'd wait behind that dumpster and ambush the prick who was following me.

As he got close to the dumpster, he pulled out his knife. The big man he followed jumped out from behind it. He was crouched low and wore a set of brass knuckles. The swing came so fast, even though he expected it, Richard didn't have time to react. The brass knuckles ploughed into the bridge of his nose so violently, Richard Brooks died instantly.

Mack caught him before he fell, the dead weight of the limp body made it more difficult. After a quick search of the corpse, he found a roll of one-hundred dollars, a white mask and an obsidian mirror. He kept the cash and smashed the mask and mirror before throwing the body into the dumpster and covered it with trash.

"Marta told me you would be looking for her. I just didn't think it would be so soon."

Hands in his pockets and whistling, he walked to his car as if nothing happened.

Chapter 27

Harriet sat on her bucket trying to fit a pipe to the steam engine but it wasn't cooperating.

"You came from here and now that you're clean and rust free you don't fit? What's wrong with you?"

Marta lay down in the grass next to her, looking up at the clouds.

Despite the large, wide brimmed hat she wore, the sun beat down on her and she sweated profusely. The repairs to this stupid tractor were taking forever and she would never finish at this rate. She wouldn't be back in Elsie's arms before they were both old women.

I bet she would still be beautiful though.

She had never done it at home, but out here, with only the memories of Elsie, she had taken to touching herself. That last night with Elsie awakened something inside her, and it needed to be released. It was all she could think about.

Marta said that Elsie was far away. She hoped that didn't mean that she moved away for good. Wherever Elsie went, Harriet would follow.

"Elsie, please come back," she whispered in a quite prayer.

She looked over at Marta, who had been too quiet for comfort. Marta was still there, lying on her back, but Harriet jumped because now that creepy pale faced girl with the dark rings around her eyes floated horizontally above her.

"MACK IS COMING BACK from work early. He's going really fast. The body is in the dumpster with bone in his brain. Pack your bags, girly. It's time," Marta said in the steady, even tones she always used when speaking for the dead.

"Pack my bags? That I understood."

She threw the stupid part she had been working on down and went up to the bedroom. She never really unpacked, so she was ready in a few minutes.

"Que esta pasando?" Lupe said, coming in to see what the commotion was about.

"No se. Marta spoke...spoke...dijo que Mack is coming home."

She didn't know how to say that last part, so she mimed a car driving and pretended to be a big man, puffing out her cheeks and trying to stand taller.

Lupe nodded and left to go find Marta.

Harriet brought her luggage downstairs and put it outside as she saw Mack's Model T in the distance, a trail of dust sprouting behind it.

A few minutes later, Mack pulled up and jumped out of the car.

"No time to waste, pack your things. You're going back home. It's no longer safe for you here."

He registered the luggage at her feet.

"Oh. Marta warned you?"

"Yup. Now let's get on out of here."

Mack threw her luggage in the back and ran off to grab a can of gasoline he kept in the barn.

Lupe ran up and gave her a bag filled with rolls and tortillas, some dried meat and a full canteen and kissed her on the cheek. A small tear rolled down her face.

"Quidado niña."

"I'll be careful. Si."

Mack came back and poured the gas into the tank under the seat.

He took Lupe aside and spoke to her in Spanish, too fast for her to understand. She was grave faced and nodded at what he was saying. He then handed her a roll of cash.

They hugged and he jumped in the car.

"We gotta go. Now."

Harriet wasted no time and jumped in, then realized Marta wasn't there. She had to say goodbye to her. She had become an odd, but dear friend in the last few weeks.

"Wait, I need to say goodbye to Marta."

"No time," he said, starting up the car.

Harriet didn't accept that and jumped out of the car. She ran for the house but noticed the front door fly open. Marta ran out of the front door with the candle she'd found in Grafton, clutched in her hand.

"You can't leave without this! Light it in the house. It'll protect you and you need to find the box!" she said, running up to the car.

She shoved it in Harriet's hand and gave her the tightest hug she ever had, then the girl let go and stepped back beside Lupe. Together, the two waved goodbye.

The car sped off as fast as its twenty-horsepower engine could manage.

"Mind telling me what's going on, Mack?"

"People are looking for you. They followed me and I don't know if they know exactly where you are, but they will soon.

The man had some dark magic with him. You are no longer safe here."

"I'm sure they know where I live. They'll have people there, too. My family's place is not safe either," Harriet said.

"For now, looks like they are sticking to the shadows. Don't want to be exposed yet. But find the woman with the burned face. Marta says she is your best protection but also the cause of your danger. There's a train leaving for up North in an hour and a half, you need to be on it."

Harriet nodded and checked the magazine of her pistol before putting it back in her pocket. Mack looked over to see what she was doing and nodded approvingly.

They drove for another half hour, approaching Hurricane when they saw a group of men standing in the road, blocking it. They all wore drab and dirty clothes and were heavily armed. There were six of them, three with shotguns, one with a Thompson and one with a huge Browning Automatic Rifle. The sixth man only had a revolver that he kept holstered.

Harriet grabbed Mack's hand and looked at him with wide eyes. He didn't look scared. He looked determined as he slowed the car.

"Can't we just drive through them? Let's go! Please don't stop. Please don't stop."

"No good, girly. That BAR will rip through the car and us like we were paper."

The man with the revolver took a few steps toward them, hands in the air.

"We just want the girl. Hand her over and you can go. We'll even forget that you killed our comrade today and you can turn around and be on your merry way. All you negroes will get yours eventually. Today, we just want her. We promise no harm will come to her."

His voice sounded so calm and reassuring, but Harriet knew he was lying.

"Here's what we're going to do, and I want no argument. Your life depends on doing what I say. I'm going to distract these men while you grab that food and water and run north. Stay to the east side of the Virgin River and follow it north. Avoid the roads because they'll be looking for you. If you see someone you're sure is safe, get a ride to a town and call your father. He'll come pick you up. But it will be safer to stay on foot. It's a long walk, but your guardian angel will help you along the way. You are smart, tough and resourceful."

"I'll give you to the count of ten to make up your mind," came the calm voice of the man in charge.

"What about you, Mack?"

"Marta told me this day would come. There would be a reckoning and it'd be time to pay up."

"Ten!"

"Marta told me everything about you and me."

"Nine!"

"Don't worry about me, girl…,"

"Eight!"

"…I knew I wasn't going to…,"

"Seven!"

"…make it out of here alive."

"Six!"

"No! Don't say that!" Harriet said desperately.

"Five!"

"I'm the reason that my…,"

"Four!"

They could hear the safeties being thumbed off.

"…sister is dead."

"Three!"

"No," Harriet pleaded, grabbing her bag of food and canteen and throwing them over her shoulder.

"Two!"

"I must atone for what I did."

"One!"

Mack threw the door open and pulled out a Colt M1892 Army revolver, firing one shot at the man with the auto rifle. The bullet entered his forehead and blew his hat off as it exited the back of his head.

"Fire!" the man in charge said, pulling the revolver out of his holster.

Harriet jumped out of the car, running and stumbling to the side of the road as shotgun pellets cracked by her, sounding like a swarm of angry hornets. She dove for the ditch as the tommy gun opened up on her.

She made it to the ditch in time as the burst of .45 caliber rounds hit the dirt where she had just been.

The men firing at her gave Mack the chance to shoot the man with the tommy in the arm, opening it up like a filleted fish and causing him to drop the submachine gun.

"Kill him first! Then the bitch!" the leader of the group yelled, his voice no longer calm.

"Run, Harriet," came a clear and calm voice in her ear.

No one was there. The voice wasn't loud, but it was firm and familiar.

She stood and ran as fast as she could, not daring to look behind her.

The booming of the shotguns was followed by answering shots from Mack's pistol until all was silent.

She ran until she couldn't catch her breath anymore and finally stopped to look back.

The two cars could still be made out in the distance, but she didn't see any movement.

"Follow the Virgin River," Harriet reminded herself.

She saw the small river up ahead in the distance and hurried toward it, looking all around her to make sure nobody could see her or followed her.

Off in the distance, barely visible, was the telltale sign of a car and it headed toward where she came from.

She hurried to the river and jumped down into the gulley. She could walk North along this river unseen. Mack's plan was the best option for now and she followed the river north, keeping it on her left, and the mountains on her right, silently crying and grieving for poor Mack.

Chapter 28

The thought of her father and brother being alive disturbed her deeply.

The will, the house, everything was part of their plot, but for what purpose? Why do they need me there? How can they control the supernatural as they do?

Elsie thought about this but could come up with no answers. She knew they didn't want to kill her, at least not outright, not yet. She also thought about how those things, those filthy people, couldn't or wouldn't come in the house even though they easily could.

It grew dark by the time the train made its circuitous route up to DC before finally turning west to get around the worst of the Appalachian Mountains.

She still felt a little sick and her rib, though feeling better, still ached. She was also still exhausted from the night before and more than anything, she wanted to sleep.

Thankfully, nothing happened during the course of the entire trip, and she was able to catch up on some much-needed rest.

The train pulled into Ogden days later, and Eslie was glad to stand on ground that wasn't swaying.

She grabbed her luggage and walked over to WR Bookstore.

Abram was there as always and greeted her like a long lost relative.

"Miss Everly! My best customer and friend! Welcome back from your travels!"

He suddenly became very sad.

"This means I have to give you your car back, doesn't it?"

"I'm sorry friend, but yes. I need my car."

"I fell in love with that car. Alas, our love was not meant to be."

"How did your research go?"

"Yes! Yes! I found many interesting things! Let me go get it. I'll be back in mere seconds."

Abram came back in with a wild stack of papers and an ancient looking book, neatly tied with a line of twine.

"Please don't lose that book. It's on loan from Brigham Young University. I had to trade several valuable books just to get access to it. I don't know what you are up to, but there is some..." He stopped to think of the right word. "...malevolent things in this research. Please be careful and please don't hesitate to ask me for help. In the meantime, here are the keys to your wonderful car, and while you are here, any books you are looking for? I have something here you may be interested in."

He pulled out from under his counter a copy of United Amateur, a New England literary journal of fantastical short stories.

"Read 'the Alchemist'. Amazing story of a rich family's demise and torment at the hands of an evil sorcerer."

Elsie snatched the book out of his hands and opened it up. She found the story and skimmed it. Author was an unknown named H.P. Lovecraft.

"Well, that's uncanny. Is there anything else by this author?"

"Not that I know of. I believe this is his first published story. His address is printed in the back. For you, this is on the house."

"Thank you, Abram. I believe I owe you payment for your research," Elsie said, taking money out of her purse.

"I can't possibly take that. The use of your car these last few weeks was payment enough. I felt like a king. Marvelous invention."

"Be reasonable, Abram. You had to trade away some of your books. I won't hear of it. Please take the money you have earned."

"No," he said, folding his arms.

After repeated attempts, she was forced to give up.

"Damn stubborn Russians."

She left the store with an armful of books and papers and went around back where her car was parked.

She drove to the same car dealership where she bought her car.

"Welcome back, Miss Everly!"

He winked and wiggled his eyebrows at her while she tried not to vomit.

"I see you have a 1918 Templar Roadster on your lot. Is it available?"

"I have some offers on it. One of the members of the Young family was looking at it, so it won't be here for long!"

"You used that same line last time."

"Yeah, but this time it's true. You know how many Youngs there are in Utah?"

Elsie genuinely laughed at his joke this time.

They haggled like last time and he ended up giving her a discount.

"Now, please deliver this automobile to Mister Abram

Dvorkin at the WB Bookstore and tell him he won it in a random raffle. If he acknowledged it was from me, he wouldn't accept it. This way we both have plausible deniability."

She left the car dealership, left Ogden and headed east to Morgan. She exited the canyon and entered the rolling green farmlands filled with cows and sheep. When she reached the exit for Morgan, she didn't continue to her house. Instead, she pulled into town and parked.

She stood in front of a large shop with a big sign that said 'Browning Firearms' in bold letters. Inside, the shop was row upon row of rifles and shotguns of all kinds and display cases showing off well-polished pistols. Several shoppers roamed around, looking at various items. They ranged from a farmer in dungarees to a high-class man and woman in fancy attire.

The young man behind the counter greeted her warmly.

"Good day, ma'am. How may I assist you today? We have the finest selection of ladies pocket pistols and target rifles in the country. Anything you would like to look at?"

Before Elsie could answer, a tall, elderly man with a large mustache and bald head walked up and put his hand on the young man's shoulder.

"I'll take it from here. This lady's not shopping for something to keep in her purse, are you, ma'am?" he said with a slight smile.

"No, sir. I am looking for something more substantial," Elsie said.

She looked around for a second.

"Can I take a look at that rifle?" she said, pointing to one behind the counter.

"You have a good eye, Miss. This is a .35 Remington Model 8. Semi-automatic with a five-round capacity," he said as he took the rifle down and handed it over to her.

She gently took the rifle from his hands and shouldered it. The balance and heft were perfect, and it fit her like a glove.

"Can you show me how to operate it?"

"Sure thing. I'd be happy to. If you'd permit me?"

She nodded and he stepped around the counter and approached her.

"If I may?"

She handed the rifle back over to him, and he showed her the safety, how to pull back and release the bolt and how to load it.

"This rifle is brilliant. I'll take two. What else do you have for the discerning woman?"

The man looked surprised, then happy.

"Why, yes, it is brilliant, if I do say so myself. For the lady that clearly knows how to handle herself, I'd recommend the Auto Five."

He went back around the counter and pulled down a shotgun from the stand and walked back over to her.

"You're not going to find any shotgun better than this. Like the rifle, this is also semi-automatic and holds five rounds. Four in the magazine, like so...," he said, showing her how to load it.

"...and one in the tube, as we say. This is the manual of arms."

He proceeded to show her how to operate it as well.

"Also, brilliant. I'll take two of these as well."

The old man raised a distinguished eyebrow but just nodded.

"Yes, Miss."

"Do you have anything that holds more rounds or fires faster?"

"If I may, what are you hunting with these in mind?"

Elsie tried to think of a reason besides the truth but

shrugged and decided to tell the gentleman. He seemed like the kind of man that could detect bullshit a mile away.

"I'm hunting something evil and malevolent that resides on my property and I am looking to forcefully evict it for good."

The old man didn't say anything and didn't move a muscle. He looked her in the eye and his gaze penetrated into her soul.

After a long stare, he turned around and went back behind the counter.

"In that case, you will be needing these."

He reached down and pulled from the bottom of the cabinet several cardboard boxes.

"In my experience, the forces of evil are disinclined to salt, and some rock salt shells for the Auto five should serve you well. Buckshot and slugs will take care of everything else. As for something that holds more rounds and fires faster, there is this," he said, taking down an exceedingly large weapon from the rack.

He placed it on the counter between them.

"This is the Browning Automatic Rifle, or BAR for short. It's 30-06, fully automatic with a twenty round detachable magazine."

He released the magazine to show her.

She picked up the big rifle and tried to put it to her shoulder. The stock was too long for her and the considerable weight caused the muzzle to constantly dip as she held it.

"While that is what I'm looking for, I'm afraid it is too much for me to handle."

"As you wish," he said, picking up the BAR and moving to put it back.

"Wait...I'll take it anyway. You never know. I'll need some extra magazines as well."

"Yes, Miss. You know, we actually had a few of these over there. I'm surprised you didn't see any."

"If they were issued to American units, I wouldn't have seen them. I joined with the French military in fourteen and treated mostly French and some British troops. I...wait. How did you know I was over there?"

"I can always tell a Great War veteran. I'll throw in the rock salt rounds for free and provide you a discount on the arms. I'll like to show you one more thing, if I may?"

From under the glass, he pulled out a brutally plain and almost rustic looking handgun.

"This is my...our pride and joy. The model 1911 .45 caliber, semi-auto pistol with a detachable seven round magazine. This is the gun our troops used over in France. A Remarkable weapon ahead of anything else out there."

"I know a woman with a taste for Browning designed pistols."

"Then you know a woman of exceptional taste," he said with a wink.

She picked it up and inspected it. The grip was far more comfortable than her Mauser and as she inspected the sights, she could tell they were superior, even if they weren't adjustable. Like the rifle, the weight and balance were superb. It was smaller, lighter and overall better than her pistol.

"I'll take four. Extra magazines and holsters if you have them."

I'm sure Harriet will appreciate these but I'm still not giving up my Mauser.

The man wrote up a bill of sale, including the holsters and hundreds of rounds of ammunition and Elsie handed him wads of cash.

"Whatever it is that is menacing you, I pray that you are safe and all goes well. If you need further assistance, my name is John and it was a pleasure to serve you. May I help you carry your purchases to your vehicle, Miss?"

"Miss Everly, but please, call me Elsie and I would appreciate the help, thank you."

John carried everything to the car himself and filled up the back seat and trunk. He then took out a rag and wiped his hands clean before offering his hand to her. She shook it with a firm grip and a smile.

"It was a pleasure meeting you," he said.

"Thank you so much. For everything."

The drive to her house was uneventful. The house was just as she left it; foreboding, malignant and intact. She could only imagine what new horrors her father and brother had planned for her.

As she pulled in, she saw that the flag was up on her mailbox. She opened it and saw that it was a letter from Harriet.

She gasped in surprise and excitement and immediately tore the letter open.

Elsie pulled the letter free from the envelope and read:

Dear Elsie,

I hope this letter is not unwanted and that you are glad to receive it. I am sorry for the way things ended that night. I was a fool for leaving you alone like that. If I was braver, I would have refused to obey my father, but I can't take back what I did. I am so sorry and can only hope you can forgive me. You are all I think about and pray we can be together again soon. I made a promise to help my uncle out here at his ranch, but once I am done, I'll be back. If you still want me, I am yours.

Yours forever, Harriet

The letter was post marked out of Saint George, Utah.

Holding back tears of joy, Elsie put the letter in her purse and drove up to the house.

She parked close to the front porch and offloaded all the weapons and ammunition into the gun safe, which left her rib aching. She kept an eye out for anything out of the ordinary, but nothing harassed her.

If something odd did happen, I suppose that would be ordinary here.

Elsie held her side went into the kitchen and picked up the phone.

Within seconds, the pleasant and professional voice of Gloria came on the line.

"Valentine Private Eye, this is Gloria speaking. How may I be of service?"

"Hello, Gloria, this is Elsie Everly."

She immediately perked up.

"I'm so glad you called. I have an update on your case."

"Please tell me you know where she is."

"Well...yes and no. Mr. Valentine and his contacts did locate Miss Harriet. She was staying with a colored gentleman named Mack, a known associate of her father's and his common law wife or girlfriend or something. It gets a little murky there.

"This Mack gentleman was found shot on the side of the road yesterday afternoon. Apparently, there was some sort of gunfight, because there were six dead bodies surrounded by bullet and shell casings. Looked like he put up a hell of a fight but there was no sign of Miss Pipper. As of an hour ago, she had not returned to the house she was staying at."

A hundred scenarios of what could have happened to Harriet flashed through her mind and none of them were good.

"Where did this happen?"

"Route nine in a big bend in the road just east of La Verkin. You know where that is?"

"I have a map. I'll find it. I'm heading down there right now. I'll find her."

"Please be careful, Elsie. Looks like Miss Harriet is caught up in something dangerous and out of control. Mr. Valentine is still working this and will find out what's going on."

"Thank you, Gloria. I appreciate that and everything you and Mr. Valentine have done."

"Be careful, hun," she said, hanging up.

Elsie went up to her bedroom and changed into her jeans, a simple button-up shirt and strapped on her gun belt. Nothing creepy had jumped out at her and no masked cultist had welcomed her, but she could feel it. She was nowhere near as sensitive as Harriet, but you didn't need to be to feel a heaviness in the air. Whatever it was, it was still here.

She went downstairs, keeping an eye out for anything abnormal, and grabbed one of the new model eight rifles and an Auto Five shotgun and loaded them. She loaded the shotgun with the rock salt shells, not sure exactly what they were for, but figured she would find out. She shoved a handful of shells into the empty pouches on her gun belt. Elsie made sure the house was locked, threw the rifle and shotgun in the back seat and took off down her driveway at full speed. She didn't have a plan but knew she would find Harriet. Somehow.

Chapter 29

Harriet had never been camping before, and she didn't see the appeal. Of course, actual camping had tents and sleeping bags, a fire with roasted marshmallows and companionship. Here, her only food was a bagged snack meant for a train ride and a canteen of water.

She figured it would be safer to move at night and sleep during the day, but the terrain was so rocky she would probably break an ankle within minutes. The moon was in waxing crescent and barely a sliver was showing, so it was dark. She had a couple of matches, but they would only last a few seconds.

Resigned to traveling by day, she settled down in a nook under an overhanging boulder and tried to get some rest.

The ground was cool, but rocks kept digging into her hip and shoulder no matter how much she adjusted. She tried to get rid of all the small rocks digging into her, but there was a never-ending supply.

She thought of Mack. She didn't see him die, but the way the gunshots abruptly ended, solidified in her mind he was dead. After all, he would have chased after her otherwise. He was gruff and not very talkative, but he was a good, kind, brave man. She had never met someone so accepting of other's differences as he was. Tears fell as she thought about a world without him in it. He gave her hope.

Harriet vowed that his sacrifice would not be in vain. She would escape and live her life to the fullest.

She allowed herself some more tears and wondered about Marta and Lupe's fate as well. What would they do if those men came after them? Would the spirits warn Marta in time? Would they be able to defend themselves?

Her thoughts were fuzzy and disjointed. Maybe she might be able to rest. She settled and tried to sleep, except something large still dug into her.

She reached down to throw the rock away, but found that whatever it was, was in her pocket. She reached in and pulled out the candle Marta had handed her.

"Thank you, Marta."

She kicked herself for not remembering the candle, lit it and started moving again, keeping crouched as she floated among the rocks. With her head down and shoulders low, the banks of the creek gully would conceal the anemic light cast by the candle.

Despite the lack of moonlight, she finally made good progress when she heard a growl.

She froze in her tracks and listened, hoping she was just hearing things.

The growl came again, and she couldn't deny she heard it that time.

Slowly, she crouched and pulled out her pistol. She brained a mountain lion before, and she'd do it again. No kitty cat was going to keep her from going home and seeing Elsie.

She couldn't tell where the growling was coming from so, she kept looking around, but still didn't see anything.

Then she saw it. Coming around the bend of the creek,

following her was a misty and vague, ghostlike shape of a large cat. It was translucent and ethereal, easy to see in the dark.

As it got closer, she felt an icy chill run through her and felt how tortured this soul was. A flash of an image came to her mind of its soul leaving its body and then forcibly being pulled halfway through the spirit world and the real world to serve in this half dead, half physical form that was pure pain and completely unnatural.

She put the gun away, knowing it would be useless. She thought about putting the candle out, but the cat already saw her and maybe the light would keep it away.

She said a quick prayer in her head because she didn't know what else she could do. She had no mystical weapons to fight spirit jaguars.

The thing stalked her, followed her and crept closer with each step.

The light of the candle was flickering from how much her hand shook, and she couldn't stop it.

"Oh, dear Father. Please deliver me from this evil. Please let me get home and please release this poor kitty kat's soul to your embrace. Amen," she whispered as quietly as she could.

The jaguar was now close enough to throw a rock at, but she remained motionless.

It crept closer and closer, and Harriet noticed something. As it got closer, the candle grew brighter and when the jaguar reached an arm's length away, the candle started to spit small, twinkling sparks that disappeared into the air.

The cat stopped and lifted what passed for its ghostly snout. It seemed to sniff the air with fast, puffing breaths that Harriet could smell and feel. The fetid breath smelled of decaying meat and grave dirt. Its ears flattened for a moment and its shoulders tensed. Harriet wondered if this was it and her luck had run out. Would the candle fail her? Would the jaguar pounce and sink its teeth into the softness of her throat?

Then the big cat kept walking as if she wasn't there.

Harriet still didn't dare to move, but as the cat went further away, the candle grew dimmer, until it was back to a normal, wobbling flame.

"Thank you, Father, and please thank Marta for me. Amen."

She waited several minutes to make sure the jaguar was gone before breathing a long sigh of relief.

Holding the candle tight like it was a rope thrown out to a drowning person, she slowly moved again, still following the path of the creek and staying behind the jaguar.

She walked most of the night and only saw the jaguar one more time. Right before dawn, it leaped out of the creek bed almost a mile ahead of her, walk off toward the mountain and disappear.

As the sun rose, she blew out the candle, said another prayer of thanks and found a nice place to rest near the creek. In a hollow, dug out from when the creek was higher, she laid down in the soft sand and instantly fell asleep.

She woke around noon when a mule deer crossed the creek, splashing loudly as it did so.

She took the opportunity to relieve herself, eat the last of her food and drink some water.

She dozed on and off for another couple of hours. When she was awake, she would peep over the creek bed to look at the nearby road. All the cars sped by, minding their own business, except for one.

Around three in the afternoon, she saw a Model T driving northbound, but it was full of men and drove slowly.

She ducked back down until it passed. She didn't know if it was the people hunting her, but it raised the hairs on her arms.

Once it became dark again, she moved, keeping that candle Marta gave her close at hand. She burned it most of last night, but it was still the same size. Not quite the miracle of the loaves and fishes, but she'd take it gladly.

She became much more adept at stumbling over the rocks, and the candle definitely helped. After a couple of hours following the creek, it turned and ran under the road through a little tunnel. It wasn't long, but she still couldn't see the other side. She listened, but didn't hear anything, so she shrugged and stepped inside.

Some kind of animal had died in here recently, because the stench still lingered. As she continued into the darkness, the faint candlelight revealed something ahead. She couldn't make out what it was, but it looked like a man sitting down. As she got closer, the stench became stronger.

Whatever it was, it leaned against the side of the tunnel and was unmoving. She approached cautiously and pressed herself against the opposite side.

"I'm sorry," came a voice so faint she almost didn't hear it.

"Is someone there?" she asked, voice trembling.

There was no answer. She approached the thing, and the candle revealed it for what it was; the partially skeletal remains of a man lay seated and leaning against the side of the tunnel, scraps of flesh and hair still clinging to the corpse.

"Tell them I'm sorry," came the faint voice again.

Harriet jumped. There was no one else in here with her. The voice came from the corpse.

"I didn't mean it," came the sorrowful voice again. As Harriet approached, she noticed the rusty straight razor in one hand and a filth encrusted bottle of booze in the other.

She kept her distance and inched past the body, finally passing and losing sight of it in the darkness.

As she continued to walk away, she heard splashing and a

scraping sound. She imagined skeletal fingers rasping against the cement and the corpse rising to its rotted feet.

"I'm so sorry!" came the voice, but now it was a loud wail. She heard halting steps splashing through the water toward her.

Harriet ran for her life out of the tunnel and didn't stop. Panting from the exertion, she looked back over her shoulder. Hidden from the light, she thought she saw the shadowy silhouette of a figure retreat back into the bleak darkness and a sad cry escaped the tunnel.

She slowed her run to a trot and then a walk so she wouldn't exhaust herself. She paused at the creek's edge to calm down and drink from her canteen. As she did so, it amazed her to discover the candle flame still flickered.

Magical candles would have to wait for answers. Here, the creek was no longer in a gulley, and following it meant she would be completely exposed. Even though she was scared to, she extinguished the candle and tried to move as fast as she could without killing herself. She kept one eye on the road and one eye on the path ahead.

Every time she saw headlights, she ducked behind anything she could find and remained motionless.

She couldn't run, but she walked as fast as she could, hoping the creek dipped back down into a gulley.

It was dark, but as far as she could see, it was all open terrain with only the mountains off in the distance providing any kind of scenery.

She continued for a couple of hours until the stream suddenly stopped.

There was a tiny pond where the stream originated but there was nothing else around. The glorified puddle was only ankle deep, so even that wasn't a hiding place. The mountains were still barely visible to the east, so she kept her right shoulder to the mountains and kept going, keeping an eye out for anywhere to hide.

She made it ten feet when a pair of headlights appeared in the distance.

The headlights rapidly approached, and she frantically looked for some place to hide. Not finding anything, she lay down on the ground and put her bag in front of her, knowing it would do little good.

She didn't want to look when she heard the car's brakes screech to a halt and excited voices carried in the air.

"Oh shit!"

Without waiting another second, she jumped up and made a run for it.

That's when she saw a luminescent, ghostly jaguar approach her, blocking any path to escape.

"Nowhere to run little coon!" she heard one of them call out.

The car doors slammed shut, and she saw four flashlights turn on and come toward her.

They took their time. They knew they had her. The ghost jaguar stood in place, not attacking but preventing her from going anywhere.

She was trapped.

"I ain't going out without a fight!"

Her dad would kill her for such improper grammar, but it looked like he'd have to wait in line.

She drew her pistol.

"Oh no, fellas! Look out! She's got a peashooter!" came a different voice, followed by laughter.

She raised the pistol, and even though she couldn't see her stalkers, she lined up her sights on the lights.

Something from behind knocked her down with a powerful force and sent her pistol skittering away.

The jaguar had pounced on her, then trotted back to where it stood before.

"Aww, the kitty cat knocked over the pussy!"

This was followed by a roar of laughter from the other three men.

Harriet heard another car door slam closed. This one came from a different location; off to her left, behind the first car.

The four men drew closer, and she heard the distinct sound of a gun being drawn from a leather holster.

"You had us out in this desert searching for you for over a day. I'll give you credit darkie, you got tenacity, but it ends here. Don't worry, you won't be alone for long. All your kind will be joining you in hell soon."

The hammer pulled back with a loud click.

She scrambled for her gun, still blinded by the flashlights pointed at her, but she couldn't find it. Her fingers and wrists tore against the rocks as panic took over. She felt the dust and small rocks cling to her hands and grind into her wounds but ignored it. She had to find the gun and did wide, sweeping arcs trying to find it as the men around her laughed. Tears of frustration, anger and fear poured down her face.

She heard another gun cock, but this one sounded like a rifle.

"Fuck you. Fuck all of you evil assholes," she said through gritted teeth.

They all laughed again as a gunshot rang out in the darkness and emptiness of the desert.

Chapter 30

The men surrounding Harriet all laughed, until the man who pointed the gun at Harriet crumpled to the ground, his head blown open like a watermelon.

The crack of a rifle shot filled the air a split second later, the laughter died instantly, and the remaining men froze.

"Nobody threatens my girl," Elsie said.

Elsie took a step to the side and adjusted her aim, lining two of them up like targets in a row. The men were perfectly illuminated by the headlights of their car and the flashlights they were holding. An easy shot.

The rifle bucked against her shoulder as another shot rang out. The men crumpled in the dirt as the one shot pierced one man through his chest and struck the second man in his throat. A torrent of blood gushed from the neck wound and the man struggled to stem the tide with his hands, but it was no use. both died in seconds.

The fourth man, eyes wide and stumbling over his own feet as he attempted to back away, tried to get his own pistol from the flap holster on his hip but couldn't manage to get it open and fumbled with it.

The ghost jaguar leaped over Harriet and ran toward Elsie, roaring with a voice that sounded like a bad wax cylinder recording of a jaguar.

Elsie calmly put the rifle down and picked up a shotgun that was lying beside her.

She snapped it up to her shoulder and fired three times in one second.

The jaguar physically reacted and leapt back as if wounded. The rock salt rounds glowed like little, malicious embers, and burned and smoked inside the misty, ghost-like body of the cat. The jaguar writhed then faded into nothing.

Elsie turned her attention from the fading ghost jaguar to the last man threatening Harriet.

The remaining man finally managed to pull his pistol from the holster and fumbled with the safety, his hands visibly trembling, even from this distance and in the dark.

Elsie fired the last two rock salt shells at the man's face.

The salt rounds slammed into his face in a spray of blood. He dropped his pistol and clutched his eyes, which were no longer there.

He fell to his knees screaming in pain.

The shotgun was now empty, and she placed it on the ground next to the rifle and drew her pistol.

She walked over to the screaming man and kicked his pistol away.

Harriet scrambled to her feet, snatched up the fallen pistol, and pointed it at the man. She breathed hard and had a wild look in her eyes.

"Who sent you? Where are the rest of your little cult?"

"Go to hell, bitch!" he screamed through ruined lips, blood and spit spraying as he did so.

"If you tell me, I'll end your suffering here and now. If you don't tell me, I'll leave you out here in the desert, in pain."

The man laughed.

"Don't you realize by now? That's what he wants. We must suffer to come unto him."

He raked his fingernails down his own face, destroying what was left of his already ruined visage.

Still laughing, he pulled out a boot knife and tried to lunge at Harriet, but it was wild flailing and nowhere close to striking her.

"Fine. Have it your way."

She squeezed the trigger and put a nine-millimeter round through the cultist's head.

Elsie was almost knocked over when Harriet ploughed into her, hugging and kissing her all over her face.

"Is it really you? Is it really Elsie? I'm not dreaming this?"

Whatever worries Elsie had that Harriet would be resentful or maybe even ashamed of what happened, were exorcized immediately.

She took Harriet into her arms, squeezed her tight and kissed her back with the same enthusiasm and need of their first kiss.

"You swore," Elsie said once she managed to break away.

Harriet did a double take and looked confused.

"What?"

"You used foul language. You used bad words. I'm proud of you," Elsie said, unable to control her smile.

"Shut up," Harriet said and kissed Elsie on the mouth again.

Elsie melted in her arms. All anxiety and fear left her body as she clung to Harriet.

"I missed you so much! I'm so sorry! I'm so sorry, Elsie! Please forgive me!"

"Huh?"

Elsie was confused. She thought that she would have to do the apologizing.

"What on Earth are you apologizing for?" she said, taking Harriet's face in both hands and looking her in the eyes.

"For abandoning you. For leaving you. I never should have, and this is all my fault. I'm sorry."

Harriet looked down, unable to look at her.

Elsie lifted her face up, within inches of her own.

"You have nothing to be sorry for. I was going to apologize to you. I thought you'd have doubts or be ashamed of what we did and our feelings...for each other."

It was Harriet's turn to be confused.

"Ashamed? Doubts? Never, Elsie. Never again will I run away from you. I'm here for as long as you want me."

"I love you and I want you forever."

Harriet broke away from the embrace and hit Elsie on the shoulder.

"Why, you little...I was going to say that to you first!" she said, laughing and crying at the same time.

"I'll forgive your unprovoked and vicious attack, but we need to be leaving. Now. Grab the rifle and the shotgun and bring them to the car."

Harriet did as she was asked and ran to grab the weapons.

Elsie went to the car the four men arrived in and searched it for anything identifying but found nothing. She got in and drove the car off the shoulder of the road in front of the four bodies to hopefully hide them from view of anyone driving by.

Elsie searched the bodies and found that one of them had a mirror and all four of them had white masks. They were the same masks the creatures that attacked her house had. The man that was about to shoot Harriet had a rolled-up wad of cash, but none of them had any identification. Their firearms were old and dirty, so she left them where they lay.

She hurried back to her car, Harriet already seated in the passenger seat, and started the engine. The V-8 roared to life, and she quickly did a U-turn, heading up north as fast as her car could go.

The sound of the engine and the wind ripping by prevented any meaningful conversation, so Elsie reached over and took Harriet's hand. Harriet in turn squeezed back and gave her the sweetest, most heart melting smile she had ever seen.

Harriet yawned and, still keeping her hand in hers, laid her head on Elsie's lap. She fell asleep instantly.

Elsie stroked her hair. She had never seen it out of her French braids, and she liked how the wild, fluffy, soft hair exploded out the back of her red bandana.

They drove until dawn and reached the Salt Lake Valley. In the light of the rising sun, Elsie was finally able to get a good look at Harriet. She was covered in dirt and the dust on her face was streaked by where her tears had fallen. Her denim was ripped in places, and filthy. She looked exhausted.

Her heart ached and wondered what hardships she went through to get to this point. Elsie thought about all the supernatural threats this poor woman had to go through since meeting her and wished she could have a normal, safe life.

"Maybe one day you will, love."

She knew her family was out there, and they wanted Harriet dead for some reason. Even if it cost her own life, she would not let that happen. Nothing would stop her from protecting Harriet and she would not hesitate to put her father and brother in the ground for good this time.

As she pulled up to the house, she realized she was glad to be home. Whatever ghosts or monsters were going to be sent her way, she had Harriet now, and that was a comforting thought.

If she could, she would have carried Harriet to bed, but instead, she reluctantly woke her.

"Harriet."

God, I love saying her name.

"Harriet, we're home. We'll get you cleaned up, pack my stuff and get out of here. Somewhere where it's just the two of us."

Harriet's eyes fluttered open, and she looked around confused.

"We are back at my house. Let's get you cleaned up."

Harriet nodded and got out of the car. Despite being exhausted and her rib still aching fiercely, she helped Harriet up the front porch and then up the stairs to her bedroom.

"There's the shower. Please feel free to use whatever you find. We'll find you some new clothes because these are done for. Once you are cleaned up, we are leaving. We can't stay here. Maybe Salt Lake would be safer."

"Why, Miss Everly, are you just looking for an excuse to get me out of my clothes?" Harriet said, looking over her shoulder coyly.

Elsie was glad that Harriet was feeling better enough to be flirty again. How she missed that.

"Do I need an excuse?"

Harriet thought about it for a second and then shook her head.

"No, why I suppose you don't."

All hints of fatigue were now gone. Harriet unbuttoned her shirt as she walked to the bathroom.

Harriet stepped in the bathroom and closed the door only part way and after a few seconds, Elsie could hear Harriet undressing.

Elsie's heart pounded at the thought.

She swallowed hard and blushed like a schoolgirl. In a way, she was. This was all new. For the first time, she didn't know what to do, so she stood there frozen.

The shower turned on behind the door.

What should I do? Would she want me to come in or would that be too forward?

To quell her nervousness, she ran downstairs to make sure all the doors and windows were locked and there were no people in masks standing around, waiting to try to get inside.

She thought of Harriet, alone and naked just upstairs and couldn't resist any longer.

Elsie stripped her own clothes off and walked up to the bathroom door.

Opening the door, she saw that Harriet was already in the shower with the curtains drawn.

She cautiously walked closer and with a hand trembling from fear and excitement, reached out and pulled the shower curtain slowly open.

Harriet was there with her back turned, holding her shoulders. Her skin was perfect and dark and glistening wet. Her shoulders were flawlessly formed with just the right amount of muscle and definition to show her strength and femininity. Her body tapered to a thin waist and the most exquisite ass she had ever seen. She had always admired Harriet's legs before, but seeing them bare, they were stunning.

"I thought you'd never come," Harriet whispered.

Elsie stepped into the shower behind her, put her hands on Harriet's shoulders and gently kissed her neck.

"Show me what you were going to do to me that night," Harriet moaned and moved Elsie's hand down her arm and slid it to her belly.

Every problem seemed to melt away as her hand moved over Harriet's perfect skin, the taut muscles of her stomach and the smooth skin below it made her moan in anticipation.

Elsie snaked her left hand around and grabbed Harriet's breast, causing a gasp to escape her lips.

"Is this where we left off?"

"Please, Elsie."

Harriet squirmed from anticipation and excitement and Elsie enjoyed Harriet's body as it writhed against her.

"Please," she whispered with a trembling voice.

Elsie obliged and moved her hand down Harriet's belly to her wet center.

Harriet moaned loudly at Elsie's touch and pressed against her.

She felt the soft, curly hair and glided a finger lightly over her.

Harriet trembled and gasped and put both hands against the wall.

Elsie pressed herself against Harriet's rear and easily slid a finger inside her, causing Harriet to loudly inhale, then moan with pure pleasure.

This was their first time together, so Elsie took it very slow. She let her finger linger before moving it in and out of her.

"I never imagined..." Harriet tried to speak between heavy breaths. "...It would be like this."

"Oh, sweetie, we haven't even started yet," Elsie purred into her ear.

"Wait, Elsie. What's that?"

"My love for you," she said as she kissed Harriet's neck.

"No. That," Harriet said as she gently pushed Elsie away and pointed to the shower curtain.

Elsie reluctantly tore herself away from Harriet and looked. Dark smoke roiled past the shower curtains. Despite the hot water and steam, the smoke brought a glacial chill that ran up her body.

"No, no, no. Not now. Harriet, we need to get out. It was a mistake coming here," Elsie said as she threw the curtains open.

Smoke snaked into the bathroom, clinging to the floor. Elsie looked through the doorway, trying to find the source of the smoke. The bathroom grew darker and chilled her skin when it touched her leg. She jumped out of the shower and saw the mirror on her vanity as it spewed a vast amount of dark mist into the house.

"Welcome home, Elsie. Welcome, Harriet. You can run from me, but I'll always find you."

The strange, androgynous voice didn't originate from anywhere, but reverberated through the room.

"I like you right where you are, Elsie. Remember the hotel and the fire? Oh, that beautiful fire. Remember how people burned alive? How they suffocated on my smoke? That was your fault. Many more will die if you try to run from me again. This is your home now."

The voice stopped, but the smoke still bellowed from the mirror.

Elsie ran out of the bathroom, naked, wet and shaking from the temperature. She grabbed a heavy, unused jewelry box and threw it as hard as she could at the mirror. The box sailed through the air and struck the mirror with a flash of light. The glass shattered and the smoke stopped pouring in, but what had already come through remained and swirled like a tempest.

"I have an idea!" Harriet said as she ran to the pile of her dirty clothes. She dug through her denim coveralls and pulled out a candle. It was small and had some sort of decoration on it.

"A candle? What is that going to do? We need to get out of here. Hurry and get dressed," Elsie said as she ran over to her dresser.

"No, I think this will work. Watch," Harriet said as she struck a match and lit the wick.

The candle blazed instantly with a shower of sparks that hung in the air. The mysterious voice shrieked as if in pain and went silent. The dark smoke recoiled against the light of the candle as if it was a living thing struck by a viper. It writhed and roiled, unable to retreat further from the light. The smoke quickly vanished and took the cold with it. Warmth and light filled the room once again and Elsie's eyes went wide at the sparking candle.

"What is that and where did you find it?" Elsie said as she reached out to touch the candle, but pulled back before she did.

"Well, I'm not entirely sure. Marta, you don't know her, she's a girl I lived with down there, she found it in a ghost town called Grafton. It was a real ghost town with real ghosts and after she found the candle a bunch of ghosts chased us, but I ran too fast and they couldn't catch us. Then, when Mack was about to take me to the train station, Marta gave me the candle, and the ghosts must've told her all about it, because the candle kept me hidden from a ghost jaguar that was stalking me. And then you came out of the darkness, guns blazing and rescued me like a knight in shining armor."

"I did, didn't I?" Elsie said with a smile.

"So, this smoke. Is this why you removed all the mirrors out of the house? This has happened before?" Harriet said as she put the candle down on the nightstand.

"Yes. I thought I was going mad the first time it happened. I wish I was. It would be so much easier than what's really going on."

"And what is going on? What's this about a hotel and a fire?" Harriet asked with a raised eyebrow.

Elsie grabbed her bathrobe from the hook on the door and sat on the bed. She patted the spot next to her. Harriet wrapped a towel around her and sat down next to Elsie. Despite the smoke and evil voice, Elsie still felt excited as a naked Harriet inched closer to her. She told Harriet everything that happened since they parted as thoroughly as she could. Harriet didn't interrupt except to ask some clarifying questions.

"So, something burned the hotel down because you left the house and a horde of filthy people in masks tried to kill you, and your father and brother are behind it? Why?" Harriet asked, putting her hand on Elsie's thigh.

"That's the thing. I don't think they are trying to kill me. They need me for something, but what this is, I'm not sure. Whatever it is, it's not good, but I think they need me scared, alone and broken."

"Okay, now let me tell you what happened to me after we were parted."

Harriet told her story and took twice as long doing it as she described everything in excruciating detail. She cried when she told Elsie about Mack's death and Elsie held her in silence until Harriet could continue. Harriet finished and laid her head on Elsie's shoulder.

"So, according to the two ghosts you talked to, some old witch knew about this evil box or something, that these cliff dwellers put in a hole in the ground and let it corrupt them and destroy them, my father somehow found it and then, I presume, they brought it here and now, according to Marta, we need to find it. Does that sum it up?"

"Yes, that about sums it up. Marta said we need to find it. Apparently, these cliff dwellers, who escaped its evil influence and went further south, are still there. The odd thing is, that is where my dad met Mack. Dad was down there with the Pueblans trying to investigate something. I don't know what, but whatever it was, they didn't like him sticking his nose in their business and they chased him away. That's when Mack found him, he was a Buffalo soldier you see, and he saved my dad."

"I've looked all over this cursed house and never saw anything resembling a stone box. Harriet, do you think your dad knows something about what's going on?"

"I think so."

"Also, you lived with a girl that talked to ghosts and could see the past and future?"

"Well, the ghosts told her stuff, and she would tell us, usually in a cryptic and indecipherable way."

"Still, that seems like that would be a useful ally to have. If they are living down there without Mack to support and protect them now, maybe we can bring them up here? My father's cult could still be after them as well. Our own personal oracle would be nice to have, don't you think?"

"The thought of both of them alone, with no support and in danger, depresses me."

"This house is too big and has plenty of room. Are you up for another road trip, my love?"

"She really is a nice girl. You'll love her. She told me you were far away, in pain and killed a maggot. Not sure what that means. She was right about you being far away. Virginia is almost as far away as it gets. I also need to talk to my father to find out what he knows."

Chapter 31

"See? It's just like your little Browning, but there is a grip safety and a thumb safety here and here," Elsie explained to Harriet as they packed the car for the trip back down south.

"I'm still sad I lost my pistol. It held a lot of sentimental value."

Her dad had given both her and her brother matching pistols for Christmas. She liked the fact that they all had that in common. It was a family thing. They buried Hyrum's pistol with him and every time she looked at it, it reminded her of him.

"We'll make fond memories with this one. This is your 1911 now. More reliable and a larger caliber. Extra magazines are in these pouches on your left side. It's going to kick more, so be prepared for that."

"You got four of these? Can I carry two?" Harriet asked.

"Sorry, all the holsters are right-handed only. Even so, it's more effective to have one gun and more reloads, than multiple guns."

"I know, but it would be so tough looking! Like a gun fighter!" Harriet said, making finger guns.

After stopping off for gas at the service station in Morgan, they were soon on their way.

A couple hours later, with Harriet behind the wheel, she took a left turn off the main road and onto a dirt road. They bumped along for another half an hour, passing another small town and then took another left. This road was even more run down and overgrown than the last one. This stretch of road seemed to be deserted.

She slowed down and pulled onto another, even smaller road. After passing a row of spruce trees, it opened up into a small town square, surrounded by several small and dilapidated houses, long since abandoned.

"What is this wonderful place?" Elsie asked.

"Welcome to the ghost town of Duncan's Retreat."

"Is that a ghost then?" Elsie said pointing to a girl standing in front of one of the houses with a battered suitcase by her feet.

"Marta!"

Harriet ran to the girl and hugged her. She was so glad to see her and didn't know what she would have done if any harm had befallen on her innocent head.

"Where is Lupe?" Harriet said as she looked around.

It was then that she noticed tears trickled down Marta's checks and her shoulders slumped.

"The bad, dirty people in masks came last night. She told me to run and hide but she didn't. She ran to make them follow her and not me. I ran and ran and hid in the house in the cliffs. Alva helped me and told me where to go, but she said the bad people in masks took my mom. They hurt her and brought her somewhere we can't see. They looked for me but couldn't find me. Alva said you were coming," Marta said between sobs and sniffs. She hugged Harriet again, clinging to her and pulling at her clothes.

"Oh, I'm so sorry, Marta. I wish we arrived sooner. We'll

find Lupe. She'll be okay," Harriet said, but didn't know if that was true.

"My God. That poor woman. I'm so sorry, Marta. We will find her, I swear," Elsie said.

"If you got here earlier, they would have hurt you, too. If we stay, dirty men in masks will come back and find me or our neighbor would eat me eventually. I need to come with you. It will still be dangerous, but better than staying here."

They heard a piercing shriek tear through the air. It sounded distant but they couldn't place which direction it came from.

Elsie pulled out her pistol and Harriet put her hand on the butt of hers.

"That's our neighbor. He lives in the hills and he's gone wendigo, so we need to get out of here. The sleeping people say bullets won't do anything and that we should run. Now that the town is empty, he's coming to sniff things out to eat. He's always hungry."

"I don't like the sound of that, love. I say we take her advice," Elsie said, holstering her gun and tossing her suitcase in the back seat.

"It's always a good idea to do what she says, once you understand it, I mean. Like I said, she gets a little cryptic sometimes. I'm driving again whether you like it or not. I love this car."

Harriet knew exactly how prophetic Marta's cryptic sayings were and she hurried to the driver's seat of the car.

"The car is yours. Now, let's go."

The almost human sounding scream sounded again, only this time much closer.

Elsie jumped in the passenger seat and looked back at Marta, who looked calm but tears still ran down her cheeks.

Harriet started the engine and peeled out of Duncan's retreat, leaving a rooster tail of dust in its wake.

Harriet looked back at the ghost town one last time, hoping to see what the Wendigo looked like, but only saw a dark shape moving around behind some bushes.

They drove back north as fast as they could, with Marta in the back seat staring blankly at the passing scenery. Harriet reached a hand back and Marta reached out to take it. She squeezed the girl's hand and continued to hold it, despite the discomfort of the position.

When they made it to the Salt Lake Valley, Harriet yelled over the wind and the engine.

"I'm going to stop by and talk to my family! I need to let them know!"

Elsie nodded but Marta didn't acknowledge.

"Let's make this quick. You still haven't found the box," Marta said in a huff.

Chapter 32

Elsie was nervous about meeting Harriet's father again. The last time didn't go so well.

She took off her gun belt and put her pistol back in her purse. She didn't want to seem threatening. Her hair was a disaster after hours of being blown by hot desert winds. Of course, no amount of primping and looking respectable could overcome a father's overprotectiveness.

Hello again, Enoch. I stole your daughter and took her virginity, but look at my hair and fancy clothes. Oh, and she's going to live with me now, a thirty-year old white woman with burn scars and shell shock. Just what you dreamed of for your daughter, right? Hope you didn't want grandkids!

Somehow, she didn't think that would go over well, but she never backed down from anything. She would face Enoch Piper and tell him, woman to man, what her intentions were. She knew he would object but Harriet was an adult and could decide for herself.

The nagging, farthest recesses of her brain asked, 'what if she doesn't choose you?'

She told her insecurities to shut up. She knew Harriet's heart now and trusted it.

Marta's head appeared between them as she sat forward.

"Harriet, you should probably hurry," she said calmly, and then sat back down.

Harriet didn't second guess or ask questions. She pushed the gas pedal and went even faster.

The city limits of Ogden drew closer, and Elsie became more nervous with each passing mile.

Harriet slowed down once she entered the city. As they drew closer to her family's house and shop, she noticed people running in the same direction.

As they reached the shop, she saw a large crowd had formed around it and blocked any view of what was transpiring.

Harriet stopped the car and jumped out without even parking it. Elsie scooted over to the driver's side and put the car in park and turned it off before it could run into something.

"What's going on?" Elsie asked.

"I don't know. Seems like trouble. Marta, stay in the car please."

Elsie grabbed her purse and rushed over to where the crowd had gathered.

She pushed her way through dozens of people, some cheering, some standing there doing nothing but looking.

When she finally got through, she saw a group of men dressed in white, with tall pointy hats and face coverings, surrounding Enoch, and all holding weapons of some kind; baseball bats, chains and knives.

Enoch was on the ground, head bleeding but conscious, holding a steel pipe and trying to defend himself.

Harriet rushed over, putting herself in between the men and her father.

One of the men, dressed in fancier robes with big, white crosses in red circles, stepped up.

"Get out of the way little girl or I'll beat you like I beat your daddy here. Not only are you colored, you're a Mormon and a girl. Three strikes and you're out! If there's one thing we hate more than Mormons, it's the coloreds, and you're both."

He laughed at his own joke.

"Leave us alone! Get out of here!" Harriet yelled, yanking her pistol from its holster.

'Oh no! The coon has a gun! We're trembling in our boots! Right, boys!"

Some people in the crowd laughed, some kept watching silently. Some watched with expressions of horror and shock on their faces. Most watched like it was a street performance, including a police officer, who stood there with a blank expression on his face.

Three of the Klan members pulled out their own pistols and aimed them at Harriet and her father.

Elsie assumed the man in the fancy robes was the leader. She shoved her way over to the man and came up behind him.

"C'mon boys, let's finish this."

Elsie took her pistol out of her handbag and placed the barrel against the back of the man's head.

"Walk away now or I give you another nostril. I mean it."

"Who...who are you?" he said with a shaky voice.

"I'm your best friend because I'm about to save your life. See that woman you are pointing a gun at? She's the best marksman I've ever seen. She killed a mountain lion at a hundred feet while on the move. She has seven shots in her pistol, and there are six of you. That's more than enough to kill all of you and put another shot into you for good measure. Now, take my warning. Leave and don't come back."

"A harpy and a race traitor. You really are a piece of work, bitch," said the leader, turning his head just enough to see her from the corner of his eye.

She heard him slowly ease the hammer back on his own gun.

"Don't think about it. I've killed men for less, believe me," Harriet whispered quiet enough so only he could hear. She put pressure on her trigger little by little.

The cop that watched from the sidelines now stepped forward.

"All right, all right. Everybody calm down. Nobody do anything hasty. Boys, you've had your fun. Now get out of here before I have to do some paperwork. If you boys come back, I'll box your ears off and run you out of town."

Elsie heard the hammer on the man's gun ease forward and click into place.

"C'mon, boys. We've made our point. Let's listen to the hag and the nice officer. We'll play nice. The Klan is here to protect good, honest people and keep America pure. Once we rid this state of undesirables and race traitors, we'll finally have a safe and free society!" he said to the crowd as if it was a recruiting opportunity.

"Go back to the South. We don't want your kind here!" said a voice from the crowd, suddenly finding courage now that the danger was over.

The crowd started to disperse.

"We have meetings every Thursday! Come join us and protect America!"

The crowd ignored him and left. The Klan members put their weapons away and walked away without a backward glance.

"If you come back, I will kill you," she said to the Klan leader in a tone that made sure he knew she meant it.

"We've made our point...for now."

They all left, leaving Harriet and Enoch alone.

Elsie rushed over to Enoch and inspected his wounds.

"We need to get him inside. Now. Harriet, help me get him up. Marta! Come with us!"

She nodded and put one of his arms over her shoulders. The two of them lifted him up. Her healing rib protested, but she ignored it, and they brought him into the house.

"Where's mom and the boys?"

"They went off to Antelope Island to look at the buffalo. They left an hour ago," he mumbled.

"We need to lay him down somewhere flat. I also need a clean needle and thread. Get some water boiling."

"Let's set him on the dining room table. What else do you need?" Harriet said, looking worried, but calm.

"Some clean towels. A large bowl of water."

"On it," Harriet said as she rushed out of the room.

She had seen this hundreds of times. Head wounds could be very serious and always bled exponentially more than they should. His head wound was a nasty gash near his temple that bled profusely. Lacerations and abrasions covered his head and arms, but none were serious. She tore a piece off her dress and applied pressure to the wound until the towels and water arrived.

Harriet arrived with the boiling water, and a needle and thread.

"This is going to hurt, Mr. Piper, so please try to stay as still as possible."

"It isn't the first time I've had to get stitches. Do what you gotta do," he said groggily.

Elsie went to work after sterilizing the needle and thread. Harriet held his hand as he gripped tightly.

The work didn't take long. Her hands knew what to do without thinking, and she had him expertly stitched up in no time.

She took Harriet to the side.

"He has a concussion, so someone will need to stay with him and make sure he doesn't fall asleep. Keep the wound clean and make sure he drinks a lot of water."

"You're not staying?"

"He's a little punch drunk right now, but I don't think I should be here when he comes to. We didn't end on the best of terms last time we met."

"No, please stay. I need you with me. I'll need your support for when he does."

"Why is that?"

"I'm going to tell my dad about everything. Everything that's been going on and everything about us."

"I see."

Elsie hesitated, but Harriet needed her.

"Then, of course I'll stay. I'll always be there for you."

Harriet snuck in a quick kiss before going back to her father's side.

Marta approached.

"What should I do?"

Elsie thought about it for a moment.

"I'd prefer it if you stayed here for now. It would be safer if we were all together."

They did not have to wait long for the rest of Harriet's family to return.

Chapter 33

When Harriet's mom came through the door, she threw up her arms, ran over to her daughter, and wrapped her arms around her.

Harriet enveloped her mom back in a bone crunching embrace.

"It's so good to see you, mom! I missed you so much!"

"I'm so glad you're back, my beautiful, sweet baby angel! Let me take a look at you."

She released her daughter long enough to look her over, then hugged her again.

"Mom, I'm really glad to see you too, but dad's been hurt. We moved him to the bedroom."

Her mom rushed to the bedroom and was instantly at his side to hold his hand.

"My dear, sweet husband. What happened?"

"Everything is okay now, Gertrude. I'll be fine. All thanks to Miss Everly here."

Enoch told her everything that happened. The Klu Klux Klan staged a demonstration outside the shop, and he went out to confront them. He yelled at them and then they attacked.

"That's when Harriet and Miss Everly arrived. Your daughter threw herself between me and them, even pointed a gun at them. Miss Everly came up behind their leader and threatened to shoot him. I'd hate to think what would have happened if they didn't show up. The townsfolk sure weren't going to do anything about it. Then Miss Everly brought me in here and patched me up as good as any doctor could."

Harriet beamed with pride at Elsie.

"Oh, bless you both. Miss Everly, thank you from the bottom of my heart for helping my poor Enoch."

She inspected the wound and the stiches under the bandage Elsie had put over his head.

"You did do a mighty fine job here. Where did a rich girl like yourself learn to do something like that?"

"French army medical corps. I was a nurse over there for the duration," she said, blushing.

"Well, bless you. I'll remember you in my prayers. I can never repay you for this. If you need anything, just ask and, if it is within my power to do so, you'll get it. You are an angel of mercy. Thank you, Miss Everly."

"Please, call me Elsie," she said, shuffling over to hide behind Harriet.

"Elsie also saved my life too, dad. I have a lot to explain, and some of it...most of it, is bad news."

"Go on then. Tell me what you need to say."

Harriet told her parents everything. She told them about the mysterious hole in the ground, the strange happenings and apparitions around the house, her time with Mack, Lupe, and, finally about Mack's death.

Her dad had to take a moment after hearing of the death of his friend.

She continued her story with her flight on foot through

the desert and about when the cultists caught her and how Elsie had rescued her.

When she mentioned the Ute that guided the old witchy woman to the obsidian box and how she took it South, he looked down, suddenly finding the floor very interesting.

"We went back to get Lupe and Marta, but Lupe had been captured by the same people that tried to kill me and we have no idea where she is. That's why we are here. We were on the way home and I was going to stop by and tell you all of this, when we saw you being attacked."

"That timing wasn't coincidence. It was providence. It seems the Lord is guiding your hands. Both of yours."

"There's more to tell, dad," Harriet said, looking uncomfortable and bashful.

"Go on dear," her mom urged.

"Well, there's no other way to say it, but me and Elsie are in love," she said with confidence. "There's no way around it and you've always known this part of me, so there's no beating around the bush. Mom, dad, I could never be happy living the way you want me to. Living a loveless marriage without intimacy and pretending to be something I'm not. It would make me die inside a little each day. I can't live like that. I can't be an emotionless machine to pop out babies and stay home and clean just to meet expectations. I can't do it. I have to do what brings me true joy. It's so rare when we find it. We have to grab onto it. And I'm grabbing on. I love her. Deeply and romantically, just so there's no confusion. So, from now on, I'll be living with her. Elsie, I mean. We'll be together. In everything."

Harriet put her arm around Elsie's waist and drew her closer, taking courage from her physical presence. Elsie, surprised at first, recovered and did the same.

Mom clasped her hands over her heart and smiled at the both of them.

Dad slumped and looked resigned with a deep sigh.

"If there is one thing I know about you, daughter, it's that you are stubborn and there is no changing your mind once you are resolved to it. I, more than anything, just want you to be happy. We raised you to be independent and strong, and it would be pure hypocrisy on my part to discourage you of it now."

Harriet rushed over and hugged both her parents in one big, all-inclusive hug. Harriet's eyes filled with tears, and she could hear Elsie sniffling behind her.

Her dad wiped away his own tears after the hug, and now looked serious.

"Miss Everly. Thank you for saving mine and my daughter's lives. But now we must turn to more serious matters. As it turns out, I know a little about the situation you find yourselves in."

"This have to do with when Mack, rest his soul, first found you down by Taos?" Harriet asked.

"Yes, it does. This was before I met your mother, you see. The church got wind of something malevolent and malicious heading this way that would threaten the territory...it wasn't a state then. Somehow, they knew the answers could be found in Taos with the Pueblan people. My companion got sick and had to turn back before we even left Utah. I was stubborn back then, even more stubborn than I am now, almost as much as you. So, I decided to carry on by myself. As you know how Mack found me, it didn't turn out too well."

He chuckled at himself, which hurt his head, so he leaned back against the pillows.

"Anyway, I made it to my contacts in Taos. They let me in but weren't overly friendly. I stayed with them for the summer. I didn't really know what I was looking for, but I kept my ear to the ground. Eventually, I started to hear the stories the children would scare each other with. They told stories of an old god. A god that haunted them in the place they came from before. It would drive men mad with greed and jealousy until they killed one another in dark sacrifice.

"Once the adults found out I was learning these tales from the children, they warned me to stop. Of course, I didn't listen. I did learn that this dark god was hidden in an obsidian stone box far to the south and was lying there, waiting for some unfortunate soul to find it and awaken it. I never found out where that was, because they chased me away."

"Did you learn anything else? How to stop it?" Elsie asked.

"Kind of. They did say you needed the obsidian box and whatever was in it. Once you had those things, you could put it back to sleep. They weren't too specific as to how though."

"Dad, do you think you could come up tomorrow and take a look at the house and the hole out back? You're smarter than me. Maybe you could help us figure it out."

"Of course. If I'm feeling well enough, I'll drive up there. If not, I'll have your mom drive me, but either way, I'll be there."

"It's getting late. I'll take care of him tonight and if those wretched men come back, I have a double barrel shotgun waiting for them. You two go home. You've had a rough couple of days. I'll bring him by tomorrow," her mom said.

"I will, but I'm going to grab some stuff from my room first."

Harriet went to her bedroom, Elsie followed close behind.

She went straight to her dresser and grabbed some clothes and her scriptures. She looked around but couldn't think of anything else to take.

"Look at all of these drawings," Elsie said.

Harriet felt self-conscious and blushed.

"Don't look at those. They are just doodles by a silly teenage girl."

"No, they are most certainly not. These are really good,

Harriet. I mean it. You should submit these to a studio. I'll help you do that."

"No fashion company is going to want sketches from a Negro, and you know it."

"There's ways around that, love."

Elsie scrunched her face and squinted her eyes at the drawings.

"Harriet...you notice anything similar about all of these fantastic drawings?"

She looked at her doodles on the walls but didn't see anything.

"All of your drawings look like me," Elsie said, pointing to each one in turn.

Harriet saw it for the first time. Almost every woman she drew was a tall, curvy blonde women. There were variations, but most of them could have been drawings of Elsie. A few of them even had her exact eyes.

Harriet chuckled to herself.

How did I never notice that?

"I guess I've been daydreaming about you for a long time, Elsie."

"When we get home, I'll make some of those daydreams come true, my love," she whispered in her ear.

She warmed up at the thought of what new things Elsie would show her tonight.

"Let's get going then."

They gathered Marta, said their goodbyes and left.

Elsie insisted they drive around the block a couple of times to make sure no more Klan members were sneaking around.

Already sick of canned food, they stopped by the grocery store to stock up, then headed home. It was growing dark by the time they arrived, and they were all tired and exhausted.

Harriet took Marta's hand and carried her suitcase upstairs to one of the empty rooms.

"This is your room now, sweetheart. You'll be safe here. We'll find your mom, don't worry. Please try to get some rest."

"You have the candle burning. That's good. Alva wondered if you would figure that out."

Marta sat on the bed, laid down and tucked her legs back. She was asleep before Harriet turned off the light.

Elsie had already snuck into the bedroom and Harriet followed.

Harriet half expected Elsie to be undressed and waiting for her, but instead found her already passed out and snoring.

She thought her little snores were adorable and lay beside her, huddled against her warmth, but couldn't sleep. Even with the candle burning, she kept an eye out for danger and worried about her family and Lupe.

HARRIET WOKE up and looked around, confused.

Elsie sat up in bed, surrounded by papers spread over the sheets.

"What are you doing?" Harriet mumbled.

"I have a pile of research to start on. Why don't you go check on Marta?"

Harriet slowly stood up, straightened out her clothes. She checked Marta's room, but she wasn't there. She quickly checked the bathroom and didn't find her there either. She was about to warn Elsie but heard Marta's voice coming from downstairs.

She found Marta sitting at the dining room table, staring at the wall, wide-eyed and blank faced.

"Marta, what are you doing down here. It's almost three in the morning," Harriet said as she looked at the kitchen clock.

"You got a lot of sleeping people in this house," Marta

said, finally breaking her eyes away from whatever she was looking at.

"I know. I can see them sometimes. What do they say?" Harriet said in a quiet voice.

"They say we are in danger. They are sad and angry but want to stop Elsie's father and brother. It was her brother that hurt them and made them go to sleep for a long time."

"Do they say anything else? Anything about the hole or why any of this is happening?"

"They can't see into the hole. It scares them. They say bad people and things go in and come out," Marta continued with her monotone voice and blank stare.

"Bad people like Elsie's father and brother?"

"Yes. Sometimes. But that's not where they live."

"Where do they live?" Harriet asked, taking Marta's hand.

"Somewhere else. A place of shadow."

"What does that mean?"

"I don't know," Marta struggled to say as she looked around the room blinking.

"How'd I get here? I should probably go to bed, huh?"

"Yes, but did the sleeping people in this house say anything else?"

"They said my mom is alive and not being hurt. She is worried about me and that we will find her soon."

Harriet smiled at the rare piece of good news. She was still worried about Lupe, but now there was hope. The ghosts of the house knew they would find her, but Harriet didn't know where to start looking.

Marta's head bobbed and her eyes fluttered.

"C'mon. You've had a long day, sweetheart. Let's get you back to bed."

Hand in hand, she brought Marta back upstairs and put her to bed, making sure she fell asleep before leaving. She loved the strange girl and promised herself that whatever happened, no harm would come to Marta.

Harriet walked back to her bedroom.

Her bedroom. She liked the sound of that.

Elsie sat on the bed with her eyebrows scrunched together and lips pursed, as she poured over the stack of papers.

"Find anything interesting?"

"Apparently, we need to find this obsidian chest or box and whatever was inside it. If we bring these two things together, we can capture or imprison this...thing. I am not sure what to label it at the moment. Your dad called it a dark god, but if it can be trapped in a box, it doesn't appear to be much of a god."

Elsie looked at Harriet and her expression softened.

"You try to get some sleep now. I'll stay up, keep watch and try to figure out how to put a stop to this."

Chapter 34

She looked over at Harriet, who had finally worn out and was asleep on her stomach, still in her clothes. She loved her back, strong yet feminine. Her eyes wandered to the swell of her buttocks, perfectly shaped, round and smooth. Harriet gave a soft moan, turned over but did not wake. Elsie refused to be distracted by that and turned back to her papers.

"Research into the indigenous mythological pantheon of pre-Columbian Mexico," Elsie whispered to herself. "Well, this sounds like a fun read."

It looked like a Brigham Young University printing of someone's doctoral research.

She read the paper and her excitement grew. She had a name. Tezcatlipoca. Smoking Mirror. The god of jaguars, magic, sacrifice, mirrors and obsidian. Her mind raced at everything that had happened to her since she came here and knew this was the being that had been tormenting her. She hurriedly read more, until she finished each of the papers and notes, leaving only the rare book that Abram procured from the university library. She picked it up and found a piece of paper marking a chapter.

"I think this is what you are looking for," said the note Abram had left for her.

Just then, she heard a gentle knocking on her bedroom door.

"Come in," she said quietly after throwing a sheet over Harriet.

Marta stuck her head into the bedroom.

"Sorry to bother you, but the sleeping people say there is something you need to see."

"Of course. Please give me a moment."

Marta closed the door, and Elsie got up. She threw on her jeans a simple shirt and strapped on her gun belt, her sore muscles and rib aching the entire time. She didn't know what the emergency was, but she wanted to be prepared regardless.

Within a few minutes she was out in the hallway and followed Marta downstairs.

Marta put a finger in front of her lips to let her know to be quiet. She crouched low and approached the large picture window in the living room at the front of the house. Elsie stealthily came up beside her and looked but didn't see anything.

"Look farther, silly. They say smoke and mirrors is out there," she whispered.

She peeked over the edge to look outside and still didn't see anything.

"Keep looking. You'll see it," Marta said

Elsie tried to focus her eyes and then she saw movement. She couldn't follow the movement or pinpoint its origins, but her eyes finally focused on the silhouette of a person standing in the field.

As she looked, she saw more people standing there. Two dozen of them so far, all lined up and encircling the house.

"Terrific. Cultists. They've done this before. If they start coming closer, I will commence firing. We have more than enough firepower here to stop them. They go down easy enough."

"It's not them the sleeping people are worried about. There's something big out there. It's big and moving around between them. I can't get a good look at it because once you see it, it's gone."

"It might be another spectral jaguar."

"No. It's bigger than that. Bigger than a house, I think. And it's fast."

"Marta, would you please go wake up Harriet and tell her to grab two shotguns and a few boxes of those salt shells?"

She nodded and hurried off to fetch Harriet.

Elsie continued to look out the window. Thankfully, none of the cultists had taken a step toward the house.

"Good. You learned your lesson last time you tried."

Then she saw it. A large, black mass darted up and moved impossibly fast, only to duck down out of sight.

"What the fuck?"

This was new. She hadn't seen anything like this before.

Harriet arrived with two shotguns and a box of ammo. She placed them on the floor.

"What do we got?"

"Come look for yourself," Elsie said and motioned for her to come to the window.

Harriet kneeled in front of the window, kept low and looked outside.

A few seconds later, she jumped back and covered her mouth.

"I saw it! What was that?"

"No idea but it's been moving around out there most of the night," Elsie said.

"They are here for me. Why do you think they're trying to kill me?" Harriet asked.

Elsie thought about it.

"It could be because you make me happy. My father is a petty and spiteful troll of a human being. For some reason, I am important, but you are expendable to his plan. Maybe he just doesn't like the color of your skin. However, the amount of effort they are putting in to try to kill you is disproportionate. Your death appears to be important to their plan, too."

"Maybe he wants you sad, scared and angry and my death is the best way to do that?"

Elsie thought about what Harriet just said.

"I do believe you are right," she said, thinking about what she just read and the one word that kept coming up in her studies: 'sacrifice'.

Before she could finish that line of thought, she heard Marta approach.

"Something is wrong. Upstairs," Marta said.

"What is it, dear? What's going on?" she said, standing up.

Marta didn't say anything. She raised a trembling arm and pointed upstairs.

She felt it before she looked. A slight humming in her ear and vibrations in the floorboards. Everything grew silent and still. Elsie looked out the window and the cultists were gone. No sign of them or the giant black mass. Every hair stood on end and her heart raced. She picked up the shotgun, took Harriet by the hand and raced upstairs. Marta followed. At the top, a sickly green light seeped from under her bedroom door.

She kept Harriet and Marta behind her as she threw the bedroom door open. It was as she left it, except for the wicked light pouring in from outside. The candle on the nightstand flickered and sparked wildly as it fought against the encroaching presence.

Through the window, a massive and ominous shape rose into view. The darkness that surrounded it blotted out light in the way that light always extinguishes the dark.

All warmth and light left her as its head came into view. It was a dark and evil sunrise. A halo of flickering and sickly light rotated around the pure white face that rose up to meet her gaze.

The white masks that its followers wore were pale imitations of their lord and master. The expression on its mask-like face was a benevolent smile, eyes mere slits of hidden mirth and contentment. The rotating halo that surrounded the face bathed the bedroom in its suffocating light and filled the room with shadow.

Its terrible and androgynous voice was thunder inside her head and caused the house to tremble around her. Harriet and Marta covered their ears and screamed as it spoke, mouth unmoving.

"WILL YOU SUFFER TO COME UNTO ME?"

Elsie heard another scream and wondered who it was, until she realized it was herself. She wailed uncontrollably and fell to her knees.

The last thing she remembered before passing out was Harriet on her knees praying and herself uttering the name of the beast.

"Smoking Mirror."

Chapter 35

Harriet woke to the sound of her father's voice and his hand gently shaking her.

"What happened here? Are you okay?" he asked, concerned.

She sat up, every muscle protested. Her head swam.

Her mom helped Elsie up off the floor and Marta stood in the doorway, eyes wide and wringing her hands.

"Are you okay?" he asked again.

"I think so," she said and tried to stand up.

Her dad helped her up and brought her over to the bed and made her sit down.

"Can someone please tell me what is going on here? I tried to call, but there was no answer, so we drove up. Marta told us a bunch of gibberish and brought us up here. You were passed out on the floor."

"I said the smoking mirror talked to you, but it went away when the other man showed up. What's hard to understand about that?" Marta said.

"It was Smoking Mirror. He…it, paid us a visit last night," Elsie said. her voice trembled as she managed to get to her feet.

Her dad nodded with a grim expression on his face, but she was in the dark.

"Am I the only one who doesn't know who that is?" Harriet asked, frustrated.

Elsie went over to the research materials she had poured over the night before and picked them up.

"The Maya worshiped a god named Tohil. The Aztecs called him Smoking Mirror. A god of night, magic, temptation, the North winds and sacrifice. His symbol is an obsidian disk...a mirror, which represents the sacred cave...or hole in the ground for all intents and purposes, and his totem is the jaguar. That is what the Aztec priests brought to the cliff dwellers and caused their destruction. My father found out about it and started a cult to worship it once again. I'm sure he thinks he can use this being and its power for his own goals, being the narcissist that he is, but he can't control this."

"The sleeping people are afraid of it. Elsie's nasty mean brother killed the 'lectrishuns...,'" she started to say but was interrupted by Elsie.

"I'm sorry, the what?"

"She means the missing electricians. The ghosts use words she sometimes doesn't know," Harriet chimed in.

"Sorry, I don't know that word, but the group of men fixing this house up. The sleeping people say that when Elsie's brother took out their hearts and they went to sleep, the smoking mirror thing woke up from its sleep. Now it's awake, but like a baby. It needs to eat and grow," Marta said, stepping away from the door, finding her courage.

"Well, that's disconcerting," Harriet said.

"Very," her dad replied.

"So, this whole inheriting a house and coming out here was just one big trap? Is that why they won't kill you? So they can sacrifice you?" Harriet asked.

"That appears to be the case. According to Aztec tradition,

every year they would sacrifice someone to Smoking Mirror, but for that year, they would be treated like royalty. Given a palace, good food and concubines. Then, on the final day, they would be paraded through the city to the temple to be sacrificed. I guess this follows the same pattern, given the nice house and money."

"So, why try to make her miserable and terrified?" Harriet asked.

Her dad puzzled on that before answering.

"Well, the Aztecs would sacrifice prisoners of war and slaves all year. Smoking Mirror doesn't have the luxury of feeding off their fear and misery, so I assume it's trying to feed off her."

"What does it eat?" Elsie asked.

"Huh?" Harriet looked back at Elsie.

"Well, Marta is cryptic and mercurial, but she is never wrong. She said this Smoking Mirror thing eats, right? What does it eat?"

Her dad stepped into the middle of the room.

"I think I have the answer to that as well," he said, hand on his chin and brow furrowed as if deep in thought.

Everybody looked at him.

"Think about it. Fear, sadness, jealousy, anger or any negative emotion. I believe this is what it feeds on and it is trying to make you into the fatted calf for the feast. It wants to drive you into the depths of terror, depression and loss, enough for you to give up and become a willing sacrifice. Your love for my daughter has turned into your greatest weakness."

"Needless to say, Harriet will need protection around the clock. She is not to leave any of your sights. There is something out there. Something evil and powerful and it's gunning for her. She won't be safe until we defeat Smoking Mirror. If we don't, our lives are in danger and all will be drowned in torment, paranoia and jealousy."

"We have a chance to stop this thing. How do we stop it?" Harriet asked.

"We need to find the obsidian box and the obsidian mirror that was in it," Elsie said.

"Obsidian mirror?"

"Yes, in the box was an obsidian mirror. It is his token and symbol. I read it in the papers Abram gave me. It represents the natal cave that all humanity sprang from. It, and every mirror are gateways into the physical world. Apparently, since my father is its chief priest, I assume he has at least one of the items."

"These things are going to be hard to find, but I think our resident oracle here can help us with that. Can't you, Marta?" Harriet said.

"I can?"

"Of course you can. Can you ask the sleeping people to find it?"

"Find what?"

Harriet had known Marta long enough not to get frustrated.

"We need to find a box. It's completely black and made of stone. Do you think you could ask them, the sleeping people, for us? Please, sweetie?"

"Oh, that. I've already asked them. They'll find it," Marta said, blushing a little. Harriet knew she liked to be called 'sweetie'.

"Aren't we forgetting something?" Elsie asked.

"What?"

"Marta said a man drove Smoking Mirror away. Who the hell was that?"

Everybody looked at each other hoping for an answer but nobody had one.

"Marta. Who was the man that saved us this morning?"

"I don't know. I didn't see him. They told me about him. He was like a sleeping person but different."

"What's one more mystery? It appears we have an ally, and we can take all that we can get. Come, let's go take a look at this hole," her dad said.

"This thing has a way of interfering with your thoughts. It warps them to bring out your darkest desires. If something hadn't stopped me, perhaps the same man that stopped Smoking Mirror, I would be dead. Guard your thoughts and if it becomes too much, please just back away," Elsie said.

Everyone went downstairs and out the back door.

The hole loomed in front of them like a malignant cancer on an otherwise unblemished body. Harriet had seen it, but she had never actually tried to get close to it. Now she knew why. Its terrible siren song pulled her thoughts to the darkest recesses of her mind, strengthening as she got closer.

Harriet's thoughts wandered as she walked down the hill to the hole.

Wouldn't your life have been so much easier without Elsie? Ever since she hired you, all that she has done has been to use you for dirty, filthy, unnatural sex and put your life in danger. You can leave now. Turn around and never come back. Leave her. She doesn't actually love you and she never will. If you stay, you could die.

Harriet burst into tears. The very idea that Elsie didn't love her and was only using her, crushed her heart. *She's a rich woman from the South. Of course she's just using you. Your dad was right. You've become her house negro. She's only bedding you because she's too ugly to get anyone else.*

Harriet screamed and fell to her knees.

"No! None of that is true! Get out of my head!"

Elsie was by her side and wrapped her arms around her.

"It's okay. Whatever it is putting into your head, it is not you. Those aren't your thoughts."

Harriet looked up into her beautiful face. A face reflecting nothing but love and tenderness.

"I don't think that about you. I promise I don't and never did. I love you and I know you love me," Harriet said, as if Elsie knew the dark thoughts that were shoved to the front of her mind.

"It is okay. I know. I think I'm okay now. I didn't expect it to be that fierce, but I know what to expect now. Let's keep going," Harriet said and let Elsie help her up.

She looked over at the others. Her mother and Marta seemed completely unaffected.

Her father, however, was.

He grimaced and clutched at his heart. Huge beads of sweat streamed down his face as he fell to his knees.

"I'll take your father back to the house," Mom said and tried to help him up.

He shook his head and stood back up.

"I'm fine. Let's keep going," he said through gritted teeth.

"Dad. Now is not the time to play hero. Get back up to the house," Harriet said with an extreme look of concern on her face.

"Don't worry about it. It'll take more than that to stop me," he said and grimaced.

They continued to the hole, approached the edge and looked down into its dark, eternal depths.

Nobody said a word, but Harriet was sure they all felt the malicious pull. Elsie had warned her that it tried to lure you in, to give yourself to it, and she felt it.

It looked so inviting.

A whispering voice creeped from the hole and gave everyone chills.

"Nechpactia nimizixmati Harriet, Enoch, Gertrude."

The voice echoed all around them and the ground trembled just enough that Harriet had to adjust her footing.

"Well, that's disconcerting," her dad said.

Harriet didn't understand what it said, but it knew her parent's names. Whatever it said, the tone made clear its malevolent intentions, as her heart pounded and she felt beads of sweat roll down her face.

"Enoch!" she heard her mother scream and turned to look at her father.

He was down on one knee, eyes shut, teeth bared and clutching at his heart.

"We need to get him away from this thing. Back to the house, now," Harriet said as she helped her mom to lift her dad to his feet.

The voices and emotions dissipated with distance from the hole. Her dad breathed easier and no longer seemed in pain. Elsie monitored his heart rate, blood flow and temperature as they walked, and Harriet was once again glad of Elsie's experience as a nurse. More than anything, she wanted to help her father, but knew he was in capable hands.

Once inside, they sat him down and Elsie put a glass of water and a couple of aspirins in front of him. After a few minutes, his breathing calmed, and the pain subsided. Harriet couldn't stop hugging him. The thought of losing her dad, especially to something like this, was more than she could bear.

"Get him home and make sure he gets plenty of rest. Needless to say, he is not to go near that hole again," Elsie said and then helped him to his truck with a promise she'd call him if they needed anything, and that he was to do the same.

Harriet watched her parents drive off with the sinking feeling she might not see them again.

Chapter 36

Elsie, after waving Harriet's parents off, marched into the house. She needed answers. Not knowing what was going on was growing tiresome, so she snatched up the book Abrahm procured for her and brought it to the library, in case she needed some of the reference books available there.

She plopped the book down on her desk and sat in the swivel chair. Blank papers and a ballpoint pen sat on the edge of the desk, ready for any notes she might need to jot down. Her mind couldn't settle down as she thought about everything that's happened to her. When she stood at the edge of her father's grave in Hollywood Cemetery, she felt surprised, but nothing else. Knowing they were out there and working to torment her further, aroused no further emotions except the steely determination to stop them. She couldn't bring herself to hate them. Love and hate were said to be two sides of the same coin, but she couldn't even give them that.

Now let's see what you are up to.

She opened the book gingerly. The pages were old and most of them had separated from the binding, but the printed words were still legible. It was the chronicles of Spanish and

Portuguese conquistadors as they pillaged the New World, compiled by a British historian who clearly admired their imperialism.

Most of the content wasn't relevant and she was about to give up hope until she found the account of Raymundo Diaz, Chaplain to Hernán Cortés. The historian had labeled this account a local legend, and as she read, knew it was true.

The account of the conquistador priest spoke of his encounter with a priest of the god Tezcatlipoca, or Smoking Mirror. Through torture and bribes, Raymundo Diaz learned of the existence of a great treasure and that the Aztec priest knew of its location. Raymundo finally tracked down and cornered the pagan priest, only to watch as the priest invoked an ancient spell, jumped through a large obsidian mirror and disappeared.

Raymundo never found the priest but according to the story, he went mad trying to discover the secret of the Aztec priest's magic for himself. However, according to legend, the priest still lives and searches for the secrets of magic to this day.

Elise wanted to read more but heard Harriet shouting from downstairs. She stood up from the desk to investigate the cause when Harriet ran upstairs and flew into the library. Her eyes were wild, and her chest heaved.

"There you are! Marta is gone!"

"What do you mean, gone?"

"I went to check on her but she was gone. I looked all through the house and can't find her!"

"Marta!"

Elsie cursed herself for leaving the girl alone in this fucking house.

How could I be so stupid?

She ran downstairs to the parlor and immediately noticed that the front door was open slightly.

Blind panic took over as she ran to the door and threw it

open. At first, she didn't see anything, then in the distance, she saw a small figure jump down into the gulley, heading for the stone building with the altar.

Her heart froze in that moment of realization.

"Marta is outside and heading for the ruins where the sacrifices happened. Let's go!"

Elsie couldn't see Marta anymore, so she grabbed one of the shotguns by the door and ran toward the ancient ruins, with Harriet close behind her. The thorns and weeds scratched her legs as she ran.

She ran along the edge of the ravine and Marta came into view. Marta approached the crumbling ruins when Elsie noticed the area around the ruins grew darker as they grew nearer. It wasn't the sky itself that became dark. The sky was still bright, sunny and warm. It was a tangible and substantial blackness gathering around the ancient place of sacrifice, as if the evil embedded there came to greet them.

She did a quick check to make sure there was already a shell loaded in the chamber of her shotgun and ran as she called out Marta's name in the vain hope she would snap out of it.

Elsie finally reached Marta just as she arrived at the decrepit ruins where Thomas had sacrificed the electricians. Lunging forward, she snatched the girl up in her arms. She skidded to a stop in the dirt and leaves, her balance heaving with the girl's weight, and for a single, breathless moment, she felt about to pitch forward into the waiting cloud ahead.

"I got you, girl. You're okay now."

The darkness formed tendrils made of shadow and slowly reached out for them both, but Elise had Marta and already backed away.

Harriet finally arrived, chest heaving as she stood between them and the darkness.

"It's...it's your brother. He's here. I can feel it," Marta said with a tremble in her voice.

"Good. Then he'll know where the box and mirror are."

There was no fear in her own voice.

This piece of shit holds no power over me anymore. Too much of my life has been spent cowering at the thought of this spoiled weakling. It ends today.

"The sleeping people in the house said the black stone box is here and the bad man that turns to smoke is hiding it. You can't hurt smoke," Marta said.

"Thomas! We know you are here! Come out and face us!" Elsie called out.

The darkness that surrounded the place swirled around them, though there was no wind or movement in the air.

"Why should I, little sister? Our dear father told me about you. How clueless you are. You are on the verge of greatness and don't even know it," came a voice from the air Elsie recognized instantly.

"That was a nice trick you pulled with that fake Harriet in my room. That was you, wasn't it? You couldn't take me by force, so you thought you could trick me? You thought I wouldn't know the difference? How's your shoulder by the way? Is that where I shot you?"

A scream filled the air as if it was emanating from the dirt and rocks itself. The sound reverberated in her head and echoed off the distant valley walls.

"I was supposed to be safe. I was supposed to be invulnerable but that pistol of yours...you have too much of a connection with it. It isn't my fault! I would have finally taken you for myself. You were promised to me! You are my reward! You are mine!"

The voice was angry and petulant and there was no mistaking it was Thomas. Elsie would recognize that whiney and sniveling voice anywhere.

"Thomas! Show yourself!"

Laughter enveloped them and vibrated in their bones.

"And why would I do that?"

"You want me, don't you? You know I want you too! How could I not?"

"I have an idea. Take my pistol and play along. Wait for the moment," Elsie whispered as quietly as possible.

Harriet nodded and as discreetly as she could, slipped the pistol from Elsie's holster and tucked it into her waistband.

The swirling maelstrom of darkness slowed and stopped. Instead of wind, screaming and laughter, a dread silence fell upon them.

"What?" Thomas sounded confused.

"I love you, big brother!"

Elsie felt the bile rising and had to swallow it down to keep talking.

"Why do you think I've only been with women? You are the only man that has my thoughts. You think I could possibly prefer her over you? You are the only man meant for me. All this time I thought you were dead, my heart was broken. Now that you are here before me, I can't hold back. I can't deny my feelings anymore."

Elsie pushed Harriet away and tossed the shotgun on the ground. Elsie opened her arms to Thomas, inviting him to her.

Harriet scrambled away, got to her feet and ran toward Marta.

"You were always meant to be with me, Elsie and I forgive you. You were acting out of fear, but there's no reason to be scared anymore. It's only natural that we be together. The same pure blood runs through our veins. Tezcatlipoca will heal your scars after you offer yourself to him. Give yourself to him and I'll give myself to you, heart and soul. I'm doing all this for you, Elsie. I can make you whole if you suffer to come unto him. I knew one day you would succumb and give yourself to me. You are mine!"

The darkness gathered around him, and his form solidified in front of her.

Thomas stepped from the darkness, looking like he hadn't aged a day and dressed in a sharp three-piece suit. He looked normal, except for the scars on his face that leaked the same sickly, pale green light that came from Smoking Mirror's halo and hurt her eyes. As Elsie watched, his form solidified and was on the verge of being completely corporeal.

"I'm so sorry I gave you those scars, brother. I was just playing hard to get. You know that. I was scared of you, of your power. I was young and you were strong and intimidating. I'll make it up to you, my sweet brother. Please come to me, my love! Take me!"

Thomas looked at her not with love, but with lust and possessiveness. He reached out to take her by the waist, but his spectral form passed through her like an electric shock.

He reached for her breasts and face, but again, he couldn't touch her. He growled in frustration.

Elsie leaned forward and whispered in his ghostly ear.

"I want you inside me," she whispered seductively.

Thomas shuddered and groaned as the remainder of the surrounding darkness coalesced into him, making him physical once more. Elsie could feel his rancid breath on her face and reached out to touch his hand. It was cold and pallid, but it was solid.

"My dear sister," he mewled.

"Now!" Elsie yelled.

A shot rang out.

Thomas made a gagging sound as a bullet that Harriet fired from Elsie's pistol passed through his neck and caused his head to jerk to the side and spray Elsie with his blood.

He put a hand to his throat and melted back into a shapeless cloud of darkness. The dark, swirling mass sprayed crimson blood and wriggling maggots as it writhed in the air like a wounded animal.

Elsie saw the blood sprayed on her wriggled with small worms and maggots. She tried to slap them off her face and arms in a panic.

The dark cloud continued to spray an inhuman amount of blood and soaked the surrounding area in a gory rain.

The blackness surrounded them and swirled even faster.

"Harriet, get Marta out of here! Go back to the house!" Elsie said as she stooped down and picked up the shotgun again.

They backed up a few feet but didn't leave.

The cyclone of black smoke and blood suddenly stopped and was perfectly still. All was quiet except the sound of her and Harriet breathing.

Harriet fired the pistol into the darkness, but the bullets passed through harmlessly.

"He's there. Pull the trigger," Harriet whispered.

"Where? I don't see him."

"Right in front of you. Fire!"

Elsie couldn't see what Harriet saw and looked around frantically for Thomas. She couldn't see him but trusted her. She pulled the trigger, firing from the hip.

The shotgun boomed, and she was rewarded when the rock salt round stopped in mid-air, burning and sizzling.

Thomas screamed in pain, and for a brief second, she could see a shadowy figure trying to claw the salt away. A heavy stream of blood flowed from his ghostly form.

She fired again, hitting him in the gut and causing the incorporeal form of her brother to fall back and disappear out of sight once again.

"Harriet, I can't see him. Where did he go?"

"He's still there. He's still straight in front of you, a few feet further back."

Elsie fired, and Thomas screamed again.

"That little bitch can see me? How?! We'll see what happens when I gouge out her eyes!"

"Elsie, he's coming right at me! Shoot him!"

She had to guess where he was, so she raised the gun to her shoulder and fired.

The shotgun went off, but nothing happened. No scream. No burning little embers of smoke and fire.

She missed.

Harriet flew back and was knocked to the ground.

She struggled to get to her feet, but something held her down.

Elsie stepped to the side to get a better angle and fired again. The blast struck Thomas once more.

Harriet, now freed, jumped to her feet, ran to Elsie's side and clung to her arm.

"You are mine, little sister!" came Thomas' voice from all around them.

The voice warbled and sounded much weaker than before. Out of the darkness, more blood gushed, and she could tell he was growing weaker. As it bled, the dark cloud grew smaller and smaller. Daylight shone on Elsie once more as the darkness retracted. It retreated and solidified until it was nothing but a frail and dead decomposing body. It hung lifeless in the air. The scars that Elsie gave him years ago were still visible on the corpse. It rotated, suspended in the air as if on a string, its dead, milky white eyes stared at Elsie.

Harriet ran up, smoking pistol in her hand and began to bat away the things that were wriggling all over Elsie.

"Get them off me!" she panicked.

"There you go. All's good, baby. We got them all off you," Harriet said in a soothing and motherly voice.

Elsie slowed her breathing and managed to calm down as she inspected herself, making sure she was clean from the disgusting things that lived in Thomas' blood.

She looked up and his body floated, suspended in the air as it slowly rotated a few feet away.

"Why is he still here" Elsie asked.

"He's still in there. The body is dead, but his soul is still clinging on," Harriet said.

"How do we put a stop to that?" Elsie asked.

"I can help with that," Marta said, stepping forward.

Before Elsie could tell her to back away, the spectral forms of several men appeared around the decrepit form of Thomas. They were transparent and still wore the trappings of their profession. Thick dungarees, caps, gloves and toolbelts decorated the ghosts.

"The electricians," Harriet whispered.

They raised their arms in unison and looked up to the sky. Writhing tentacles of dark mist snaked out of Thomas's body and flew up, following the ghost's gaze. The strands of smoke quickly disappeared as the sun evaporated the darkness away.

The body twitched and let out a long breath as what passed for Thomas' soul left its corpse. The body finally fell to the ground and crumbled into dust and ash, the slight breeze scattered what was left over the grassy fields. The ghosts of the sacrificed electricians smiled at each other, then faded from view until they were gone.

Elsie walked over to the disintegrating body and spat on it with all the contempt she could muster.

"You fucking monster. I hope you burn in hell."

Harriet put her arms around her and dug her face into Elsie's neck and let her know she was there.

Marta walked up to the pile of ash and looked at it like it was an interesting bug and shrugged.

"The sleeping people told me to come here. The thing you

are looking for is in there," she said and pointed to the ruins where Thomas had made human sacrifices years ago.

"I didn't see any obsidian stone box in there when I looked last time," Elsie said, voice trembling.

The things she had to say to her brother troubled her far more than being forced to kill him. She wanted nothing more than to shower, get clean, curl up in Harriet's lap, and forget about what had happened. The thought that she was related to that creature disgusted her.

Harriet walked over to the ruins and looked in. Confusion spread over her face.

"I don't get it. I don't see anything."

"Alva says to look closer and close your eyes, dummy. Sorry, she said dummy, not me."

"That doesn't make any sense, but I'll give it a try," Harriet said and closed her eyes.

She scrunched up her eyes and concentrated harder, then opened them again.

"I still don't see anything."

"She says don't force it. She used a word I don't know the meaning of, but it sounded mean, so I won't repeat it."

"Fine."

Harriet closed her eyes once again. This time she did not look like she was concentrating. Several minutes passed in silence before her arm raised and she pointed to what Elsie thought of as the altar in this wicked little ruin of a temple.

"There. I can see it plain as day."

Harriet walked over to the altar and moved her hands, as if to pick some invisible thing up. Once she touched it, it became visible to everyone.

A roughhewn, obsidian stone box with four rings on each side appeared in her hands. No decorations were visible, and it was smaller than she envisioned; only one by two feet.

"That's it. That's the box," Harriet said with finality.

Elsie rushed over and with some effort, lifted the lid.

Nothing was inside. Elsie sighed and returned the lid.

"My father has the mirror. We need to go get it now."

"I figured as much. I wouldn't expect them to hide both of these things together. That would have been too easy," Harriet said.

"I guess we are going to have to do this the hard way. Go in and get the mirror and excise my father like a cancer."

"Go in where?"

"Into the mirror in the attic."

"What are you talking about?"

"I need to finish reading the book Abrahm procured for me. There was an account of a priest of Smoking Mirror that could travel through mirrors. Maybe my father found a way to do the same. He seems to exercise a large amount of influence through them. Let's go back to the house for now. I have a question for you, Harriet."

"Yes?"

"Why didn't you shoot Thomas in the head? It would have ended him much more quickly."

"Oh, that. I tried. The sights on your Mauser are terrible. Get a better gun."

Chapter 37

Harriet ate dinner as she watched Elsie read. She had a plate in front of her but hadn't paid any attention to it. She didn't know if it was because Elsie was too engrossed in her book or because she was disturbed by the events of the day.

The woman she loved had just been forced to kill her brother and so far, had been very detached from it. If she had to kill her brother, she'd be an emotional mess, even if he was a spoiled deviant like Elsie's.

Of course, Elsie had killed men before, so maybe it gets easier? Maybe an emotional breakthrough will come later and if it does, she'll be here for her.

She herself was barely holding it together. Remembering the dark and misty form of Thomas on top of her, trying to gouge her eyes out, was almost too much. She really didn't feel like experiencing something like that again, especially so soon. She noticed her hand tremble as she lifted the fork to her mouth. Thomas's leering face appeared in her vision again, and she lost all appetite.

She looked over at the mysterious black box they found, now sitting on the dining room table. She expected it to be menacing and give off an aura of evil and darkness. But no. She didn't feel anything as it sat there, nothing more than a plain old stone box.

"You think they'll try to come after it?" she asked.

"Excuse me, what?" Elsie said, snapping out of it.

"Do you think they'll come after the box?"

"I'm sure they will try," Elsie said, taking another small bite of her food for the first time.

"Why am I the only one concerned?"

"You're not. I'm deeply concerned. You think I want to die? Hardly. But we are as prepared as we'll ever be. We have the candle. If a horde of cultists try, we'll gun'em down. If that Smoking Mirror thing shows up, not much we can do. Maybe the candle will keep it at bay. Maybe my pistol would hurt it, like Thomas talked about? Maybe it's a spirit and our rock salt rounds would work? Or just hope that mysterious stranger shows up and drives it off again," Elsie explained.

"That's...a terrible plan."

"I didn't say it was a plan, but it's all we got, unless I find something in this book about how to kill an Aztec god."

"What about you, Marta? How are you doing?"

Harriet looked over at her and the ghost girl; Alva floated behind Marta. Her huge, dead grey eyes stared at nothing. Her spirit faded in and out. Sometimes she looked solid and other times she was barely visible, even to Harriet.

Marta shrugged.

"I'm okay. The sleeping people here are happy now that Elsie's brother is gone. They are happy so they left. They were nice. Alva says that Elsie's daddy is very angry and will try to get the box tonight."

"I'll go hide it in our bedroom and keep reading," Elsie said as she stood from the table, leaving her dinner almost untouched.

She scooped up the stone box in both hands and marched

upstairs with some grunts and groans. Harriet's own plate sat almost untouched but she waited for Marta to finish eating before standing. Harriet gathered the plates and went to the kitchen. She washed the dishes and put them away as she thought about facing Elsie's father and what kind monster he'd turn out to be. She was lost in thought when a small pebble hit the window above the sink and startled her.

It was dark outside, but the lights inside made her see her own reflection. When she turned off the wall switch, the room was thrown into darkness. Through the window, she strained to see who could have thrown the rock. Two figures stepped into view.

It was Leroy and Orson, her two little brothers.

Leroy put his finger to his lips and motioned for her to come outside.

Harriet dropped the dish towel on the counter and hurried to the front door. She stopped herself before she touched the knob.

"It's a trap," she told herself.

Harriet went to the parlor and grabbed a shotgun. She opened the door a little and peeked outside. She didn't see anything, so she opened the door further.

Still nothing.

She kept low and tried to stay as quiet as possible. She crept around the porch over to the side where the kitchen window was and looked around the corner of the house.

Her two little brothers stood there, looking at the kitchen window. They stayed motionless, except for their hands, which twitched and convulsed as if they had a mind of their own and wanted to wrap their fingers around the first throat they could find.

Harriet closed her eyes and tried to open her mind like she did when she found the obsidian box. Concentration wasn't the key. All she had to do was shift her perception and open up her mind.

All was dark, but as she opened her mind's eye, her two brothers shifted into focus, two beings of light in a field of blackness. Only now, they didn't look like her brothers. She could see their true nature. They looked like fly larva that grew misshapen and Ill-proportioned limbs and giant spikes for teeth. They had no eyes, and their heads consisted of nothing but giant, fanged maws that pulsated open and closed in anticipation of their next meal.

Harriet recoiled at the obscene creatures and knocked her shotgun on the side of the house, causing a loud noise.

The creatures turned their translucent, eyeless heads toward Harriet, gave a loud and angry hiss, then turned and ran off on all fours into the dark night.

Harriet hurried back inside and locked the door behind her. She said a quick prayer in her mind as she tried to control her heavy breathing.

The phone in the kitchen rang, startling her further.

Harriet went to the kitchen and answered the phone.

"Hello? Who is this?"

There was a strange, muffled sound on the other end, like the phone was being brushed against fabric.

"Return the box, Harriet. You don't know what you are dealing with. Put it out on the porch and no one will get hurt," came the stern voice of her dad.

Harriet didn't for a second believe it was him.

"That's a pathetic attempt. You try to trick me with some maggots dressed like my brothers and now this lame attempt right after? You must be scared and desperate."

"Bring me the box," came a familiar, strange but calm androgynous voice.

It was Smoking Mirror.

"Bring me the box and I will spare you the slow and agonizing torment I have set aside for you."

Harriet's voice broke when she responded.

"And if I don't?"

"Then you will suffer and die in ways that your kind haven't envisioned yet. The ones you care for will also suffer painful and gruesome deaths, devoid of dignity and mercy at my terrible hands. My hands are everywhere."

"What if I plan to seal you up in this box before you can hurt anyone else?"

"You can try. Maybe you will succeed. It has happened before but my hands, my followers and loyal slaves, are numerous and always find me. I have destroyed many earthly kingdoms. I was ancient and beyond days when I brought down the haughty Minoans, powerful Hittites and the scholarly Harappans. They all knew my face and my hands and suffered as the Mayans and Aztecs did. My hands have always been with mankind and always will be. I will rise by their endeavor to crush mankind's achievements. Your nation is ripe for the plucking. Give me the box now and I will spare you and your loved ones the fire and blood that is to come."

"And what makes you think I'd trust anything you say? You are an evil being, a fallen angel and nothing but lies and foulness. I'd give you the box and you'd still sacrifice Elsie, kill me and destroy everything around you. Instead, I propose this: We seal you up in your little box and put you to sleep. Then, we'll hide the box somewhere nobody will ever find it. There will be no stories or clues for your little cultists to follow and dig you up. The only people that will know will be me and Elsie and when we return to the dust from which we come, all mention of you, all hope of anyone finding you, will die with us. That is the deal. That is what you are going to get from us. Then, for good measure, we'll find your followers and hunt them down until they are wiped off the face of the Earth. An avenging angel will be visiting you soon. Back to the outer darkness from which you came, beast!"

Harriet slammed the phone down, all fear replaced by righteous indignation.

Elsie stood in the doorway of the kitchen with a shocked look on her face.

"Did you just tell a god to go to hell?" Elsie asked, stunned.

Harriet thought about it for a second and nodded her head.

"That is no god, but yes. Yes, I did."

"Good job."

"I probably pissed him off though."

"Good. Let it know what it's like to be angry and scared for once," Elsie said.

"It really wants that box. Is it safe here? What can we do with it?"

"We just need to keep it out of their hands until we can get the mirror and put this thing back to sleep. It's also close to the candle, which hasn't died down one iota yet, so I think that'll protect it, too. As for getting the mirror, I think I know how to get it, I just don't know how to stop him once there. However, I heard a saying many times while I was in France: No plan survives first contact with the enemy. So, maybe we shouldn't overthink this one. Maybe we should go in and improvise. It's hard to plan for something we know nothing about anyway."

"That's a good point, but we should try to prepare for whatever comes at us. I don't think bullets will help us this time," Harriet said, slipping out of her clothes and getting into bed.

"That brings me to another point. Thomas said something about my pistol. He said that I have a connection with it and that's why I could hurt him,"

She pulled the pistol from its holster and inspected it as if she was seeing it for the first time.

"I bought this pistol off a British officer while I was still recovering from…"

Elsie trailed off but the look on her face didn't betray what emotions she was feeling.

"I bought it so I could kill myself with it. At the time, I liked the irony of dying by the pistol that saved my life, but it's not so funny now. I was going to do it, you know. That night. I had the barrel against my head and finger on the trigger. Something stopped me then and has stopped me every time I've tried to do it since."

"What was that?" Harriet said softly, not trying to interrupt.

"Hope."

Elsie rushed over to the book she had been reading and opened it up.

"Here! In the vague and brief description of the ceremony to seal Smoking Mirror, it mentions a talisman, but it doesn't give a description. We have to strike the mirror with the talisman and place it in the box. I didn't know what the book meant, but I figured we could find or even make one. I also assumed my father would have one on him, being the new high priest of Smoking Mirror and all. If this bastard soaks up negative emotions, then maybe a talisman of good emotions will hurt it. It has always been there for me. Looks like it will serve me in this, too."

"That is good news. We have a weapon that can hurt it and a talisman to put him away for good. Now, come to bed. We had a big day today and we have a bigger one tomorrow."

Chapter 38

Elsie had been studying since she woke at four in the morning. She needed to find the right incantation and then memorize it. Since the book Abram had procured at the university library treated all Reymundo Diaz' accounts as tall tales and folklore, it didn't bother getting too detailed about the specificities.

She did, however, find a phrase that kept repeating throughout the book in regard to Smoking Mirror. It wasn't his axiom, 'we are his slaves, by whom we live'. It was another phrase:

"Ia Ia. In ie tlecujlixquac, in ie tlamamatlac. Itech naci in Tezcatlipoca. Hail. Hail. Already at the edge of fire, already at the stairway. I join Smoking Mirror," she said, speaking the strange words out loud.

The small electrical nightstand light flickered and grew dim. A wave of nausea struck and doubled her over.

The words on the page seemed to glow with a faint but brief unearthly green light.

Elsie tried to shake off the effects of the incantation. She felt sickly and just plain wrong but as she took deep breaths, the effects faded.

"I assume I found the right incantation."

Elsie sneaked out of the bed, trying not to wake Harriet and grabbed a small mirror from a drawer in her vanity. She propped it up so it stood on its side.

She stood in front of the mirror and steadied herself, ready for anything that might happen and repeated the incantation.

She felt sick again, though not nearly as bad as the first time.

The mirror in front of her turned black, but not an ordinary black. It was the complete absence of light and a profound depth of all-encompassing void. She stared into it, watching the slight movements inside the blackness, as if it were a great maw opening to swallow her whole.

"I don't feel so good, baby," Harriet said in a confused and sleepy voice.

"It'll pass quickly."

"What are you doing?"

"It's okay. It's all under control. I think."

Harriet noticed the mirror and recoiled, drawing the sheets around her like armor.

"What's going on?" she asked, with wide eyes and quick breaths.

"There's no danger. Just watch."

Elsie picked up a mostly used tin of foundation from her makeup drawer and gently tossed it at the mirror.

It flew through the air and disappeared as it touched the nothingness.

"What we have here, my darling, is a doorway to where my father resides and to the mirror he hopefully possesses. Once we are ready, we'll all go through and confront that bastard."

"I wonder if Marta could see what's on the other side.

Some reconnaissance would be a great help before we jump into a magic portal completely blind."

"Good idea. Let's see if she can help us out."

Harriet dressed in the same sailor suit she wore on the picnic but with a gun belt strapped around her waist and a 1911 tucked in the holster.

Elsie thought it was an odd choice and gave her a quizzical look.

Harriet noticed she was being stared at and figured out it was because of her wardrobe.

"What? If I'm going to die today, I want to look cute," Harriet said with a shrug.

"Nobody is dying today," Elsie said.

"What do we do with Marta while we go in to confront your father? We can't leave her alone. She's such an innocent and vulnerable person. She could be captured or killed or just wander off, and either of those two options I couldn't live with. Look what happened after we left her alone for just a few minutes last time. Heaven help us, but it is our job to keep her safe. She didn't ask to be a part of all this," Harriet said.

"We should bring her with us. If she can talk to spirits and stuff, maybe it'd be a good idea to take her along," Elsie said.

They gathered Marta and ascended up to the attic. The three of them stood in front of the mirror, determined. Elsie tried her best not to show her fear, but the tremor in her hands gave her away. She had something to live for now and wanted nothing more than to keep Harriet safe.

Thoughts of running somewhere far away and leaving all of this behind filled her mind, even though she knew it wouldn't work. Smoking Mirror and its cult would find them. Her father would find them.

"I hate the idea of leaving the box here, even with the candle to protect it," Elsie mumbled.

"The candle is here and it's hidden. It'll be safe for now. We better hurry though."

Elsie checked the chamber of her shotgun for the tenth time and let out a long breath.

"Marta, can your friends see into the mirror? Can they tell us what's going to happen?"

Marta shook her head.

"No. They only see this world."

"Everyone ready?" Elsie asked, keeping her eye on the mirror.

Harriet nodded and Marta looked around bored and distracted.

"Good enough."

Elsie reached out, threw the blanket off the mirror and tossed it to the side.

The mirror sat unchanged, but an ominous feeling filled her heart with dread.

Elsie cleared her throat.

"Ia Ia. In ic tlecujlixquac, in ie tlamamatlac. Itech naci in Tezcatlipoca."

The mirror's reflective surface turned into a black void and the air around her thrummed with pulsing energy.

Before she could talk herself out of it, she stepped forward and walked into the mirror.

Chapter 39

Fingers of burning cold caressed her skin as she stepped through the mirror into another world. It took a minute for her eyes to adjust but when they did, she found herself in what looked like a small, picturesque town.

The streets were bare rock and dirt, but the buildings are what disturbed her. The buildings and houses were shaped like a sleepy, Mediterranean coastal village, complete with tiled roofs, pillars, porches and verandas. The difference was, and what gave Elsie a cold shiver, the buildings were devoid of all color and made of wispy, pure black shadow.

Every building and every detail were discernable, but the edges were fuzzy and gave the town a look that a good, stiff breeze would blow the whole thing away.

Tendrils of shadow played off the edges of the roofs as if they blew in a nonexistent breeze.

Elsie looked behind her and saw a great stone archway that marked the beginning of this town and the edge of this world, because there was nothing beyond it, just the dark void of the open mirror.

"What am I looking at?" Harriet said as she appeared next to her.

"It's an entire town made from shadow. Did he build this all somehow? Is this something he saw once and copied it here?" Harriet stammered, the nervousness showing in her voice.

The Architect of Shadow.

"There are no voices here," Marta said.

The door of a house they stood next to opened and a figure walked out. It looked to be made of the same substance the buildings were made of, but pure white. It was female and completely nude. Also, like the buildings, every detail could be made out. What was more disturbing was the fact she had no eyes, just empty sockets.

The shadow person ignored them and walked by, headed for the center of town.

"Let us follow it and see if it leads us to my father," Elsie whispered.

They followed the figure and kept a safe distance. More of the shadow people came out of the buildings, joining each other in the streets, all headed for the same place.

They were now surrounded by hundreds of shadow people but were completely ignored, as if they didn't exist.

Elsie bumped into one, a man, and felt a solid presence. They might look like they were made of shadow, but they were physically real.

Elsie noticed that every male looked like an Adonis, while every female looked like an Aphrodite. If they were real people, they would be perfect physical examples of the human form.

"This is really creepy," Marta whispered.

"Architect of Shadows. I can see why he calls himself that now. This is his dream world he created," Elsie whispered back.

They followed the crowd to what looked like a town square. There was no tumult or press of bodies. Thousands of the shadow people thronged the square and around a giant statue.

The statue looked like her father but wore what looked like Aztec priestly robes. One hand held a mirror and the other held javelins or arrows.

The shadow people fell to their knees in silent supplication and raised their hands to the statue as if in worship.

"So, this is your father's made-up dream world?" Harriet asked.

"He is nothing if not consistently narcissistic."

"Look at that," Harriet said, pointing up.

Over the horizon of buildings and houses, Elsie saw a hill out past the town, covered in mist. On the hill was a giant mansion of impossible and contradictory architecture of no known style.

"That would be where he is," Elsie said as she pushed her way through the crowd in the direction of the mansion.

Past the town square, the crowds thinned out. Elsie looked back and the shadow people revilers had started a massive and violent orgy at the base of the statue. Limbs flailed as they pressed against each other noiselessly. The shadow people, one after another, climbed the statue and flung themselves into the throng. There was no effort to catch them, and their bodies crashed into the ones on the ground, where they would be pulled apart by the crowd. Tendrils of smoke leaked out of the severed limbs in place of blood, and the body parts were then used as weapons or for sexual gratification.

She had to look away quickly, as what little she saw sickened her.

They made their way through the empty streets and soon came to the edge of the town. A long and winding road lead up the bleak and barren hill to her father's mansion.

"Marta, how are you holding up?" Harriet asked as she wrapped her arm around her shoulders.

"I'm okay. There are no voices. No sleeping people here. It's quiet but I've seen that house before. In a dream. There's a monster inside."

Elsie knew that already. Her father was a monster in every sense of the word.

They began the long trek up the hill. Her pocket watch had stopped working and no sun shone to judge the passage of time. Since there was no sun, there was no warmth. But it wasn't cold. It was nothing. There was no sensation. No life.

Elsie thought that if Harriet had this same power, she would have created a landscape of vibrant color, warmth and full of life. Her father chose to create something distant and lifeless, only suitable to fulfill his carnal desires and to be worshiped.

"Architect of shadows my ass. Let's go finish this," Elsie said.

After what seemed like hours, they made it to the top, tired and winded.

They took a few moments to rest and catch their breath before approaching the mansion.

The mansion, like everything else, was made of shadow. Every brick and stone looked flawless and was rendered in exquisite detail in the dark and misty matter. The closer she inspected the mansion, the weirder it became. At first glance, it looked like everything else in this odd world. But every time she turned her head, she could see the shadows move and flow like water around rocks in a stream. The angles and geometry were all wrong and impossible in the real world, and her head hurt the more she looked.

She tore her eyes from the evil place and with her head down, approached the front door.

The front doors were gigantic, and Elsie instantly recognized them. They were modeled after the doors of the Roman Pantheon.

A house of gods. Of course he'd do that.

She raised a hand to try to open them, but the doors swung open on their own before she could.

They looked at each other but none of them knew what to say.

"I guess it's no surprise he's expecting us," Harriet said and walked in.

They walked cautiously into the mansion. Inside, the furnishings were real. They were not made of shadow and mist but, had obviously been brought from the real world. Elsie recognized the portrait of her great grandfather, a Southern plantation owner whom her father idolized. The rest of the furnishings looked new, as if they had never been used. She doubted he received many callers.

An androgynous white shadow figure walked into the room. Like the others, it had no eyes. It also had no arms but wore delicate and feminine jewelry around its slender waist and neck.

It bowed to them, and then walked back from where it came.

"Why, ain't it a courteous little shadow demon," Harriet said in her best Southern Belle voice.

"Should we follow it?"

"He knows we are here. Maybe he wants to make a deal? Whatever happens, let's remain calm. If he wants to talk, let him talk. Maybe we can get more information from him. I'll try to do most of the talking, you all keep an eye out for the mirror," Elsie whispered.

They followed the shadow thing down the hall and through a great pair of polished mahogany doors. Inside was a lavish and gaudily decorated drawing room. A cyclopean fireplace took up most of the opposite wall and bookshelves occupied the remaining wall space. A carpet, similar to the ones in her own house, covered the floor and several high-backed leather chairs formed a rough circle in the middle of the room.

"Come in. Have a seat and make yourselves at home, honored guests."

Elsie walked into the circle of chairs and saw her father.

He wore slacks, a smoking jacket with an ascot and fuzzy looking slippers. A giant cigar hung out one side of his mouth. A bottle of whiskey and a small glass of ice sat on a small, round end table next to him. A second edition copy of 'The Count of Monte Cristo' sat in his lap.

"Welcome to my humble abode. I've been expecting you. I have seats for each of you. Please, don't be shy. Make yourselves at home. Refreshments?"

Several shadows lined against one wall. All wore butler or maid uniforms, only they were bare below the waist. Each one held a silver tray with different foods and drinks.

"You...you tried to kill me and now you want me sit down and have a damn sandwich?" Harriet said, doing a bad job of holding her temper.

He chuckled as if he just heard a slightly amusing joke.

"Oh, come now. That's water under the bridge. Never take business personally. I know I don't. I never used to let anyone not of the master race into my house, yet here you are, an honored guest."

"Why, you slimy piece of...," Harriet started when Elsie held up a hand for her to stop.

Elsie took a seat opposite to him, trying to act as nonchalant as possible with a shotgun cradled on her lap.

"Ah, and the little retarded spic oracle girl. You especially have been problematic for us."

Marta didn't respond. She trembled and hid behind the chair Harriet stood next to. Harriet had refused to take a seat.

"I thought not. Oh well. You know, I was very saddened to

hear about the death of Thomas. Oh, the tears I shed for that boy. He was loyal but he was always weak. I admit, you continue to surprise me, daughter."

"I'm glad I can keep you on your toes then, father."

"I blame all that time away from home. I see where I made grave errors in your upbringing. If I knew then what I know now, I would have educated you at home. Instead, you were exposed to the lies of Jews, race traitors, sub humans and now you've made yourself a whore to one."

"Funny how education is anathema to your philosophy. Truly, only the ignorant would believe in you."

Walter Everly paused and a dark look broke through his calm and cordial countenance.

"I will remind you, you are still guests in this house and you will not speak to me in that manner."

"Why don't we get down to brass tacks then? You obviously want to talk, otherwise you would have had your fantasy world here attack us on sight. So, what is it you want?"

"Getting down to business. That's the Everly in you. Yes, let's get down to business then. My patron, Smoking Mirror, as you know him by, knows all and sees all. We know you understand our purpose, to bring him back to life. He is but a shell of his former self. We can't do that without you. I am willing to cut a deal with you. You give yourself up. Let me cut out your heart and replace it with something much more powerful, and you will be given life again. Eternal life. You will be Smoking Mirror's avatar and mouthpiece in his world to come. You will topple empires and gain the riches of the world and dominion over mankind. All the undesirable races will eventually be sacrificed and fed to our lord, but we'll let you keep our dear Harriet here. I'll even let her family live if that makes you happy. You can have it all and keep your loved ones safe. Live with the woman you love in absolute wealth and power for all eternity, because you will be immortal like me. I can't die. Every wish you ever had will be fulfilled, if you would just submit. No more fear, pain, death, heartache and no more nightmares. Can you imagine? Who in this world has ever been given a chance such as this? The power of the mirror will be yours, too. You can create your own worlds. Every inhabitant will be at your beck and call. The corrupt empires of man will fall, as they have been orchestrated before. No more greedy capitalists! No more cabal of Jewish conspirators! No more diluting white blood with filth! There is nothing so pure as to fulfill your every desire!"

He sat back in his chair and puffed his cigar, a smug look on his face.

"Well, that is quite the offer, father. Just so I am aware, what is the alternative? What happens if I refuse?"

"That's easy. I will have my slaves hold you down as I force you to watch me torture, rape and kill Harriet, in that order, until you agree. I have absolute power here and the mirror grants me just a small fraction of my lord's power. But you, you can have it all!"

"Why me? Why couldn't you sacrifice yourself and gain the world? Why go through all of this?"

"It's not that simple, child. There is an order of things. The rights and rituals must be observed. Even Smoking Mirror can't break some rules, and I am his chief priest, so I must abide. I can't have his powers, but I am granted the power of the mirror, and as you can see, I am beyond human. I'm a god here. You will be his voice and have the power to do his will. Thomas was too weak willed to be a vessel for our lord. It requires a strong will and intelligence to be an avatar for a god. I naturally have that in abundance, but it is not my place."

"So Smoking Mirror, as powerful as it is, still has to follow rules? So, it has a boss? You worship a servant? An underling? Why don't you worship what Smoking Mirror obeys?" Elsie said as she looked around the room nonchalantly.

Walter did not like that at all. He puffed on his cigar angrily.

She used this time to try to find the mirror. It was too big to keep in a pocket and he would keep it near him at all times. She couldn't stall him forever and time was running out.

She could see Harriet and Marta whispering to each other. She hoped they had a plan.

"Because it is so incomprehensible that it is above notice. Even the prayers of the gods themselves don't catch its ear, let alone prayers of insignificant specks like humans. It is vast and infinite. It's all knowing and all powerful, but it doesn't acknowledge lesser beings. It's the insane god. Better to worship something that actually listens and can grant blessings and give you power. It simply is, and its high priests around the universe interpret its insane ramblings, and all obey whether we realize it or not. If you listen carefully, you can hear the music it makes."

Elsie did try to listen. At first, she heard nothing, but as she filtered out the ambient sounds of the fireplace, her breathing and beating of her heart, she did hear something. She heard what sounded like distant and eerie trumpets or flutes. It was a quiet cacophony, and as she listened harder, the noises of the trumpets melded into a mad babbling and mumbling. It was insane and incomprehensible, but she heard it. She heard a voice. A great and terrible voice that filled her with dread.

She threw her hands over her ears, fearful that if she heard any more, she would lose her sanity.

Walter laughed.

"You heard it. Good. That's a sign that you are meant to be the vessel for Smoking Mirror. Its voice follows me wherever I go, but I've learned to drown it out. I actually met a group of people in the depths of the Persian desert that could hear it and worshiped it. They were dark and mad priests of a dying religion, hunted by the emperors and mullahs over the centuries, until only they remained. They called it Azothoth and only the truly insane worship it."

"Are there other such gods as Smoking Mirror?" Elsie asked, now a little shaken.

The revelation of a being such as that existing terrified her, but she needed to know more.

Walter Everly leaned forward with a smile on his face.

"More than you will ever know."

He laughed at Elsie's discomfort and leaned back.

"Come now. We've done enough catching up and family bonding. What path do you choose? Do you come of your own free will, gladly accepting the riches and power of becoming a vessel for a god? Or do you choose the difficult path, which is long and perilous and ends up with the death of your friends and you begging to be sacrificed just to end the pain? I need an answer."

"What was that first option again?"

Walter stood up and threw his copy of 'The Count of Monte Cristo' into the fire.

"A book written by a subhuman and filled with sapphic references. Of course you'd like it, you little slut. Enough stalling! What say you?"

"Here's your answer, you son of a bitch!" Elsie stood up, yanking the pistol from its holster. The world seemed to slow down as she listened to the barrel slide against the dark, worn leather of the holster. The satisfying release and silence as the barrel escaped its confines let her know to rotate the pistol forward and punch out. The front site lined up on her father's chest and she smoothly and effortlessly pulled back on the trigger. The bolt flew back and the pistol bucked in her hand. She stroked the trigger ten times, keeping the sights on her father. As she did so, all her practice paid off, as all ten rounds found their mark.

Walter fell back into his chair, grunting from pain. His wounds sprayed dark and partially congealed blood infested with maggots everywhere. The thick and ropey strands spewed from his chest, hanging in the air as if gravity failed.

Little tongues of fire licked out from the bullet holes. He yelled to his slaves.

"Grab them! Don't let any of them go!" Walter Everly screamed.

White and hazy, but impossibly strong hands grabbed her, pinned her arms and wrapped her in a vice-like embrace.

Elsie struggled, but they had her. She could not escape.

Chapter 40

"You...you tried to kill me, and now you want me sit down and have a damn sandwich?" Harriet said, trying her hardest not to shoot him in the face with her shotgun.

They needed time to find the mirror, and making him angry wouldn't help.

She refused to take a seat, mostly because he asked, but also because if things went sideways, she would be ready to run.

Harriet didn't pay attention to what Walter Everly was saying. She was too busy looking for where he would hide the mirror. Her guess was that he had it on him. Something that gave him this much power would be with him at all times. He would never part with it.

Elsie and her dad talked back and forth. She did a good job of keeping him occupied.

Marta leaned over and whispered.

"Can you use that same trick you used to find the box?"

Then Harriet remembered how she'd found the box and took a deep breath to relax. She let her mind expand without forcing it and released something deep inside herself.

Her sight came to her. Everything appeared as vague outlines and shadows, except for people. She could see people in every detail, except she saw them how they really are.

She looked at Elsie. She was bright and strong, and in this second sight, she had no scars. She glowed like an angel. There were cracks, however. It was as if she was made of porcelain and there was a network of spider web cracks all over her. She looked so fragile that Harriet was scared to touch her in case she fell apart.

Oh, my poor Elsie.

Marta shined like an angel as well, but without the cracks or bruising or darkness. She was a pure soul, but as Harriet looked closer, she could see that parts of her mind were closed, as if they were imprisoned behind locked doors. Harriet wondered if those doors could be unlocked somehow.

What a great mind that would be.

Then she looked over at Walter Everly and froze in place. What sat in that chair was not a person. It was a desiccated corpse.

The mummified flesh stretched too thinly over his bones. His hair was sparse and hung in matted clumps. He had no eyes, just empty voids that looked as if he had scratched or clawed his own eyes out years ago. The emptiness of his sockets cast a dark light on everything he gazed upon. That wasn't what was most disturbing to Harriet. In the middle of Walter's forehead, was a great, inhuman eye, living and pulsating. It had one big pupil in the center and several smaller ones that would appear and fade away seconds later. The eye constantly moved and twitched but thankfully wasn't looking her direction.

She looked away for a second to gather her courage, then looked for the mirror once more.

Walter and Elsie still talked, then Walter stood up angrily and yelled at Elsie.

There!

When he stood up, she could see the small table on the other side. On top of the table was the mirror. This evil creature was using it to put his drinks and ashtray on.

Walter continued to yell at Elsie, so they didn't have much time. She was about to sprint for it, to try to grab it, when she felt a pull at her sleeve.

Harriet opened her eyes, vision returning to normal.

Marta pulled on her with one hand, and in the other hand she held both the spirit candle and a match.

"You forgot to bring this. It will protect us."

Marta nodded at Harriet and urged her to take it. She kissed Marta on the forehead and took the candle.

Harriet heard several gunshots and Elsie yelled something. She looked quickly enough to see Walter fall back into his chair and knew she had no time left.

"Grab them! Don't let any of them go!" Walter Everly screamed.

Harriet lit the candle.

The light that came out of the candle burst like an explosion, blowing away and dispersing the mists that made up this sick fantasy world like a hurricane. The walls of shadow disintegrated around her as if they never existed.

Several of the disturbing shadow people that had grabbed and held Elsie, ceased to exist when the light hit them. The entire building disappeared except for the chairs, tables and throw rugs that Walter had brought here from the real world.

Walter Everly's façade disappeared too, and everyone could see his true and monstrous self. Nothing hid what he truly was now.

Harriet shoved the candle into Marta's hands and picked up her shotgun. Walter rose to his feet and knocked the drinks and cigars off the little table at his side.

"He's going for the mirror!" Harriet said as she raised the shotgun and fired two of the salt rounds into him.

Walter recoiled. He stepped back and clutched his skull-like face.

Harriet rushed in and grabbed the mirror from off the table, held it to her chest and ran.

"Let's get out of here!" she shouted.

She stopped to make sure Marta followed and saw Elsie shoot Walter again and knock him down before she started to run. Elsie let her shotgun dangle on its sling and tried to reload her pistol as she rushed by Harriet.

"Stay in the light of the candle. Stick together!" Harriet shouted as she took up the rear, close to Marta, who was holding the candle up like she was the Statue of Liberty. The candle caused the shadows to retreat, as darkness always does before the light.

They ran down the hill when Walter burst through the shadowy ruins of his mansion in pursuit of them on foot. For a withered corpse, he ran inhumanly fast.

When Walter approached, Harriet fired two rounds at his legs, which caused him to stumble and fall. He was quickly back on his feet, but it created some distance.

Walter leaped down the hill and jumped impossibly far, higher than any human could. He tried to get ahead of them, but Elsie shot him out of the sky like she was skeet shooting. He tumbled out of the sky and landed hard several feet behind them.

"Nice shooting!"

"Thanks," Elsie said breathily, trying to keep up.

They approached the town. The streets filled with the pale shadow people, arms raised and running toward them.

"Let's go around. We won't be able to make it through that," Elsie said.

"No time. The candle is from this place. It doesn't burn

down in our world, because it's not from there, but it is burning down now. I don't think we have time to go around," Marta said in a calm, soft voice and pointed to the diminishing candle.

To Harriet's horror, the candle had melted and grew smaller by the second.

"But don't worry, the light will protect us," Marta said and walked down the street, as a hoard of shadows came toward her.

"She hasn't been wrong yet," Harriet said and followed her.

They kept within the soft glow of the candlelight as the shadows rushed to meet them and crashed into the light like waves against a breaker.

The buildings and the people all melded into a terrible titanic force, a massive living darkness. It surrounded them and moved against them as it tried to break through the light. A spectral face or arm would appear to reach for them, but was banished by the light.

Harriet lost sight of Walter in the darkness. The candlelight didn't stop him, and with his inhuman might, he could overtake them and seize the mirror again.

"Everyone stop for a second," Harriet said as she closed her eyes and opened her mind again.

The swirling vortex of shadow disappeared, and she saw the world as it was, a flat and barren wasteland.

Walter Everly had come up beside them and tried to sneak ahead of them, using the shadow as concealment.

"There you are," she said as she raised the gun to her shoulder.

Walter must have heard that because even with a face of dried, dead flesh, he looked surprised.

He was even more surprised when she shot him in the face, and he tumbled backward.

"Wait, we have the mirror now. Can't we control the shadows?" Elsie said.

Harriet looked down at the mirror in her hand. She raised it to the sky and concentrated, trying to command the shadows.

Nothing happened.

She lowered her arm and looked at the mirror, hoping for instructions or something, but it was smooth and plain obsidian.

She tried again. This time she calmed her thoughts and tried to open up to it.

The shadows continued to beat against the barrier of light, giving no heed to her attempts to control it.

"I know what to do. If you will permit me," Elsie said and took the mirror from Harriet.

She held the mirror in front of her and repeated the same chant that opened up the mirror that brought them here.

"Ia Ia. In ie tlecujlixquac, in ie tlamamatlac. Itech naci in Tezcatlipoca."

The roiling and churning shadows instantly stopped. The skeletal form of Walter appeared out of the darkness and ran for the mirror, a look of sheer panic on his dead face.

"NO! Give that to me!"

He reached for the mirror when Elsie stepped forward and swung her shotgun like a baseball bat and struck him in the face with a loud crack worthy of Babe Ruth.

The dry and brittle skin split, the skull cracked open from the impact and knocked the dead thing back to the ground.

Harriet fired her last round and blew off Walter Everly's hand. She watched in horrid fascination as his skull and skin knit itself back together, and his hand reformed.

"Shadows! Attack Walter Everly and don't let up. Hound him for eternity! Rip and tear him!" Elsie yelled to the void around her.

Harriet noticed his wide eyes and open mouth as Walter realized what was about to happen. He stood up and began to run faster than any human could, but it wasn't fast enough. The shadows that made up his sick and twisted fantasy world swirled around him like a dark and malevolent tornado, flaying the dried flesh from his bones. As quickly as the darkness pulled him apart, his flesh came back to him, reforming where it was violently pulled apart.

Walter Everly was caught in an unending cycle of torn flesh and pain, with no escape. His screams came and went like a skipping record player, as his throat was ripped out and reformed, over and over again.

"Let's leave the monster to his fate and go home," Elsie said with a sneer.

With the town gone and all the shadows tormenting Walter, the only thing left standing in this nightmare world was the stone arch that brought them here.

They approached the archway and stopped in front of it.

"Let's go home and end this once and for all," Harriet said, looking at each of them with a smile.

They stepped through the archway and found themselves back in the attic and in front of the mirror, just as the candle sputtered and died.

Chapter 41

Elsie turned around, faced the mirror and looked at it with a funny expression on her face. She then kicked it, knocking it to the ground, shattering it into hundreds of pieces.

"Good riddance," she said and turned back around.

"So, now that we have the stone box and the mirror, what do we do now?"

"Well, according to the book, we need to approach as close as possible to Smoking Mirror, chant his name, strike the mirror with the talisman and seal up the mirror inside the box."

"That's it?" Harriet said incredulously.

"That's what the book says," Elsie said.

"After all this time, being harassed by spectral cats, cultists trying to kill me, nightmares made real and an ancient god knocking on our window, we just put a mirror in a box?"

"Nothing left but to give it a try, I guess," Elsie said with a shrug.

"Let's get this over with then," Harriet said, heading downstairs.

Elsie went to her bedroom and grabbed the book and read the chapter about the ritual one more time. She knew it by heart, but wanted to make sure there were no mistakes. After reading the passages again, she grabbed the stone box from the hiding place beneath the floorboards under the bed, and brought it outside to the back porch, in clear view of the hole.

Marta stepped out onto the porch. Alva floated on her stomach, following behind her.

Elsie jumped when she saw Alva, as she always did. Something about that ghost didn't sit right with her.

Alva's pale face turned to face Elsie, her grey, dead eyes stared at her, boring into her before finally looking away. Elsie shivered.

After several minutes, Harriet approached.

"It knows we have the objects to put it away again, so do you think it'll try to stop us?" Harriet asked.

"Maybe we should reload those shotguns and bring them along. Just in case. Maybe bring the BAR, too."

"Good idea. I'll be right back," Harriet said, turning around and going back inside.

Harriet came back with an armful of weapons, all loaded and ready to go.

"Okay, let us go down and finish this, ladies," Elsie said as she stepped off the porch.

Elsie led the way as she made her way down the hill. She could feel the malign pull of the hole on her thoughts as she got closer. Each step closer brought more wicked and dark thoughts to her mind. The thoughts of Harriet not loving her or just wanting to use her, were easy to disregard this time. However, images of Harriet and Marta being killed in front of her in the most horrible ways, caused her to double over and fall to a knee. Tears rolled down her cheeks and she tried to fight off the images that bombarded her mind. The influence of Smoking Mirror was so intrusive and powerful, it felt like icy, dead fingers scratching her mind.

She looked over at Harriet, who still had a hard time with her own demons. Her face scrunched up and she whispered "no, no, no" to herself as she walked.

Marta was just fine, as always. She had no demons, dark thoughts or haunting past that bothered her. Alva floated beside her and held Marta's hand.

Elsie managed to stand back up, bolstered by Harriet's and Marta's courage. As they drew closer, she felt a rumble in the Earth. It was barely noticeable at first, but it grew until she had trouble standing. The others had trouble standing as well, and crouched low or took a knee.

Elsie put the obsidian box on the ground before she dropped it, and also took a knee to keep balance. The box vibrated and she was glad to be rid of it. The prairie grass and weeds underneath the box withered and died when it touched the ground. Elsie took a step back.

A low roar rumbled from the hole that grew louder and louder with each second. As Harriet listened, the roaring sound wasn't from one source, but from hundreds of voices, screaming in torment and anguish.

"Let's do the ritual right here. I don't think we should get closer. Marta, stay back. If something happens to us, run," Elsie yelled over the din.

Before Elsie could respond, the earthquake and the deafening cacophony suddenly stopped.

Elsie looked at Hariet in confusion and fear when suddenly, the hole exploded in a great geyser of corpses. Hundreds of naked and partially clothed bodies erupted from the hole, some flew a hundred feet into the air before crashing down onto the ground like heavy, wet, pounding rain. Though they wore white masks, these weren't like the cultists she encountered before. These were dead bodies. Dried and decayed corpses. The corpses, all in various stages of decomposition, lay still after they fell.

Elsie froze.

Her thoughts were torn back to that chilly day in November 1916 near Gommecourt, France, after the Battle of the Somme. A temporary field hospital had been established and she and the other nurses inspected the battlefields, looking for wounded. Because of the brutality of the battle, no quarter was given and no truces agreed upon to collect the dead. Bodies, some burst open from laying in the sun, others torn open by shrapnel and bullets and now covered in early morning frost. Over a million bodies scattered over the corpse of what used to be a beautiful French countryside. The horrific vista of the aftermath of the Battle of the Somme was nothing compared to the smell.

That same smell spewed from the hole and the corpses. The sense of smell had the ability to rekindle memories like nothing else, and Elsie was there again, standing on the battlefields of France, surrounded by the dead.

Just as she did on that day, she stood paralyzed, unable to comprehend the scope of inhumanity. She wanted to run, to escape this vision of hell, but couldn't. Her own mind betrayed her and forced her to look upon the worst mankind had to offer. Unlike the Somme, these corpses began to move again.

"Ritual! Now!" Harriet said, looking over at the field littered with dead bodies.

Elsie couldn't respond as she faced the horror of the Somme and this new terror simultaneously.

"Elsie! The Ritual!"

The first bodies to land, slowly moved and stood up. They raised their smiling white masks to meet their gazes.

Elsie didn't think of beautiful movie stars like she was taught. She thought of Harriet's face until she could move again. Slowly, she remembered where she was and kneeled down beside the box.

Every corpse stood, hundreds of them scattered around, and they stared in their direction.

"Um, Harriet? Make sure that BAR is ready. I think we are going to need you to keep them off me," Elsie said, taking her pistol out of the holster.

The animated corpses moved toward them in a lumbering and uncoordinated gait at first, then moved faster and faster as they gained their feet.

Harriet extended the bipod and lay on the ground behind the huge automatic rifle.

Elsie hit the mirror with the butt of her pistol as the book said, placed the black mirror into the box and covered it with the lid.

The corpses ran closer with each passing second. Harriet opened fire on the things, but she turned her gaze to the closest ones, all of which seemed to run for Elsie. She put the front sight of the BAR on the closest one and pulled the trigger. The bullets blew off the top of its head and it fell into the grass. With each burst of the powerful weapon, chunks of meat and limbs flew into the air, with sprays of putrefied bodily fluids. It was like a scythe harvesting wheat. Scores of the things fell and were either replaced by new ones or rose to their feet once more to lunge forward.

"Tezcatlipoca! Tezcatlipoca! Cochi! Cochi!" she chanted, over and over again.

The corpses rushed forward, Elsie felt the Earth stop shaking and the box ceased vibrating. The obsidian box flashed with a blinding white light as waves of energy flowed through her body and gave her a sense of weightlessness. Smoking Mirror rejoiced as one of the corpses slammed into her Its fetid breath made her gag, as clumps of skin and dried flesh came off in her hands. She struggled against its weight and tried to fight it off when she realized it wasn't moving.

It slumped, unmoving.

She threw the body off her and sat up.

All the corpses had fallen to the ground, lifeless once more.

"I think it worked," Elsie said, dumbstruck.

Harriet jumped to her feet and clapped for joy.

"That was a little too close," she said as she wiped her forehead.

"Look," Marta said. She and Alva both pointed to the corpses that littered the ground.

The hundreds of corpses broke apart into little pieces that floated off into the air like ashes in a fire, until there was nothing left and the fields were clear.

Elsie, in happy shock, looked around.

"We did it! We did it!" Harriet cheered.

As Elsie shouted for joy, she noticed something about the hole change. It pulsated, as a sickly green light spilled out.

"Um, I think somethi...," Harriet began to say.

Harriet didn't get to finish her sentence as a giant, clawed limb covered in black, desiccated skin, reached out from the hole and grabbed her, pulling her in, where her cries faded into the void.

Elsie screamed.

Chapter 42

"Harriet!"

"Smoking Mirror has her," Marta said as she pointed to the hole.

As Elsie looked, another great, black and multi jointed arm erupted from the hole. It slammed to the ground and caused the earth to shake. It grabbed the obsidian box and dragged it into the hole.

That same laugh as before, the laugh of earthquakes and rumbling boulders emanated from the hole once more.

Elsie stood there, transfixed by the sight before her, as her heart dropped to her feet and she fell to her knees. Harriet was taken. Taken by that thing, down into its hole.

She hit the ground with her fists and screamed silently through clenched teeth.

A voice came from the ground as it shook, and it pierced her mind. It was the same strange voice she heard that night. It was Smoking Mirror.

"Hello, Elsie."

"Give Harriet back to me," she said, seething.

"You know what I want, Elsie Everly. Come and meet me. I won't hurt you or Harriet. Yet. She is safe with me for now. I promise. I want you. I need you," it said in a mewling and pleading voice. "I have so much to show you. To do to you. You will have the world at your fingertips, if you but come talk to me face to face. So, come. Please come. But come alone. I cannot guarantee the safety of your friends if they enter my temple."

"Give her back now or I will kill you," she growled.

"You can try, Elsie Everly. You can try but you cannot kill what cannot die."

She got up from off the ground and rushed back inside, Marta close behind her.

She tied her hair back with a large ribbon and hurried to the kitchen. She wanted to jump down into the hole and rescue Harriet right now but knew that wouldn't work. She needed help if there was any chance of getting her back alive.

Elsie grabbed the black candlestick style phone and dialed the operator. After a minute, she was patched through

"This is Enoch of Piper and Son. How can I help you?"

"Enoch, it has Harriet."

There was a long silence before Enoch answered.

"I'm on the way," he said and hung up.

Elsie was about to step away, but she noticed a card sitting next to the telephone that had sat there undisturbed for weeks. It was Samuel Richard's number.

She dialed the operator again, gave the number on the card and waited.

After a few minutes, the bored voice of the operator responded.

"Sorry, it appears the person you are trying to call is not answering."

"Shit," Elsie said as she hung up.

She gave the situation a moment of thought.

"Marta. Come with me. We are going on a little walk."

"Okay," Marta whispered.

She grabbed a rifle, took Marta by the hand and walked in the direction of Samuel Richard's house. Despite being her closest neighbor, he was still half-mile away. She walked as fast as she could, while keeping an eye out for cultists or monsters. Marta easily kept up with her. Most of the time, Elsie couldn't figure out what Marta was thinking or feeling. She seemed to live in perpetual bliss and ignorance. Now, it broke Elsie's heart to see her scared and worried.

As they approached Samuel's farm, Elsie noticed a column of smoke rising from the direction of the house. It was much too large and dark to be from the fireplace.

Elsie ran forward and as she crested the hill overlooking the farm, she stopped.

Bodies covered the fields in front of the farm as the house burned. Elsie didn't want to, but she walked down the hill with the muzzle of her rifle sweeping back and forth. She had to know what happened. There were dozens of bodies, most of them wore white masks and were riddled with bullet holes. Others did not. A plain woman in a pretty dress lay face down in a pool of blood.

"Marta, turn around. Please don't look at this."

Elsie had seen horrors, but seeing Samuel's sons unmoving in the lush, swaying grass nauseated her. She emptied the contents of her stomach and dry heaved as she cried. Marta, also crying, approached and patted Elsie on the back.

After a while, she regained enough composure and continued to the house. The smoke and heat from the blaze prevented her from getting close to the house and she assumed Samuel was inside.

"He's around back," Marta said.

Elsie nodded and walked around to the rear of the destroyed house. At first, she didn't see him, but a ragged cough drew her eyes to a man leaning against the tire of an old truck and a lever action rifle in his lap.

"Did I do it? Are my wife and kids safe?" Samuel Richards wheezed through the blood gurgling through his sucking chest wound.

Elsie gently put the rifle down and kneeled in front of Samuel. She remembered her bedside manners and lay a reassuring hand on his shoulder.

"They are safe, Samuel. They made it out and are waiting for you. You did good. Now lie here and get some rest, then you can see your family," Elsie lied in the most reassuring voice she could muster.

"Bless you, Elsie. Oh, look. Here they are..." Samuel whispered with his last breath as his body went limp.

Samuel died with a peaceful expression on his face and Elsie closed his eyes.

BACK HOME, Elsie paced in the kitchen, trying to clear her mind. She needed to be clear-headed if she was going to rescue Harriet. If she had to give up her own life to do so, so be it. She was ready to leave this life so many times before, but to die to help Harriet is more than she could ask for.

She said a simple prayer. She asked that Harriet and her friends be safe and that she be able to save her. She said 'amen' and took Marta by the hand and marched out to the barn. There, she found ropes and chains and dragged them out to her car. They threw them in the trunk and drove the car around the house, through her fields and parked in front of the glowing, pulsating hole.

"Marta, listen very carefully. I'm going to need your help.

I'm going to show you how to operate this car. I'm going to need you to lower me into the hole and pull me out."

"I know how to drive. Mack taught me. I know what to do. I have Alva and an army of ghosts to protect me up here. Go in there and save Harriet, please," Marta said.

Chapter 43

Elsie held onto the ropes as the car backed up and lowered her down further into the glowing hole. As she descended, the dark thoughts, nosebleeds and pain vanished, and she sighed in relief.

Elsie trembled in fear, but not for her own safety. She didn't care about that. She was terrified of the idea of Harriet being harmed. The thought of anyone else dying scared her too, as she thought of poor Samuel and his family. She could not imagine a world without Harriet in it. That's not the world she wanted to live in.

The hole seemed to go on forever, but the soft, green glow grew brighter as she was lowered down.

After what seemed like hours, her feet touched solid ground. Elsie looked down and her feet pressed against a damp dirt floor that led to a tunnel where the glow was coming from.

She looked up, and to her surprise, the entrance of the hole only seemed to be twenty feet above her head. She could see Marta looking down at her.

"I made it down safe! Be ready!" Elsie called up.

Marta nodded and pulled back from view.

"I assume I go that way," Elsie said, looking down a tunnel of which she couldn't see the end.

The tunnel looked like it had been freshly dug, but not by man or machine. It appeared a giant worm had crawled this way and devoured the very earth it moved through.

Puddles formed everywhere from the constantly dripping ceiling, but whatever putrid and stinking liquid it was, it wasn't water, and had the foulest look and odor to it. With morbid curiosity, Elsie looked closely at the liquid and recoiled when she saw miniscule worms flailing about. They were the same worms that infested Thomas's blood. She remembered how the vile creatures covered her and wriggled on her skin as panic threatened to encompass her. She looked away as she practiced her breathing exercises and finally calmed down.

"Whatever you do, don't let this drip on you," Elsie said to herself with a trembling voice.

The glow became brighter, and soon Elsie could see runes or glyphs carved into the walls, ceiling and floor of the tunnel. They resembled the geometric patterns of the odd throw rugs that littered her house. She vowed to throw them away if she made it out of here alive.

The symbols began to glow and pulse, increasingly faster as she drew near the end of the tunnel. There was no point to being stealthy, so she hurried her pace toward Harriet. She had no idea what to expect on the other end of the tunnel.

The tunnel opened up into a vast cave. Massive pillars of stone supported the impossibly tall ceiling, and the cavern resembled a perverse and unholy cathedral of darkness and filth. The pillars lined up in rows and rose hundreds of feet. Wicked symbols lined the walls of Smoking Mirror's sanctuary. The smell was damp and putrid, like rotting meat left out to spoil in the rain. Elsie had to keep herself from gagging. Rotting corpses of unknown things were scattered everywhere and most seemed as if they had been gnawed on by a great beast.

The glowing symbols were not the only source of light. Smoking Mirror, in all its unholy majesty, lay on a cyclopean stone pedestal on the opposite side of the cave, where a pulpit would normally be. Its ever-revolving halo of sickly light illuminated the cathedral of filth and caused her stomach to rebel more than the putrid and rotting cadavers.

The Halo orbited the massive white mask-like face of the evil god. Shapes, symbols, numbers and letters from long dead languages decorated it. What looked like planetary orbits and star charts appeared and disappeared in the slow turning of the Halo. The mask showed a content, almost smug look as it gently smiled down at Elsie.

Smoking Mirror's body was a massive and bloated larval form that protruded with oddly jointed, spindly limbs that jutted out from every angle. Some ended in feet or claws, while others ended in almost human looking hands. She noticed that one leg ended in a bleeding stump that constantly dripped with a pale, milky ooze.

The entire body stretched almost fifty feet long and resembled a maggot that had been roasted over a fire. The skin was black and cracked all over and flaked away in sheets and slivers of what looked like obsidian.

The stench of rotting meat and feces assaulted their senses and Elsie was forced to control her breathing to avoid vomiting again. It only became worse as they drew closer to the evil being that had tormented her.

"Am I not magnificent? Do you not tremble in awe at my beauty and might? Bow and worship me. Suffer to come unto me, little ones."

Smoking Mirror's voice echoed all around and caused the ground to shake.

Elsie covered her ears and gritted her teeth against the sharp, pulsing pain its voice brought.

Smoking Mirror gave a chuckle that sounded like a million little bells chiming.

"Sometimes I forget how fragile your ears are. My voice is the voice of the North Wind. The roar of the Jaguar," it said, in a much quieter voice, though still ear-achingly loud.

"Where is Harriet?!" Elsie called.

Smoking Mirror ignored her.

"I really should thank you, Elsie Everly. You have been of considerable assistance to me. I was going to kill that bothersome father and brother of yours. Walter and Thomas Everly were becoming very tedious. It defies all imagination that they had the audacity to think they could control me. Me?!"

That last word became an animalistic roar that rang inside Elsie's head.

"They served their purpose, however. They gathered my slaves and set up the sacrifice. You, Elsie Everly. You, the perfect vessel of my will and glory. They thought they would use me to wipe out the inferior races of man. Elsie Everly, I will tell you what I did not tell them."

It leaned forward, its haloed head moving on a massive, pulsating neck.

"All the races of man are inferior to me, so all will serve me or perish."

It leaned back and chuckled again.

"I was going to kill them after I sacrificed you, but you saved me the effort."

The light from its halo flashed bright and crackled with energy as dozens of men and women appeared from out of nowhere, lining the walls of the chamber, surrounding her.

"Behold, my slaves. Witness my domination over them and see the fate of all mankind."

They wore the familiar masks and filthy clothes. Some

were armed with knives and clubs. Every mask reflected an expression of rapture and bliss. Two of them brought a palanquin with the obsidian box and laid it in front of their god.

"The ritual to put me to rest was written by my most loyal servant, the priest Reymundo. He wrote that account at my behest so anyone foolish enough to attempt sending me away would only serve to waken me further, if I had devoured enough fear, hatred and jealousy. Now, I need one last thing, my beloved Elsie Everly. I need your will. Your body. Your desire to serve me. I know not why you fight me for I will give you the world. The riches of the kingdoms of men. Their fear and awe and their flesh will be yours."

Smoking Mirror held out a hand and opened it up like a flower petal. Inside was Harriet. She appeared unharmed but was unconscious.

"You can have the seer, Harriet. She will be yours for all eternity. She will never be sick or grow old and will be by your side until the sun grows cold and the Earth perishes. All you must do is submit. Submit your will to me willingly and all this will be yours. I must have a sacrifice."

"All of this is dependent on me saying yes? On my willingness to let you kill and enslave mankind? That is a terrible plan. I can see why you have been sleeping for hundreds of years. All I have to do is say no. You'll kill Harriet and I'll go back to the house, where I am sure you will continue to torment me, but all mankind will be saved. What is the worth of my life and Harriet's life compared to the lives of the entire human race? That is not even a decision."

The masked face of Smoking Mirror now showed an annoyed expression, though Elsie never saw it change.

"I know you, Elsie Everly. You love this woman. You would not see her harmed."

Another thin and oddly jointed limb moved and took Harriet by one arm, while another limb held her by the other, suspending her in the air as if she was being crucified. Elsie thanked God Harriet was still unconscious.

"Have you ever torn the wings off a fly?" Smoking Mirror asked, its expression one of deadly mirth now.

"I have not, because I am not cruel. I am, however, pragmatic. It makes no sense to sacrifice the world for one or two people, assuming you even honor your word. I mean, I am sure you said the same to my idiot father and brother. Unlike them, I am not an idiot. So, if you will not give up Harriet, I will be leaving now," Elsie said and turned around.

She wasn't going to leave. She would never leave Harriet. The creature was right about that. Instead, she was going to rescue Harriet or die trying. There would be no agreement.

"Perhaps you imagine I am bluffing? Perhaps you would prefer a demonstration?" the thing asked.

Demonstration?

Elsie didn't like the sound of that.

"Bring her forth."

Two cultists brought in the unconscious form of a pretty, dark skinned woman with long hair, wearing what looked like a torn and tattered colorful dress.

"This is Guadalupe Adriana Monica Chavez. She is a friend to Harriet, and it will vex her greatly to know that you were the cause of her demise. What will Harriet say when she finds out that you could have saved this poor woman who befriended her?"

Before she could respond, Smoking Mirror reached out and grabbed Lupe with such speed and strength, it knocked the cultists holding her across the room and slammed them against the far wall in spatters of dark, ropey blood.

Lupe, to Elsie's horror, woke up and screamed. From the odd angles of her arms and legs, crushed underneath the iron grip of Smoking Mirror's fist, every bone in her extremities had been broken.

Elsie wished that Lupe had remained unconscious.

Smoking Mirror lifted Lupe's broken body above him like a Roman emperor eating grapes and squeezed.

Lupe screamed for only a second more before the life was crushed out of her and her bodily fluids poured into Smoking Mirror's wide, gaping mouth.

A great tentacle of a tongue snaked out and lapped up the viscera that fell on its horrid face.

Once every last drop of blood and bile was extracted, it dropped the mangled body of Lupe into its Maw. Elsie didn't see the mask change, but it now showed a content and satiated expression as the sound of meat and bones being chewed filled the cavern.

Smoking Mirror now wore an angry expression on its mask and held Harriet's unconscious form in front of it.

"I am a benevolent god and will give you one more opportunity. Submit or you watch the seer being slowly pulled apart before I devour her flesh. I know your fears. I know your jealousies and anger. I have tasted them. It is these things that have woken me enough to bring us to this point. Submit and she lives. Then I will awaken to my full glory, a being of blinding light to drown out the sun. I will not be caged in this form forever. I will be free. By this, I know you will not sacrifice this woman. I have swum in your dreams and tasted your desires. I know you, Elsie Everly. Here she is. Here is your seer. I knew you were the worthiest of being my avatar. With you as my mouth and my hands and fulfilling my will, I will be blessed by great Azothoth, blessed be all who hear the music. No more games. Submit to my will or Harriet Piper will spend eternity in pain, in an endless cycle of madness and unspeakable agony. This is your choice."

Smoking Mirror raised several of its hands and faced upward in dark adulation of its master.

"If I refuse, are there others that can take my place?" Elsie asked, keeping her eyes on Harriet.

"There are always others. It will take time. But I want you, Elsie."

"If you know my emotions, then you know this one; disappointment."

Elsie pulled her pistol out of the holster and fired at Smoking Mirror's face.

Smoking Mirror recoiled, more out of surprise than pain, and dropped Harriet. The bullets caused no damage to its mask-like face, which now held an expression of disappointment.

"Do not harm the sacrifice," it said in an almost bored voice.

The dozens of cultists, as if guided by the same hand, ran toward Elsie as she made a dash for Harriet, reaching her first.

She looked her over, just as she would have if she was a new casualty brought into her field hospital. There were no outward signs of trauma, but she was alive and breathing.

Two cultists with angry looking masks ran toward her. Elsie took a quick second to aim and fired one shot into each of their heads, shattering their masks and dropping them to the floor instantly.

Elsie reached down and struggled to pick Harriet up. She had plenty of experience moving limp and unconscious bodies, and thankfully Harriet was a lot lighter than most of the soldiers she had moved. Her rib, still not healed, shot searing pain through her body and took her breath away.

She holstered her pistol until she could get Harriet up on her shoulder, then used all her strength to get to her feet, ignoring the pain.

A filthy and almost corpse-like figure ran toward her, clothes too rotted and tattered to tell when or where it came from, was almost on her. She did the only thing she could, she punched the thing in the face with the palm of her hand. Its head snapped back and it clumsily fell to the ground. Elsie drew the pistol and shot another couple of cultists that were getting too close, but more took their place.

Smoking Mirror sat back with a pleased expression on its rigid mask of a face.

Elsie fired the remaining clip into Smoking Mirror's face. Small entry wounds sprouted, but quickly disappeared and Smoking Mirror laughed.

"That won't work on me, Elsie. Relent. Be my sacrifice."

It roared in mirth and rose up on its multitude of feet and reached its full height. Its head now almost touched the ceiling of the chamber, while the halo spun faster and faster.

Elsie ran as fast as she could, but Harriet slowed her down tremendously. With a quick glance back at Smoking Mirror, she saw a large, black, boney hand, mere feet away reach for her. She found the strength to run faster.

The exit grew closer. Almost within reach.

Something grabbed her ankle in a vice-like grip and caused her to trip and spill Harriet on the ground. She looked back to see a dirty, skeletal hand coming out of the ground. Another hand broke through the surface and then pulled itself up from the dirt. Its face was covered in a white mask and bore an angry expression.

"Well done. The weapons of your age are a wonder, but nothing compared to my power," Smoking Mirror said

It raised three of its arms to the sky and every cultist that had been cut down by her bullets, twitched and stood back up on their feet. Some of them picked their masks up off the ground and put them back on, and within seconds she was surrounded.

"Valliant and noble effort. This is the most entertainment I have had since I watched those cliff dwellers gnaw the meat off the bones of their children," Smoking Mirror said and giggled.

Elsie punched the cultist that held her in the eye. It let go and she scrambled for Harriet. She reached her and covered Harriet's body with her own, as more of the things came toward them. She waved the pistol at the things surrounding her, daring them to come closer.

She felt a massive, piercing pain explode near her temple as she fell face first onto the ground. A cultist stood over her, leather sap in hand. It reached for its mask and took it off.

It was the clerk of the Ute Trading Post, who also attacked her on the porch, his long hair and face even filthier than the last time she saw him.

"Remember me? Last time we met, you shot me," he said as he kicked the Mauser out of her hand and sent it skittering across the ground, far from her reach.

He raised his arm as if to strike her again, but an enormous black hand enveloped him and crushed him in an instant, rancid blood and organs spewed between its fingers. Elsie heard a loud and violent pop as the cultist's head burst, showering Elsie with bits of bone and grey matter.

Smoking Mirror withdrew the bloody hand and licked the viscera off with a long, lolling tongue that dripped with blood.

"I said, do not harm the sacrifice," it said reproachfully.

Another cultist took his place and crouched on top of her. It was the female that she had shot through the window.

"Looks like you should have taken me up on my offer. I could have been anything you wanted. Now I'll be your captor," she said as she squirmed suggestively on top of her.

"Do you know why you failed, Elsie Everly?" Smoking Mirror asked.

It cocked its head as if it waited for an answer.

"Fuck you," she managed to spit out, while struggling against dozens of hands holding her down.

"Sacrifice. You don't have the will and force to make the sacrifice necessary to put me away. You were doomed to fail and destined to be mine."

"I would have sacrificed myself! You know my thoughts and dreams. It would have been easy for me," Elsie called out.

"I know. You are brave and strong. You would do anything for your love. For your friends. But you must know that I would never have permitted that. Can't you see that I never wanted to harm you? I have servants and servants unseen in vast numbers. Your life is guarded and protected until you break to my will and sacrifice yourself at the proper time and in the proper manner. That time is now. Bring her and Harriet Piper to me. I will break Harriet and you will bow to me and be mine, for all eternity."

Chapter 44

Harriet came to in a daze. Her head swam with pain and confusion as she realized she was on a damp, dirt floor.

The sounds of yelling and fighting surrounded her but she couldn't make out who was involved. The last thing she remembered was they'd completed the ritual to seal Smoking Mirror away, but then something went wrong.

Something went very wrong, and she couldn't remember what it was. She managed to get to her knees and sat up. Her head swam and she almost keeled over.

There is Elsie, but why is she on the ground, and who are all these people?

Her memory and wits snapped back into focus as she saw her love being tackled by a dozen filthy people wearing masks.

The ritual didn't work.

With that thought, she raised her eyes to the other side of the room and saw it. The thing with the white face that visited them that night. Smoking Mirror itself, in all its hideous and infernal glory.

Her body shook uncontrollably, and she willed herself to move, but couldn't.

"Keep her down this time. If you fail to do so, I will devour your flesh and spirit. I don't want any more surprises," came the rumbling voice of Smoking Mirror.

As Harriet tried to stand up, she noticed Elsie's Mauser pistol discarded on the ground mere feet away. Her vision blurred and she found herself on the ground again. She couldn't walk, but she tried to crawl to the pistol. If she could grab it, maybe she could help Elsie.

She looked at the gun and hoped she could somehow will it into her hand, but it lay there, motionless as her body refused to cooperate.

A pair of work boots and dungarees stepped into her vision and stopped in front of the pistol.

A calloused, dark hand reached down and gingerly picked it up.

She looked up and saw her dad.

He looked down at her with a sad smile on his face.

"Hello, stubborn daughter of mine. Please take care of your mother and brothers for me and tell them I love them. I love you so much, Harriet."

He gave her a reassuring smile before he walked toward the hulking form of Smoking Mirror, calm and dignified.

"Dad! Where are you going?" is all Harriet could think to say.

"Enoch! Get Harriet and get her out of here!" Elsie called.

"You. Be good to my daughter," Enoch said, and stood boldly to face Smoking Mirror without a hint of fear.

Smoking Mirror regarded him as if he were an insect.

"Please tell me you have come to plead for your daughter's life. I adore a good groveling. You were not invited though. If you get on your knees and beg like a dog, I might make yours and your family's suffering short."

"You don't frighten me, you miserable worm. You have

been stopped before and you will be stopped again," he said in a loud and powerful voice. One that commanded respect.

Harriet could have sworn the ground shook when he spoke and as she focused her blurry vision, she saw somebody, another man, standing next to her dad, but she couldn't make out who it was. He was also tall with dark skin, and he had a hand on Enoch's shoulder.

Hyrum?

Smoking Mirror's sickening laughter filled the cavern and his slaves laughed with him.

"You? You are going to stop me? A lone, old man walks into my temple and thinks he is going to defeat me? I am not sure if you are delusional or just an idiot like the oracle girl, who's mother I devoured, but either way, this will be most entertaining."

"I am not delusional. I am not an idiot, and I am not alone. A sacrifice is required to seal you away. A sacrifice you will have!" he said in his booming voice.

Enoch ran toward the obsidian box.

"Stop him!" Smoking Mirror roared.

Harriet could feel the fear and desperation in its voice as it realized the threat Enoch presented.

The cultists that had Elsie pinned, rose to their feet and ran toward Enoch.

Harriet still had trouble moving and tried to get up but couldn't. She fell back down but tried to stand again as she reached for Elsie. A strong hand wrapped around hers and pulled.

"I have you," Elsie said as she lifted her off the ground and put her arm around her shoulder.

"We need to get out of here. Now," Elsie said as she tried to run and pulled Harriet with her.

"But, my dad!"

Elsie looked pained and looked down at the ground as if she was ashamed.

Her gaze went back to her dad, who now stood over the obsidian box.

"Dad! Run! Get out of here!" Harriet screamed.

Smoking Mirror raised a twisted and blackened fist to smash Enoch into oblivion. The deformed fist swung down like a giant hammer and promised to destroy everything in its path, but the man who stood next to Enoch calmly raised a hand, caught Smoking Mirror's fist and stopped it instantly and without effort.

The masked face of Smoking Mirror looked surprised, but raised three more fists to bring down on Enoch Piper.

"Elsie! Take care of my family!" Enoch yelled and put the barrel of the pistol to his heart.

"Dad! No!" Harriet screamed.

She didn't understand why he was doing this and wanted him to run to her and to safety.

He closed his eyes, and with a serene look, pulled the trigger as a dozen hands tried to grab him. Harriet saw her father's blood, his life, exit his body. Images of her gentle father flashed through her mind. She remembered how patient he was when he taught her to ride a bike, despite putting a dent in their mailbox with her head. Her love of engines and the joy of fixing things was because of him. The courage to be herself and to love Elsie, was because of him.

Harriet saw her father's last act. The cultists went limp and lifeless before they could grab him. Enoch's lifeless body fell onto the obsidian box, his blood poured into it and overflowed, dripping over the sides.

Her father was dead, and she screamed. She found no words as the breaking of her heart escaped her lips and filled the cavern. Harriet tried to push Elsie away and run back to where her dad, the man who had taught her everything, lay motionless, surrounded by the worst this world could bare upon him. Harriet was still too dazed to resist Elsie, who bore her away further from her dad.

She didn't know how to continue without her father. He had always been there for her at every step of her life. He patched up her cuts and skinned knees and told her everything would be okay when she came home from school crying because the kids made fun of her.

That serene smile filled her mind, and she wanted nothing more than to see it again as she screamed and cried.

"This can't be happening! Elsie, take me back! Now! Daddy!"

Elsie held her tight but remained silent, though Harriet could see the tears on her face as well.

The mysterious man that accompanied Enoch was gone and Smoking Mirror sat still on its dais, frozen in place with its fists still in the air. The halo around its head stopped revolving and grew dim. This threw the unholy cathedral into darkness. The halo cracked and shattered into small shards as it disappeared into thin air.

All the cultists fell, lifeless once more, sustained only by Smoking Mirror's now absent influence. Smoking Mirror itself crumbled into dust, the white mask of its face had fallen to the ground, revealing a giant maw with crooked and malformed wormlike teeth, and hundreds of now dead, glossy eyes.

She lost sight of it as the tunnel and everything was thrown into darkness. The mysterious glowing glyphs all around them flickered out and died one by one. As the lights winked out of existence, cascades of dirt and rock fell behind them. Gouts of putrid liquid poured down from the ceiling and Elsie darted between them as if they were acid.

"This way! Hurry up!" Marta yelled from the edge of the hole.

Rocks and dirt collapsed around them, and Harriet noticed everything behind them was disappearing at an incredible rate. As the tunnel broke apart, it also turned into void. A great nothingness chased them as the rocks fell.

They reached the area under the hole, and Elsie placed Harriet on her feet but held her steady. She quickly tied the rope around both of their waists and gave a tug.

Elsie grabbed onto the rope and yelled.

"Pull us up!"

She heard the car engine bellow as it pulled away from the hole and lifted them up.

Harriet looked down as the void, now only feet away from them, approached rapidly.

Elsie held on to the rope with all the strength she had left, while she tried to keep Harriet from hitting the walls. She must have noticed the quickly vanishing hole because she yelled for Marta to lift them up faster.

They crested the edge of the hole and quickly crawled away from it with Marta's help. She grabbed and pulled them as far away from the hole as fast as he could.

Elsie was on Harriet, checking her vitals and feeling for any wounds.

"Harriet, I'm so sorry about your father. I'm so sorry. I'm here for you. I'll always be here for you."

She burst into uncontrollable sobbing once more as Elsie wrapped her arms around her.

Once out of the hole, it disappeared completely, leaving nothing but pristine and unblemished land.

The man that walked in with Enoch and protected him against Smoking Mirror's might, appeared and stood over her. He leaned down to whisper in her ear. The voice was deep and calm and sounded pleased.

"You did good, little sister. I'm proud of you. Take care of each other and live the best life."

"I will. I promise," Harriet said as she melted into Elsie's embrace.

Acknowledgments

Thanks to my long-suffering wife Cindi, who put up with me during this process and without whom, none of this would have been possible.

My sister Shannon who's support, knowledge and experience as an author was invaluable, deserves so many thanks.

Jennifer, my sister from another mister, was my partner in crime throughout the writing of this book. I could not have done this without her.

Thanks to my twin brother Zach. I just wish he was alive today to see how much he has inspired me.

Thanks to Larry Correia, Steve Diamond and their Writer-Dojo podcast. They taught valuableblessons and de-mystified the dream of becoming an author.

Thanks to Dave, who had to listen to me rattle on about this book for the last two years. Sorry brother.

About the Author

The first movie I remember watching as a kid was the 1982 film *The Thing* with Kurt Russell.

Apparently, my older brothers' favorite past time was showing me and my twin age-inappropriate movies. However, this did create a love of horror movies very early on and which soon branched out into a love of horror books. My mother read us Stephen King's *Skeleton Crew* as bedtime stories and I was hooked.

While attending Southern Virginia University, my twin brother and I took writing courses by the incredible author, Orson Scott Card. We learned so much and my brother began writing novels immediately and wrote several before his death. He gave me the courage to take up his torch and start writing my own books. I love sci-fi and fantasy, but wanted to return to my roots and write what I was raised on. Horror.

> Josh is a natural story teller, who's knowledge of history go hand in hand to produce an original and thrilling horror novel that is hard to put down.
>
> — Larry Correia

Wicked House Publishing

Come find us!

Amazon: Wicked House Publishing
Mailing List: Sign Up Here!
Facebook Group: The Wicked House Cult of Slightly Insane Readers

Made in United States
Troutdale, OR
07/06/2024